What people are saying about …

JUSTIFIED

"Down-home as Friday night football, volatile as a coiled rattler, *Justified* is an emotional journey through scandal and heartbreak to forgiveness and grace. Denman's work is achingly honest, witty, and it plucks at the heartstrings. I'm a huge fan."

Candace Calvert, bestselling
author of *By Your Side*

"A small-town romance with a universal stick-to-your-soul message about the beauty of grace and the acceptance of a second chance. With an exceptional voice for story, Denman has created characters who will own your heart before the last page is turned."

Nicole Deese, Amazon's bestselling author of
the Letting Go series and *A Cliché Christmas*

"Varina is an incredible talent, and without a doubt this second book will bring the reader hours of enjoyment. I've been waiting for it, anticipating it, and now I have it in my hands. Three cheers for Varina Denman and *Justified*—well worth the wait."

Joseph Courtemanche,
Commotion in the Pews blog

What people are saying about …

JADED

"Small-town flavor, real-life issues, romantic, funny, and poignant—hope with a hint of a drawl. Denman's fresh voice is a delight, and her debut is a winner."

Candace Calvert, bestselling
author of *By Your Side*

"In her debut novel, Varina Denman tackles tough subjects in a contemporary setting as she weaves a story of memorable characters with the secrets that haunt them. With touches of humor and an air of mystery, *Jaded* may trigger a few of your own questions about spiritual truths and the accountability of church leaders. A nicely paced small-town tale. I look forward to more stories from this gifted storyteller."

Carla Stewart, award-winning author of
Stardust and *The Hatmaker's Heart*

"A compelling story with truth tightly woven at the core, Ruth Ann and Dodd's journey will stay in your mind long after the last word is read, and it will challenge you to look at others and the world through different eyes. A powerful debut novel."

Anne Mateer, author of *Playing by Heart*

"Varina Denman's *Jaded* showcases the talent of an author who is unafraid to inflict truth upon her characters as they journey from prejudice and naïveté toward acceptance and the rawness of knowledge gained through pain. Relevant and real, this emotive debut subtly strikes at the heart of what keeps so many people at arm's length from God and provides a satisfying romance that keeps the pages turning toward its hoped-for happy ever after."

Serena Chase, author of *The Ryn* and contributor of the *Happy Ever After* blog at *USA Today*

"*Jaded* is a poignant story of old scars and new hope. Through the journey of one wounded family, the transformational powers of forgiveness and genuine faith become clear. Varina Denman's fictional small town could be any town, and many readers will recognize the all-too-human challenges facing today's churches."

Lisa Wingate, international bestselling author of *The Prayer Box* and *The Story Keeper*

"Varina captures your heart in this journey of love, pain, and intrigue. Captivated by the town's mysterious past, caught up in the suspense, and lost in forbidden romance, you'll never be prepared for what happens next. Read this book. You will not regret it."

Don Brobst, MD, author

"*Jaded* is not only a soul-stirring tale of transformational love, but it's also a bridge—one that stretches the delicate divide between hurt and hope. The empathy and grace of Denman's skilled pen will carry far beyond these characters and into the hearts of her readers."

Nicole Deese, author of the Letting Go series and *A Cliché Christmas*

"*Jaded* is an emotionally-charged masterpiece that sinks into your soul and challenges you to see beyond the pitfalls of religion. The small-town setting, remarkably real characters, and meaningful theme of forgiveness makes this book a 2015 must-read."

T. L. Gray, Kindle bestselling author
of the Winsor and Set Apart series

"Trapp, Texas, is a town where football and gossip are king and queen, secrets are kept and told, and nothing changes—until it does. Denman has given us a story as rich as a chocolate sheath cake with characters as familiar as an old pickup truck and with grace as broad as the flat fields of cotton. Recommended!"

Bill Higgs, author

JUSTIFIED

A NOVEL

VARINA DENMAN

transforming lives together

JUSTIFIED
Published by David C Cook
4050 Lee Vance View
Colorado Springs, CO 80918 U.S.A.

David C Cook Distribution Canada
55 Woodslee Avenue, Paris, Ontario, Canada N3L 3E5

David C Cook U.K., Kingsway Communications
Eastbourne, East Sussex BN23 6NT, England

The graphic circle C logo is a registered trademark of David C Cook.

Scripture quotations or paraphrases are taken from the following versions: Holy
Bible, New International Version®, NIV®. Copyright © 1973, 2011 by Biblica,
Inc.™ Used by permission of Zondervan. All rights reserved worldwide. www.
zondervan.com. The New American Standard Bible®, Copyright © 1960, 1995
by The Lockman Foundation. Used by permission. (www.Lockman.org.)

LCCN 2014957982
ISBN 978-0-7814-1216-2
eISBN 978-0-7814-1326-8

© 2015 Varina Denman
Published in association with the literary agency of The Blythe Daniel
Agency, P.O. Box 64197, Colorado Springs, CO 80962-4197

The Team: Ingrid Beck, Jamie Chavez, Nick Lee, Jennifer
Lonas, Helen Macdonald, Karen Athen
Cover Design: Amy Konyndyk
Cover Photos: Getty Images (Thomas Barwick), Veer Images, iStockphoto

Printed in the United States of America
1 2 3 4 5 6 7 8 9 10

032015

For those who try too hard

*He saved us, not because of righteous things we
had done, but because of his mercy.*

Titus 3:5

CHAPTER ONE

My world shattered last winter. A hairline crack formed, and my life perched on the edge of an abyss, set to topple at the slightest breeze. But instead of a breeze, I got a whirlwind … in the form of a positive pregnancy test.

Of course, that wasn't supposed to happen. Not to me. But when my world finally ceased its roiling, I barely recognized myself—or my thoughts and feelings—because my new life had become an inverted image of what it was before.

Now I sat on the hood of Velma Pickett's old, maroon Chevy, waiting for the sunrise, and rubbed my palm across the curve of my stomach. "Don't worry, little guy. It's not your fault." I say *little guy* because I had the sonogram. Saw the picture. And it figures I'd bring another man into the world. Even though I wanted this child more than I imagined possible, I prayed he wouldn't be like his daddy. Or mine.

My new rent house perched fifty yards from the edge of the Caprock Escarpment, a chalky, bronze declivity dividing the flat-as-a-board tableland of the Llano Estacado, with the rolling plains hundreds of feet below. I could see for thirty miles, and I drank in the unbroken terrain as it transformed from shadows to sunshine.

And I tried to figure out my life.

I'd been trying for almost eight months, and so far I'd determined three things. I could survive without my parents' help. My heart wouldn't break if I never saw Tyler Cruz again. And I could and would make a home for my child.

I shifted on the car hood and peered down at the fading streetlights of my hometown. In a few minutes, the glow of dawn would eclipse the artificial light, and Trapp, Texas, would momentarily disappear. Good riddance.

Already the horizon glowed orange, and I sipped my iced coffee, letting its bitterness relieve the effects of the smothering heat. August had always been a source of pleasure, with its parties and cookouts, but now that I had no central air-conditioning or ceiling fans or swimming pool, fall looked better all the time.

I opened the Bible app on my cell phone and read my new favorite verse. *Children are a gift from the Lord.* I whispered it into the warm air, reminding myself that even though I hadn't followed the proper time line; even though I had disgraced my family, my church, and my community; even though this baby had turned my life upside down … my little man was a gift.

It had taken me quite a while to accept that fact. I cried the entire first trimester and threw tantrums during the second, but now that the baby could kick some sense into me, I realized for the first time in twenty-one spoiled-little-rich-girl years, my life would have purpose.

The good Lord—cranky as He was—had gifted me with a mission I hadn't thought to ask for. Not that He had rewarded my sin.

On the contrary, I felt the sting of His punishment daily when people in town greeted me and then discreetly turned away. Last week my only remaining friend, Ruthie Turner, told me I'd get used to all that. But I wasn't so sure.

The ever-brightening sky continued to pull the sun above the ground, illuminating miles of uneven pastureland and revealing all its browns and greens, which gradually appeared from the blackness. The wind whipped past me, slacking as though an oscillating fan had turned from high to low and causing my hair to hover above my shoulders before falling weightlessly down my back. I breathed deeply, inhaling the scents of cedar and sage, and waited for the sunshine and wind to erase my insecurity.

I shouldn't have cared what people thought, yet the pious opinions of my parents and a handful of church members chafed my guilt like a new saddle. It didn't matter if they never spoke the words, gave the looks, cast the blame, because I knew what they were thinking. I knew they expected me to marry Tyler Cruz. I knew they thought a wedding would cover a multitude of sins. I knew, in their eyes, marriage was the only way out of my mess.

I knew it … because I was them.

The sun poised golden above the horizon, seeming to buckle its seat belt before sliding boldly into the sky, but it didn't lighten my mood. I slid from the hood, turned my back on the rising sun, and studied the house, now bathed in morning fire.

The paint had long since peeled from the wood siding, the roof slanted precariously over the front porch, and a mesquite branch rubbed against a side window, screeching like the ghost of a centuries-old resident.

If my parents ever saw this house, they'd have a cardiac arrest. Their barn was nicer.

My sandals crunched dry grass as I dragged myself into my new home. My little guy deserved better than this.

But I probably didn't.

CHAPTER TWO

Tyler Cruz stalked diagonally across two plots at the Snyder Cemetery. *Idiot lawyer. Senseless will.* But his *dad* ... his dad had triggered a defensive reaction within Tyler that had him growling like a cornered javelina. Good thing the old man had already died, or Tyler might have taken a sledgehammer to him.

Anger pressed against him as he stood at the center of the grave, panting. A steady rhythm pounded his temples, and the skin on the back of his neck grew moist from sweat, yet he forced himself to settle down. The will didn't matter. He could work with it. When he met his lawyer that morning, he had imagined leaving the office with the bulk of his family's estate, and he still would. Eventually.

His boots sank into the soft mound of dirt, and he asked himself why he had come to the cemetery. *Such a female thing to do.* Mothers or girlfriends or wives, left with empty arms, might stand by the graves of their *loved ones* and bawl enough tears to green the dry West Texas grass.

Tyler's eyes were dry.

He hadn't come because he missed his dad. He came because this was the last place he had seen Fawn. She had stood near the back of the crowd at the funeral—looking as if she could pass out from the summer heat—while he sat in a folding chair under the canopy. At the time, he figured it served her right, but in the past hour, he had developed a change of heart.

He looked down and noticed two flower bouquets, now brown and brittle, left on either side of the tombstone by grievers the morning of. Tyler squatted with an elbow to his knee and pulled a stem from one of the cement vases. Without thinking, he waved the corpse silently back and forth and remembered Fawn years ago in a high school play, dressed in pink fluff and holding a magic wand between her fingertips. *Glinda, the Good Witch*. He crushed the flower petals in his fist.

Four months ago, the woman had infuriated him as much as his father ever did. She had done it quietly out at the ranch, but she might as well have taken out a full-page ad in the county newspaper. Everyone for miles around knew he had been rejected. They knew Fawn had turned her nose up at his family's millions and swore a blue streak that she'd never take him back. But none of that mattered now, because Tyler was man enough to forgive her.

He released his grip, allowing the bits of dried flower to sift through his fingers and fall to the base of the granite marker. It might take a while, but he could woo her back.

After all, she needed him. Her privileged upbringing hadn't prepared her for parenthood, especially not as a single mother. Not that he had been raised any differently, but he would have enough money to make up for it. Fawn, on the other hand, wouldn't get ten cents from her uppity, Bible-righteous parents, even though they had it to give.

A chuckle rose from deep in his throat as he brushed trembling palms against his jeans. Fawn wanted him to think that her pregnancy had somehow made her self-sufficient, defiant, even tenacious, and perhaps he had wondered about that at first.

But when she showed up at his father's funeral, she nullified all the verbal claims she had made about their future. She exposed her subconscious feelings, her naive simplicity, her yearning for things to be set right.

And she proved to Tyler that he still owned her.

CHAPTER THREE

"I can't believe you went to Byron Cruz's funeral."

I sat stiffly on a denim-covered futon in the waiting area of Sophie's Style Station while Ruthie Turner reprimanded me. "You went too."

"I'm not carrying his grandchild."

"That's the point. I'm practically family."

Her voice lowered. "But you don't *want* to be part of that family."

"No, I don't, but that doesn't change the facts. My baby is a Cruz whether I like it or not."

A sarcastic snicker slipped from Ruthie's lips like a stifled hiccup. "Poor kid."

I inspected a cricket near my foot before reaching for a tattered fashion magazine. Ruthie's comments rankled, but I took the criticism as well as my pride would allow. After all, she'd stuck around when my sorority sisters flurried away like startled quail. But we were unlikely friends.

She was a grocery-store clerk desperately in need of a manicure, working nights and weekends to put herself through college, and I was the holier-than-thou daughter of the wealthiest man in Trapp. But somehow Ruthie found it in her heart to forgive my family for our sins against hers when I toppled from my imaginary pedestal and landed splat on the ground at her feet.

I'd say we were best friends, but that sounds all cute and confident and united in purpose, which we weren't. The only thing holding us together was my upside-down life, because we both knew I would flounder without her by my side tutoring me in lower-middle-class survival.

Flipping the pages of the magazine, I boasted, "I scrubbed the windows on my house."

"The place is falling down, and you clean the windows." Ruthie's tinkling laughter caught the attention of Sophie Snodgrass, who paused with a lime-green roller suspended above the hunched shoulders of a tiny old woman whose name I couldn't remember.

"Fawn Blaylock washing windows? I can't picture it." Sophie's jaw worked a wad of chewing gum like one of my father's Hereford cows, and she lifted an eyebrow at her gray-haired customer.

I answered Sophie lightly, brushing off her insulting tone. "The view is the only thing the property has going for it."

"That's not true," Ruthie said. "Your place is cozy, and with your fancy things, it practically looks like something on HGTV."

Bless Ruthie Turner.

Even though she considered my house a dump—and told me so—she would never stand by and let Sophie do the same. None of my "fancy things" had been allowed to leave my parents' house. Instead, Ruthie and I drove to garage sales, collecting tacky household items, which her cousin delivered in his pickup truck.

I lowered my head. "Mother would just *die*, wouldn't she?"

"Eew, don't think about your mother," Ruthie said.

The woman in Sophie's chair chimed in. "How's your mama doing, Fawn? I haven't seen her in town for weeks."

Her question startled me, partly because I never dreamed the old woman could hear my private mutterings to Ruthie, and partly because I had no answer for her—I hadn't spoken to my mother lately either.

A second elderly woman appeared from the corner bathroom, inching toward a hair-dryer seat with her four-pronged, aluminum cane clicking along the linoleum. "That's not quite right, Sister," she said slowly. "We bumped into Susan Blaylock last week in the United grocery. In front of the freezer where they keep the orange sherbet."

"Oh, that's right. She wore high heels on a Tuesday morning."

I lifted my magazine slightly and whispered, "Remind me of their names."

Ruthie turned in her seat as though she were looking at something on the street. "No idea. I always call them Blue and Gray." She winked before wandering to the air conditioner, where she held her hair away from her neck so the frigid blast could dry her skin.

Blue and Gray? I frowned, wondering if she was referencing the Civil War, but when she crossed her eyes and tilted her head toward the hair-dryer seat, it all made sense. The woman in front of Sophie had gray hair, but her sister's hair held a tinge of blue from too much dye.

I bit my lip to keep from laughing.

"Fawn, honey," Gray said as Sophie pulled the last roller from her hair. "I remember when your mama married. Seems like just last week."

Blue gave an airy whistle. "Susan and Neil Blaylock's wedding was the most highfalutin event Trapp's seen in fifty years."

"Maybe sixty." Gray scrunched her nose. "And I bet Fawn's marriage to the Cruz boy will be even fancier."

A sickening knot tightened my insides. Apparently the news of my newfound independence hadn't completed the local gossip circuit yet, though from the look on Sophie's face, the hairdresser was bursting to share the news.

The sweet sisters continued their conversation, oblivious to the tension in the room.

"Like mother, like daughter."

"Sure enough, the apple doesn't fall far."

I crossed one knee over the other and sent the futon's uneven legs tapping back and forth like the pendulum on my parents' grandfather clock. The words of two batty old women shouldn't have bothered me. Everyone from Trapp to Tahoka had already pointed out that my unplanned pregnancy and hurried wedding plans echoed that of my parents.

Sophie peered at me with wide eyes. "Fawn? Are you and Tyler a thing again?"

I wanted to crawl under the futon. Or leave the building. Or move to another state. A haircut shouldn't have been so much trouble.

Ruthie huffed. "Sophie, you know good and well Fawn broke it off with Tyler Cruz for good."

"Well, who am I to say?" Sophie busily teased a lock of Gray's hair into a tangled frenzy.

Blue sat up straight, stretching her withered frame to peek at me over the edge of the counter. "I bet he was unfaithful to you, wasn't he, dearie?" She seemed to imply that if Tyler would sleep with one woman out of wedlock, he would certainly sleep with others.

I lowered my gaze to the floor with an air of mournful loss. I didn't want to lie to the old woman, but I wasn't about to admit the real reason I backed out of my engagement. So far, the truth hadn't come anywhere near the gossip chain—evidence of Tyler's interest in keeping it under the radar as well. In fact, I wouldn't put it past him to have started the cheating-groom rumor. He knew as well as I did that people around here wouldn't forgive abusive behavior nearly as readily as they overlooked promiscuity.

"That's the natural way of men." Gray held up a crooked finger for emphasis. "Can't trust 'em from here to the porch and back."

She coughed as Sophie sprayed her head with a can labeled *Big Sexy Hair.*

"You're all done, sweetie." The hairdresser gently shooed Gray out of her seat while Blue used her cane to pull herself up.

"You and the preacher still wasting time with college?" Blue asked Ruthie. "The two of you ought to be settled down by now."

Gray's palm rested on the counter, and she seemed to use it for balance as she looked back over her shoulder. "Now, Sister, you know how things are these days. Like on the television shows. A woman has to have a career first."

Sophie held the door open. "Ladies, I'll see you again next week. Same time."

I stepped around the puttering women and wondered if the hairdresser was anxious to get me captive in her chair. I mumbled to Ruthie, "I'm beginning to remember why Mother always took me to the spa in Lubbock."

"Welcome to the working class."

I settled into Sophie's throne as she approached. "What can I do for you, Fawn, hon?"

A brief explanation quickly set her to work on my split ends, and soon her gentle combing and snipping relaxed my nerves. I closed my eyes, hoping she would let me enjoy the goose bumps tickling across my scalp.

"Oh, sorry." She yanked a tangle, and when my eyes popped open, she asked, "So you're living up on the Cap?"

"Yes, ma'am."

"But I see you're still driving Velma Pickett's car."

"That's right."

"Ansel and Velma were awful hospitable to board you while you worked things out with your folks."

What was she getting at? Not only had I not worked things out with my folks, but my moving in with the Picketts was old news. "I talked it over with Ansel and Velma, and we agreed I should have my own place before the baby comes. That's why I rented."

Sophie's response came so quickly, her words tripped over mine. "Someone sat in this very chair the other day saying they knew the reason that house has been vacant so long."

"*Sophie ...*" Ruthie plopped into the hair-dryer seat. "This sounds like something you shouldn't bring up."

"Why shouldn't I bring it up?"

Sophie's movements grew rapid and jerky, and I began to fear for my hairstyle. "I've probably heard it already," I said.

"Oh, I doubt it. You never would have moved there."

The lingering scent of *Big Sexy Hair* stung the back of my throat, but I accepted it along with Sophie's prattle. Another layer of my sentence.

She paused in her work, clearly waiting for us to ask for details, and when we didn't, she blurted, "The place is infested with rattle-snakes. I heard the last tenants moved to Oklahoma after they found their six-year-old daughter dead one morning … with a rattlesnake coiled on her pillow."

"That's not true, and you know it." Ruthie looked as if she might slap her.

"Well …" Sophie's bottom lip pooched. "I heard there were tons of—"

"But nobody ever *died*."

The hairdresser lifted her chin. "So you admit there are snakes up there."

"Of course. We live smack in the middle of rattlesnake country, but don't start telling Fawn wild stories."

"I've heard all the stories." A small foot or hand or elbow poked my insides, reminding me to keep things in perspective. "But I've been there a week, and I haven't seen anything but scorpions and tarantulas.

"Did the owner mention snakes?" Sophie turned her head so quickly, her bobbed hair whipped against her cheeks.

"I haven't met him."

She dropped her hands to her sides. "Then how did you rent the house?"

"Ansel knows him." I adjusted the vinyl cape hanging from my shoulders. "I don't know where the man lives. Dallas or Austin, I guess."

"Ruthie, do you know who he is?"

"No, but if he's a friend of Uncle Ansel, he's probably supernice."

I ran my thumb across the stubble on my knee. I hadn't told Sophie everything, but Ruthie knew the sole detail that redeemed my ratty little shack on the Caprock. The owner offered to let me stay there rent-free for two months if I cleaned the place up, and the financial break would make a difference.

Sophie stood motionless with her eyebrows bunched together in concentration. "Let me see if I've got this straight. You're willing to live alone in a snake-infested dump because you're too proud to live in Tyler Cruz's enormous mansion?"

Ruthie slapped her palms against her thighs. "Sophie Snodgrass, Fawn's house may not be as nice as what she grew up in, but she sure as heck doesn't need any help from Tyler."

"Oh, he's that bad, is he?" Sophie chuckled, then squirted gel into her palm and began working it through my curls. "Maybe that boy wants to do right by Fawn. Have you ever thought about that?"

Ruthie snorted.

"He doesn't," I moaned. "When I broke it off with him, he didn't argue. He seemed relieved."

"Not that it's any of your business." Ruthie scowled at Sophie, and the hairdresser's lips momentarily wadded into a tight pucker before she smiled down at me.

"Well, I'd bet money you misjudged the boy. I'd wager he's concerned for his little family."

"Why on earth would you say that?" Ruthie's voice rose. "He hasn't shown an ounce of interest in Fawn or the baby in months."

Sophie wrinkled her nose at Ruthie's reflection in the mirror but then made eye contact with me. "I just think you're wrong about that." She looked pointedly out the front window to the street.

The vinyl cape around my shoulders acted as a barrier, trapping warm air against my torso, but when I looked past the front counter, chill bumps shimmied up my arms and legs as though I had stepped outside during a cold snap.

Tyler stood on the curb leaning against Velma's Chevy, waiting for me.

CHAPTER FOUR

"Hey, babe." Tyler didn't so much as glance at Ruthie when she stomped past him on her way to the diner. Instead, he kept his eyes trained on me, humming the words softly as though approaching a spooked colt. "Was hoping I'd run into you."

My breath caught in spite of my defensiveness. His unexpected appearance, the low timbre of his voice, and the term of endearment worked together to transport me from Trapp's quiet Main Street to a dozen different places he and I had experienced together.

His black hair had grown longer across his forehead, and he had muscled up, but the biggest difference lay in his eyes. They didn't mock as much as they once had, though a glimmer of self-importance remained, and a protective shield hardened around my heart.

"You found me." I wanted to wound his confidence with a glare, but I couldn't muster it, and I let my gaze wander to his truck parked nearby. A pair of binoculars lay on the dash, and I wondered if he'd been hunting recently.

He rapped his knuckles against the hood of the Chevy. "Classy ride. Your dad still holding your Mustang hostage?"

I didn't want to discuss my car, or my parents, or any other controversial topic. I didn't want to talk to him at all. Without a doubt, half the Dixie's Diner patrons across the street were ogling us while they shoveled chicken-fried steak into their mouths, and I wouldn't have put it past Sophie to video the event from her post at the salon. "What do you want, Tyler?"

His eyes roamed a circle around my face, bounced to the Gucci bag hanging from my elbow, and then deliberately examined my body from neck to ankle.

I instantly regretted my choice of clothing, knowing my baggy shorts and oversize Texas Tech T-shirt did nothing for my new body type. *But I shouldn't care.*

He nodded. "You look *good.*"

The emphasis he placed on the last word indicated surprise, and my palm quivered with the urge to slap him. "Right."

"Fawn … *babe* … don't stay mad. I miss you something fierce."

The scent of his Dolce and Gabbana cologne flashed a string of memories across my heart. A lingering hug after a fraternity social. A candlelight dinner on the balcony of his father's house in Snyder. A midnight swim in my parents' pool.

But once he found out about the baby, it had taken him weeks to speak to me and two months to stand up and propose. I fingered a curl hanging near my shoulder. "I'm doing fine without you."

"You can't be having an easy time of it."

Of course not. I lived in a shack without enough money for groceries or doctor bills, but I'd rather live alone than with someone I couldn't depend on. "Like I said, I'm doing all right."

He shoved his hands into the pockets of his cargo shorts. "I shouldn't have been drinking. I never meant to hurt you."

We had danced this number before, breaking up because of his lack of self-control and getting back together because of my need for security. Five times I forgave him. I could count on the fingers of my right hand the number of times I took him back, but once he endangered our baby, I vowed I wouldn't continue the count on my left.

"It won't happen again." He ran his palm across his forehead, and his hair fell back into place exactly the way it had been. Shiny, straight, unchanging.

"That's what you said last time."

"But things are different now. You and the baby mean everything." He peered at me through his eyelashes. "Please forgive me."

The muscles behind my knees weakened, and I shifted my weight. "I've never heard you apologize." *Not to me or anyone else.*

"It's about time I did."

Something in the droop of his shoulders chipped at my resolve, but I hugged myself to mask the effect.

With his middle finger, he poked my abdomen. "How's our little bundle?"

"It's a boy."

"Seriously?" His eyes puzzled. "That's cool. If we're going to have a baby, I'd want it to be a son." He seemed to realize too late the double edge of his statement and did his best to recover. "Are you happy about it?"

I blinked into the wind. "I can't wait to hold him and rock him and all that."

"Sure." Tyler looked down the street, hesitated, then squinted back at me. "The kid got mentioned in Dad's will … Nothing to speak of, but as soon as he's born, there'll be papers to sign."

I hadn't considered Byron Cruz's will. The man had treated me as an inferior, and when he died, I figured my child hadn't crossed his mind. "Sorry I didn't call when he passed."

The glass door of the diner jangled open, and an elderly couple ambled out and to their car.

"No big deal." He brushed his fingertips across my arm. "Can we go somewhere to talk?"

"Better not. Ruthie's waiting for me."

He cut his eyes toward the diner. "She's probably got her eye on me."

"Ruthie and twenty other people." We were standing on Main Street. The news that Tyler Cruz and Fawn Blaylock had spoken would be all over town by sundown.

"I don't see why you hang with her, Fawn. She's not like us."

My spine bristled. Ruthie and I shared a rocky history, but over the past several months, she and her family had done more for me than anyone else. "Meaning?"

"She's hardly even a Christian. And her family's a mess. You shouldn't get tangled up in that."

"She comes to church now."

"Ah … right. With her preacher boyfriend."

"I'd better go." I hurried across the street, but he jogged after me.

"Can I call you sometime? To talk about the baby and see if you need anything?" His words spilled over one another as though he were frantic for me to hear him, to acknowledge his feelings, to love him again. To share our son. That's what it sounded like, but did he mean it?

I despised him for pressuring me to sleep with him—even though I did it willingly and would agree with anyone who called me trash—yet in the midst of my strong feelings, it broke my heart to think of my little man growing up without a daddy. The baby deserved better. I glanced at the diner's tinted plate-glass windows, feeling like an actor on a reality-television show, wanting the studio audience to choose my fate.

If someone had asked me that morning if I would ever speak to Tyler again, I would have said, *Not in a million years.* He had gone too far, left my heart battered and my cheeks bruised. Yet here I stood not only speaking to him but considering letting him call me.

A good Christian would keep on forgiving, but when I looked back at him, a hint of nausea grazed my insides. He seemed to be inspecting my clothing, and then his eyes bounced to the diner windows, and he squared his shoulders.

He would never change.

Even though my life was falling apart, I hadn't given up my dream of a happy ending. A future involving roses and candles and sweet, kind words, not vanity and drunkenness and abusive rage.

"No." I opened the door to Dixie's. "Don't call me."

CHAPTER FIVE

When I walked through the entrance of Dixie's Diner, most of the merry patrons returned their attention to the piles of food in front of them, but a few couldn't keep their eyes from ping-ponging back and forth between Tyler and me as he pulled away.

The only person openly glaring was Ruthie.

"Sit." The wooden legs of the chair across from her grated against the floor as she shoved it with her foot. "What did the undependable, shallow egomaniac want?"

I glanced at the two women on each side of her—Ruthie's aunt Velma and her mother, Lynda—and wished we were alone. Tyler's appearance rattled me, and I would have liked to discuss it with my friend … but not her entire family.

I eased into the seat, scooting back an inch to account for my swollen belly. "I don't know what you mean."

"Don't play stupid." Ruthie smirked.

Velma's plump palm patted my arm. "Aw, Ruthie, give the girl a break. Plain as day the boy caught her off guard."

A grunt of disgust came from Ruthie's mother, but she didn't look up from the laminated menu. She merely raised one condescending eyebrow and tucked her hair behind her ear. I never knew what to make of Lynda Turner.

My mother once described her as an unambitious small-town floozy, but Mother, understandably, was biased.

Velma Pickett, on the other hand, she described as *homemade soap*—functional, old-fashioned, not much to look at. But ironically, Ruthie's aunt Velma, more often than her mother, caused a stifling wave of guilt to press against me like a sauna. Even though she hadn't set foot in a church building since her marriage to Ansel thirty years before, she still had more jewels in her crown than I ever would.

All three women shared the same skeptical brown eyes, compelling me to open my own menu. "Tyler asked about the baby. He didn't want anything."

"Tyler Cruz?" Lynda finally spoke. "Wanting nothing?"

Ruthie glanced at her mother out of the corner of her eye, but she didn't rebuke her the way she often did.

"The man doesn't exactly have a good track record for love and devotion," Lynda said.

She had worked at the diner over a year, so she had no reason to read that menu. She merely used it as a prop to hide behind, like a hot-wire fence separating her from the rest of the world.

I pressed my lips together to keep from snapping at her. The woman had every right to hate my family. Especially my father. "I know Tyler's a mess, but so am I."

"No, you're not," Ruthie said. "You're making something of your life and taking responsibility for your actions." Her head jerked to the window. "He's only flumping along doing whatever feels right in the moment."

"You don't even know what he said."

"I bet I can guess." Lynda slapped her menu against the table. "He loves you, he wants to do right by you, he misses you. And the best line … he'll never let it happen again."

I squirmed in the wooden chair. "What makes you think he said any of that?"

"She's heard it before," Ruthie said with an implied *duh* in her tone.

They were ganging up on me. "He apologized for what happened in April."

Lynda's eyes rolled so dramatically, they seemed to pull an exasperated sigh from the depths of her lungs. "Good grief, those two men are just alike." She glared desperately at Velma. "How can she not see it?" Lynda didn't wait for an answer from her sister but stood and stalked out of the diner.

As the cow bell on the doorframe clanked against the thick glass, indignation swarmed through my lungs like a cloud of angry bees. No matter how well Lynda Turner knew my father, she didn't have the right to criticize him.

Velma tsked as the waitress approached, and I quickly skimmed the menu for the lowest priced item. "I'll have the fried zucchini."

"She'll also have an order of chicken and dumplings," declared Velma to the waitress, "with okra and corn on the side. Same for me."

"Me, too," Ruthie said.

The baby chose that moment to kick me in the ribs, and I sat up straight and rubbed my side. "Thanks, Velma."

She watched me as she sipped her sweet tea and then set her glass down with a thump, obviously forging the conversation in a new direction. "How's your new home?"

The woman could read my moods like a gypsy fortune-teller. "I get lonely out there."

"I can come over more often." Ruthie's statement seemed to double as an unspoken regret for her mother's outburst.

"You come over plenty." I fiddled with the silverware bundle on the table. "I just miss campus life."

Ruthie raised an eyebrow. "Partying and spending money?"

"Don't be ugly." The older woman's chin jutted, and I got the impression she expected Ruthie to apologize then and there.

"She's a Blaylock, Aunt Velma. She can't help it."

"For crying out loud, Ruth Ann."

But Ruthie hit the target. I missed my right-side-up world, and my stubborn will was bucking the changes. "I'm not like my parents … I mean I'm not like my father."

"Oh, Fawn." Ruthie rubbed her palms over her face. "It's not your dad that has Momma upset. It's you."

Velma chuckled. "My sister might not show it, but she cares."

I almost laughed out loud. Lynda Turner cared for me about as much as a hawk cares for a field mouse. "Yeah, right. It's obvious from the kindness she's shown over the years."

"That's Lynda, darlin'," Velma soothed. "Her love's prickly, but it doesn't make it any less real."

A tractor rumbled down Main Street, and I gazed at it blindly, lost in thought. A person like me, with only one friend—two if I counted Velma—had no room to be picky when it came to affection.

"Well, at least your mother speaks to me," I said. "That's more than I can say for mine." I took a sip of ice water, and as its cool wetness washed the soot of bitterness from my lungs, I said a silent prayer, thanking God for these women He placed in my life. It was true Ruthie looked down on my sorority sisters, her aunt Velma naturally upstaged me and my sinful ways, and her mother resented my father so much she could never forgive, but the three of them cared about me.

Certainly they weren't the people I would have chosen for the job, but nevertheless, they were all I had. And their words of concern, painful though they were, floated around in my brain the rest of the day.

CHAPTER SIX

For the first time in my life, I had a job, and—wouldn't you know it?—I was surrounded by men. When Dusty Burnett, from the feed store, insisted he needed some accounting work done, I assumed he asked me as a favor to Ruthie's uncle Ansel, but after inspecting his books—four spiral notebooks filled with pencil scratches—I could see the man truly did need help.

So every weekday morning at seven, I parked Velma's Chevy between the tractor implements in the parking lot, climbed the loading ramp past crates of livestock feed, and made my way through the dimly lit sales floor to Dusty's closet-sized office, where I crunched numbers, reviewed purchase orders, and organized files until noon. I loved the work, putting my college accounting classes to use, and took advantage of the opportunity to forget my troubles.

The downside? Customers—mostly men—sauntered through the store, a few of them greeting me, others ignoring me awkwardly, most of them paying no attention whatsoever. I had always enjoyed a certain reaction from men, but since I had gotten pregnant, their eyes skimmed past me. I felt like a jar of peaches on display at the youth fair, inspected for color, taste, and texture, then set aside in a dark cupboard until winter.

I lifted my gaze from the computer screen and noticed Clyde Felton out on the sales floor. The man's muscular frame seemed to fill the entire back corner of the store as he casually studied a display of seeds and glanced at me every few seconds.

Great. Of all the men in town, only the convicted rapist paid attention to me. With his dirty-blond hair pulled back in a short ponytail, he didn't look as rough as usual, but when he saw me watching, he shuffled out of my line of sight.

I dropped my head in my hands, running my fingernails through my hair before gripping handfuls of curls at the base of my neck. The good Lord would probably strike me dead for my vanity.

"You don't look so good."

I jerked my head up, only to see Ansel and Velma's grown son. My shoulders relaxed. "Oh, I'm all right, Coach Pickett. Taking a break."

"I told you to stop calling me Coach. You graduated from high school three years ago."

"I'm trying, but *JohnScott* just sounds wrong."

I didn't really know Ruthie's cousin except as my high school history teacher. Even though I'd lived with his parents for the past seven months, I mostly stayed locked in the spare bedroom with a box of tissues. Nevertheless, the coach and I developed a light friendship over evening meals, which he habitually ate at their house. He lived in a manufactured home on the back of their property, and Velma said she saw no sense in him cooking a random nibble every night when she planned an entire spread.

He rested a fist on the doorframe. "Mom's Chevy running all right?"

"Seems to be." I gently swiveled my chair back and forth.

"Might need Freon soon."

"Okay." I had no idea what he meant by Freon, but I didn't ask. "Thanks for helping with the garage-sale furniture."

"Yep." His eyes traveled around the store before he looked back at me. "Your front steps could use a little repair. Thought I'd slap a few boards on there before somebody gets hurt."

"There's no need for that, Coach Pick—*JohnScott*. The steps are fine."

"They're not." One side of his mouth lifted, creating a set of smile lines on that cheek, but I didn't mind him laughing at me.

When I sat in his classroom my sophomore year of high school, most of the girls tittered because he was straight out of college, attractive and single, but I hadn't paid him any mind. In the first place, he was Ruthie's cousin, and back then, the two of us weren't on speaking terms. And in the second place, I didn't see the point of wasting my time on a teacher.

Now he reigned as the head coach of the Trapp Panthers football team, still attractive, still single, and if I hadn't been in my current situation, I might have finally considered him worth the effort. But I didn't have that luxury. The most eligible bachelor in Trapp wouldn't settle for a pregnant college girl like me.

So I opted to ignore his smile lines and the soft curls teasing out from under his cap. Instead, I appreciated his kindness, because Coach JohnScott Pickett represented one of the few people who treated me exactly like he used to.

He nodded his chin in greeting to someone around the corner. "Fawn's working here now."

The sound of boots dragging on concrete signaled the approach of another man, and then Clyde Felton peered at me over the coach's head. "Sure enough," the ex-convict grumbled. "How you doing, Miss Blaylock?"

My lips fumbled a reply, but Clyde didn't wait for my babbled response.

"You'll be at the diner, Coach?"

"I'll be there." JohnScott's gaze followed the older man out the front door, and when he looked back at me, his smile lines disappeared. "You don't like him much, do you?"

I fingered a stack of receipts. "They convicted him. I'd be a fool to ignore his past."

His long arms folded lazily across his chest. "Why do you act like that?"

"Like what?"

"You know what statutory means, right?" Suddenly he took on the role of teacher, patiently explaining a lesson I hadn't quite grasped the first time around.

"Coach Pickett, I don't care if they were dating. The girl was still underage."

"Huh." Silence vibrated the room until I met his gaze, and when our eyes locked, he chuckled. "The way I see it, the only difference between his situation and yours is that you're a few years older than his girlfriend was."

I felt naked, visible not only to every man in the store but to every person in town. In the county.

I dropped my hand to my abdomen in a reflexive attempt to hide my sins, but JohnScott Pickett only shook his head and smiled. As though it might take me a while to learn today's lesson, but I would eventually get it in the end.

CHAPTER SEVEN

I sat on the third pew from the back in our white-frame church building and counted the number of women who passed me without speaking. So far, seven. Not that many, but considering there were only eleven females in the building, seven represented a fairly high percentage.

If someone asked them about it, they would have been shocked by the accusation, so unaware were they of their behavior. But I had been in their place before, throwing stones. Back in high school, a friend's parents got a divorce, and I treated her differently afterward, because I didn't know what to say.

Now I found myself on the dark side, paying penance.

Ruthie sat next to me, and her boyfriend, Dodd Cunningham, stood at the end of the pew, greeting his congregants as they entered the small chapel.

"Good morning, Mrs. Reeger," he said. "It's good to see you today."

"Hello, Dodd." She shook his hand. "Ruthie." She nodded politely, then cleared her throat and continued down the aisle.

What a jerk. I decided to ignore them all.

"Don't let them get to you." Ruthie adjusted her skirt. "Things will be better. Remember how they were when I came back."

"Hardly the same. Most of them went out of their way to be kind."

"Bless their hearts, they did." She chuckled under her breath. "They were so kind, it seemed … *unbelievable.*"

Dodd's eyebrows pressed together, but soon his reprimanding scowl evaporated into a smile. "Ladies, things are not as bad as you make them out to be."

"He's always telling me that," Ruthie said.

The preacher bent down until his lips were next to her ear, but he spoke loud enough for me to hear. "Be a good girl during worship, and I'll give you a treat afterward."

She turned her head so their mouths were inches apart. "What will you give me if I'm not good?"

The exchange took only a few seconds, but it served to remind me the Trapp congregation hadn't had a single minister for as long as I could remember—maybe not ever—so when the baptized believers walked past our pew, they already had a lot to chew on before they ever got to Ruthie and me.

"I can't believe you're making out in the church building." Dodd's younger brother sidled into the pew next to us, his jaw hanging open. "Preachers these days."

"It's about time you got here, Grady," Dodd said. "Where's Mom?"

"Water fountain, but as soon as she gets here, I'm telling."

The gentle banter of the brothers put my nerves at ease, but when I noticed my mother in the foyer, my muscles tightened.

"Grady, stop tattling." Milla Cunningham sat next to Grady and opened the worship bulletin to scan the announcements. "Just when I think you've outgrown that."

"But if Dodd will flirt with Ruthie right here in front of everybody, there's no telling what he'll try when we bow our heads to pray."

Milla ignored him and smiled at Ruthie and me. "I hope my sons haven't been too obnoxious."

"Not any more than usual." Ruthie stuck her tongue out at Grady.

My mother came through the doors next, floating down the aisle like a beauty queen. She maintained her arrogant flair, but my father's absence from worship rendered her actions shallow and artificial.

"Good morning, Susan." Dodd smiled, but he didn't hold out his hand. Undoubtedly he had been left hanging too many times and had learned to avoid the gesture.

"Hello, Dodd." Her nose tilted above the rest of us, and our entire pew watched silently as she glided to her usual seat.

Mother's behavior sent my heart plummeting, but a slow rhythm of pity beat against my rib cage. Pity because she sat alone, without my father on the pew next to her.

Dodd walked to the front as the congregation began to sing "Wonderful, Merciful Savior."

An occasional friend of my mother, Pamela Sanders, patted Dodd on the back as she and her husband scooted into the pew in front of us, late as usual. I smiled. For years they blamed their tardiness on their teenage daughter, but now that she was away at college, they had no excuse.

"Morning, Brother Cunningham." The wooden pew creaked as she turned around and raised her voice to be heard above the singing. "Fawn, how you doing? You feeling all right?" She reached for my hand and gave it a squeeze.

"Yes, ma'am."

"You look lovely today. Pregnancy sure does agree with you." She blinked twice, then turned to Ruthie. "How's your momma, sweetie? She doing all right?"

Ruthie shrugged, seemingly unconcerned with the looks we were getting from a few rows up. "Oh, you know. Momma never changes."

Pamela nodded with a knowing frown. "Well, you tell her I said *hey*. Tell her I think about her often."

"I'll do that, Pamela."

Mrs. Sanders turned to face forward, and as she did, I realized my heart had lightened. This simple, bumbling woman was *good*. And kind and thoughtful and Christlike, and surprisingly I admired her.

In my upside-down world.

But Pamela Sanders wasn't the only one topsy-turvy. Like the reflections in a fun-house mirror, Ruthie and my mother were warped distortions of what they had been a year ago. The girl I had always been expected to scorn was now my friend, and instead of me shunning Ruthie, my mother now shunned me.

Pamela turned around once more and patted Ruthie's knee, speaking in a loud stage whisper. "I heard about the Panthers being picked for state, and I don't doubt that cousin of yours could do it."

Grady leaned across me. "Coach Pickett says with the roster he's got this year, any coach could take them." His eyes cut toward Ruthie. "But I wouldn't go that far."

"Naw, me either," Pamela said. "JohnScott brings the team together." She nodded firmly, then started singing.

But I stopped. At the mention of his name, I pictured my old history teacher leaning against the doorframe at the feed store, pointing out the similarities between me and the rapist Clyde Felton. JohnScott Pickett hadn't been a Christian very long, but he had certainly caught up to the rest of us, slicing me down with a mere cut of his tongue. Thank goodness he didn't worship in Trapp.

His accusation had hit its mark as intended, keeping me awake two nights running, but I hadn't yet spoken to him about it, neither to apologize nor to defend myself, and I might not ever. Probably he had already forgotten the incident.

Dodd strode to the pulpit, where he smiled at the congregation. Smiled and meant it. That was the refreshing difference about Dodd. He was real.

And he belonged to Ruthie.

I peeked at her out of the corner of my eye, wishing I weren't envious of her right-side-up life. Granted, she didn't have money or any of the pleasures it could buy, but she had her uncle Ansel and aunt Velma and JohnScott. And she had a mother she could relate to.

But my deepest shade of green resulted from Ruthie's relationship with the preacher.

Dodd's voice carried across the room as he gave his opening remarks, told his icebreaker joke, and launched into a lesson from Genesis. Adam and Eve and their fall from grace.

Don't get me wrong. I did not have feelings for Dodd, but I longed for the security a man could give me. And love. And trust. Dodd's ambition might not ever provide a cushy income, but his faith would keep him anchored by her side and loving her like Christ loved the church. And Ruthie didn't even realize what she had.

I sighed and rubbed my pinky against my stomach. Tyler could buy me anything I ever wanted—houses, cars, clothes, toys for my baby. But he would never be a spiritual giant, even though he'd been raised in church three times a week. Over and over, I had chosen him, but now in my upside-down state, I found myself yearning for the opposite. The impossible.

Dodd stood calmly with his fingertips pressed together at his waistline. "We all have our own serpents leading us away from the light." He spoke gently. "Yours might be a person or a situation in which you find yourself. Or it could be nothing more than your own thoughts pulling you away from the Lord."

Or it could be all three. My shoulders relaxed into putty, like they did when mother's massage therapist worked on them at the spa, and I felt the urge to lie down on the wooden pew and drift into a restful sleep that would take me closer to God. But that never worked when I'd lie on my garage-sale mattress up on the Caprock, so it wouldn't work here, either.

I closed my eyes. If anyone saw me, they would think I was sleeping in church, but for once, I didn't care what they thought. I just wanted to pray.

I told God about my loneliness, and I begged Him not to leave me. I had studied the Scriptures since I was a toddler, so I knew all about God being omnipresent, omnipotent, and omniscient.

Supposedly He would be with me. Always and forever. By my side.

I just couldn't feel Him.

A pudgy finger poked my knee, and I opened my eyes to see Pamela Sanders turned around in her pew yet again. Her shoulders bounced as she giggled.

I ran my hand across my forehead. Maybe someday I would be more like Pamela. Maybe someday I would stop calling people names like *jerk* and start loving them right where they were, even if they fell asleep in the pew. Maybe someday I would be as good a Christian as I used to think I was.

No wonder Pamela confused my prayer for a party-girl's nap. I hardly recognized myself.

CHAPTER EIGHT

JohnScott would have kept an eye on Fawn Blaylock even if his parents hadn't insisted he do so, but he never intended to repair her steps with her away from the house. She might view it as too familiar. Or an invasion of her privacy. Or poor manners. But if he was honest with himself, he had to admit another reason he regretted not catching her at home.

He unloaded lumber onto a bare spot in her yard on Sunday afternoon, and then he set to yanking the three boards off the front steps. They were so rotted, he could have done it with his bare hands, but he used a crowbar instead, enjoying the work.

He pulled the last board loose and tossed it onto a pile behind him, then peered into the shadowy crawl space beneath the house. Daylight shone through an uncovered opening at the back corner of the building, and he made a mental note to cover it later. No need to invite wildlife to nest beneath Fawn's feet.

He chuckled. Fancy little Fawn was out of her element living here. Sure, she'd been raised in the country, but not alone. Neil Blaylock ran his ranching business like a well-oiled machine, with hired hands doing most of the labor.

JohnScott retrieved a circular saw from the cab of his truck and unrolled an extension cord before scanning the porch. He groaned. Of course the old place wouldn't have an exterior outlet. He gripped a post and pulled himself up onto the porch. Maybe she'd left a window unlocked. He tested two by the front door, but from the looks of it, they were cemented shut with layers of house paint. The panes had recently been scrubbed clean, though, in stark contrast to the rest of the house.

Fawn and her view.

He turned to survey the landscape. Jagged uplifts, shallow ravines, and choppy fields created a crazy patchwork quilt of muted earth tones far below. And through it, Highway 84 snaked down the Caprock, curled through the low-lying buildings of Trapp, and slinked away into the distance.

He shook his head. Maybe the girl had a point. He might consider living in harsh conditions if it meant he could wake up to that panorama every morning.

As an afterthought, he reached for the doorknob, growling softly when it turned in his hand. "Fawn …" He swung the door open and stepped into her living room, scoping the walls for outlets. In the end, he scooted the loveseat away from the wall to access a plug behind it.

Surveying the room, he realized she needed a rocker for the baby, but then he smiled. He couldn't picture Fawn in a rocking chair.

She had made the place homey since he'd dropped off the garage-sale furniture, though the temperature inside the house still made him sweat. An oval rug partially covered the worn hardwood floors, and one of his mother's crocheted afghans rested on top of the loveseat where the stuffing fluffed through the upholstery. He could tell Fawn burned scented candles to mask the stale odor from the house being shut up so long.

The bedroom was just as plain. Fawn and Ruthie found a mattress at a garage sale, but with no frame or box springs, the bed rested right on the floor. Fawn covered it with a not-too-ratty quilt, but the pillow looked as flat as a pancake. She probably had to fold the thing into a ball just to get comfortable.

His chest tightened in shame as he realized *he was snooping.* He turned and tossed the end of the extension cord across the porch and closed the front door behind him, having no trouble maneuvering the cord beneath it. He cringed as a tiny mouse followed him outside.

Swinging down to the ground, he reached for a board, but just as he positioned it to make a cut, he noticed a cloud of dust approaching. He bent to make the quick slice, and then lay the board across the support beams to test the length. He turned in time to see Fawn's maroon Chevy, his mother's car, slow at the bend in the road.

His parents were crazy about her, a fact that surprised them as much as him. When she turned up pregnant with no roof over her head, Dodd Cunningham had asked them to take her in, but their decision had been swayed more by their animosity toward Neil Blaylock than their compassion for his daughter. They hadn't expected to take to her like they did.

"Hey, Fawn." He reached for a fistful of nails as she got out of the car.

"There's really no need for this, Coach Pickett." She walked toward him carrying a brown paper grocery sack and her snazzy handbag.

"There is." He hammered two nails in place. Fawn must have been seven months along by now—maybe more—but other than her midsection, she didn't look pregnant at all, and sometimes he imagined her pulling a volleyball out from under her shirt and laughing about the joke she had played on all of them. He looked at her. "How are things?"

"I think the air's out on your mom's car."

He smiled but didn't let her see. "Might be the Freon."

"Oh, right. You mentioned that the other day." She hesitated at the vacant steps, then scooted onto the porch on her bottom and swung her legs around. "You shouldn't have torn off all the steps," she said. "You could just replace the one."

"And come back when the others give way?"

"I wouldn't mind." She went in the house, leaving the door wide open behind her.

He considered closing it, but the measly air conditioner wasn't running anyway. She walked into the kitchen, tossed her purse on the table, and moved out of sight. What had she meant by *I wouldn't mind*? His stomach tensed.

Truth be told, he wouldn't mind either. At all.

But Fawn was one of his students—or had been—and it felt wrong to even toy with the idea. Besides, he had no business taking a shining to a single, pregnant girl. Especially a Blaylock. He scoffed at the possibility as he ran his hand over a board, snagging a splinter.

Fawn called from the house, "Want some iced coffee? It's mocha."

"Sure." He pinched at the tiny sliver in his skin, but his fingers were too big and his fingernails too short.

"Splinter?" She squatted to hand him a glass.

"Yep." He lifted the coffee to his lips and watched her over the curve of the plastic cup as she turned his palm back and forth. Her delicate hands were still cool from carrying the glasses, and her long fingernails tickled his palm.

He pulled away. "It's nothing."

"I've got tweezers."

"So do I, back at the house." He set his coffee on the porch and reached for another board. "By the way, Dad said the owner of your house is sending a couple window units."

She gasped. "Air conditioners?"

"Yep."

She leaned her head back and laughed softly. "Thank. You. God."

She had fumbled her blonde hair into a mess on top of her head, but a few stray curls clung to the moist skin on the side of her neck.

JohnScott concentrated on the steps.

"I'll install them as soon as they come in."

"*Yep*," she teased.

He ignored her. "So you're taking some classes this semester."

"Start tomorrow."

"How many hours do you lack?"

"A million." She paused, and JohnScott wondered if she considered him nosy. She shrugged as though she had nothing to lose by disclosing her plans, but she didn't look at him. "I'm not really sure what I'm going to do. The baby and I can't live off my feed-store salary." Her bottom lip quivered once before tucking beneath her teeth. "But I've got a lot of options, right?"

Twenty questions popped into his head. How much money would she need? Could she stay in college with the baby? What options was she considering?

He nodded. "Yep."

"Coach Pickett, stop saying *yep*." She slapped her hands against the porch, and her blue eyes sparkled with teasing laughter.

He rose to his full height and lifted his chin in a challenge. "Only if you stop calling me *Coach Pickett*."

Her nose wrinkled. "I forgot about that. I'm supposed to ignore your age and treat you as an equal."

He stuck a nail between his teeth, preparing to cut the next board. "I'm not that old," he said around the nail.

The squeal of the electric saw temporarily cut off the conversation, but she picked up again when it silenced. "If I'm twenty-one ..."—she counted on her fingers—"you must be, what? Twenty-eight?"

"Seven."

"That's practically thirty."

He enjoyed her taunts but wished he didn't. "I see what you're saying, Fawn. Thirty is fossilized."

She raised her palms as though he'd stated a fact that couldn't be debated. "*Yep.*"

He reached for his cup. "What year were you in my class?"

"Sophomore. Sixteen years old."

That made him feel even worse, and he took a long drink to avoid looking at her. He remembered her in his class. Bubbly, happy, immature like all the others. "You changed sometime after that," he said.

"What do you mean?"

He lifted his cap and scratched his head, questioning why he had mentioned something so personal. "You sort of … stopped smiling as much."

"Did I?"

JohnScott couldn't read her expression.

She squinted at the clouds, wrinkled her nose, shrugged. "I think I got snottier my junior and senior years."

His laugh came from deep in his lungs, releasing some of his tension. "Well, I didn't want to say so."

"I was awful, wasn't I?"

"Of course you were awful. You were a teenager."

She smiled as she stood to lean against a post and look out over the mesa. "You don't seem that old anymore."

At her words, his heart throbbed against his chest, and he almost fumbled his cup. But when he looked up at her, she stared absent-mindedly into the distance. She hadn't meant anything by it.

He bent to grasp a hammer. "Maybe I feel old because I hang with Clyde so much."

She crossed her arms then, and JohnScott realized he had made her uncomfortable again, like the other day at the feed store. He hadn't intended to get in her face about Clyde, but her attitude about the ex-convict tugged at his sense of justice.

She swirled ice in the bottom of her cup. "Clyde Felton is old enough to be your dad." She said it lightly, as though to keep the topic safe.

"Not quite. He's only a few years past forty, so unless he did the hanky-panky at fifteen, it wouldn't pan out right."

"Not a pleasant thought."

A drop of defensive adrenaline leaked into his veins. "Because it's hanky-panky or because it's Clyde?"

"Both." She rotated slowly, scrutinizing the porch and deliberately turning her back on him.

JohnScott decided to give her a gentle nudge. "He's old enough to be *your* father, though. You being such a spring chick and all."

"Eww."

The drop of adrenaline increased to a steady stream, and he tossed his hammer on the porch. "Has he done something to offend you?"

Her eyes widened. "Well, no. Not personally."

"Has he ever been kind to you?" He knew the answer.

"I suppose so."

"Then what's the hang-up?"

"For goodness' sake, Coach Pickett, he went to prison."

"Well, he's out now. And he repented."

She stomped into the house and returned holding the end of the extension cord. "You don't have to be so touchy about it."

He stared up at her, frustrated with himself because he still found her attractive. "Clyde's a friend of mine."

Her expression softened, but only slightly. "I'm sorry, JohnScott. I'm just tired."

When she shut the door behind her, JohnScott's insides exploded, and he yanked the orange cord, gathering it into a swirl.

So disappointing.

Fawn was no longer the pious brat he had taught in high school. Now that she viewed herself as an inferior Christian, she had actually started becoming a better one. A humble one. A woman he considered worthy of admiration.

Yet every so often, the old Fawn showed up and stuck her little nose in the air, as though to keep herself from becoming too clean. And during those times, JohnScott regretted his parents' attachment to her. He regretted his promise to keep an eye on her. And he regretted the way her smile made him feel.

CHAPTER NINE

The coach got on my nerves. As I drove into town late the next afternoon, I thought about his visit. I appreciated him fixing my steps, but I got the feeling he had assigned himself to watch over me when I didn't need, or want, the attention. And he always seemed to be laughing at me.

I pattered into the Trapp Laundromat carrying a flimsy plastic basket full of secondhand maternity clothes Velma had scrounged. As I lifted the lid of a washer, I thought of the designer brands I used to wear. Closets full. I gripped a T-shirt by the shoulders, scrutinized it, then shoved it into the machine.

I missed the designers. When I left home, Mother had been gracious enough to send my wardrobe, but my Miss Me Jeans and Anthropologie dresses were currently stuffed in a closet, waiting for the day I got small again. I wiggled my toes in my sneakers. At least my Kate Spades still fit.

I kicked them off and settled into a blue plastic chair in the corner, easing my back pain. The soapy, clean scent of detergent cleansed my mood, and I settled down with my history textbook, but soon my attention wandered from the dull pages to a poster hanging on the bulletin board to my left. The homecoming street dance. Ruthie and Dodd would probably go. I would stay home.

Traffic passed the front windows. Mostly pickup trucks. A few SUVs. A delivery truck headed to the United grocery. But then my mother's Audi crept by, stuck behind a slow-moving cattle trailer. My father sat behind the wheel, his eyes focused on the bumper in front of him, but Mother pointed at my Chevy and pursed her lips.

Wouldn't they have been shocked if they could see me? Barefoot and pregnant. My dad had used that phrase to describe me, and at the time I found it offensive, but now I only snickered. He had been right after all.

About some things.

I ran my finger down the page and began reading again. He hadn't been right about the church. He'd said they would cast me out with the other sinners, yet I had been there every time the doors opened. The members had limits to what they could overlook, but apparently I fell within the boundaries of grace. Or maybe my last name simply granted me special treatment. I wouldn't be surprised.

The Laundromat door swung open, and the shrill blast from a train two blocks away disrupted the monotonous churning of the washer.

My mother.

She flashed a fake, almost desperate smile that sent a metallic taste to the roof of my mouth. "Fawn, honey." Her gaze bounced from me to the old machines to the dirty floor, where powdered laundry soap gritted beneath her sequined sandals.

My tongue felt swollen and dry in my mouth. "Hello, Mother."

She scrutinized the wall above my head. "Are you well?"

"Awesome." My remark came out more sarcastic than I intended, but the irony of my mother asking about my welfare was just too much.

And yet I wanted her to care.

She stepped forward as though to sit next to me, but my legs were draped across the seat. Instead, she perched two seats down and peered at my feet.

She would view my behavior as rude—rebellious—and she really didn't deserve that. After all, she hadn't kicked me out of the house. She merely went along with it, so submissive she couldn't stand up to her husband.

Not even for me.

Turning, I tucked my feet beneath my chair, and Mother managed to convey both approval and disgust with her lipstick smile.

"Are you still staying with Ansel and Velma Pickett?"

"No, I've got my own place." If she'd socialized with the working class, she would've heard it by now.

Her eyes widened in surprise. "How can you—" She looked away, unable to hide the raw emotion. Something like jealousy. "Where?"

"It's a small house up on the Caprock, half a mile past the scenic overlook. It's not much, but it's all right for the baby and me." I peered at her, evaluating her mood and weighing my options. "You could come up sometime. To see the place." I laughed, feeling exposed. "I make a mean iced mocha."

She ran her fingertip along the edge of my book resting on the chair between us. "I … I know that house. I've been there."

I held back a laugh. She couldn't have surprised me more if she'd stood on a washer and danced a schottische. Even though she had lived in Trapp her entire life, my mother never set foot in real estate less than a certain square footage.

"You've been in that house?"

She snatched at her purse. "Your father insisted I give you some cash. It's not much, but it will help with rent and groceries." And just like that, her stoic indifference fell into place.

"I'm not taking his money." I couldn't take it. My father made it clear there were expectations attached to anything I accepted from him.

"Fawn ..." She dragged out my name, shredding my nerves as she pulled me through memories of arguments.

"He can't even bear to look at me, Mom."

Her shoulders dropped a half inch. "He's not heartless, only disappointed."

"He's always disappointed."

She almost leaned back in the blue chair but caught herself before her tanned shoulder made contact. "I know."

Yes, she knew exactly what I meant. We may have never enjoyed the kind of mother-daughter relationship where we stayed up late and discussed girl problems, but we could empathize about my father without ever speaking a word.

"I ran into Lynda Turner," I said. It was a low blow, and I knew it, but the endless list of forbidden topics had worn on me during our short separation. "Tell me what he did to that woman."

My mother inspected the cuticle of a painted fingernail. "I don't see how that matters."

"Obviously it matters to Lynda."

"Then ask her, not me."

"I shouldn't have to." I leaned back so forcefully, the plastic popped, and I wondered if I had broken the blasted chair. My mother never really talked to me. When my pregnancy test came back positive, I thought we might finally have common ground, but no, she only pulled further away.

"Calm down," she purred. "The fact is, your father dated Lynda Turner when we were young, but he broke up with her to date me." She rubbed her cuticle again, adjusted her blouse, cleared her throat. "But I wouldn't mention it to him if I were you."

She left something out, I knew it. Her explanation sounded too simple, too clean, and way too forthcoming. I knew better than to think they had kept a simple love triangle a secret for so many years.

"How is Dad?" One little question with many layers. *Is he well? Has he humbled himself at all? Has he hurt you lately?*

"He's fine." Her face matched the plastic seating, hard and cold.

I noticed him on the sidewalk then, dragging his boots arrogantly as he spoke into his cell phone. *Always the businessman.* He kept his back to the window, head held high, laughing.

I cut my eyes back to my mother. "Nothing's changed?"

Her gaze skittered to the sidewalk, and she lowered her voice. "He may never come back to church, but he apologized to the preacher."

"Well, that's a start."

"It's huge," she snapped. "These things take time, Fawn."

These things. Things like change. Like forgiveness. Like heartfelt repentance. I wondered if *these things* would happen in my lifetime.

"Will he ever speak to me again, or is he just going to send cash through you?"

"He's coming in here, actually. He has something to say to you."

Her voice faltered, matching the trembling in my legs, and I almost felt bad for giving her a hard time. But not quite.

As if on cue, he sauntered through the Laundromat door, setting off a chain reaction of heat up my neck and cheeks. In contrast to my mother's entrance, he looked at nothing in the room but kept his eyes focused on me. "Good God, Fawn. Surely you've heard of dry cleaners."

A nervous chuckle forced itself, unbidden, from deep in my lungs. "Good to see you, too."

"Your mother says you talked to Tyler."

My washer finished its cycle. "We've had words."

"Good."

He paused, and one of my bare feet vibrated against the metal bracket that bolted the chair to the floor. I knew he was deliberately stalling, waiting for me to look at him. My father had always demanded eye contact, but I didn't want to give him that much power.

My foot bounced slightly, and the row of plastic seats shook from the movement. I locked my knees together, willing my muscles to comply. My mind rebelled against him while my body yearned to obey … out of sheer habit.

I lifted my eyes to meet his, and he nodded his approval.

"In spite of the depth to which you've lowered yourself, you and Tyler are still a match. You should do what you can to make things happen with him."

"Make things happen?" His words struck me as crude, but he waved away my question.

"You know what I'm saying. He'll take care of you ... and your child." He said the last words as though they were a disease that must be dealt with. "In the meantime, I'll see you have what you need." He cocked his head toward my mother. "Did you give her the money?"

"I tried."

Everything always came back around to money. "What about love, Dad? Does that matter at all?" To gain confidence, I fled to the washer and lifted the lid.

"Apparently you loved him enough to sleep with him. Surely you can muster enough love to marry him."

"Neil ..." My mother moaned.

"Don't get me wrong, Fawn. I'd be tickled pink for you to live happily ever after, but you're not living a fairy tale." His key chain jangled. "Tyler Cruz wants you, and I don't see any other men standing in line."

A drop of sweat trickled down the back of my knee. "Well, Dad. Now that you put it that way, you've made me all mushy inside." I pulled wet laundry from the washer, dropping each item in the basket at my feet.

"Don't be sassy." Mother hissed the reprimand as she stood, but I had already heard it in my head.

"She can't help it, Susan." He lurched away from me as though to distance himself from my shame, and Mother followed after him, straightening her back uncertainly.

And then they were gone.

A hot breath of air gusted from the sidewalk as the door closed behind them, and already a grin covered my father's face as he lifted his chin in greeting to a passing friend. But Mother, ever the worrier, glanced back at me with a pained expression.

I peered down at my bare feet, embarrassed they had seen me like this, figuring it only added to my father's perception that he had been right all along. My damp clothes lay heaped in the basket, needing attention, but I ignored them and stumbled to a chair.

Slipping on my shoes, I rested my elbows on my knees, head in hands. I had loved Tyler once. Maybe I still did. He understood the deal about my parents, and he always shared my dreams and worries.

But he had broken my trust. Not once or twice but over and over.

The first time, our junior year in high school, he spent thirty minutes with Hannah McGready behind the show barn at the stock show, effectively ending the ten months we'd sat next to each other in church. The second and third times, he screamed hateful things at me, once when we were alone and once in public. After that, there was Ashley Alvarez my first year at Tech.

But the fifth time, he struck me. And to make matters worse, the preacher had seen it. A few days later, when Tyler denied the baby was his, I thought I would never take him back, but he had come to me, heartbroken and sincere. And he seemed so sorry.

But then he hit me again. He hadn't hurt the baby, of course—Tyler would never do anything except slap my face—but I couldn't get over the idea of it. The thought of him lashing out when I carried something so precious—a tiny person who needed to be protected and nurtured.

I called off the wedding that day because a hungering desire had welled up inside me. A yearning to be protected and nurtured myself … and *cherished*. But nobody had come along to do it.

In the past few months, I had demanded to do things on my own, trying to prove I didn't need Tyler, and certainly didn't need my parents. Yet I hadn't proved anything. Not really. Ruthie took me to garage sales. Velma loaned me her car. Coach Pickett repaired my steps. But I never stopped needing someone. I merely transferred the caretaking obligation to my new friends.

The baby kicked, and I pressed a palm against the movement, wishing Tyler could somehow become everything the baby and I needed. "I know, little guy. I've made a mess of things."

CHAPTER TEN

Twenty minutes later, Ruthie sat cross-legged on a washing machine while I checked messages on my phone. I'd dumped my laundry in a dryer, then watched the clothes swirl while I relived my parents' intrusion. When I finally snapped out of my pity-induced trance, I called Ruthie to come keep me company.

"Which do you like better—ball gown or mermaid?" she asked.

I glanced at the bridal magazine open across her lap. "My favorite is Empire. Fitted at the top but not as dramatic as trumpet."

Ball gown, Empire, mermaid, trumpet—all styles of wedding dresses familiar to me from the years I'd anticipated a marriage proposal from Tyler.

Everyone had anticipated it. A huge ring, a huge wedding, a huge fuss.

I leaned against the change machine. "Has Dodd asked you … anything?"

"Not officially, but we've practically planned the wedding."

"But you're both staying in school, right?"

"Of course."

"So what are you planning?"

"Just a small ceremony in Uncle Ansel and Aunt Velma's backyard."

"Their backyard?" I turned the idea over in my head, knowing everyone would expect the minister to marry in the church building. "I like it."

Ruthie's smile wavered. "This is going to be my day, not the church's."

"Right." The raging fire between the Turners and our small congregation had gradually diminished over the past few months, but there still remained a slow burn that would take years to extinguish.

Her shoulders drooped apologetically. "Do you still think about a wedding?"

My core suddenly felt cavernous, but I chewed my peanuts, swallowed, shrugged. "If I ever get married, we'll run off to the courthouse by ourselves, then go on an exotic honeymoon and lay around half naked for a week."

"The scandalous vacation sounds amazing, but the justice of the peace? I know you, and you're a church-wedding type. No matter what order you're doing things."

"I don't know. These days I think more about finding a man than planning a wedding." I wadded my wrapper and studied the resulting cellophane ball. "Besides, everyone would talk."

"Who cares?" She held up her right hand in what looked like an *Okay* sign, except her pointer finger and thumb were separated.

"Is that supposed to be a panther claw?"

She frowned at her fingers. "No, it's WC for *Who cares?* See, these three fingers make the *W*, and the pointer and thumb make the *C*. If I could make an *S* and a *U* with the other hand, I could give you *Who cares? Shut up*."

I threw my trash in her direction, but it fluttered to the floor halfway between us as the door of the Laundromat banged open. We both startled.

Tyler strolled in wearing cargo shorts, a polo shirt, and leather slides.

A low-pitched humming filled my ears and vibrated my skull. It was too much, seeing Tyler. Now. Right after my parents.

"What are you doing here," Ruthie said flatly.

Tyler's mouth curved into an easy smile that showed his teeth. "Checking on my girl."

I had always liked his teeth. Almost perfectly straight, but not quite. One tooth in front slanted ever so slightly, and it gave him a rakish look.

Ruthie glared at me. "You're back together?"

"No," I said quickly.

"We're working on that." Tyler's words overlapped mine as his gaze dropped to my stomach. "Are you all right, babe?"

"I'm good." When my dryer stopped spinning, the room filled with thick stillness. I picked up the laundry basket and scuttled to the back wall.

"Don't you have somewhere you need to be?" Ruthie asked him.

Tyler stared at her for a count of three before he spoke. "Yes, when a man has the amount of property my father left me, it requires fairly intense management skills. I wouldn't expect you to understand."

"Yet here you are … at the *Laundromat*."

He had never gotten along with my friends. Not in high school. Not in college. Not now. He turned his back to her. "Are you busy next Monday?"

Ruthie stepped around him. "We have class."

My laundry crackled as I pulled it from the dryer. Ruthie was up to something, but it didn't matter. "I have a doctor's appointment."

"What time?" Tyler asked.

"Eleven."

"Perfect. We'll go together."

Ruthie's voice sliced. "Are you asking her or telling her?"

"Dads are supposed to go to these things. Seems like you would be impressed."

I bent down to pick up my basket and noticed Tyler's neatly trimmed toenails. "It's all right, Ruthie."

He glanced at the basket in my arms. "Let's grab lunch after and hit a few stores. You could use a couple new outfits."

A tiny voice in the back of my head said he couldn't be trusted, but a louder voice reminded me he loved me, in his own way. "I need to think about it."

"No rush. I'll call you." He smiled his almost perfect smile as he pushed through the door.

It happened so fast. He spiraled in then out in less than five minutes, and my heart and mind spun in crazy circles, unable to make sense of it. As he walked across the street, I gripped the laundry basket and watched him, wondering if his body language might reveal his intentions.

He waved at Old Man Guthrie, so maybe he had become more caring. And surely his steady gait indicated a greater sense of purpose.

Ruthie cleared her throat. "He's bribing you with clothes."

I plopped the basket down and started folding laundry, not wanting to discuss it, but after a few minutes, she moved to stand across the counter.

Her hand rested on a laundry cart, and she squeaked it an inch forward, an inch back. "He bumped into you the other day at the diner, and today he *happens* to see you at the Laundromat. Is he stalking you or something?"

"It's not like that."

She raised an eyebrow in typical Ruthie fashion, and an invisible cord tightened around my neck. She meant well, but I needed to go home, sit on my porch, and stare over my cliff where I could see for miles. Where I could breathe.

"He doesn't even live in Trapp. What are the odds?"

"Snyder's forty-five minutes down the highway, not on another continent.

"Fawn?" She leaned on the counter and looked deep into my eyes. "Run. Away."

The cord around my neck snapped, and emotions spewed from my mouth. "That's easy for you to say. You're dating a minister, for goodness' sake, but your selfishness won't allow you to stand in someone else's shoes for five minutes. Not mine and certainly not Dodd's." I dropped a shirt and bent to snatch it off the floor. "Did it ever occur to you that Dodd might *want* to get married at the church?"

I regretted my words, yet I couldn't hold back. All the tension I stifled toward my parents and Tyler hurtled toward Ruthie. Not because she deserved my anger or warranted my tantrum but because she was safe.

I slammed folded clothes into the basket. "After all these years, you finally came back to the church and immediately started criticizing all of us." My voice took on a slight whine. "And you don't even realize you have *everything*."

Ruthie looked bored. "You're just weirding out because of your dad and Tyler." She scratched her head. "Didn't somebody say those two were a lot alike?"

I slumped over the counter, resting my head on my arms.

"Forgiven," she said.

I raised my head. "What must people think of me? In a month I'm going to be a single mother working at the stinking feed store."

She slowly raised her hand and gave me her made-up WC symbol, then mouthed the words *Who cares?*

CHAPTER ELEVEN

Tyler couldn't stomach Ruthie Turner. She had latched onto Fawn like a tick and would undoubtedly suck every drop of common sense from her. But Fawn had always allowed her friends to do that, clinging to them as though she couldn't stand on her own.

He would set Fawn straight, though.

Tyler pulled to the side of the road and punched his phone. "Sure enough. I found her right where you said she'd be."

Neil Blaylock's mutterings on the other end of the line brought a smile to Tyler's lips. Fawn's dad undoubtedly thought he had Tyler wrapped around his little finger.

"Did you talk sense into her?" Neil asked.

"It'll take me a few days to get her on the line, but I'm working on it."

"My daughter's no good on her own. Never has been."

Tyler looked across the street to where Neil and Susan Blaylock sat in their car. Fawn's mother fluttered her hands, and Tyler could hear her over the line, whining about love. He chuckled. "She won't be alone much longer."

Neil raised a palm to silence his wife, and Tyler heard him mumble, "He loves her, all right? We've established that fact."

"Tell your wife I love Fawn more than life itself."

Neil squinted at him from across the street.

"I saw it in a movie one time."

Neil lowered the phone to the steering wheel and turned to Susan. "He says he loves her more than life itself."

The woman's shoulders melted. Lord, she was pitiful.

Neil put the phone back to his ear. "I don't care what words you use, but you've got to convince her. Fawn deserves the best, and you're it."

Tyler questioned the man's intentions. Neil was a Christian, a husband, a father, but he was a rancher first, and Tyler knew he wanted more than a good match for his daughter. He wanted a solid connection with the power behind the Cruz name.

"I wouldn't have it any other way." Tyler nodded, using Neil just as much, if not more, to get what he wanted.

Fawn couldn't stand to be in the same room with her parents, but she always tried to milk them for approval. *Good luck to her.* He'd tried the same thing with his own father, and a lot of good it did.

Neil started his car, and it settled into a dull purr. "She's refusing to take my money, even after all that complaining about me not helping her." Tyler could see Neil's jaw clench, even from so far away. "But that could work to your advantage, I suppose. Without my help, she'll need you even sooner."

Susan snapped at him, louder this time. "Not everyone marries for money, Neil."

Tyler reached down and pulled a can of beer from the ice chest on the floorboard, hiding his smile. The Blaylocks could really get off on each other once they got going. Susan's eyes became slits, and she glared at her husband. Tyler found it humorous, but he knew once he was married, he would have to teach Fawn to show him respect.

"Oh, shut up." Neil didn't look at his wife, only lifted his chin to Tyler. "Let me know if you need any help. I already put in a good word."

"Don't worry, sir." Tyler opted to use the formal title, continuing the charade. "I love your daughter, and I'm determined to win her back."

"Well, you might want to hurry it up. She ought to be married before the baby comes."

"I see what you mean." Tyler had every intention of marrying Fawn before the baby came. That way there would be no doubt of his son carrying his name. He popped open the beer can. "Yes, sir. Before the baby comes. You can count on it." He tossed the phone on the seat, then tilted his head back to let the liquid cool his throat.

He stretched the truth when he swore he loved Neil's daughter, but he figured he could work up to that eventually. Or maybe he loved her already. He wasn't sure what that felt like, but something burned inside him. Now he just needed to convince her, and the first thing on his list was to figure out where she was living.

He took another swig of beer, started the truck, and pulled confidently onto the highway leading up the Caprock.

CHAPTER TWELVE

Friday night I went to the Panthers' first football game of the season, feeling old and pregnant. Cheerleaders a few years younger than me flipped head over heels down the track while I sat in the stands with Ansel and Velma and all the other parents. For once, I was grateful to see Lynda Turner climbing up the bleachers with a cardboard tray of nachos. Ruthie's mother didn't look a day over twenty-five, and when she sat down next to me, I felt the average age of our group drop dramatically.

"Is Ruthie coming?" I asked.

"No, she and Dodd went to a concert in Lubbock."

She closed her mouth around a cheese-covered chip, and my stomach complained. So far my nose had alerted me to every morsel of food in our section of bleachers, including a bag of buttered popcorn, a hot dog topped with mustard and onions, and two dill pickles.

"You eat before the game, Fawn?" Velma adjusted her cushioned stadium seat and poked Ansel to do the same.

"Frozen dinner."

"That don't count, girl. You go get you something else."

Once again, she read my mind. "I'll wait till halftime. I don't want to miss anything." I loved the pigskin sport. I didn't understand the subtle details of every play, but I had a better-than-basic understanding of the strategy.

At the moment, the Panthers were leading one touchdown to zip, and Coach Pickett—*JohnScott*—sent in the second-string offensive line to rest the starters. I saw no real risk in that move, even this early in the game, because the second string played almost as tough as the first. Trapp High School hadn't had a team this strong in years, and I smiled thinking of how much fun JohnScott would have coaching his way through the play-offs.

He stood on the sideline with his arms crossed, silently concentrating on his boys and ignoring the hubbub of activity around him. The entire town showed up for home games, but JohnScott might as well have been alone with his team. His ability to block out the crowd was legendary, one reason he had become so good at his job.

Ansel leaned forward, picked up an empty Dr Pepper can, and spit tobacco juice into it. "That boy of yours could use a trim, Velma."

The three of us immediately evaluated JohnScott's hair. He wore a Panther snapback pressed all the way down to his ears, but curls sneaked from beneath its edges.

"Sure enough, he could." Velma dropped her palm to her knee. "That's one more thing I need to tend to."

"It's about time you let that boy grow up." Lynda tossed her empty nacho container under her seat. "He can go to Sophie over at the Style Station, like the rest of us."

Ansel grunted.

"Now, Ansel, you be nice." Velma leaned toward me and snickered. "Sophie cut Ansel's hair last year when I came down with the flu, and he hasn't gotten over it yet."

"Almost talked my ears clean off." He spit in the can again.

I smiled, unable to picture either Ansel or JohnScott trapped in Sophie's chair beneath a leopard-print cape. I glanced at the coach. He wore a red Trapp High School polo shirt, tight across his shoulders and arms, and gray coaching pants that were none too baggy. As he stood next to two of the assistant coaches, I compared them limb for limb and remembered why my sophomore friends giggled in class.

"Lord have mercy, here comes Grady." Lynda scooted two inches to her right to shorten the gap between her and the aisle, but Dodd's brother headed toward Ansel, walking across benches as if they were stepping-stones in a stream.

The old man muttered Grady's name without looking at the boy. "You just getting here?"

"Yes, sir. I had to tend to a few things." Grady leaned forward and attempted to make eye contact with Lynda, who pointedly ignored him.

Velma looked between the two of them suspiciously. "There something you're wanting to tell us, Grady?"

"Well, now … no." He glanced at Lynda again. "I wouldn't want to bring something up if it weren't the right time."

My head turned left then right as I watched the two of them, and Velma's did the same. Ansel, on the other hand, kept his eyes focused on the game, spitting into his can.

"Oh, for crying out loud," Lynda said. "I know about Dodd's plans."

Grady grinned. "In that case, I might as well tell you Dodd's proposing to Ruthie tonight."

Velma gasped. "You don't say! How's he going to do it?"

"Boring." Grady shook his head. "Dinner at Red Lobster and a concert after. We'll be lucky if he even gets down on one knee."

"Ruthie won't care," Lynda said.

My silence embarrassed me, and I blurted, "I'm so happy for them!" The words came out high pitched and graceless, but nobody seemed to notice. Velma fired three more questions at Grady and Lynda while Ansel smiled so broadly he almost lost his wintergreen snuff.

Everyone seemed pleased. Except me.

But Dodd and Ruthie went together like tortilla chips and *picante* sauce. It was expected. And planned.

And perfect.

As jealousy invaded my heart, I shoved it back down, like stuffing a queen-size pillow into a shoebox. Just when I thought I had it under control, it would spring back up in my face.

Another Panther touchdown interrupted their glee, and we stood and cheered as the band played the fight song, the cheerleaders did backflips, and two air horns sounded from the top of the stadium. JohnScott remained oblivious to it all, still standing placidly on the sideline with his arms crossed.

The assistant coach to his left gave someone in the stands a thumbs-up, and my face warmed as I imagined JohnScott turning to look at me. Absurd.

"You'll be next," Lynda said as we sat back down.

At first I thought I hadn't heard her right. Probably she was talking about Tyler, but I didn't want to get into another debate. "I don't know about that."

She rested her feet on the bench in front of us, then leaned her elbows on her knees. "You know, Fawn, some things are worse than being alone."

"Why do you dislike Tyler so much?"

She sighed. "I don't want to see you turn out like Susan."

Lynda never spoke of my mother, and the sound of her name coming from Lynda's lips tugged at memories locked deep inside me. Memories of my girlhood when Ruthie and I had been playmates, and our mothers had tolerated each other for the sake of our friendship.

But that was years ago. "You hate my mother."

"No," Lynda said sharply. "I hate your father."

I thought she would deny her feelings or soften the wording, and her ready admission sent a chill down my spine. Ever since my dad stepped down as elder at the church, I'd known about the friction between my parents and Lynda—the whole town did—but there were a lot of things I didn't know. I would have to fish.

"I don't blame you. Mom told me what he did to you."

She turned and looked at me then, peering into my eyes as though she were looking for an explanation. She shook her head. "No, she didn't."

"Um ... yes, she did." I frowned uncertainly. "She said my dad broke up with you so he could date her."

She snickered. "Susan's too much of a coward to tell you the whole truth. And way too proud."

"Well, if you're so brave, you tell me what happened."

I expected her to lash out or stalk away in anger. Or maybe, just maybe, get riled enough to accidentally let something slip.

She turned to me with sadness in her eyes—the last thing I expected.

"Oh, Fawn." She sighed heavily. "It's not mine to tell. If it was, I would've told you years ago."

CHAPTER THIRTEEN

At halftime I leaned against the chain-link fence at the end of the field, nibbling a hot dog. I could have taken my second dinner back into the stands, but my frazzled nerves needed a break, and I chewed slowly to prolong the peaceful lull I found away from the crowd.

Junior high girls walked the track in front of me, little boys played tag behind me, and old men leaned on the fence ten yards down, undoubtedly hashing and rehashing the first two quarters of the game. But I felt removed from them all. Even as the Panther band marched across the field, their brassy tones seemed muted and distant.

I put the last bite in my mouth and chuckled. Only a few days ago, I missed my sorority lifestyle, but now I found myself hiding in the end zone, in plain sight, mind you, yet separated from all the excitement. I began to wonder if I should go back to the stands with Ansel and Velma or hide awhile longer or slip to the parking lot and go home.

"Hey, babe. You shouldn't be down here all by your lonesome."

I jerked slightly as Tyler leaned against the metal railing next to me.

"Sorry if I scared you. I got here late and noticed you standing over here. Everything all right?"

Define all right. "I was eating. I'm hungry all the time." My stomach grazed the chain-link fencing, reminding me of my distorted figure.

"No big deal. You're pregnant." His voice, encouraging and kind, renewed my self-esteem, and I straightened slightly.

I bumped his shoulder with my own. "Someone from Snyder is bound to find out you showed up to support the Trapp Panthers."

He smiled as though he'd been caught in a petty crime. "I'm not sure anyone in Snyder cares. Or to be more accurate, I'm not sure I care if they care."

"Good for you." My fingers almost curved into Ruthie's *Who cares?* symbol, but I stopped myself. Even with Tyler in a generous mood, he would never appreciate cheesy humor.

As the two teams huddled outside the field house, we leaned with our elbows on the fence, side by side, not looking at each other. Tyler had lost the cocky desperation of the Laundromat and now seemed more like himself. Relaxed. But he had always been more appealing with no one else around.

The Panthers ran past us with their cleats slapping the pavement as they chanted a threat to intimidate the opposing team. They needn't have bothered. The write-up in the county newspaper left every team in the district quaking.

The coaches half walked, half jogged with the boys, and as they passed by, JohnScott looked at me. I smiled and lifted my hand to wave, but he kept running and showed no sign of recognition. Probably he hadn't seen me.

"You look tired, Fawn." The fence clinked as Tyler shifted his weight. He had been watching me, and I didn't notice.

"The baby wakes me up at night." My hand fell to my abdomen. "But once I'm awake, I start tossing and turning, and he gets still again."

Tyler's eyes softened. "Sounds like he wants you to rock him back to sleep."

I laughed softly, feeling his familiarity settle over me. This was the Tyler I used to know. Who cried at his mother's bedside when she got sick and showed so much tenderness, I hadn't wanted to hold back any part of myself.

I missed that Tyler.

"He's awake right now. Do you want to feel?"

"I'd like that." He turned toward me and hesitated, so I took his hand between my own and pressed his palm against the firmness of my side, where I had last felt the baby's movements.

Tyler's other hand found its way to the small of my back, and we stood motionless for several seconds, him staring into space as he concentrated on what he felt, and me watching him closely so I wouldn't miss any sign of acceptance that might flitter across his face.

Suddenly the baby kicked hard against his daddy's hand, and Tyler smiled. "He's got my attitude." He laughed out loud, and his fingers rubbed my back, above the waistline of my jeans. But then his smiled eased, and his hands dropped to his sides. "I'm sorry about everything, Fawn."

I gripped the metal pipe running along the top of the fence, ignoring the junior high girls who were ogling us. Tyler had said those words to me on the street in front of the diner, but now he actually meant them. I could see his regret and feel his pain, and I had the overwhelming urge to comfort him. Neither of us had asked for this new life. Neither of us knew what to make of it.

A touchdown took our attention back to the game, and we peered over the fence at the players knocking against each other in celebration. As they lined up for the extra point, my gaze drifted to the sideline. The cheerleaders had quieted for the kick, and Coach Pickett stood as rigidly as ever, arms crossed. But just as the ball sailed through the upright posts, I thought he turned his head to look toward the fence. At me.

I did a double take, but he had already started yelling directions to an assistant coach.

"I was serious about taking you to your doctor's appointment." Tyler's shoulder brushed mine. "It would mean a lot to me."

I pictured my doctor's office and the other pregnant women with men by their sides—holding hands, fetching cups of water, giving support—and a missing link in the chain of my confidence snapped into place. "It would mean a lot to me, too."

Tyler released a long, slow breath. "I'd like to spend time with you away from the doctor's office too. I miss you."

His words didn't affect me as much as his body language. His posture cried out in desperation, and his eyes begged me not to abandon him. He looked exactly this way at his mother's funeral back in junior high, and more recently, at his father's. My parents weren't dead, but they had all but abandoned me, and Tyler's expression of helplessness instilled in me a sense of unity.

"I miss you, too." My resolve melted. I knew what I could expect from him, and even though it didn't compare with the perfect life laid out in front of Ruthie, it might be close enough to perfect. At least my baby would have a father.

Tyler's sad eyes turned up at the corners, but not enough to transform into happiness. "Why do we do this to each other?"

As the band played a drum roll for the kickoff, he gently slipped his arm around my back. "Old habits, I guess."

"Fawn?" His voice broke. "I promise I won't hurt you again."

I'd heard that before, but this time it sounded different. Either he meant it more or I wanted more desperately for it to be true. The baby kicked again, seeming to remind me, as though I could ever forget.

My mind and body were weary from months of anxiety, but Tyler's gentle promise felt good against my soul, ringing with the clear tone of good intentions.

I believed him.

But I had to draw the line in the sand. "This is the last time. If you get drunk again, if you make a scene, if you hurt me … it's over for good."

"That won't happen." When he kissed the top of my head, the junior high girls giggled, but I didn't pay any attention. *Who cares?* I smiled, enjoying the familiar scent of his cologne, the secure feel of his muscular arm behind me, and the soft whisper of his breath against my hair.

I could have stood like that at the fence all night, but after a few minutes, he pulled away and intertwined his fingers with mine.

Just then, the opposing team's fans cheered enthusiastically, drawing my attention back to the game as I wondered what could have happened so soon after our last touchdown.

I scanned the field, and my mouth fell open.

They had scored against us.

The wire of the fence pressed my skin as I gripped it with my fingers. Since the Panthers were slated for state, the area papers had speculated we might go all year without being scored on. Yet here we were—our first game of the season—giving up six points already.

The other team's band, cheerleaders, and fans—good grief, *their entire team*—went berserk. The noise level rose obnoxiously while our fans watched in stunned silence. As the ball sailed through the goalposts for the extra point, every face in the stadium—whether from glee or from mourning—studied the opposite end zone.

My heart hurt for our team, but I had the most compassion for JohnScott, who would undoubtedly be criticized by half the town. And they wouldn't be kind about it. I scanned the sideline until I located him, but then a chill raced down my spine.

He stood with his feet planted shoulder width apart, fists on his hips, but instead of being turned toward the other end of the field, he looked straight at Tyler and me.

He jerked his head away quickly, and I told myself it probably hadn't been what it seemed.

But when he glanced back a second time, I knew it wasn't my imagination.

CHAPTER FOURTEEN

They say boredom can drive a person insane, and I seemed to be testing the theory. Saturday afternoon, I lay on the loveseat, twirling a ruffled throw pillow above my head and wishing for something to do other than homework.

I had worked at the feed store a few hours that morning, and every man who entered the place speculated to the owner about Friday's game. They all had an opinion about what went wrong. Of course, the Panthers won the game by a margin of thirty-five points, but the fact we hadn't routed the opposing team bothered the locals.

And it bothered me, too. But I chose not to think about it, and by the time I got home, I had pushed the game and the coach far into the back of my mind.

Rolling to my side, I sipped iced coffee through a straw, swishing the sweet mocha across my tongue while I wondered, yet again, what my life would be like if I hadn't gotten pregnant. Tyler and I had so much in common. Wealth, religion, status. The similarities in our families had brought us together, and high expectations had kept us that way. Now we had the baby, and being with Tyler seemed the only justification.

When I heard the rumble of a car approaching, I rose on one elbow and saw Coach Pickett's green step-side pickup rounding the bend in the road where it curved near the drop-off.

I met him on the front porch. "What brings you all the way up here?"

JohnScott lifted his ball cap and swiped his arm across his forehead, revealing a serious case of hat hair. "Dad wants you to have his old recliner."

My gaze slid past him, and I noticed Ansel's brown La-Z-Boy wedged in the bed of the truck. "Doesn't he need it?"

"Mom talked him into getting a new one. Been after him for years."

I hesitated, wondering if I had room for the huge chair, almost large enough for two people.

JohnScott's eyebrows shrugged. "It's a rocker."

I nodded, suddenly excited about the worn piece of furniture and the possibility of rocking my baby. "Awesome, JohnScott. Tell your parents thanks."

He frowned at a distant point to the side of the house. "While I'm here, I thought I'd clear some of this …" A sweep of his hand indicated my front yard.

"You mean the piles of brush?"

"And the lumber." He nodded toward the far corner.

My face warmed. "It's practically a junkyard."

"Not for long." One side of his mouth lifted in an easy grin.

"JohnScott, you fixed the steps just last week. You don't need to spend another day working here."

"I don't have practice on Saturdays." He rubbed his flattened palm against his shoulder. "If I don't find something to do, I'll likely die of boredom."

"Okay, but I'm helping you. Let me put on some boots."

I stepped into the bedroom and tugged on my worn ropers. I knew exactly what the coach meant about boredom. Even though the idea of JohnScott cleaning up my yard humiliated me, I couldn't pass up the opportunity to busy myself.

Five minutes later, I came out of the bedroom to find the recliner neatly positioned in front of the window with the loveseat pushed along the side wall. I ran my hand across the velour and inhaled the comforting scent of Ansel and Velma Pickett's farmhouse. More than once I had seen the two of them sitting in the recliner together, Velma's legs draped over Ansel's knees as they watched television.

I had never seen married people act like that until I lived with the Picketts. They were so comfortable with each other. Not at all like my own parents.

My gaze drifted to the window, where I could see JohnScott pulling brush into a pile at the edge of the yard. He might have sat in this recliner with an old girlfriend.

My thumb fingered a worn spot on the headrest, and my face warmed for the second time in fifteen minutes. I should have been picturing myself rocking my baby in this chair. Instead, I imagined what it would be like to sit there with JohnScott, my legs draped over his knees.

I exhaled in disgust and jerked the door open, joining the coach outside as he picked up an armful of debris.

"You don't have to help me, Fawn."

I forced a light tone that probably didn't sound natural. "You're saying you would get done quicker if I got out of your way."

"No." His eyes smiled, and his lips tried not to. "I reckon you're not used to this type of work."

I pulled my curls into a wad at the nape of my neck and captured them with a tie. "I never helped Dad on the ranch, but I watched him. Does that count?"

"I just watched you put your hair up, but I wouldn't have any luck if I tried to do it myself."

I fingered a curl that had already escaped from bondage. "Not the same." I yanked a mesquite branch from a tangled mess, but when I tossed it onto the coach's pile, a thorn scratched my finger, and I winced.

"I see what you mean." He lumbered to his truck and brought back a pair of men's leather work gloves. "These won't fit, but they're better than nothing."

The gloves smelled of cattle feed and creosote, but I slipped them on, bending my elbows and holding my hands aloft so they wouldn't slip off. "Such a nice scent."

The coach shook his head as he unrolled a garden hose, testing the water supply before he lit the brush on fire. He mumbled some-thing about cheerleaders.

"What did you say?" I mustered a defensive tone. "I'll have you know I cheered for Trapp, and I'm proud of it. That's how I learned what I know about football."

"Did you seriously just tell me that?" He transferred brush to the burn pile, the smoky scent of burning mesquite already filling the yard.

"Why shouldn't I?"

He adjusted his cap, apparently trying not to laugh. "I'm the head football coach, so I know you were a cheerleader. And I rest my case."

"You weren't the head coach back then. Just an assistant."

He only grunted.

"What did you mean anyway? About me being a cheerleader? I don't see what that has to do with anything."

"I'm just saying ... you're a girlie girl."

I clamped my hands around a two-by-four and dragged it across the yard. "If you're trying to insult me, you'll have to try harder."

"Simply stating facts." He took the board from me. "You really could let me do this."

I sighed, tired of his teasing. "I want to help," I said firmly. "Just because I never worked physical labor, doesn't mean I didn't want to." A flame edged away from the burn pile, and I stomped it with my boot. "Mother hardly even let me work around the house."

The coach sing-songed, "Cheerleader ..."

"But I did learn to cook a few things in Family and Consumer Science class. Ms. Fuentes could dish out a mean enchilada plate."

He paused in his work. "You cook enchiladas?"

"When I'm provoked, yes."

"Huh."

He thought I couldn't cook. "What did that *huh* mean?"

"I'm wondering how I might I provoke you."

"I owe you a lot more than an enchilada."

"You don't owe me a thing." He retrieved a shovel from the back of his truck and stirred the fire. "Seen any rattlers?"

I wrapped a ponytail holder around the wrist of one of my gloves to keep the blasted thing in place, and then rolled a deteriorated log toward the fire. "No, and I'm not going to talk about snakes or we'll jinx it."

"Girl, this place is already jinxed. Clyde said boys from the Sweetwater Rattlesnake Round-Up used to come out here every year, trying to find the den, but they never could."

I turned around, intending to stomp away from him, but pain radiated from the side of my foot. I yelled, plopped down to the ground, and tossed my boot all at the same time.

JohnScott watched me for a second, then bent to retrieve the boot and held it upside down, giving it a little shake until a scorpion fell to the ground.

"Kill it," I screamed as I rubbed my foot. "Kill it dead!"

He ground his heel into the brown, crusty shell, then handed me my footwear. "You okay?"

"I hate those things." I removed my sock and blew on my foot. "Did it crawl up my boot?"

"Could've been in there the whole time. Come on. I'll get you an ice cube."

I clambered to my feet and limped to the front steps, where I held the coldness to the sting.

Coach Pickett chuckled.

"What are you laughing at?" I didn't look up.

"Kill it? Kill it dead?"

His teasing irritated and soothed me at the same time. "A reflex reaction."

He sat on the porch, stretching his legs down the steps, and suddenly I reverted to a ditsy teenager who couldn't handle a bug bite. But it was more than the scorpion. It was my life. It was Tyler and the baby. My parents. It was Ruthie and Lynda Turner and the upside-down position of my life.

He cocked his head to the side. "You stopped smiling."

Across the yard, the fire crackled away from the burn pile, gobbled up a few blades of grass, then scurried back. Just like my parents. They showed up in town, devoured my confidence, and went back home. I squinted at the cloudless sky. "I saw my parents a few days ago. My father wants to give me money."

"Hmm."

"It's guilt money, of course."

I didn't look at JohnScott, but I could tell he studied me. "Explain."

I brushed away a layer of dust on the gray boards beneath me. "He's trying to buy me off."

"How do you know he's not sincere?"

"He always throws money at problems." I frowned. "And usually they go away, but not this time. If he wants to ease his guilt for the way he treated me, he can apologize."

The coach scratched his hairline. "Does he do that?"

"There's always a first time."

"But you could use the money."

"It's not enough to make a difference anyway. Might buy a week's worth of groceries." I huffed. "Apparently I'm not worth a substantial investment."

He removed his hat and did that arm-across-the-forehead thing. "Maybe that's the best your dad can do right now."

I didn't like his attitude, so I changed the subject. "I go for another checkup Monday, and Tyler's going with me this time."

He responded with a low hum in his throat, but it felt like an accusation.

"It's not like we're getting back together for sure," I rattled. "But I owe him a chance."

"Do you?"

"For the baby, at least."

He shrugged. "Dad said you would have a hard time quitting Tyler."

"Ansel said that?"

"Yep. I swear there's a therapist inside those overalls."

I pulled the holder from my ponytail, letting my hair fall down my back so I could rebundle it and tie it more securely. "My dad never dreamed I would *quit* Tyler. He said we were bad for each other in all the best ways."

JohnScott bent his legs and rested his elbows on his knees. "Strange concept for a dad."

I rose, balancing on my good foot and wondering why I had confided all this to him. "Put that cap back on your head. Your hair looks like a scoop of chocolate ice cream." The top lay matted with sweat, but the sides fluffed in uncontrolled curls. "In fact, you might want a haircut soon."

"You sound like my mother."

I smiled, thinking of Ansel and Velma's discussion about Sophie. And then I looked up at JohnScott. For a reason I couldn't figure, I felt a juvenile need for his approval. Some sign that he didn't find me absurd, and that he could possibly deem my shattered life acceptable.

But he only turned away and walked back to the fire.

CHAPTER FIFTEEN

Tyler and I sat side by side in the Lysol-scented waiting room of the obstetrician's office. He had picked me up in his spotless truck, made small talk on the hour-long drive to Lubbock, and ushered me into the office as though he owned the place. Now we stared at the large-screen TV, watching two sea horses mate.

He grunted.

I considered frowning at him, but a middle-aged, pregnant woman sitting across the room lowered her parenting magazine and did it for me.

"Sorry." He laid his arm across the back of my chair.

But I didn't really mind Tyler's crass behavior. I was just glad I wasn't alone.

"What do you think the baby will look like?" I rubbed a hand across my inverted belly button.

"I don't know. Us?"

"But will he look more like me, or you, or one of our parents?"

"He can't go wrong either way." Tyler's eyes drifted to the television, where hundreds of tiny, fully-developed sea horses shot from the male's swollen belly.

Tyler shook his head.

I snatched a magazine from the coffee table and buried my nose in it, but then a door at the side of the room opened, and a nurse called my name.

She led us to a pink-and-blue exam room that smelled like rubbing alcohol and felt like a walk-in refrigerator. Then she weighed me, took my temperature, and checked my pulse. As always, the speed with which the woman marshaled me through the office made me feel like a cow being driven through a chute at the livestock auction. "It means a lot that you're here, Tyler."

"Sure." He pulled a metal chair forward and sat near my knee, which caused him to look up at me at an angle. "I wouldn't have it any other way."

I pretended to study a poster showing the monthly stages of pregnancy, and I wished we had the type of relationship where I felt comfortable sitting in silence.

Tyler pressed a warm palm against my calf to stop the nervous jitters that tapped my flip-flops against the footrest. "The street dance is this Saturday, Fawn. Can I pick you up?"

I opened my mouth to answer but heard my file slide from its resting place on the other side of the wall, and then Dr. Tubbs entered, along with a breeze of cold air and the aroma of onions.

"Hello, young lady. You're looking well." He held his hand toward Tyler. "I don't believe we've met. I'm Harrison Tubbs."

"Tyler Cruz."

"Cruz ..." The doctor squinted. "Are you any relation to the rancher?"

"My father." Tyler lifted his chin, and on the inside, I did the same.

"Sorry to hear of his passing." The doctor's eyes softened earnestly—a facial sympathy card—then he nodded. "Glad you could come today." He turned his attention to me while Tyler resumed his seat beneath us both. "Any problems this month, Fawn?"

"I'm not sure. The other day I had a few pains."

"Did they feel like monthly cramps?"

I glanced at Tyler and nodded.

"Ah yes. Those are Braxton-Hicks contractions. Nothing to worry about. Now that you're in your third trimester, it's your body's way of getting ready for labor." He smiled. "Any other concerns?"

"Nothing besides being hungry all the time. And really, really tired."

The doctor grinned. "Both are perfectly normal effects of a healthy pregnancy." He put a chubby hand on my shoulder. "Lie back on the pillow, and let's hear the heartbeat."

When I lifted my shirt to expose my abdomen, Tyler looked on with silent interest. I felt my neck flush when I remembered the small stretch marks rippling across my skin. I had found some lotion to make them invisible, but after two weeks of use, I couldn't tell a difference.

The doctor swiped a handheld probe across my midsection, and I shivered.

"Sorry. I know it's cold." He cut his eyes to the side and listened to the sounds coming from the plastic monitor.

But they weren't the right sounds. Usually the persistent whoosh of my baby's heartbeat filled the small room, but today I heard only an occasional thump along with the amplified movements of the device itself.

My fingers found the edge of the paper tablecloth, and I poked my thumbnail through it. "Something's wrong."

Instead of answering, the doctor shifted his attention to my other side, and he stared into the corner of the room, giving all his attention to the small device in his hand.

My ears became sensitive radar, searching for my baby's heartbeat but only finding other muffled sounds. A droning voice down the hall, the clank of the scale, water running. My heart seemed to struggle to pump blood through my veins, and I stared at the ceiling in frozen shock. And still the sounds coming from my body were wrong.

Dr. Tubbs finally spoke. "I'm getting an irregular heartbeat, Fawn, but before we panic, let's get Regina in here for a quick ultrasound." He stepped into the hallway, leaving the door open.

I lay on the table, my face turned toward the wall while three tears dripped sideways to puddle on the paper pillowcase. My eyelids squeezed shut, pushing the doctor and his machinery out of my thoughts, and I wished I were back home in my shack, lying in Ansel Pickett's recliner, where I could see my view.

My hand gripped the paper until it tore away from my grasp. I hadn't talked to God much lately. Or read my Bible enough. Or volunteered to teach Sunday school. But I dressed modestly now, and I stopped drinking and using bad words, and I wanted to be a good mother.

Fingers of guilt strangled me, barely allowing air in and out of my lungs as I choked on silent sobs. I cried for my baby, but I longed to be held like a baby myself. To have someone who could make this go away. To be rocked and cuddled and comforted. And saved.

Tyler cleared his throat. "Come on, Fawn. The doctor said not to panic."

I opened my eyes and focused on the sonogram machine by the side of the bed. I had forgotten Tyler was even in the room.

I turned my head to see him casually scrolling through his phone messages, and I realized if I stayed with Tyler Cruz … I would always be alone.

CHAPTER SIXTEEN

"Oh, Fawn, I would have been scared to death."

I couldn't look Ruthie in the eye when I said, "It helped to have Tyler there."

Late Tuesday, the two of us sat on the edge of the cement holding tank in the side pasture at Ansel and Velma's house. Our feet dangled in the hazy, green water while I replayed my horrible visit to Dr. Tubbs. "But when they did the ultrasound, everything looked normal. Dr. Tubbs said the lotion I used interfered with the Doppler."

Ruthie became unexpectedly quiet, staring into the cold well water. "That must have been terrifying." She lifted her eyes. "I'm so sorry."

Her compassion startled me, and I blinked. Ever since I left the doctor's office, my tears flowed easily, sometimes from the roar of heartbreak, sometimes from the echo of relief.

She squeezed my hand and slid into the shallow water, four feet deep. "Man, it's hot today." She moved slowly to the middle of the concrete tank, stirring up moss with each step. "I wish we were at the lake instead of here."

Usually by the first of September, the temperatures in Trapp dipped into the nineties, but our little town continued to hit the century mark daily. The cement-sided cattle trough didn't compare to the swimming pool I grew up using, or to Lake Alan Henry, where Ruthie spent countless summer Saturdays with the Picketts, but it cooled my feet nonetheless. I figured I would eventually get used to its murky water and the goldfish flicking past my ankles. In the meantime, I couldn't bring myself to get all the way in. I told Ruthie I didn't have a proper swimming suit, but truth be told, I didn't want to get dirty.

"So, tell me about your date with Tyler. After the doctor's appointment?" Ruthie floated on her back.

"It was *not* a date," I insisted. "But he took me shopping afterward and bought me several maternity outfits."

"Did he say why he's acted like such a moron for the past year?"

I trickled water down my arms. "I've decided to forgive him."

Her voice clipped, but I had a feeling most of her impatience lay with me, not Tyler. "You're going to fall in the same trap again."

"A child needs two parents."

She looked away from me and squinted into the sun hanging low in the sky.

I shouldn't have said that. Ruthie's father left years before, and she still hadn't healed from the damage he caused. "I'm sorry, Ruthie. I wasn't thinking."

She swam away from me, and then turned. "Okay, then. My tattered childhood is evidence that a child needs two parents, but your father daily proves not every man is sufficient for the job."

"Tyler isn't as bad as my father."

"Tyler's a mean drunk."

I counted to ten. "You're right, but when he's sober, he's not a bad person."

She tilted her head back in the water, soaking her hair so it would fall smoothly down her back. "Are you just interested in him because the church expects you to be?"

"No," I said quickly. "I don't care about that anymore."

"Good." Ruthie gave me the *Who cares?* sign. "But you're still stuck in some kind of victim mentality."

"You listen to too much talk radio."

"You could call them and do a show."

I wished we would talk about something else, because every time I thought about Tyler, I felt like I was riding the Ferris wheel at the tricounty fair. Only this time, instead of clinging to my mother's hand, I was all alone.

"Can you help me out this week? Ansel had me take the Chevy to a mechanic in Lubbock."

"Changing the subject, are we?"

I lifted a shoulder.

"What's wrong with the Chevy?"

"The air conditioner is out. Something about a compressor. They said it'll be ready Saturday."

She frowned. "Dodd and I can take turns getting you to classes this week, but I don't know about Saturday."

A rustling sound behind me caught my attention, but before I could turn, a tanned male body barreled across the yard, whooping as loud as a Santa Fe train engine. He set one foot on the side of the holding tank and did a front flip, landing on his back and splashing water all over me.

Grady.

Dodd called from the barbed-wire fence where he and JohnScott were climbing over the metal stile. "Sorry about that, you guys. I try to leave him at home, but he keeps following me."

I wiped water from my face while Ruthie laughed. "You can only do so much."

She leaned out of the water and kissed him, causing Grady to make a gagging motion with his fingers. "Ruthie, you and Dodd are so cute, I could puke."

I smiled at Dodd. "Congratulations on your engagement. Ruthie told me all about it. She's a lucky girl."

"I'm the lucky one." He stepped into the water and stood behind Ruthie, wrapping his arms around her waist and leaning over to nuzzle her neck.

JohnScott, standing to the side with his hands on the wet cement, shook his head at me and shrugged.

"Dodd, you are *not alone*," Grady said loudly.

"You're just jealous." JohnScott chuckled. "Get yourself a girlfriend."

"Coach Pickett's got a point." Dodd pulled Ruthie to the side of the tank opposite JohnScott.

Her back was still pressed against him, and she giggled softly before focusing on me. "Fawn, Grady is going to be Dodd's best man, and—"

"Because I am the manliest man in the world," declared Grady.

"The manliest man without a girlfriend," crooned JohnScott under his breath.

"You don't have a girlfriend either, Coach. I thought we were united in this fact."

"He's the head coach," Dodd said. "That gives him an automatic man card, with or without a woman by his side."

"Anyway ..." Ruthie looked at me. "I wanted to wait until Dodd was here before I asked you. Would you be my maid of honor?"

I felt my mouth curve upward in a smile, and I thanked God for the reflex action. I felt numb. I had planned on being a bride, not a bridesmaid, but so much had happened in the last year, my heart didn't know what to feel. But numb was good. Numb was easy. Numb was safe. "I'd be honored, Ruthie." I cringed as I pictured myself in a tent-sized maternity gown. "When is the date?"

"Sometime in November. After your baby comes. Ansel and Velma's yard will be awful that time of year, but there's no way we're waiting for spring."

Dodd buried his face in her neck again. "We're certainly not."

"Please. That's disgusting." Grady groaned and went underwater.

When he resurfaced, Ruthie spoke softly to Dodd but loud enough the others could hear. "Fawn was just telling me about her doctor's appointment. The baby's heartbeat sounded irregular at first, but when the doctor ordered an ultrasound, everything checked out good. It was just a problem with her lotion."

"Oh, man," Grady said. "I'm sorry."

Dodd nodded. "Glad everything's all right."

The coach turned his back to us and sat on the edge of the holding tank, staring across the pasture. If he heard the discussion, he gave no indication, and a noticeable lag in conversation followed. Apparently he didn't care to hear the boring details about my office visit.

Grady's eyebrows bounced three times, and then he eased toward JohnScott with only his head above the water, a mischievous grin on his face.

JohnScott glanced over his shoulder right as Grady pulled him backward into the water, dunking him as though in baptism.

The coach came up coughing, then stood and shook his head twice, slinging water out of his curls. "Grady, be glad you're not playing football under me anymore, because you'd be running laps for a year."

"I thank the good Lord for that every day."

"That bad?" JohnScott asked.

"Worst experience of my life."

I smiled, knowing Grady had idolized Coach Pickett since the day they met. "We don't believe that, Grady. Not for a second."

"Fawn?" Grady stood straighter and peered at me. "It's about time you got in the water too."

I held out my palms. "I'm good right here."

"Okay." All four of us looked at him, surprised he backed off so quickly, but then he cocked his head to the side. "You don't want to get in. Fine." He swept his hand through the water and splashed me full in the face, taking away my breath. "But you didn't say anything about getting wet."

"Stop it, Grady. She's pregnant." Ruthie splashed him, and Dodd joined her.

Soon water was hitting me from every direction, and I held up my arms to shield myself. After a few seconds, I realized I would be less of a target in the water, and I slid off the wall. The skin on the back of my legs hurt from being pressed against the cement for so long, but the water felt good. Someone, probably Grady, kept splashing me in the face, so I submerged and swam a few feet to the left, hoping he would give someone else his attention. I surfaced and wiped water from my eyes, only to receive another faceful. I submerged again and swam farther around.

With five adults in the small tank, I kept nudging into legs. I groped for the cement side, careful not to bump my head on the rough hardness, then rose out of the water, but only so far as my nose.

I found myself looking directly into Coach Pickett's eyes, inches away from me. His nearness embarrassed me, and I desperately wanted to look away, to hide behind something so I could escape his penetrating gaze, which seemed to expose my faults. But I couldn't move.

The flurry continued around us as we both looked at each other in surprise. We were so close, I could see drops of water on his eyelashes. I clutched the cement with my fingertips, as he rose slightly above the water. His eyes roamed down to my mouth, in and then out of the waves, and I held my breath.

JohnScott looked like a different person. Wet and startled and no longer my history teacher or the head coach or my friend's cousin. But someone else.

Someone interesting.

He pushed off the cement wall and swam away from me.

When the splashing settled, I crouched at the far side of the tank, trying to calm the butterflies flittering in my stomach. I stood up, pulling my wet T-shirt away from me, then once again perched on the edge of the tank. I avoided eye contact with all of them and wondered if any of them had seen.

Grady flipped in the water, attempting to stand on his hands, and Dodd and Ruthie laughed together on the other side of the tank, sharing a few kisses. Apparently they hadn't noticed.

I couldn't look at the coach.

But maybe I'd read more into it than I ought to. Maybe he hadn't noticed anything peculiar. Maybe we simply bumped into each other.

Probably, it was *nothing*. Nothing at all.

I swung my legs over the side and stepped toward a lawn chair to retrieve my sandals. "I better get home."

As Ruthie voiced her objections, I finally glanced at the coach, but when my eyes met his, he turned away.

Shame settled over me like a warm mist, and stifling heat pressed against my chest, reminding me of a sauna Mother and I had sat in too long on vacation one year. By the time we left the room, I was light-headed and almost fainted.

I wanted to faint now, to succumb to blessed unconsciousness. Because whatever happened between JohnScott and me in the water was definitely not *nothing*.

CHAPTER
SEVENTEEN

JohnScott installed my new window-unit air conditioners one evening while I was at class, leaving a note apologizing for not catching me at home. But he knew my schedule.

Whatever.

My house was remarkably cooler, but the refrigerated air left me feeling like smut because the coach couldn't bear to be in the same room with me. After dinner I escaped my guilty conscience and settled on a kitchen chair that I pulled to the back porch. The tableland on that side of the house, unlike the front, stretched into the distance, as flat as if God had poured a concrete slab all the way from Trapp to the top of the Panhandle. Squatty cedars and sagebrush grew near the house, but beyond them lay the first of countless cotton fields, where a green John Deere tractor spent the day rumbling in monotonous rotations.

The scent of freshly plowed earth reminded me of my father. Except his tractor was a Kubota, not John Deere, with an enclosed, air-conditioned cab so he could work in a comfortable, isolated cocoon.

My phone chirped in my pocket. A text from Ruthie saying she and Dodd couldn't take me to get the Chevy at the repair shop on Saturday morning, but JohnScott would pick me up at ten. Oh joy.

A pair of scissortails swooped back and forth above my head, their yellow bellies plump and full of bugs that otherwise would have found their way inside my house. A pain suddenly shot through my right calf, and I flexed my foot, trying to ease the muscle cramp. These were happening more often lately, and my doctor had given me the profound advice "That happens sometimes," which seemed to be his diagnosis for many of my pregnancy symptoms. I had learned not to take myself too seriously.

When the cramp intensified, I slammed my glass of iced coffee down on the porch rail and pulled my toes toward my shin as I massaged the rock-hard muscles of my calf. After a few moments, the pain eased, but every time I released my foot, my calf would tighten again. Gingerly I put weight on my leg and hobbled down the steps into the backyard to walk it off.

I stopped at the corner of the house, resting my hand on the rough wood of the siding as my muscles cramped again. I bent to knead my calf but tensed when I heard a hollow shaking behind me. It started as a timid chirrup not unlike a cricket but quickly increased to a threatening vibration that sent goose bumps up my spine. I knew that sound.

My leg immediately turned to granite, but I took a slow, painful step away from the diamondback rattlesnake. A sudden movement would be dangerous, but even my slow progress caused another more intense shake of its tail.

The back porch loomed to my left, and in one swift yet lumbering motion, I grasped the railing and stepped up with my good leg, raising myself three feet above the ground. As I awkwardly climbed over the rail, another rattle sounded, less threatening, and then it stopped altogether.

I leaned over the rail to locate the reptile but saw only a rectangular opening on the side of the house. Some sort of access to the open area beneath. The snake must have been resting there to escape the heat of the setting sun. Well, it would have to find another place to cool off. I gently bit my bottom lip, remembering Sophie Snodgrass's stories.

I had seen snakes on my family's ranch, but I'd never had to deal with them myself. My father or the foreman usually shot their heads off with a twenty-two, but one time a small rattler ventured into the yard when all the men were at work, and our maid took after it with a garden hoe. She chopped until the animal resembled ground meat.

I considered the hoe option but didn't want to get that close. Besides, I didn't have a hoe. I stepped off the porch, took a wide path around the corner, and peered under the house into the darkness.

Sure enough, a midsize rattlesnake lay coiled in a small mound, relaxed and resting. The diamond design on its back alternated its gray, black, and white pattern, and the now-silent tail protruded from the center of the scaly pile, ready to shake again should the snake feel threatened.

I would have to stand there and keep an eye on it while I called someone to come kill it. If it got away, I would never be able to go in and out of the house knowing the thing slinked around the property.

My father was out of the question. He would use the incident as ammunition, firing even more condescending remarks my way.

Tyler would undoubtedly know how to kill a snake, but he lived all the way in Snyder.

And since it was a Thursday, Dodd and Ruthie had classes at Tech. Not that they could help anyway.

Ansel would have come in a heartbeat, but Ruthie had been describing him as more and more feeble lately. I hated to be a bother.

That only left one person in my short list of friends, and I dreaded calling him.

For a few seconds I considered the fiasco at the holding tank, but then I pulled my cell phone from the back pocket of my shorts and knocked my pride down a few notches. JohnScott probably considered me a flirt, but he could shoot the head off a snake from twenty feet, without a hitch.

Fifteen minutes later, his truck sped into the front yard, and my body reacted as if a professor had called my name to stand and recite the Gettysburg Address.

I checked on my reptile friend, but he hadn't moved at all. Not when I slipped into the house to use the restroom. Not when I retrieved my glass from the porch rail. Not when I sneaked a few bites of cake.

I stepped around the side of the house but stopped short when I saw who the coach had with him.

"Clyde and I were eating at the diner when you called." JohnScott lifted his chin as he walked across the yard. "Hope you don't mind I brought him with me."

"Of course not," I lied.

"He knows about diamondbacks."

I seriously doubted the middle-aged man knew much about snakes, since he'd been locked up for twenty years. Perhaps JohnScott had brought him along so the two of us wouldn't find ourselves alone with an awkward topic looming over our heads. If that were the case, I applauded his judgment.

The ex-convict stood by JohnScott's truck with his back to me, and I tried not to stare at the tattoos running up and down his arms. When he turned, he held a long pole and a burlap bag.

I tapped my foot. "You brought a gun, right?"

JohnScott crossed his arms, but Clyde only looked between us with a humored smile on his face. "How are ya, Fawn?"

My cheeks warmed at my rudeness. "I could be better, but thank you for coming."

"Aw … that's okay. I kind of enjoy wrestling rattlers."

"You do this often?"

He glanced around the front yard. "Before I get into that … where is the critter?"

"Oh, it's back here under the house. Hasn't moved since I first found it." I turned toward the side yard, walking briskly.

"Hold up there, Fawn." The coach jogged two steps and brushed my elbow with his fingertips. "Let's take things slow."

"Fine with me, but the thing's not going anywhere."

As we crept toward the back of the house, I said, "So you're going to shoot it, right?"

Clyde's gaze roamed back and forth. "No reason to kill the beast flat out when we can snare her."

"You mean, like, catch it?"

Clyde chuckled as though he knew an inside joke, and he held the pole like a walking stick, only the pole had some sort of pincers on the end. His bent posture, coupled with the shaggy, blond hair shielding his face, reminded me of a lunatic in a horror movie.

I pointed to the open space at the corner of the house. "It's in there."

The two men inched toward the crawl space while I sipped coffee and speculated about JohnScott's impression of me at the holding tank. He didn't act like he remembered the embarrassing episode at all.

"I didn't take the time to go out to my house for my gun." JohnScott spoke without turning around, and I noticed the brand of his jeans. They fit more snugly than Tyler's. "We were two streets over from Clyde's trailer, so we picked up his gear. Lucky it worked out this way."

"Lucky?"

"Yep." He turned and scanned the ground around me. "Because your rattler took off."

My scalp prickled. "What? It was there a second ago."

I stepped toward the open space, but Clyde raised a palm. "Why don't you get on the porch." As an afterthought, he stepped to the corner of the house and inspected the raised platform, the railing, even the covered ceiling. He turned to me and glided his hand through the air like a used-car salesman. "Please."

I glanced at JohnScott, who couldn't seem to take his eyes off the ground, and then I returned Clyde's smile. "Certainly." I didn't like the idea of Clyde taking charge no matter what kind of experience he had. "So how do you know about snakes?"

The coach's gaze left the ground long enough to roll his eyes at me, but Clyde only sidestepped to the crawl space and squatted slowly, giving the impression of a tall elevator lowering to the bottom floor. He peered inside. "There we go, JohnScott. She only moved back a ways, trying to find a cooler spot. It's hot as blazes out here." He got down on one knee, leaning closer to the opening and extending the pole slowly into the shadows. "Watch out now. I'm going to pull her toward me with the J-hook, so I'll have more control."

The coach put his weight on his back foot in case he needed to bolt, while Clyde continued to speak smoothly. "I've shore enough wondered about that serpent in the garden of Eden. Evil little thing. But this one?" He jerked the pole, then flipped a handle on the end. "This one ain't evil." He stepped back from the house, and the rattlesnake writhed on the hook, clamped in her midsection. "This girl's just a little riled."

"Whoa," JohnScott said. "That happened so quick, I barely saw what you did."

Clyde's description of this girl being a little riled seemed a gross understatement as the reptile flopped and jerked on the end of his pole, the tail now pulsing angrily and filling the hollow beneath the house with its enraged clamor.

Fingers of unease inched over my scalp, leaving me chilled in the warm afternoon air.

"Nothing to it," Clyde said. "The main thing is to keep her at the opposite end of the hook. She can't strike that far, so you're safe as long as she's at the other end. Then you simply move her around a bit until you can clasp her in your tongs. But not too close to the head. Don't want to kill her. Not yet anyway."

I peered over the porch, realizing I had gripped the railing until I had a splinter in my palm. "Am I missing something? Why do we not want to kill it?"

Clyde motioned for JohnScott to fetch the bag, which looked like an oversize pillowcase. Then he maneuvered the snake into it, released the clamp, and pulled drawstring. The bag jerked once before going motionless. "Aw, Fawn, she'll probably end up dead, but I've got a friend that can milk the venom first. And another that'll want the hide for belts and such."

"Milk the venom?"

He hummed a yes. "They use it to make antivenin."

"To treat bites?" asked JohnScott.

Clyde nodded, continuing to search the area around us. "The good Lord provides."

I hadn't expected Clyde Felton to hiss religion at me. I'd been a Christian my entire life, and he only recently found God in a prison cell. I curled a strand of hair around my finger, realizing I didn't know how long Clyde had been a Christian. "I don't think God would mind if we killed one snake."

"It might be more than one, I'm thinking." The way his neck jutted forward got on my nerves, and he still searched the grass as though Godzilla might jump out any minute. "Yep, there's her mate." He gestured to a pile of logs twenty yards to the side of the house. "They often run in pairs. That one's found a cool spot in the shade of the woodpile."

Shivers went up my spine as I followed his gaze, and I began searching the yard myself.

JohnScott shook his head. "Good thing you came with me. I never would've known to look for a pair." His I-told-you-so smirk didn't go unnoticed, but maybe I deserved it.

"And it's a good thing we didn't bring a gun. The shot would've scared this one away." Clyde rested a fist on his hip. "You tackle this little boy, JohnScott. Might as well learn."

The coach looked from the snake to Clyde, then down to the clamp on the end of the pole. "When I shoot them, I don't have to get that close."

Clyde laughed. "I know, but as long as you keep him a pole's length away, you're all right. It's not like he can fly."

I sought safety on the porch again, glancing at the crawl space as I walked past.

The coach took a deep breath and let it out. "All right, Clyde. I'll do it." He reached for the J-hook. "But stay close, so if I mess things up, you can snatch the pole."

"Aw, you ain't gonna mess up. Piece of cake."

The two of them walked toward the woodpile, and I wondered what would happen if they were bitten. I had never heard much about people getting struck by rattlesnakes. Lots of rumors over the years, but nothing ever came of them.

Clyde squeezed the coach's shoulder. "You're more likely to get struck by lightning than a snake."

JohnScott glanced at the sky above his head, sprinkled with cotton-ball clouds. "Not today, I'm not."

"Use your hook to uncoil him, then reach in and pick him up."

In five seconds, the second snake squirmed in the clamp, and JohnScott whooped. "I can't believe I caught a rattlesnake. Fawn, look at this thing."

I looked at it all right—from the safety of my perch on the railing, which may or may not have been strong enough to support my weight.

"Fawn's hiding over there on the porch." Clyde smiled, prompting me to climb down.

Clyde took the J-hook and explained the mechanics of getting the angry snake into the bag.

My teeth grazed my bottom lip. "So Clyde, tell me again how you know about this sort of thing."

"My grandpappy." He picked up the weighted bag, and we followed him to the front yard. "He used to compete every year in the rattlesnake round-up over in Sweetwater. Sometimes brought in a couple hundred diamondbacks in one weekend."

I shivered, but neither of them noticed.

"He said I had snake eyes. Since I'm color-blind, I see the varmints easier than most people. Anyway, at twenty-one, I led a hunt on my own." He gently laid the snakes in the back of JohnScott's truck and winked at me. "After that, I took a short break ... But this past March, I went back to the round-up again. Turns out hunting's like riding a bike."

My pulse slowed as my pride slithered into the grass. "Well ... I'm glad you came."

JohnScott peered at me from behind Clyde's back. He only met my gaze briefly before looking away with a stifled smile, but I thought he might finally have shown that tiny bit of approval I'd been hunting for.

CHAPTER EIGHTEEN

JohnScott hadn't mentioned taking me to Lubbock to pick up the Chevy, and Saturday morning I half hoped he had forgotten. I poured a glass of milk and unwrapped a strawberry Pop-Tart, but then I saw his truck creeping up the drive.

In a peculiar way, I wanted to see him. I was mortified when I thought about the electric current that shot through me when we were swimming, but the way his eyes twinkled as he snared that rattlesnake made me want to sit and talk to him, get to know him better, discover what made him tick.

Ridiculous.

It took me a minute to open the front door—the lock had been acting up lately—and when I finally got it open, he stood at the bottom of the steps with his hands shoved in his pockets. "Brought you something."

He brought me a gift?

He stepped to his truck and opened the door. "Come on, boy."

Nothing happened, so I stuffed the last of my toaster pastry into my mouth and followed him. I peeked into the cab and saw the Picketts' old blue heeler lying on the seat with his head on his paws. The dog's eyebrows lifted when he saw me.

In the seven months I'd stayed with the Picketts, I'd grown accustomed to the black-and-gray cow dog that habitually lay as a permanent rug on Ansel and Velma's back porch, tired and slow.

"You brought Rowdy? But we're going all the way to Lubbock."

When the coach snapped his fingers, Rowdy raised his head but didn't move. "It'll do him good to be off the porch." He whistled sharply, and Rowdy stood, picked his way across the seat, and lumbered to the ground, where JohnScott patted his head.

I had never been much of an animal person, but Rowdy held a special place in my heart. When I first moved in with the Picketts, I had been a flurry of tears and panic, and the dog had sat next to me, resting his head on my leg and watching me with his friendly silver eyes.

I squatted next to him and scratched behind his ears.

JohnScott shut the truck door with a snap. "I figured he might stay up here for a while. Keep you company."

"No way." Even though I loved Rowdy, I didn't want a dog. "Who would take care of him?"

"It crossed my mind you could."

"I don't know, JohnScott. I'm not much for taking care of things." He stifled a laugh.

"What?"

He studied a red-ant bed four feet away. "Might not hurt to get some practice, ya think?"

"No." I frowned at the dog. "But thanks anyway."

"Aw, Fawn." He removed his cap. "If I take Rowdy home, he'll just hate it."

I crossed my arms. *He wanted the dog to babysit me.*

The coach stepped onto the porch, slapping his hand against his thigh so the dog would follow. "Know what else he hates?"

"I can't imagine."

"Snakes." He said the word subtly, like an afterthought.

I glanced toward the corner of the house, around which lay the exposed crawl space and woodpile. Even though the odds of my finding another rattler were small, a canine snake alarm would give me peace like a monitored home-security system.

JohnScott crouched on the raised porch next to the dog, and when he looked at me, our eyes were level. "All right if he stays?" he asked.

Once again I morphed into my sixteen-year-old self, sitting at a student desk while Coach Pickett explained the importance of studying history. "Okay. Thank you."

He transferred a bag of dog food from his truck to my kitchen, filled a Cool Whip container with water, and patted Rowdy on the head. "Feed him twice a day."

And that was that. I had become the proud owner of a four-legged senior citizen.

But as we drove away from the shack, I didn't know which made me more uncomfortable—leaving a flea-carrying animal in my house or climbing into the truck with the coach.

After thirty minutes, we were halfway to Lubbock, near Slaton, and JohnScott had only spoken once. When I asked about the offensive line during the previous night's homecoming game, he rambled about strategy for five minutes and then settled back into silence.

The scent of hay mingled with coffee reminded me of his parents' house, but I didn't ask about Ansel and Velma. Apparently we needed to clear the air, but if I waited for him to say something about the holding tank, I'd likely be waiting until I was old and gray like Rowdy.

My stomach did a flip. "JohnScott?"

He jumped as though I had woken him from a deep sleep, and then he cleared his throat. "Clyde was helpful the other day, wasn't he?"

I sighed. Right when I found the courage to broach the subject, he started talking about something else. "Oh … yes, I suppose."

"You don't like him."

He didn't sound judgmental or condescending, but I suddenly wished my prejudice wasn't so transparent. "I like him all right." I rubbed my thumb against the rough upholstery.

A smiled played around JohnScott's lips. "Why do you do that?"

I pulled my hand away from the seat. "What?"

"Act all snobby. You're not like that at all, once you let your shield down."

"My shield?" I wasn't sure where this conversation was going, but it seemed safer than what I'd been about to bring up.

"I guess it's a shield," he said. "You throw something up in front of yourself when you're around other people. But when you relax, like now, you're a different person. You smile a lot more."

His evaluation was dead accurate, except for one thing. I was not relaxed at the moment. "It's easier that way," I said with an offhand tone as I resumed thumbing the seat cushion, wondering if I might wear a hole in it that would match all the others.

"Explain," he said.

I didn't want to explain. And honestly I never even tried to figure it out. "I'm sort of shy, I guess. Way down deep. And it's easier to be standoffish than risk talking to people and being rejected. Snobbiness generally scares people away."

He nodded. "Or repels them."

He said the words softly and yet they sliced through my pride like a scythe. "Well, yes."

We fell into silence again, JohnScott rubbing his chin and occasionally removing his ball cap, and me wanting to somehow crawl into the floorboard and hide. *I shouldn't have told him that.* This felt worse than bumping into him in a wet T-shirt.

"I'm kind of unsure of myself too," he blurted. "I probably hide it behind sports talk. If I feel skittish in a group, I bring up football, and then I can pretty much outtalk anyone in the room."

I smiled, and then the smile turned into a laugh. "JohnScott, you're the least insecure person I've ever met. Seriously."

The corner of his mouth pulled up, and he looked at me sideways. "Maybe I hide it better than you."

"Name one thing you're apprehensive about," I challenged. "But you have to give supporting documentation. I want proof this weakness exists."

His arm lolled over the steering wheel, and he sighed. He opened his mouth to speak, and then closed it. "All right," he finally said. "I'm shaky around women."

All the giggles that had been building up in my lungs quickly dispersed to my nerve endings, and I clenched my hands tightly in my lap.

"And supporting evidence?" He sounded as though he was smiling, but I couldn't bear to look at him. "I never date. That should be proof enough."

I forced a chuckle, but it had way too much air involved. "At least you're not a snob." Such a silly thing to say, but my brain addled.

Apparently my statement caught him off guard, because he laughed loudly. "I like you with your shield down, Fawn."

Silence swelled in the cab.

It seemed we had simultaneously noticed his reference to *liking me*, and neither of us knew what to say next. Of course, he hadn't meant he liked me in a romantic way, only that he liked me better than the stuck-up version of me he had taught in high school.

I felt sorry for him then, squirming and gripping the steering wheel, and I figured I should do something to let him know I didn't think he liked me ... like *that*.

I pinched my bottom lip between my teeth. "I'm sorry about that day at the holding tank."

"I don't know what you mean."

I stared out the side window, watching cotton fields blur past the pickup. "I almost bumped into you ... trying to get away from Grady." I straightened the leg of my shorts, smoothing the fabric until it lay flat against my thighs. "I wanted you to know it wasn't deliberate. I have this thing about dirty water, so I didn't open my eyes." My voice tapered off.

He cocked his ear toward his shoulder, staring down the highway. "I didn't notice anything."

I felt three inches tall. *I spent days worrying about it when he hadn't even noticed.*

"Okay." He spoke loudly, then corrected his volume. "Maybe I noticed, but I didn't know if you noticed, to tell the truth. I hunkered down because of the splashing and didn't see you coming."

"I didn't see you, either."

"Yep." He ran the back of his hand across his mouth. "And then when you popped up next to me, you sort of took me by surprise."

"Me, too." I remembered the way his eyebrows softened as his gaze roamed to my lips. He had looked like he wanted to kiss me.

I blinked. Hard. I didn't need to be thinking like that.

"I should be the one apologizing," he said. "You'd think I'd never been that close to a beautiful girl. And then I just left you there." His gaze bounced to me, then quickly away. "Please don't think I'm a cad."

The cogs in my brain began to spin, frantically processing the fact that he had called me beautiful, and I wasn't even sure he realized he had done it. I curled a strand of hair around my finger and gently pulled, harder and harder, until my mind came back to reality. "You're not a cad, Coach Pickett."

The whiteness around his knuckles disappeared as he eased his grip on the steering wheel. He glanced at me, and his half smile created a series of lines on his right cheek.

No, JohnScott Pickett wasn't a cad. Not at all.

CHAPTER NINETEEN

As streetlamps flickered on, I walked with Tyler down the middle of Main Street, which had been barricaded for the homecoming street dance. My steps naturally synced to the beat of the country-and-western band, and I recognized the lead singer who had graduated from high school with my mother. I said a silent prayer, thanking the Lord my parents always stayed away from this type of civic gathering.

Since our trip to Lubbock that morning, Coach Pickett's smile lines had flashed across my memory, but I shoved the image deep into the back corner of my consciousness, where it belonged.

I was such a hypocrite.

I demanded Tyler behave in such a way as to regain my trust, yet I abused his faith by not only noticing another man but entertaining innocent yet persistent thoughts.

It wasn't as if the coach noticed me back. Not unless I was wet and six inches in front of his nose, which decidedly made him uncomfortable enough to point out that he *did not date*. And it didn't take a genius to realize that if he ever overcame his insecurity and asked someone out, he would not choose a woman with this many complications.

I kept my thoughts deliberately focused on Tyler.

He leaned toward me with his lips at my ear, and I imagined his breath smelled like beer. But he wouldn't be drinking. He had promised me. "You thirsty?" he asked.

"I'd only have to go to the bathroom. I better wait."

He led me to the stop sign, where I leaned against a red pumper truck from the volunteer fire department. As always, they parked their equipment downtown as a safety measure, as well as to add to the festivities.

I could feel people watching us, some whispering, others talking indiscreetly.

"I knew they'd get back together."

"Cut from the same mold."

"She'd be a fool to let him get away."

Tyler put his arm around my shoulders and squeezed.

A few couples were already dancing on the wide brick boulevard, the old-timers wearing boots and jeans, the younger people in shorts and sandals. I fell somewhere between the two, because I had slipped on a baggy maternity dress, which made me feel like a health-food green girl, while my custom-made Lucchese boots brought back memories of honky-tonk nightclubs.

Tyler rested his foot on the bumper of the truck. "You look pretty tonight."

"I'm as wide as a barn."

"Don't say that. There's nothing more beautiful than a pregnant woman."

He held my gaze while I silently weighed the possibility of him quoting lines he had heard in movies. But he sounded sincere.

Sophie Snodgrass marched toward us and ran her fingers through my hair. "Seen any more split ends, darlin'? I sure hope I got 'em all." When she grinned at Tyler, she reminded me of a donkey. "How you doing, son? I see the two of you are spending time together again. I suppose the wedding bells will ring soon—"

"No plans to speak of," I interrupted.

Tyler pointed his finger at her and smiled. "But if we make any rash decisions, you'll be the first to know, Sophie. I promise you that." He took me by the hand. "Fawn, let's dance a few."

I didn't really want to dance, because I had never gotten good at it—besides, I couldn't see my feet—but I wasn't about to pass up the opportunity to escape Sophie.

Soon Tyler led me in a clumsy two-step, no better at dancing than I was. "We'll give them something to talk about."

Clearly he wanted to be seen with me, but I had to admit, I enjoyed being seen with him, too. His tan skin, black hair, and firm muscles drew the attention of most of the females on Main Street, and his bank book drew the attention of the rest of them. But even though his looks and money were appealing, it was the familiar way his arms wrapped around me that settled my worries and calmed my fears.

"Excuse me." A tap on my shoulder brought me out of my daydreams, and Grady Cunningham grinned at Tyler. "Could I be so bold as to break in and steal your partner?"

Tyler's fingers squeezed my hand. "She's all mine tonight. I'm selfish like that." Then he danced me away from the college boy, who clutched his chest as though he'd been shot.

"You were never good at sharing your toys," I said.

"Not a chance."

I glanced back at Grady as he pulled Ruthie onto the dance area. "Dodd and Ruthie are engaged now."

"No kidding."

"They're getting married in Ansel and Velma's backyard."

We maneuvered awkwardly around a slow-moving elderly couple. "I've never seen the Picketts' place. What's it like?"

"A pasture."

He chuckled. "I'm guessing that wouldn't be your ideal wedding venue."

"Not quite." I fingered his collar, trying to calm the flurry in my stomach.

"Let me guess." He pressed against the small of my back, pulling me closer to him. "I bet you would choose some fancy outdoor garden or a grand ballroom with chandeliers." He grinned. "Everyone in West Texas would show up, all with outlandish gifts for you."

"I don't need gifts, just a roof over my head and food on the table."

"Well, you'll likely have a lot more than that." The song ended, and he led me back to the fire truck. "Stay here, and I'll go get you a bottled water."

He walked away, smiling, and a slight hum of doubt swept through my mind. I wondered if I would ever fully trust him again, but Velma would tell me not to borrow tomorrow's trouble.

When the next song ended, Grady appeared by my side. "Your bodyguard's gone. Dance with me."

I looked toward the concession stand but didn't see Tyler. "He'll be back any minute."

His head lolled forward as though in despair.

"Sorry, Grady."

He wandered away, and soon I saw him dancing with a high school girl whose name I couldn't remember. Three songs later, he scooted past with Ruthie, and she called out to me, "You're not dancing."

I shrugged. "Waiting for Tyler."

But obviously Tyler had gotten sidetracked. I walked a wide circle, looking for him, and the longer he stayed gone, the bigger the cavern of concern grew in my heart.

I returned dutifully to my post by the fire truck, determined to wait him out, but Grady bounded to my side again, clicking the heels of his boots together. He held his elbow toward me. "May I have the honor, fair maiden?"

I turned my back on my worries and curtsied. "Thank you, sir."

He led me to the far end of the street, away from the stage with its loud speakers, and I walked backward in a slow circle as he led me in some sort of homemade dance step. *The preacher's little brother couldn't dance either.*

"I'm glad you came." His unusually sober tone surprised me. "I was afraid you'd stay locked up all alone like you did at Ansel and Velma's. It was like you were punishing yourself for being bad."

"Maybe I was."

"Well, you're not a bad person, and you don't need to be in time-out."

I squinted. "Have you been talking to Coach Pickett?"

"No, why?"

"He says the same thing." I parroted the coach, "Love the sinner, hate the sin."

"He knows what he's talking about."

"But he doesn't have to be so pushy about it."

"Don't I?"

JohnScott's voice startled me.

He was leaning against a telephone pole, and Grady and I had stumble-danced past him.

"Coach, we're not talking about you," Grady called.

"I heard you." He took my hand from Grady. "My turn."

"I'm not done with her."

"Sure you are, little mountain boomer." He curled me under his arm. "Go find some other kids to play with."

As Grady stuck out his bottom lip, I focused my gaze on my hand, held firmly in JohnScott's.

The coach led me confidently around the dance area while I examined my feelings. I had come to the dance with Tyler and had every intention of finding him again, but a quiver of energy bounded around my lungs and gave off tiny explosions every time I looked at the knuckles of the coach's hand.

His knuckles.

This didn't feel right. I shouldn't be experiencing tiny explosions from anyone other than Tyler. And Tyler would not like me dancing with JohnScott.

A chill went up my spine.

"You all right?" he asked.

"Oh, sure." I looked over my shoulder, scanning the crowd.

"I saw him down a side street, behind the bounce house." He looked over my head, lifting his chin in greeting when he caught someone's eye.

"Saw who?"

He looked down at me with an amused smile as though I were a child telling a white lie.

I sighed helplessly. "What was he doing?"

"Does he know you're here?"

"We came together."

His eyebrows twitched, and he frowned slightly.

"What?"

He twirled me then, making the move seem effortless as we temporarily separated. When we came back together, he kept his eyes above my head. "Let's dance a few songs. You deserve to have a good time since you got all gussied up." He released my waist and held me at arm's length, his gaze wandering across my dress.

How did he do that? How did he look at me without that drooling animal expression other men had? "One more song."

He nodded. "How's Rowdy?"

"He's keeping an eye on me."

He twirled me again, and as I spun beneath his hand, I wondered if he were watching me, but when he pulled me back into the crook of his elbow, he seemed to be looking everywhere else.

I stared at his shoulder, disgusted with myself. Of course he hadn't been watching me. This was JohnScott Pickett, for heaven's sake.

But since he determinedly avoided looking at me, I took advantage of the opportunity to inspect him. Something seemed different, but I couldn't quite place it. His fingers pressed into my side, signaling me to veer to the left around a slower couple, and as we did, a horsefly landed on his temple. He shook his head and released my hand to swat it away, then resumed his previous control.

"You got a haircut," I challenged.

"I cut a heck of a lot more than one."

When I shook my head at his corny humor, he smiled, almost apologetically.

His hair was still long enough to curl, but now the curls seemed in a controlled formation. "I like it." I fought the urge to touch his hair, to feel the texture, to see what would happen if I ran my fingers through it.

He cleared his throat. "There goes Tyler."

Without thinking, I dropped my arms to my sides and took a step back.

The coach's eyes widened, and for a split second, he stood with his arms suspended as though I had vanished into midair.

I imagined a hint of hurt in his eyes, and I took a shallow breath and looked at the ground.

"I'll show you where I saw him," JohnScott said. "But let's snatch you a bottle of water first. You look warm."

As soon as he mentioned water, my thirst exploded, and I followed him dutifully through the crowd. I uncapped the bottle, and as he craned his neck to find Tyler again, I downed the entire sixteen ounces without once lowering the bottle from my lips. I tossed it in a nearby trash barrel as JohnScott laughed. "Need another one?"

"No, I'm good."

"There he is." JohnScott turned his back to me and walked toward the post office, his long strides leaving me running to catch up.

Tyler didn't notice me at first. "Wassup, *Coach*?"

I grimaced. Tyler habitually called JohnScott *Coach* behind his back. A slam. JohnScott had never been his coach, and Tyler wouldn't respect him even if he had.

"Bringing Fawn back to you," JohnScott said. "You seem to have misplaced her."

I studied a string of vehicles parked along a side street.

"Shoot, she always finds her way back." Tyler belched. "She's like that. Low maintenance."

My vanity splattered across the asphalt parking lot, and I wanted to lock myself in my little house and never come out. I should have known Tyler's drinking was out of control. I should have known he didn't love me enough to change. I should have known it was too good to be true. My friends had told me as much.

But my friends didn't understand the pull.

Tyler hooked his arm around my neck. "Time for us to go."

I tried to push him away, but his arm lay too heavy on my shoulders. "You're drunk."

"And I bet you're gonna start whining about it any minute." He raised the pitch of his voice to an annoying falsetto. "Tyler, I'm so *disappointed* in you."

I ducked out from under his arm. "Get away from me."

He gripped my forearm, and his fingers dug into my skin. "Now … that's no way to talk to your baby daddy."

I felt sick. People as far away as the stage were turning toward the commotion, and I only wanted to get away from Tyler, away from Trapp, away from all of them. I wanted to go somewhere far away where people didn't know me, where boyfriends didn't drink and fathers didn't abandon their children.

"You're scaring her," JohnScott said calmly.

Tyler blew a puff of air through his lips, spraying me with spittle. "You don't know much about women, *Coach*."

For an instant I thought of JohnScott when he admitted his fear of dating. The nausea building in my stomach morphed into anger, and I growled, "Shut up. JohnScott's twice the man you are."

Tyler's palm popped loudly against my cheek, knocking me off balance as pain splintered from my jaw to my ear. My shoulder slammed into JohnScott's chest, and his arms steadied me. But once I gained my footing, he gently pushed me away.

"Coach Pickett ..." Tyler's voice sounded surprisingly clear for someone so drunk, and since the band just finished a song, his words rang loud through the downtown area, gaining the attention of the few remaining citizens who weren't already watching. "Get your hands off my woman."

JohnScott's hand rested beneath my elbow, and he was bending slightly, checking on me, so when Tyler reared back and pummeled him below the chin, JohnScott didn't see it coming, and his head snapped to the side.

The coach's fingers slid from my arm as he fell hard to the ground.

CHAPTER TWENTY

Dodd and Grady physically restrained Tyler to keep him from kicking JohnScott in the ribs as the coach lay sprawled on the post-office parking lot. They gripped Tyler by the arms and walked him up and down the sidewalk until he stopped cursing and fighting them.

My cheek stung from Tyler's palm, but my dignity stung far worse, and I turned my back on the crowd. I should have helped JohnScott get up. I should have apologized, but half the Panther football team rushed to the coach's aid as soon as Tyler threw the first punch.

"I'll give that low-life cattle prodder what's coming to him!" yelled Sophie's eldest son as he pulled JohnScott to his feet.

The hairdresser answered him just as loudly. "He's got a lot of nerve coming to Trapp and messing with our coach."

But JohnScott put an abrupt halt to his team's taunts with a few short words, and Dodd and Grady loaded Tyler into his fancy double-cab truck to drive him home to Snyder. Ruthie followed in Dodd's El Camino so they would have a way back to Trapp.

"Fawn, honey, you all right?" Sophie patted my shoulder.

"I'm just so … embarrassed." I stepped to the side of the shrubbery at the corner of the building in a feeble attempt to shield myself from view.

Sophie followed. "That boy's always been a drinker. I'm not sure but what you're better off without him." She swept a stray lock of hair from my forehead with her long fingers. "Thinks he's better than the rest of us. I mean I'm sorry for his losing his father and all, but that only goes so far, you know. He ought to be drying himself out by now. And certainly ought to be treating you with respect."

JohnScott emerged from a huddle of teenagers. "You boys go on about your business."

"But, Coach, we can't let him get away with that. It ain't right." A burly senior thrust his jaw out, but JohnScott answered sharply, hands on his hips.

"Anyone who retaliates will run laps on Monday." His gaze swept the players until every pair of eyes lowered from his stare and a collective sigh of disappointment shushed through the team.

Sophie clucked her tongue. "Now, Fawn, don't you take Tyler back after this. I don't care if you are about to pop, he needs to know once and for all that he can't go around treating people like dirt."

Her words rang in my ears like the droning whine of a mosquito, and I began to wonder how I could get away from her, but more important, how I would get home. Desperate to escape the town's prying eyes, I considered JohnScott, weighing the possibility of asking him for a ride, but the coach turned and walked briskly toward the United with two players tagging along behind him. He didn't so much as glance back at me.

My already bruised ego took another hit, and I blinked three times to keep from crying.

Sophie's eyebrows rose slightly, and then her expression melted into disappointment. Apparently she had been hoping the coach would offer me a ride as well, and she hummed slightly as though my status had been knocked down another notch.

When my cell phone vibrated, I expected it to be Ruthie. Instead, it was a text from the coach.

Head toward Aunt Lynda's house.

I stared at the phone.

I didn't want to go to Lynda Turner's house. She would only say *I told you so*, and she would be right.

Sophie leaned forward, trying to see my screen and speaking with syrupy sweetness. "Darlin', do you have a way to get home?"

"Yes." I backed away from her. "Thanks, Sophie."

"Let me know if you need anything," she called. "I'm always around."

I strode quickly down Main Street, and the only thought in my brain was to get away from the street dance. I needed to be alone. To hide. To think. I turned onto Avenue S and immediately felt the safety of its shadows. After walking half a block, I leaned against a tree trunk near the sidewalk, obscured by the near pitch-blackness.

Later, without a doubt, I would cry, but for now the invisibility of darkness comforted me, and I closed my eyes and let the stillness settle like salve. My nerves calmed, and my pulse slowed, and I gingerly touched my tender cheek.

I wanted to hate Tyler.

I should have hated him, but I found myself making excuses for him. He had been under a lot of stress since his father died—not to mention the baby—and those two things could cause a person to lean on the bottle.

I let my head fall back, tapping it against the rough bark of the tree. *Bump, bump, bump.*

No.

There weren't enough excuses to explain away Tyler's behavior, but even more than that, there was no excuse for me repeatedly taking him back. This had to stop.

So I would be raising a child on my own. *Big deal.* I wasn't the first single mother on the planet. If others could do it, so could I.

Of course, I didn't want to be alone, but it would be better than being with a man I couldn't count on. I glanced down the street, where I could see Lynda Turner's porch light shining. Ruthie's mother had told me, *Some things are worse than being alone.*

With Tyler's slap still lingering on my cheek, I was finally convinced of the truth in Lynda's words.

A vehicle approached slowly from a side street, and as it drew closer, I recognized it as JohnScott's truck. He stopped long enough for me to get in, then drove in the opposite direction from Main Street.

"Sorry I left you," he said, "but we probably didn't need to be seen leaving together. You all right?"

"Yes." I answered him readily enough, but then I began to wonder. *Maybe I'm not all right.* This didn't feel like the other times Tyler and I had broken up. It was far more painful. And foreign.

And permanent.

As we approached the outskirts of town, I noticed a group of stragglers at the Allsup's, and I lay down across the seat. I didn't want to be seen with JohnScott.

Maybe the coach understood, because he didn't say anything as we drove up the Caprock. His truck windows were down, and the wind whipped through the cab, blowing away my jumbled thoughts and brushing against my tense muscles. By the time we stopped in front of my shack, my hair had blown into a tangled mess, and I fingered it to one side as I sat up.

We both stared out the front window as the engine idled.

"I'm sorry," I whispered.

He grunted. "Not your fault."

"He hit you."

JohnScott rotated his jaw. "You know? I haven't taken a punch in a long time."

I stared at the dash, frowning at the glowing lights until they blurred from emotion.

"No, wait," JohnScott said. "Last season, I got in a tangle of players at the end of the Denver City game and ended up with a concussion and a couple broken ribs." He killed the ignition. "That was worse than this, because those boys knocked me out cold."

I opened the door and slid from the truck, unable to find humor in his attitude, and realizing, with a shock, that my greatest emotion was not that of loss. Yes, I would break up with Tyler once and for all, but more than sadness or humiliation or regret, I felt anger. Intense anger.

At myself.

JohnScott got out of the truck, and with both doors shut, we were left in the pitch-blackness of a new moon. There were still things that needed to be said, and I rested my elbows on the hood, wishing I had left the porch light on.

"Why are you with him?" JohnScott stayed on the opposite side of the truck, and even though I couldn't see him, I imagined him leaning on the hood like me.

"I'm not anymore." I released a long breath. "I never should have been with him in the first place."

I could hear the coach rubbing his whiskers. "Do you love him?" he asked.

"Well, that's the million-dollar question."

"I'm sorry. It's none of my business."

No one had said that to me in a while. It seemed everyone considered my life their business. "It's all right." I turned and leaned with my back against the truck, staring toward the edge of the Caprock to my sacred view, now hidden in the night. I longed for a full moon so I could feel the openness of the landscape. So I could escape. "I thought I loved him. But maybe I was just addicted to the idea of him."

The engine clicked as it cooled, settling down in the same way my thoughts were settling into logic. "I don't want my child to grow up in two separate households, and I thought we could make it work. He loves me, I know he does." I heard a desperate whine in my voice and corrected it. "But now I realize he's not capable of loving me … the right way."

"You've come to terms with a few things."

"I had a short discussion with a mesquite tree back in town."

His boots gritted against sand as he stepped around the truck, and he leaned against the hood next to me, joining me to gaze into the darkness. "So you're done with him."

"It won't be easy, but yes, I'm done." Pounds and pounds of bad decisions lifted from my chest, and for the first time in months, I felt light and free.

We stood there in silence for several minutes before JohnScott asked, "How old were you when you first got together?"

"Sixteen." I chuckled. "His *bad-guy* persona appealed to me back then."

JohnScott paused, seeming to think about something. "So you don't really know what it's like to date a *good guy*."

His words rubbed—it was one thing for me to call Tyler a bad guy but something else for JohnScott to do it—but I couldn't argue. "I suppose."

"I don't mean to offend you, but guys like Tyler need a daily kick to the groin until they figure out how to treat a woman."

"What's your point?"

He shifted. "He ticks me off, treating you like dirt. And in front of everybody. I had half a mind to let the team work him over."

"You don't mean that."

He sighed. "No, I would never do that because I'm *the good guy*. The one who always follows the rules, always does the right thing, always walks away from a senseless fight. Yet Tyler hurts you over and over and over."

I pursed my lips. "Well, I can hardly blame him this time. I should have known better."

"*Of course* you can blame him." He cut a sigh short in disgust. "Stop playing the victim."

"What do you expect me to do?"

"Don't look back." He raised his voice, but it traveled over the cliff, swallowed up in nothingness. "Quit settling for the likes of Tyler Cruz. You deserve better than that."

"Tyler is more than what you saw tonight."

"He's only as good as his worst day. You said yourself, he has a bad-guy persona."

My anger toward myself quickly paled in comparison to my mounting irritation with the coach. "Yes! Tyler's a bad guy, and I'm the stupid little girl who took him back *six times*."

"You're only stupid if you take him back a seventh time, Fawn."

"Well, I don't plan on it," I snapped.

His voice sounded gravelly, laced with aggression. "Then you should date someone else for a change."

"Who would date me, JohnScott? What kind of person would want me now?"

"Maybe someone like me!" He slammed his palm against the hood of the truck, and I jumped.

Silence hung heavy between us.

I held my breath as shock caused my anger to slither away unseen. *Someone like him?* Someone like JohnScott Pickett. My mind raced through the past few weeks of swimming and cleaning my yard and catching snakes. Every word he said to me rang in my ears in shouts and whispers and questions. He couldn't have meant it the way I wished he did.

But then his hands gripped my shoulders in the darkness, and he frantically inched them up my neck to the sides of my face, finding my lips with one of his thumbs before pressing his mouth firmly against mine.

It started quickly. Unexpectedly. One second we were sort of arguing, and the next second he was kissing me. My first thought was that his mouth felt different than Tyler's. His lips were softer and more full, and he tasted vaguely of Dr Pepper and Juicy Fruit gum.

A voice inside my head said, *I shouldn't be doing this*, and I kept my arms folded over my chest. But as one of his hands slid through my hair, gently working a tangle through his fingertips, I couldn't come up with a reason to hold back.

Every thought of Tyler disappeared in the warmth of JohnScott's lips and the intensity of his kiss, and I hesitantly wrapped my arms around his waist while the ringing in my head yielded to a beautiful song of emotion.

CHAPTER
TWENTY-ONE

I told no one about the kiss.

The next afternoon, I sat in a metal folding chair at my baby shower in the tiny fellowship room in the back of the church building. I ate cake with sugary frosting and wished I didn't feel like smut.

JohnScott's kiss ended as quickly as it began, and he broke away from me, seemingly startled by the predicament in which he found himself. He ushered me to my front door while he mumbled apologies. He was sorry for kissing me, and sorry for his lack of self-control, and sorry for his absence of tact. He opened the door, and the dog brushed against his leg, prompting him to back down the steps, apologizing again—for what, I wasn't sure—but by the time he sped out of my yard, I was completely convinced that JohnScott Pickett was very sorry.

Sorry he had touched me.

The church ladies, in belated kindness, blessed me with a baby shower, and as I opened bag after bag of diapers, wipes, and little clothes, I imagined their unspoken accusations echoing off the walls.

"You're thinking about something." Ruthie popped a pillow mint in her mouth. "Tell me."

"I'm thinking my life's a mess. You wouldn't understand."

"Oh, that's right." She nodded. "I have *everything*."

"Everything except money."

She held her fingers in the *Who cares?* symbol. "I can still understand your problems."

Pamela Sanders stopped in front of my chair and patted my knee. "We can all understand your problems, darlin'. What that boy did to you in town last night was a flat-out crime. And what he did to Coach Pickett was outrageous." She turned to Velma, two seats down. "You've gotta believe me when I say the church is behind our coach one hundred percent. It's a crying shame what happened to your boy."

Velma shook her head. "JohnScott's a good man, but trouble seems to find him no matter what."

Ruthie's mother, sitting between Velma and me, had kept her eyes on her plate for the past hour, but she now lifted them. "Thank you, Pam. We do appreciate the kind words about our family."

Lynda and Velma surprised me when they showed up for the shower. Neither of them had been in the church building for years, and Lynda had all but sworn she would never set foot there again. Their presence flattered me, but at the same time, I felt like a fraud, surrounded by JohnScott's cousin, aunt, and mother.

My own mother slipped into the room, and a momentary hush fell over the fluttering mouths, but then the conversations continued at an increased pace as the ladies tried to camouflage the pause.

I stepped to the punch table, feeling the childish need for my mother to tell me things were going to be all right. "Hi, Mom."

"I heard what happened last night."

A protective shell fell in place around my feelings. "You and everyone else."

"It'll clean up easily enough." She scooped two almonds with a teaspoon and placed them gingerly on her glass plate.

"I'm tired of cleaning it up."

Empathy flashed across her face. "But you love him, Fawn."

"I'm not sure I do. I'm not sure I could survive Tyler's kind of love. Sometimes I feel like I'm going crazy."

Her lips screwed into a pout. "Don't be silly."

Lynda appeared at my side. "We all feel that way sometimes, don't we, Susan?"

My mother's eyes snapped. "I don't know what you mean."

"Sure you do. Talk to the girl for once."

Mother glared at Lynda, then turned away and went to sit next to Milla Cunningham.

Bless Dodd's mother. The woman had taken it upon herself to minister to my cranky mother when the other church ladies weren't really sure what to do with her. As a result, Milla spent more time with my mother and less time with me, but we seemed to have an unspoken agreement that it was best under the circumstances.

Lynda pretended to admire the decorations on the serving table. "Don't feel bad telling your momma about Tyler. She knows exactly how you feel."

"What do you mean?"

Lynda let out a breath. "They called it acute depression, and she had to be hospitalized for a while. I'm not saying you're depressed.

Clearly you're not. But your mother knows what it's like to be overwhelmed."

"Why are you telling me this?"

Lynda lifted her gaze from the sugary blue-and-white cake, peered sadly at my mother on the far side of the room, then frowned determinedly into my eyes. "Because I've been on that ship too, Fawn." She shook her head. "A lot of people have."

CHAPTER
TWENTY-TWO

Where was God?

Monday morning, Labor Day, I sat on the hood of the Chevy, picking at the polish on my thumbnail and waiting for Him to show up.

Probably He was angry. Even though I turned my back on some of my sinful behaviors, greed had driven me into another scandal with Tyler, and I hadn't even prayed about it. Not much anyway.

In general, prayer was a new thing for me. I had been raised in the church, perfect attendance three times a week and years of potluck meals, but in spite of that, I hadn't developed a faith of my own.

I lifted my hair to the top of my head and fanned the back of my neck. If I didn't shower soon, I wouldn't be ready when Dodd and Ruthie picked me up for the softball game. But I shifted to a more comfortable position, gifting myself five more minutes as I considered the terminology. *A faith of my own.*

I heard that phrase in sermons, read it in blogs, and listened to it in Christian songs on the radio. And I recognized it in myself. Once I started looking.

And I started looking about the time I left home. I don't mean when I went to college because nothing changed then. But when my parents kicked me out of their house? That's when I started questioning God, wondering why I couldn't feel Him. Yes, *feel Him.* According to the sermons and blogs and songs, God could be felt. He could be heard. And if I believed strongly enough, He could be seen.

But so far, He hadn't shown up.

He hadn't been at Ansel and Velma's house either, in their guest room where I first started fumbling with prayer and cried and moaned and pitched a fit. I had expected Him to show up immediately, and when He didn't, I longed to ask for Velma's advice. But I didn't. Even though we talked about every topic under the sun, religion was off limits. The Picketts were still trying to make sense of JohnScott's baptism last year.

Ruthie was no help either. I tried to talk to her about God a few times, but she could hardly understand the *faith-of-my-own* dilemma. She had been going to church such a short time, she couldn't understand the habitual boredom I felt every time I entered the building. Or worshipped. Or prayed.

"God?" I leaned my head back and stared at a puffy, white cloud. "I get the feeling I should have talked to You about Tyler a while back."

Nothing. My words floated over the cliff, dropped straight down fifteen feet, then tumbled end over end down the sloping terrain until they came to a stop two hundred feet below.

Maybe I should speak more confidently. Boldly. Assuming God would grant my requests. But no, I'd heard strong Christian women in the Tuesday-morning ladies' class praying soft and humble prayers, and they seemed to be feeling His presence constantly.

"Anyway, I'm sorry I didn't consult You about Tyler, but now … what am I supposed to do about JohnScott?"

I ducked my head. How could I expect God to answer? I carried one man's child, yet somehow attracted the attention of another. And I enjoyed it.

Maybe I had a thing about sin.

I shoved my curls out of my face and frowned at the cloud. "Okay. So I don't deserve a man, but could You at least help out with my bills? I can't take care of this baby all by myself."

In slow motion, the cloud slid to the left, mocking me with silence, and I jerked to my feet, wincing as the backs of my thighs stuck to the metal hood. I cursed, kicked the bumper, then slumped against the driver's door and sobbed.

CHAPTER
TWENTY-THREE

JohnScott pulled to the side of the road, slid his truck out of gear, and leaned his head against the back windshield, wondering if he would see Fawn today. Ever since Saturday night's street dance, she had invaded his thoughts to the point he couldn't concentrate. But fortunately, he'd been on the tractor most of the weekend and hadn't had much to think about.

Except her.

As two more vehicles parked, he thrust his door open and plastered a smile on his face. "Hey, Clyde. You ready to play some softball?"

"Might as well."

They had met at the overpass on the edge of town, calling a few friends and spreading the word. Even though Trapp boasted a Little League field, the gate remained chained nine months of the year because of a political mix-up, forcing pickup games to be held at the intersection of Highway 84 and Farm-to-Market 288, where the two roads created a knoll, perfect for use as a baseball diamond.

JohnScott transferred four bags of feed from the bed of his truck to the grassy area, creating three bases and home plate, while a plastic trash can lid marked the pitcher's mound. More cars pulled off the road, some with players, others with spectators, and soon tailgates lined the makeshift field, creating two dugouts and a series of bleachers.

When Dodd backed his El Camino between JohnScott's truck and Clyde's old sedan, the coach immediately noticed Fawn's long blonde hair in the passenger seat. His pulse raced, but he turned away quickly, holding a baseball bat at each end and using it to stretch his shoulders.

Dodd called to him as he lowered his tailgate and pulled an ice chest to the back. "J.S., I say you and I should be team captains."

Ruthie wagged her finger. "You're picking me first."

Dodd raised an eyebrow. "I never said that."

JohnScott peeked at Fawn, but she had turned away from him to watch Grady as he talked to an elderly man. She pulled her hair back in a ponytail. Surely she didn't intend to play. He frowned at Dodd and tilted his head toward Fawn, questioningly, but Ruthie popped him on the shoulder. "Fawn, my cousin doesn't think you should play."

JohnScott's stomach tightened as if his team had just lost the state championship, and when Fawn glared at him, he thought he would've preferred losing a game, if he had been given the two options.

"I'll be on Dodd's team," she quipped.

"No way." Dodd wrapped an arm around Ruthie. "I've already got one weak link."

She smiled, but JohnScott noticed she only looked at Dodd and Ruthie. "I'll have you know I played softball in high school and intramurals at Tech my freshman year. Even if I can't run at the moment, I can still knock the occasional home run."

The preacher held his palms up in surrender. "But still, I only want one of you."

Ruthie kissed him on the cheek. "And you're stuck with me." They walked toward the pitcher's mound while Fawn crossed her arms in a pout.

A small, faint bruise lay across her cheekbone, barely visible beneath a thick layer of makeup, and when JohnScott saw it, he had the overwhelming urge to protect her. She seemed so fragile. And sometimes naive.

"You could get hit in the stomach with a ball," he challenged.

"In all my years of playing softball, I've never been such a bad player that I could actually miss a ball coming straight at me." She still kept her eyes diverted.

"Okay, fine." JohnScott slid his hand into his baseball glove. "But if you're going to be on my team, you can't refuse to look at me for the entire game."

She blinked twice, and her gaze flitted to his knees, sending a burst of energy through his muscles.

"I ... don't know how to act," she mumbled.

"Neither do I, and it's my fault. I'm sorry."

"You mentioned that." She turned her back on him and walked to Ruthie.

JohnScott could have kicked himself. They had been good friends, and he, like an idiot, had messed that up. Only a few moments before he kissed her, the poor woman had been slapped, betrayed, and humiliated by her boyfriend, and JohnScott hadn't slowed down long enough to consider all the reasons for him to keep his distance.

Dodd and Ruthie's easy banter settled his nerves, but at the same time, their comfortable relationship shone in stark contrast to his and Fawn's. But he could repair the damage he had done. He would show her they could be friends, even if he had acted like an adolescent schoolboy strung out on hormones.

Clyde held a bat toward Fawn. "Just try to hit the ball, and then run like a jackrabbit."

"We don't have to worry about her making contact with the ball," JohnScott said. "But I'm not sure I want to see her running like a jackrabbit."

"Aw, now." Clyde chuckled. "Forgot about that."

As JohnScott watched Fawn's back at home plate, he could see why Clyde forgot. She swung the bat in a slow arc, and from this angle, she didn't look pregnant at all. She even had a bit of a waistline. His gaze dropped to the curves of her shorts as she swayed, but he pulled his attention away, scolding himself.

He didn't see the bat connect solidly with the ball, but it sailed high into left field, a little short. Fawn jogged to first base and stopped as Dodd fumbled the ball, picked it up, and threw it home.

The huddle of players around JohnScott cheered.

"She's our secret weapon," he called to Dodd.

"A pregnant girl who runs like a duck?"

Fawn laughed from first base. "I don't run like a duck." She shrugged at Ruthie. "Do I?"

JohnScott's nerves settled as he stepped to home plate, hoping he didn't make a fool of himself. Football was his game, not baseball, but sometimes he got lucky at bat. He glanced at first base, and when he saw Fawn staring at him, it charged him with adrenaline, but he quickly reminded himself she *ought* to be staring at him. He was batting, for heaven's sake.

The pitch flew right over home plate, and JohnScott connected with it, hitting it high in the air. Holding his palm to his forehead, he followed the ball as it soared over his head to drop onto the frontage road behind him. Foul ball.

As Grady chased it, JohnScott called to him. "You might want to stay over there until I'm finished batting."

"Turn around and hit backward," Grady said.

"Not a bad idea," JohnScott chortled.

As predicted, the next hit also sailed in foul territory, but the third slammed over Ruthie's head in right field and turned into a clean home run.

JohnScott sailed around the feed bags, catching up to Fawn and sweeping her into his arms to carry her across home plate. Her giggles only made him run faster, and when he set her down, they both stomped on the feed bag.

"Two to zip." JohnScott put his thumbs in his ears and wiggled his fingers at Dodd.

"You wait, J.S." Dodd shook his head. "The best is yet to come."

JohnScott pulled a Gatorade from the ice chest in the back of his truck, then sank onto the tailgate next to Fawn. "Be sure and keep drinking. You don't want to get dehydrated."

"Dehydration isn't going to be the problem. You thought of everything except restrooms."

"I suppose the cedar tree I used won't do."

She made a face. "Definitely not."

"If worse comes to worst, take my truck to Allsup's on the edge of town. Can you drive a standard?"

"Of course."

A car honked as it passed, and JohnScott, along with several others, responded by lifting a hand in the air. But when he glanced toward the highway, he recognized the F-150 as Tyler's, and he spoke quickly. "Hey, Mom and Dad are missing you. Can you come tomorrow night for dinner at my place?"

Her forehead wrinkled slightly, but then a swell of yelling brought their attention back to the game. Clyde was strolling around the bases, guzzling from a bottle of water, having just hit a home run far across Farm-to-Market 288.

"I'd like to see your parents, JohnScott."

He gripped the edge of the tailgate as he grinned over Clyde's home run, but then he slowly turned his gaze back to Fawn, forcing his actions to appear casual and unbothered. Her makeup had run slightly, and the bruise on her cheek was more prominent. He worked his sore jaw back and forth absentmindedly, wishing he could have been the one to bruise, not her. He didn't realize he was staring until Clyde sat on the tailgate between them and spoke to Fawn.

"Seen any more snakes?" He pushed his hair out of his eyes.

"No, and I don't expect to."

"Best be on the lookout just the same. Back in the day, there were lots of critters out at that place."

"So you've heard the rumors."

"They weren't all rumors. A team of hunters used to make a special trip to your place every year during the round-up." His voice softened. "But even if there are more diamondbacks out there, they won't bother you none unless they feel threatened."

"But if a team came out, they would have gotten all the snakes, right?"

Clyde shifted on the tailgate, and JohnScott and Fawn lifted up, then down. "Well, that was a long time ago."

"Which makes me think the stories don't apply anymore," she said.

"Not necessarily." He spoke slowly, and JohnScott could tell his friend didn't want to scare her. "Rattlers live in dens, and the odds of every last one of them getting caught is slim to none. Usually at least a few are left behind."

"Well, you guys got two the other day."

"Yes, but …"—Clyde ran a hand over his chin, causing a scratchy sound—"they keep coming back to the same den, sometimes for years, having babies."

JohnScott could see the gears turning behind Fawn's eyes. He kept his mouth shut though, glad she had finally humbled herself enough to carry on a conversation with the ex-convict.

"Okay," she said. "Let's say there were two snakes left behind. If both of those came back every year and gave birth to a baby snake, then after a year, there would be four snakes. And after two years, there would be six."

Clyde sighed and seemed to choose his words cautiously, as though he were about to step on a diamondback himself. "Well, there's a couple things you have to think on."

"Such as?"

"Well, that second year, the babies would be having their own babies."

"Of course." She lifted a hand and let it fall against her knee. "So the growth would be exponential."

JohnScott thought he saw her shiver as she considered the numbers behind it.

She massaged her lower back. "You said there were a couple things to think about. Do I even want to know the other?"

"I reckon not." Clyde paused, watching the frolicking on the baseball field for a few minutes before speaking softly. "When diamondbacks give birth, it ain't just one."

"How many do they have?"

"Anywhere from three or four up to …"—he scratched behind his ear—"ten. Maybe twenty."

"Oh my God." Fawn slipped off the tailgate and turned to face him.

"Now, like I said, you don't need to be scared." Clyde spoke quickly. "Even if they're out there, they don't want a fuss any more than you do. Just give them some space."

She stared, speechless, and JohnScott wanted to wrap his arms around her and tell her she didn't have to stay in that mess of a house.

"JohnScott brought the dog out there, right? Dogs can smell 'em."

"But Rowdy is like … nine hundred years old," Fawn protested.

"That doesn't matter," JohnScott said. "He can still bark."

Clyde smiled, and then sobered again. "If you come up on a critter, do what you did the other day. Freeze, get your bearings, and then back off slow. Odds are, the snake will want away from you, and then it'd be a footrace to catch him."

She sat back down, rubbing her palms up and down her arms as though she were cold.

Clyde peered across the makeshift softball diamond. "You don't have to stay out there, sweetie. Ansel and Velma would take you back in a heartbeat."

JohnScott cut his eyes toward Fawn. Two weeks ago, Clyde Felton referring to her as *sweetie* would have elicited a violent scowl, but now she only frowned in concentration.

"I need to prove I can take care of myself."

JohnScott's insides filled with clay. *Surely she wasn't talking about him.*

Clyde grunted. "Your mom and dad?"

"*Yep.*" Now she was mocking him. "You have no idea."

"Oh, I bet I do." Clyde chuckled. "I bet I do."

CHAPTER
TWENTY-FOUR

The restroom at Allsup's was only a half step above the cedar tree JohnScott mentioned, but at least it had toilet paper. As I came out of the store, I immediately noticed Tyler at the gas pumps, and the confidence I felt at the ball game dwindled. I didn't want to talk to him—or ever be seen with him again—but I had to get it over with. I stopped at the front bumper of JohnScott's truck and waited.

Tyler replaced the nozzle on the gas pump, then smiled as he sauntered toward me. His good looks reminded me why I had dated him in the first place, in the midst of rebelling against my parents, against the church, against all the expectations burdening me. I had latched on to him with the fervor of a drowning child.

But I had grown up since then.

"You're driving the coach's truck now." A glimmer lit his eyes. Maybe jealousy. Maybe disgust. Definitely anger.

I felt as though I had been caught red-handed stealing a pack of cigarettes. "He offered." I gestured to the store behind me. "Too much Gatorade."

"Babe ..." He lowered his eyes, looking at me through his eyelashes. "You've got no business playing softball in your condition." His gaze roamed across JohnScott's truck, and his eyes softened as though he were forcing himself to stay calm. "You haven't been answering my calls."

I fingered the warm hood ornament and didn't answer.

"You're upset." He stifled a laugh.

"I can't ignore your behavior at the street dance."

"Fawn ... *come on* ... Your old coach has been filling your head with ideas."

"JohnScott had nothing to do with it."

His glee from a moment before transformed into spite. "When did you stop calling him Coach Pickett?"

"Why do you care?"

He smiled at a blob of gum on the pavement. "I don't want him to take advantage of you." His gaze bounced to my waistline, and my anger swirled like a dust storm.

"I'm not a tramp."

"No, you're not, but the man's been working at your place too much."

"How would you know?"

He shrugged. "People are starting to talk. Everyone's saying you're after the coach."

"That's not true." If that rumor had been flying around, I would have known. Ruthie would have heard it at the United, and JohnScott would have already taken flack about it from the Booster Club.

I opened the driver's door but didn't get in. Instead, I used the door as a shield. I had to get this over with. I had to end it.

Tyler lowered his head, not cowering to me, but low enough he appeared contrite. "I'm sorry about the street dance, Fawn. The booze made me step out of line." When I rolled my eyes, he continued quickly. "But I've given up on drinking once and for all because you and the baby deserve better than that. Can you forgive me?"

I held up my hand and tapped my fingers against my thumb.

When Tyler stepped around the door, I thought he might slap me again, but then his eyebrows drooped, and I had a startling realization. He strategically calculated every move, right down to his facial expressions. How had I never noticed it before?

"I know I messed up again," he said, "but I love you, Fawn."

I scooted back on the seat, putting more space between us. Being aware of Tyler's strategy didn't completely take away his power over me. "This isn't love."

He looked away, blinking into the breeze, and his eyes reddened around the edges. *Almost real.* "You're going to leave me again. You're breaking up."

"I think that's best."

Desperation flashed across his face. "We'll slow down."

I answered hesitantly, but as I spoke, my shoulders relaxed. "To be honest, I think we're only together because of the baby, and that's not a good enough reason."

"It's what God would want."

"No." I glanced at the gas pumps where two people were filling up. "It couldn't work, Tyler. We've already tried it, and it's over."

A train chugged on the edge of town, its whistle stalling our discussion and giving me a chance to calm my racing pulse. I had done it. I had ended things with him, and I already felt better, more free and healthy. My initial reaction was to call Ruthie, but when I stopped to consider my priorities, I realized I wanted to tell JohnScott.

Tyler nodded, accepting my rejection stoically, but his hands gripped the frame of the driver's door so tight, I imagined the steel buckling under his fists.

CHAPTER
TWENTY-FIVE

In the seven months I lived with Ansel and Velma Pickett, I never ventured to the back pasture to the coach's mobile home. Even though it could be seen from Velma's back window, I hadn't bothered to notice the way the double-wide lay nestled between a mesquite thicket and a shallow ravine. Or that he had built a large wooden deck for a front porch, where two tall-backed, wooden rockers now sat. Or that the place was immaculately well kept.

As I parked Velma's Chevy on the circular gravel drive, a small herd of cattle gathered near the stock pond a hundred yards away. Not at all what I expected.

The way my mother's nose wrinkled any time she said the words *trailer house* had always given me a certain impression about people who lived in them. As I made my way up the steps, my hand brushed the stained wood of the handrail, and I realized my negative opinions might have been unfounded.

The front door opened, and JohnScott's father stepped onto the deck. "Haven't seen you lately, Miss Priss."

"Hello, Ansel."

He put an arm around my shoulders. "You and the wee one doing all right?"

"Dr. Tubbs says everything is coming along right on track. Still a few more weeks." The gentle compassion on the old man's face nearly brought me to tears, and I looked away quickly.

"Better come on in the house. Velma and the boy are about done in the kitchen."

I followed him into a spacious living room that opened directly into an eating area. Past a low counter with bar stools lay a brightly colored kitchen, where JohnScott and Velma bustled.

"Hey there, Fawn," Velma called as she withdrew a pan from the oven. "How's Rowdy?"

"As lively as ever." The dog had become a good friend, calming my fears that came from living alone, but I felt silly telling the Picketts that, so I kept it to myself.

JohnScott carried a large pot into the room. "Red beans and french fries." He set it on the table and inhaled deeply. "Doesn't get any better than this."

As we sat down, I felt as though I were returning home after a long absence, even though I had never set foot in the house, and the Picketts had none of the characteristics that mattered to my biological family—money, status, power.

The table had been set neatly with dark, octagonal plates, quite unlike Velma's mismatched dinnerware, but I recognized her corn bread in a dented metal cake pan.

"Velma, what makes your corn bread taste better than any other I've eaten?"

"Well … it's Mexican corn bread."

"Chili powder and processed cheese." JohnScott grinned. "That coupled with the greasy fries makes for a heart attack waiting to happen."

I passed JohnScott the potatoes, and our hands touched, but I ignored the electric current it sent through my fingers. He had given me the distinct impression he viewed the kiss as a mistake, and we were returning to our previously scheduled friendship. And that seemed fine with me. I had made a big enough mess of my life without adding more gossip to the fire.

"Now wait." He stared down at the red platter in his hands. "We're having *Mexican* corn bread and *french* fries. Is that culinarily acceptable?"

"I think you mean *culinary*, Son." Ansel sprinkled grated cheese over everything on his plate.

"How on earth would you know?" JohnScott asked.

Ansel pointed his thumb at Velma. "Rachael Ray. Channel eleven."

"You watch cooking shows?" I spoke with my mouth full.

He set his fork down on the edge of his plate. "Now, sweetheart …"—he wagged a crooked finger at me—"I never said I watched it."

Velma waved her fork. "Ansel thinks she's cute."

The old man blew air through his teeth, dislodging a tiny speck of food, which landed on his bottom lip. He wiped it slowly with a plaid cloth napkin. "I said her chicken-fried steak is cute."

"I can't believe my dad watches Rachael Ray." JohnScott smiled at me, but his eyes sobered. "Dad's been taking some time off during the day."

"Aw … nothing to speak of." Ansel moved food around with his fork, like a child in trouble at the dinner table. He speared a fry. "It helps to rest for a spell after lunch. Kinda nice how it's been working out." His lips trembled in a smile. "I get to spend a little time with … Rachael."

If Velma had been standing in her kitchen—her usual post—she would have popped Ansel with a rolled-up dish towel. In lieu of her weapon of choice, she wadded her napkin and threw it across the table.

Ansel shook with silent laughter, and JohnScott leaned toward her. "Mom, you've got your work cut out for you."

"You'd think I still had one child left at home. His body's wearing out, but his mind is getting younger all the time."

JohnScott watched his dad for a moment and then rubbed a hand over his jaw. "Would you consider hiring a teenager to take over some of the work?"

Ansel's chin jutted to the side. "No, we're doing fine, JohnScott."

The fact that Ansel said *no* instead of *naw* and *JohnScott* instead of *Son* spoke loudly to me, and when I glanced at the coach, I could tell the verbiage didn't go unnoticed by him either. The muscles in my neck tensed. I had never heard the Picketts disagree on anything except sports.

Velma pushed her chair back and announced, "I brought Mississippi Mud."

"Wait a minute," I said. "Mexico. France. Now the Deep South?"

"It's just wrong." JohnScott shook his head sadly.

"We're international chefs," called Velma from the kitchen.

As the coach removed plates from the table, Ansel leaned toward me. "The owner of your place contacted me again."

"Oh?"

Ansel took a toothpick from a tiny glass in the middle of the table. "Said he might as well cover your rent from here on out. Place ain't worth much anyhow."

The muscles along my spine relaxed without warning, pushing air from my lungs. "For how long?" I whispered.

"Long as you're out there, sounds like."

My hands lay in my lap, and the baby rested firmly against my arms as though he were nestled in my embrace. "Does this man know me, Ansel?"

He picked his front teeth with the toothpick and then held it between his lips, moving it to the corner of his mouth, where it bounced as he talked. "He says he's good for the utility payments, too." He reached for his fork and cut into the gooey chocolate-and-marshmallow dessert as Velma and JohnScott slid into their chairs.

I blinked. "Why would he do that?"

"He's a good man," Velma said.

I rubbed my palm across my stomach.

"He says it's because he's a Christian." Ansel's fork clinked against his saucer as he set it down. "I take that to mean it's the right thing to do."

The baby shifted, and a foot or a fist moved from my right side to my left. I shouldn't have cared what the man's motives were. He had provided me with a home for my baby. I ran a hand across my little man and laughed out loud.

All three Picketts looked up from their dessert plates and smiled along with me.

CHAPTER TWENTY-SIX

Even though the Picketts' down-home goodness made me as comfortable as a feather bed, I couldn't relate to them. I felt insufficient, as though my arrogant roots had lifted me high above this sweet family, and I could only look down on them from my perch, not clearly seeing or hearing them. And definitely not feeling them.

As Ansel and Velma hobbled down the road toward their house, I opened the door of the Chevy, and it moaned softly. "Thanks for dinner, Coach."

JohnScott gazed after his parents with his brow wrinkled, but when I spoke, he spun around. "Where do you think you're going?"

"Home. I've got a paper to write."

"And leave me with all the dishes? You've got nerve."

"Oh …" My face warmed. "I could stay and help."

"If you insist." He pushed my car door shut and climbed the three steps to his porch, firm and sturdy like the steps at my house. "You wash," he said. "I'll dry and put away."

"What if I don't want to wash?"

"You don't know where to put away." He started the hot water running and then reached into the refrigerator, pulling out a bottle of Dawn dish detergent.

"You keep your soap in the refrigerator?"

"I hid it from Mom. Otherwise she would stay and do the dishes. The woman's a workaholic."

"You know what they say about that …"

"What?" He opened a drawer and took out a cup towel.

"It takes one to know one." He spun the towel, winding it into a weapon, but I shook my head. "Don't even think about it, JohnScott."

"Your water's about to run over."

"I'm not turning around until you uncoil that towel."

He looked down at the terry cloth strung tightly between his fists, then to the sink behind me. "It's going to make a mess on the floor."

"You can clean it up yourself. With that towel."

He relented, relaxing his shoulders. "I don't know what you're talking about. I would never attack a pregnant woman."

"So, you admit you'd attack me if I wasn't pregnant."

"Sure," he said without hesitation. "You're beginning to understand me."

Emptying ice from the glasses, I submerged them in bubbles, enjoying our light banter even though my pulse raced. I felt myself falling for him, like the crush I had on Leonardo DiCaprio in sixth grade. And like the actor, Coach Pickett lay out of reach. "I understand you a lot better than I did three weeks ago."

"Meaning?" He stood next to me, taking soapy glasses from my hands to rinse under the running water.

"You're worried about your parents."

His mood shifted. "Dad's getting old fast. Mom's a good bit younger, so she tends to him, but I don't know what she'll do when he needs more care."

"They seemed defensive when you mentioned it."

He laid the wet glasses on a wooden drain rack. "He doesn't want to give up any control before he has to."

"That's understandable. He can still do a lot on his own."

"How am I supposed to know what's too much?"

I rinsed a plate. "Maybe you're not."

"What do you mean?"

"Your dad can still decide for himself." I turned back to the sink to avoid the coach's penetrating gaze.

"You think I'm overreacting."

"No," I said quickly. "You're concerned about your dad, as you should be, but they don't need you to make decisions for them yet."

He leaned his hip against the counter. "How do you know these things?"

"I don't know." Looking into his eyes, I saw the compassion he held for his parents, and I wished I had a smidgen of it for my own. His eyebrows puckered, and he smiled, reminding me of the feel of his lips on mine.

He cleared his throat loudly, and the plates clattered as he slid them into the cabinet. "You're probably right."

The comfortable feeling I'd enjoyed all evening disintegrated as a brick wall fell between us. If we were going to maintain our friendship, we'd have to pick at that wall one brick at a time.

"Thanks for helping with the dishes." He folded the towel and hung it neatly on the handle of the oven.

I followed him out the front door, but once we were on the deck, he gestured to the rocking chairs. "Can we sit and talk a few minutes?"

I eased into the closest chair, getting a feel for its balance as I studied JohnScott and tried to get a feel for him, too. He sat down, leaned forward, and crossed his bare feet at the ankles.

He laughed lightly, then paused and picked at something on the arm of the chair. He laughed again and finally looked at me. "I'm really sorry about Saturday night."

I sighed. "You said that. Several times. It never should have happened."

He stared at me then, and his eyes filled with something deeper than sadness. The expression made me antsy, and I wished he would look away.

"I didn't mean I'm sorry I kissed you. I'm just sorry I did it at such a bad time, when you were upset." He leaned with his elbows on his knees, rubbing his hands together. He looked up at me hesitantly, then back down to his hands. "So you wish it hadn't happened."

I didn't know what to say. Since that night in the dark, I had thought of little except JohnScott Pickett—even to the point I hadn't dwelt on my breakup with Tyler—but I couldn't figure out what I thought about that kiss. If I told him I wished it hadn't happened, I would have been lying, but if I said I was glad he did it, I would have been just as untruthful. I shrugged. "I didn't say that. Exactly."

"Yeah, I don't know what to think about it either."

I inhaled a shallow breath, then released it slowly. "I thought you regretted it."

"No." He smiled, and the lines on the side of his face made me tingle. "Oh no." He leaned back in the rocker, relaxing into the wooden curves. "I only wish it weren't so complicated. Imagine it. *You* ..." His eyes pierced mine, conveying his understanding of the complexity of my situation, the baby, my parents, Tyler. "You with ... *me*." He shook his head, and in the droop of his eyes, I recognized the acknowledgment that both our lives would be dramatically affected if something happened between us. "You're not ready for a relationship with me or anyone else. And I'm not sure I should even ask that of you. Now or ever."

I rested my head against the back of the chair and closed my eyes for a few moments, agreeing with everything he said, yet feeling a flame of hope had been snuffed out. "It's over with Tyler." I don't know why I spoke those words right then, other than to reassure myself that JohnScott believed it. "I'm embarrassed I ever took him back."

He jerked his head and frowned at me. "Don't be embarrassed about that. You felt you needed to give it another go."

"But ... I think deep down inside, I knew he wouldn't change ... that he *couldn't* change." My chair gritted against the boards of the deck as I rocked, but I stilled my movements as my true motivations came into focus. "For some reason, I felt bound to him. I guess it's because of the baby."

JohnScott moved one of his shoulders in a circle, a nervous shrug. "It's not just that." His gaze dropped to his knees, and I thought he blushed. "You and Tyler have a physical bond now because of … well … you know. But it's a spiritual bond, too—which is even stronger—so it's only natural you would feel that way. And for him to feel that way about you." His voice tapered off.

As warmth washed over my face, I turned away from him and pretended to inspect the herd of cattle grazing on the other side of the barbed-wire fence. His statement broke open the protective shell of my emotions, leaving me vulnerable and exposing one of my greatest fears. "Will I always feel bound to him?"

He inhaled deeply and thoroughly, and when he exhaled, I sensed sadness for my past, regret for his own, and hope for both of us. He spoke softly. "When I was in college, there was this girl." His gaze slid away from me, to the safety of the herd. "I wasn't a Christian then, and I guess I didn't have any reason to wait. Of course I knew I should respect her—*and I did*—but we were both consenting, and we thought we were in love." His eyes grew distant. "I know I was."

A hundred questions leaped into my brain, but I held my breath, hurting for him, wanting to tell him we should talk about something else, yet yearning to hear whatever answers he had to offer me.

He stretched his legs in front of him, breaking the awkward spell that had been cast. "For years I imagined myself still in love with her, and maybe I was a little bit. But then Dodd started talking to me about Jesus. And forgiveness." He chuckled. "And we had a lot of late-night conversations about me and my sordid past."

I tsked. "Sordid?"

"Yep." He smiled, and his cheek wrinkles flashed briefly, but then he sobered. "Turns out those spiritual bonds are a lot harder to break than the emotional ones." His eyebrows lifted sadly. "And I don't know … Maybe they never completely go away. But that doesn't mean either of us are bound to our past mistakes." He shook his head. "God washes it away."

A lifetime of Sunday sermons echoed in my mind, and I heard our little congregation droning the hymn "God Shall Wipe Away All Tears," but my heart couldn't quite believe it. I shook my head. "I've been going to church all my life, sitting by my parents, reading the Scriptures, singing the songs, but only lately have I started to come close to God."

JohnScott tilted his head thoughtfully, and a corner of his mouth wrinkled in a hesitant smile. "Maybe we're both starting off brand new."

CHAPTER
TWENTY-SEVEN

Tyler gripped the binoculars resting in his lap as he eased his truck into the scenic overlook on a curve a mile from Fawn's shoddy house. The field glasses were powerful enough to see for miles, and Tyler needed to see far and clear because he had determined to set things straight with Fawn, get her to love him again. Even if it meant sitting on a cement picnic table day and night, he'd keep an eye on her.

He let the pickup door shut behind him with a soft click.

Tyler loved his truck—the one thing his father had given him before he died, and the only thing that didn't come with strings attached. Tyler leaned against the bumper and crossed his arms. The morning air chilled his skin, but the warmth of the engine penetrated the back side of his Levi's.

Fawn liked him in jeans. She said he filled them out like a man ought to. The girl had always been a pain in the neck, but she still had a way of getting him roused.

He peered across the ravine as a light popped on at Fawn's place. Right on time. Up before six. He'd gotten used to seeing that light every morning, and he'd enjoyed watching her, studying her, following her.

But she'd better not hook up with JohnScott Pickett again. Tyler had wanted to shake her by the shoulders when he saw her driving that man's truck. Her pale fingers wrapped around the steering wheel, and Tyler could only imagine her slender thighs pressed against the seat cushion. She would smell like *him*. Like cheap cologne and sweat. Like the coach.

Tyler shoved away from the truck and raised the binoculars. The house lay in darkness except for two windows, the kitchen and living room. He hated going in that junk of a house. The old place might topple at any minute, and it disgusted him—the lengths to which she would go to claim her independence. He didn't blame her for putting distance between herself and her parents, but turning her back on Tyler irked him something fierce.

He lowered the glasses to fiddle with the dials. Something was off, too blurry. When he brought them back to his eyes, he smiled. Fawn stood at the kitchen sink, the window positioned for a perfect view. She looked like she might be filling up a pitcher. Not surprising. Iced coffee, with all those fancy ingredients she added. He used to hate the way it made his truck smell. Girly and weak.

And Tyler wasn't weak. His father had seen to that. Work. Work. Work. "That's how a man makes something of himself, Son." The phrase had been drilled into Tyler's brain, always with the token sign of affection tacked on to the end.

But his father had gone and left him alone.

Tyler gripped the fiberglass, fouling the adjustments, but then he calmed and corrected the focus to bring Fawn back into view.

His dad's last will and testament left everything to Tyler. Sort of. The house, the property, the business, all the money would be his, but even in death, his dad was forcing Tyler to work for the inheritance when rightfully it belonged to him already. There was nobody else. His mother had long since abandoned him in death. No brothers or sisters, thank God. No grandparents.

But some things never changed.

Like the twenty-two rifle on Christmas morning his freshman year of high school. Dad told Tyler not to come home until he bagged a duck. Took two days.

Merry Christmas, Son.

Fawn waddled past the living-room window and out the front door, and Tyler's pulse quickened. *Lord, she's pretty.* A lot of good it did her, though. She looked like a fattened hog in that outfit. He examined her clothing and appreciated the quality of the binoculars. She wore denim shorts and a huge T-shirt, and Tyler questioned why she hadn't put on one of the maternity outfits he had bought her, if only to maintain a sliver of dignity. Instead, she looked as if she'd walked straight out of the Goodwill on the wrong end of Lubbock. She made him look bad.

He would have to talk to her about that.

She stomped across the weeds, and Tyler noticed the Gypsy Soule flip-flops she loved so much. He smiled. She hadn't lost all her style.

As she left the glow of the porch light, the binoculars proved useless in the blackness, but in a few minutes, when the sun came up, he would be able to see her again. Sitting on the hood of that old Chevrolet.

If it had been Tyler, he would have relaxed with a beer, but he knew Fawn turned her nose up to alcohol. Sure, she shared a few bottles with him over the years, but Tyler always knew she looked down her nose at him because of it. Rebellion drove her to drink, but piety prevented her from enjoying it.

He lowered the binoculars and crossed his arms as the sun peeked over the horizon. He scoffed. Fawn and his father would have made quite a pair, because both were driven to do the right thing—at least in appearance—and his father knew it. His blasted will stated Tyler could claim his inheritance once he married and secured an heir. Not only did his father expect him to work for the money, but he wanted him to take Fawn back. Even Tyler's lawyer deemed it unusually old-fashioned, but the overpaid legal beagle couldn't come up with a way around the addendum.

But no matter.

A muscle twitched across Tyler's jawbone. Fawn Blaylock with her curly hair and long legs and cynical smile occupied his thoughts twenty-four hours a day, seven days a week, and he wanted her worse than he ever wanted anything in his life. More than alcohol or money or sex. He wanted her to be his for life.

Because he loved her.

He cackled at his father's ignorance. Dear old Dad tried to force Tyler to take Fawn back, when actually, Tyler had planned to have her all along. His dad only added icing to the cake, causing Fawn to serve a dual purpose in his life.

Now his woman would not only feed his craving, but she and that baby in her gut would be his ticket to a life of ease.

CHAPTER
TWENTY-EIGHT

The earthy scent of the feed store, along with constant thumps and bangs of merchandise being loaded into farm trucks, distracted me from my work in the dusty office. I stared at the screen of the company laptop while I nibbled a granola bar and tried to keep my mind focused on invoices instead of JohnScott.

What a strange conversation we'd had. I left his double-wide not knowing where we stood, but not worrying about it either. In the end, I think we agreed we were mutually attracted to each other, but that neither of us needed a relationship. Especially me.

I suppose I felt relieved, in a way, to have broken things off with Tyler and temporarily put JohnScott out of my mind. I rested my forehead in my hands as a preterm contraction tightened across my midsection. Give me a break. JohnScott was *not* out of my mind.

Please God. Help me. Forgive me. I'm so sorry. I'll try harder.

A knock on the open door caused me to jerk my head up.

"Are you sick?" My father stood in the doorway, gazing at me with a blank expression, my mother a few feet behind him.

"No." I blinked away moisture in my eyes, surprised they would be at the feed store. Dad usually sent his foreman. "I'm fine."

"How's the child?" he asked.

I straightened a stack of papers on the desk. My father had never made reference to the baby, only my state of pregnancy, and his question put me on the defensive. "He's fine."

"Good." He stood with his hands on his hips, a cement wall for me to pound my fists against, but then his gaze dropped to the floor for a split second. "And how's the job?"

He wanted something, and I knew it had nothing to do with my health or my job. "I enjoy organizing."

His fingers toyed with the buttons of his polo shirt. "I ran into Tyler yesterday."

Well, that explained it. "You ran into him." A more accurate statement would have been that Tyler tattled on me—because I'd been misbehaving, driving the coach's truck, breaking up with Tyler.

"He stopped by the ranch," Mother mumbled, and when I looked at her closer, I noticed she'd been crying.

My father waved away her comment. "He's worried about you."

"I'm all right."

"Of course you're all right." His voice rose. "But you've been talking nonsense."

I stared at a printed advertisement of a rodeo cowboy tying up a calf. Caught halfway standing, the leathery man extended his arms as the calf struggled against tight ropes. I didn't answer.

"Look at me, Fawn."

I begrudgingly looked his way. Like I did in seventh grade when he lectured me about disrupting my Sunday school class with too much giggling.

"I understand if it takes you and Tyler a while to work out the kinks. He's had an enormous weight on his shoulders since his dad passed."

I gazed at his forehead. We had perfected this routine until neither of us had to stop and think how to push the other's buttons, but as always, he remained the domineering father and I his rebellious child.

He exhaled, and a string of words tumbled from his lips. "Your mother wants you at the house. Won't shut up about it being your home, and she's probably right for once. It's time you came back."

"Please come home," my mother whined.

I stood slowly, tired of being beneath my father and tired of him manipulating my mother. Years ago the two of them had urged me to date Tyler, and now they were urging me to get back with him. My father had kicked me out of his house, and now he had changed his mind. I may have been worthless in his eyes—and in my own—but I had to break free from his control.

"No, Dad."

He studied my crossed arms, my jutting chin, my defiant eye contact that he craved so much. Then his face darkened. "You can't keep living up on the Caprock. Especially after ..." He gestured toward my stomach.

"I can survive on what I make at the feed store."

He glanced at the sales floor before moving in front of my desk. "You're not being fair to Tyler. Come stay at the house until the two of you smooth things over. Your mother has your room made up and a few outfits picked out."

"No." My knees trembled, and I eased myself down to the chair. I wanted to stand firm, stare him down, tell him off, but I didn't have it in me. "I'm a better person on my own."

"Right now, you need guidance and support, and your mother and I can give it to you."

His words rubbed a blister on my heart. The two of them didn't know the first thing about support, and if he interpreted guidance as coming to my workplace for a father-daughter talk, he had a lot to learn. "No."

He stiffened. "Dusty barely pays you minimum wage. How will you manage?"

I ran my finger over a swirl in the wood of the desk. "The owner of my house is giving me a break on the rent." I didn't go into detail.

My mother gasped and clutched the doorframe, and my father clenched his fists so hard, his entire body shook. You would have thought I had told them I sold cocaine door to door for extra cash.

"What?" I lifted my hands, then let them fall to the desk. "Tell me what I've done this time."

My father's anger burned so violently, the whites of his eyes turned pink. "You shouldn't even be in that house." He slammed something down on my desk, then turned and pushed past my mother, who had the back of her hand pressed over her mouth as though she might be sick.

Funny. Their behavior didn't have the usual effect on me because I didn't understand what motivated it. I counted to ten, and Mother still hadn't moved a centimeter.

A flash of blue caught my eye near the laptop, and I reached down to pick up the object my father had thrown down. I fingered it, clinking it between my fingers.

My key chain with its blue-and-gold Tri Delta fob reminded me of my past interests, my past life, my past self. Attached to it were all my old keys, right where I had left them. House key. Barn key. Car key. I held my right-side-up life in the palm of my hand.

"Mom?"

A farmer on the sales floor peeked at us, and I felt exposed once again, for the entire town to see my failures and to judge whatever just happened with my parents.

"He'll calm down after a while." She stepped toward me, but she didn't sound overly confident in her assessment.

"What's wrong with him?"

"It's nothing. He's upset because I've been nagging him to help you."

"That's not what that was about. Why doesn't he want me to live in the house on the Cap?"

She tightened her lips, as though an honest explanation might escape her mouth if she didn't hold on tight. "I used to know the owner. But I don't anymore."

"You mean there's a different owner?"

She shook her head, and her dangle earrings jiggled against her neck. "It doesn't matter. It happened a long time ago."

I began to realize my mother's past might be even more scandalous than my own, and I pleaded with her. "Tell me what happened. Lynda Turner said you were treated for depression."

A long honk sounded from the parking lot, and Mother's body went rigid. But then her face took on a determination I didn't often see, and her shoulders relaxed. "It was before you were born." Her lips turned up in a smile, and she squeezed my hand. "I have to go now, but know that I love you."

"What did he do to you?" I whispered.

She shook her head. "He didn't do it, Fawn. I did it all by myself."

CHAPTER
TWENTY-NINE

"I'll go to church with you if you go to church with me."

JohnScott's challenge seemed innocent enough when we were talking on the phone, but as I left the adult Bible class at the Slaton church, I decided I should have viewed it as less of an invitation and more of a dare.

Even in Slaton, twenty-five miles from Trapp, the baptized believers had heard about the Cruz boy knocking Coach Pickett to the ground. The high school football teams in the two towns were hard-core rivals, but the Slaton congregation still claimed JohnScott as an adopted orphan all their own.

And they were none too sure what to think when I showed up Wednesday evening, sitting between him and Clyde, and looking up scriptures in my well-worn NIV. They politely introduced themselves, welcomed me to their fellowship, and made appropriate small talk. Then they buried their noses in their study guides and scratched their perplexed little heads.

"You should smile more," JohnScott said as we stood on the lawn after the service.

"She's been smiling," Clyde said. "Sort of."

"Those aren't real smiles." JohnScott clasped his hands in front of him and curled his lips tightly—absurdly—showing no teeth and no smile lines. "She's got her shield back up, Clyde. Safety first."

I couldn't help but laugh at the ridiculous expression on his face. "Oh, shut up, Coach."

"That's much better, thank you."

Clusters of people stood on and around the porch, laughing and talking, and the minister stepped toward us, greeting JohnScott and Clyde, then extending his hand to me. "It's good to have you with us tonight, Fawn."

"Thank you." My gaze darted to Clyde briefly. The two men looked to be about the same age, and I wondered if they had known each other before Clyde's prison stay.

"Your dad and I go way back," he said.

My dad?

"We used to attend lectures together years ago. I was sorry to hear he stepped down as elder over there in Trapp, but I understand he had personal issues to work through." He scratched the side of his neck and lowered his voice. "He's in my prayers, Fawn, and I trust he'll come back to the church when the time's right."

My insides twisted into a knot, and I felt my lips curving into a tight smile exactly like the one JohnScott had mimicked. "Thank you."

"And give Dodd Cunningham my best wishes when you see him next." He patted my arm and then called over his shoulder as he walked away, "He's an excellent preacher."

Three people turned to look our way before returning to their own conversations.

"Look at that, Clyde," JohnScott mumbled to his friend. "Poof. Her smile's gone again."

Clyde nodded. "It's that shield you were talking about."

My heel tapped silently against the grassy soil. "What do you expect me to say to that?"

"Aw, Fawn," Clyde said. "Buster didn't mean anything. That's just his way of saying he's real sorry for what happened last spring and all. I know for a fact he prays for your daddy all the time."

I studied the minister, now bending down to listen intently as a child spoke. He seemed kind enough. In fact, everyone at the church had been nice to me. Yet I still felt an unspoken condemnation, and my gut reaction blamed them for my own guilt.

I squeezed my eyes shut for a moment, and when I opened them, Clyde and JohnScott were both watching me and grinning. "You're right," I admitted. "It's a shield. I don't know why I do that."

"I do it too." Clyde chuckled. "Uh-oh. I'd better get out of here before JohnScott asks me to share my feelings." He lifted a hand in a parting gesture.

"Hey," called JohnScott. "You want to ride with me to Lubbock Saturday morning? I've got to get supplies to repair the crawl space out at Fawn's house."

"I wouldn't mind helping," Clyde said, "but I'm scheduled to work at the DQ."

We watched as Clyde loped to his car, leaving us alone.

Only a handful of churchgoers remained, and JohnScott and I wandered toward the parking lot. "I'm sorry if Buster upset you."

Buster's comments hadn't bothered me nearly as much as the whispers I imagined behind my back. *But maybe those weren't real.* I ran my teeth across my bottom lip. "I guess he just surprised me. Hardly anyone mentions my dad, especially at church."

"Must be awkward."

"Yep."

Smile lines spread across his cheeks, and I found myself wanting to trace them with my fingertip, but when we rounded the corner of the building, he stopped and his eyes widened. "You got your Mustang back."

"My parents brought it by the feed store."

He studied me, lifting his eyebrows as though he knew I had left something out.

"And they offered me money again." I sighed. "Dad even said I could move back home."

JohnScott didn't answer right away, so I opened the car door, wanting to escape the conversation without escaping him.

"Fawn, that's big."

My right foot lifted to the floorboard, but I remained standing. "I'm not moving in with them, and I shouldn't take his money."

He rolled his head back, staring at the sky, but then snapped his eyes back to me. "You've been praying?"

"Of course." I slid into the role of rebellious student.

"Well, what have you been praying for?"

Looking down at my Tri Delta key chain, I mumbled, "For a way to support my baby."

When he didn't reply, I raised my head.

His palms were lifted in the air, and he gave me a *you're-such-a-dufus* look. "You asked for it." He leaned against the hood of my car with such force, my foot slipped from the floorboard.

The whole ordeal made me want to move to Alaska. It made me weary. "He could be trying to bribe me."

JohnScott took a deep breath that calmed me as much as if I had taken one of my own. "Fawn, you prayed and God answered. Just because you take your parents' car, or their money, or eventually move back into their house—"

"I won't."

"Okay, probably not. But you can let them help you."

"I can't trust them."

"You don't have to. Just respect each other."

"Respect." My veins slowly filled with lead. "They don't respect me."

"But you can respect yourself."

I rested my elbows on the top of the door and covered my face with my hands, wishing I could cover my entire body. "But I feel so ashamed. So guilty."

"Fawn?" He waited until I met his gaze, then he held my eyes with his until the lead in my veins began to lighten. "You shouldn't feel guilty."

"Guilt is the emotion all my decisions are based on."

He stepped to the other side of the door, placing his hands around my elbows. "Guilt isn't an emotion, Fawn. It's a state of being, and you're not in it."

"I am." I shrugged. "I'm guilty of fornication, of dishonoring my parents, of selfishness."

"Last time I checked, you asked all concerned parties for forgiveness. Including God."

"Well, I sure don't feel forgiven."

"Just because you can't forgive yourself doesn't mean God hasn't forgiven you. He washed your sins away long ago."

I looked into his eyes, I felt his touch on my skin, I heard his words ... and I almost believed it could be true.

CHAPTER THIRTY

Saturday morning JohnScott sped toward Lubbock, intending to purchase supplies for Fawn's place, but all the while questioning if he had any right to court her. He glanced in his rearview mirror. Other than another pickup half a mile back, he had the road to himself.

He attached his cell phone to his car stereo and fumbled with it until Josh Turner's deep bass filtered through the speakers, and he wondered if Fawn liked country music. He had never asked her. Probably she liked pop, or rap, or something crazy like classical. He scratched his ear. Probably he couldn't stand whatever music she listened to.

He made a mental list of the supplies he would need to fashion a removable cover for the crawl space. Plywood, two-by-fours, nails, maybe some paint. But the whole house needed to be painted, and he hadn't signed on for that. So maybe no paint.

He frowned, wondering for the hundredth time if there might be more snakes. Clyde had told him the best way to rid a property of snakes was to eliminate the food source—in this case, mice— and he had done what he could. He'd also removed piles of debris that created nifty hiding spots, and he had cut back tall grass in the corners of the yard. A pile of rocks still remained out back, and of course, the woodpile. If a snake came within a twenty-mile radius, it would gravitate to that rotted wood.

He pulled into the Home Depot parking lot, grateful the store wasn't busy so early in the morning. He could fetch the supplies and get out to Fawn's house before the sun rose too high. He entered the store, thinking how she would have iced coffee waiting when he took a break. He'd rather have sweet tea, but he would never tell her that.

After loading lumber onto a flat cart, he pushed the cumbersome load toward the aisle where the nails were found. As he rounded the corner, he almost ran into another customer, and he swerved to avoid hitting him. "Sorry about that."

"Well, hey there, *Coach*."

JohnScott looked up, instantly on guard. "Tyler." He yanked the cart to the side of the aisle. "What brings you all the way to Lubbock on a Saturday morning?"

Tyler's gaze traveled slowly across the wood. "Looks like you got yourself some lumber."

"Sure enough." JohnScott ran his palm along the rough board. "Now all I need is nails. How 'bout you?" He opted to ask his original question once more before abandoning it.

"Picking up some gear for the ranch. Always needing something."

"I see." But JohnScott didn't see. If Tyler needed supplies for the ranch, he'd have a cart, or at least a basket, or an inventory list to place an order. "Same with our place. Always needing something."

Tyler's lips curled away from his teeth, and JohnScott wondered how he got them so unnaturally white. "Now, *Coach*, your family has what? A couple hundred acres? It's hardly the same." His grin lessened. "Is it?"

JohnScott began to comprehend Tyler's intent, but they weren't going to debate whose ranch was bigger. He might as well be back in second grade, arguing about Transformers or bicycles or lunch boxes. "No, our ranches are quite different." He gripped the handles of the cart, signaling his exit. "I'd better get going."

"I'll mosey along with you while you find your nails." Tyler walked next to his cart.

The kid wasn't drunk this time, but he was up to something.

Tyler motioned to the nail display. "You need a box? Or just a handful?" He reached into a drawer and withdrew two four-inches nails. "What kind of project are you working on?"

Apparently Tyler knew JohnScott had been working on Fawn's house, so he decided to get it out in the open. "Today I'm covering a crawl space on Fawn's rent house. She had a rattler under there a couple weeks back."

"She told me about that snake. Set her off pretty fierce."

The fact Tyler didn't mention the second snake proved Fawn hadn't talked to him. "Yep."

Tyler shoved the nails back in the drawer. "You seem awful bold, tending another man's woman. Asking her to church with you."

JohnScott tensed, surprised Tyler had already heard she went to church with him. It had only been three days. He decided to ignore the comment and focused on something else that bothered him. "She's not your woman."

"You've seen her lately. I think I've left my mark on her, or have you not noticed ..."—his boots gritted against the cement floor as he repositioned himself—"her body?"

Fire shot through JohnScott's rib cage, and he had the urge to hit Tyler. To pound his face over and over until that stupid grin fractured. Until his teeth were no longer unnaturally white, until his mouth stopped talking.

But more than anything, he wanted to get out from under Tyler's scrutiny, because JohnScott felt his face flush at the mention of Fawn's body. He was appalled not only by the degree to which he had noticed her but that Tyler had guessed it as well.

He lowered his head. "I'm just helping her get the place fit to live in."

"I can take care of her on my own, *Coach*. I don't mind if you repair the stinking crawl-space cover. It'll save me the trouble of hiring it out, but after that, stay away from her." He grinned like a demon. "She's my property."

For weeks JohnScott had been questioning his own intentions, his propriety, his Christianity, but Tyler had pushed him too far. "Actually, no."

"What?"

"You haven't been taking care of her. I have. But I'm not doing it because I want something from her. I'm doing it because it's the decent thing to do. So no, she's not your property. And I don't think she needs you at all."

Tyler clenched his fists and took a step toward him.

"Surely you're not going to fight me in the middle of the Home Depot." JohnScott laughed even though he wanted nothing more than to hit him. "Tyler, I've got no beef if Fawn wants to be with you. I'm not standing in her way, but if you need to fight someone, fight yourself. Fight *for* her. Show her you want to be what she needs."

Tyler smirked. "I thought you said she doesn't need me."

"She needs a lot, but it doesn't necessarily have to come from you."

"So you're saying you and your dinky job can provide for her as well as my family's millions."

JohnScott shook his head. "You don't get it. She doesn't need millions. She may think she does, but she doesn't. She needs a man."

The fury on Tyler's face didn't dampen JohnScott's determination. On the contrary, it convinced him he hadn't been wrong to discourage Fawn's relationship with the guy. And Tyler's threats didn't lessen JohnScott's growing feelings for her, as Tyler undoubtedly intended. Instead, the instinct to protect her clamped onto his heart like a vise, driving him to defend her with the intensity of an offensive lineman protecting the quarterback.

He pushed the cart toward the registers, half expecting Tyler to tackle him from behind, but when he got to the end of the aisle, he glanced over his shoulder, and Tyler had gone.

He took a deep breath, then paid for his items and pushed the cart out the door in time to see Tyler's truck speeding out of the parking lot.

JohnScott frowned. Tyler hadn't purchased anything. As far as JohnScott could tell, he hadn't even looked around. Tyler's truck stopped at a red light at the corner, and JohnScott remembered the vehicle behind him on the way to town. It could have been Tyler's— the color was right—but surely not. That didn't make sense.

He loaded the lumber in the truck and pushed the cart back into the store with a sinking feeling he had made things worse for Fawn. He supposed he would have to explain it to her, but that would be the easy part. Figuring out what to do with the protective instinct exploding in his brain? That would be something entirely different.

CHAPTER
THIRTY-ONE

"Figured you'd be out here, Fawn. Watching the sunrise."

JohnScott had come by my house first thing in the morning, and I could still hear the drawl of his voice. He measured the crawl space and asked if I'd like to ride into Lubbock with him, but I said no. I had too much homework.

But it wasn't true.

I wanted to spend time with him, ride with him in his old, beat-up pickup, and inhale his masculine, outdoorsy scent. I wanted to follow him through the store and trust his judgment on the purchases for my house. I wanted to touch him.

So obviously, I couldn't accept his invitation.

Examining myself in the bathroom mirror, I tugged on my hair, which had lost its highlights, then ran both hands across my abdomen. I slumped against the tile wall, cool in the warmth of the house, and wished I could turn off my thoughts. Thoughts of JohnScott Pickett.

Sliding to the floor, I rested my head on my knees, but only for a second. My body didn't have room to be folded in such a way, and the baby kicked, prompting me to lower my legs and sit cross-legged.

Rowdy, watching me from the doorway, whined softly.

"I know, buddy. I'm on the bathroom floor again."

Dropping my hands to my sides, my fingers touched a clear plastic ring I'd pulled from a can of shaving cream earlier in the week, and I glanced at the trash can, out of reach. Tyler would hate that my house wasn't neat and tidy. I set the ring on the edge of the bathtub and wondered how JohnScott felt about messes. And babies. And me.

I shook my head. Sometimes I imagined long and hard what it would be like if I hadn't gotten pregnant, but I never went so far as to wish it were so. Until now.

When I heard his truck in the yard and the squeak and thud of its door, I hauled myself up from the floor. "Your old owner is back from the store, Rowdy." It took me a while to find my favorite flip-flops, but I finally located them in the closet. Pregnancy must have affected my memory, because I didn't even remember putting them away. I habitually left them against the wall by the bedroom door. Pausing, I gazed around the room, wondering what else I had forgotten.

The dog and I walked out the back door and around to the side of the house, where JohnScott had two sawhorses set up near the crawl space.

"Good game last night? I'm sorry I missed it."

"Stomped 'em. And we had a pretty good show of support for an out-of-town game."

"Did you try the new play?"

"Worked like a charm." He powered on the saw, and it rang through the morning breeze.

When he shut it off, the air snapped with silence. "Thanks again for everything you've done out here."

"I've enjoyed helping." A smiled played at his lips, and he picked up his metal tape measure, checking his work against figures scribbled on a notepad he pulled from his back pocket. "I ran into Tyler at Home Depot."

"That's strange."

"A little too strange, if you ask me."

"What do you mean?"

"I'm probably being paranoid, but I can't figure the kid in Lubbock on a Saturday morning."

"Did you talk to him?"

"Sure did."

"And?" Sometimes getting JohnScott to talk was like coaxing honey from an onion.

"He didn't seem to like the idea of me working out here."

"Too bad." I sipped my drink, crunching a piece of ice.

"So you really broke it off with him?" JohnScott had his back to me, so I couldn't see his expression.

The wind blew my hair out of my face, and I closed my eyes, wishing I had never known Tyler and imagining the air cleansing my conscience of familial expectations, religious propriety, class distinctions.

"I know my parents want me with him, and the church, maybe even God. But I'm done." I opened my eyes and found him watching me, and when he went back to work, peace settled over me like sunshine, instilling me with a sudden jolt of confidence. "I want someone else."

He was halfway straightened, as though he had frozen while in the process of standing up. He held a pencil in his hand, and his eyes focused on my left shoulder as if he couldn't bring himself to make eye contact, as though my words might be a spell in jeopardy of being broken.

I said nothing else, just looked at him, waiting. If I knew the coach at all, he would ponder my words for a few seconds.

He shook his head briskly, either in acknowledgment of my statement or to clear his thoughts. His attention fell rigidly on his project as he fitted the door to the opening, screwing in the hinges, fashioning a brace to keep it tight against the wall of the house. He didn't say anything, but two more times he shook his head.

When he began packing his gear, my confidence dissolved into a puddle. On trembling legs, I slipped through the back door to lean against the refrigerator until I stopped shaking.

I fixed two iced coffees, then watched from the front window as he made trips to his truck. This morning he would finish the work on my house, so we wouldn't necessarily be seeing each other often. If I avoided him in town, things might not be awkward between us.

My gaze drifted past his truck, and far in the distance, Flat Top Mountain rose boldly above the plains, reminding me of a time my father and his ranch hands had ridden horses to its base. He let me tag along, and since he didn't often do things just for fun, the venture stuck out in my mind. I loved this country. Sweeping views and rocky terrain gave it a wild, sometimes dangerous feel, and my life seemed intertwined with its fierceness.

The back door opened and closed, and I watched mutely as JohnScott's gaze bounced around the kitchen before he located me in the living room. He blinked slowly as though steeling himself for an undesirable task.

"Listen, JohnScott." I picked up his coffee. "Don't worry about what I said."

I held the glass toward him, an icy peace offering, but he didn't take it. Didn't look at it. Maybe he didn't even see it.

"Fawn?" His voice caught. "You know that day at the holding tank?"

My heart collapsed.

I could imagine his next words, but I had to answer him anyway, follow this conversation to the end, take my medicine. "Yes."

"I've been thinking about that day. Because that's sort of when this started."

I nodded but said nothing as I set his glass on the coffee table and cradled my own between my palms.

"I know we've already hashed through it, but something's been gnawing at me." His voice drawled more than usual. "I was dishonest. I didn't tell you what I really thought that day."

My hand settled on the back of the recliner, steadying me, grounding me, keeping me from running out the door.

He laughed in a nervous way, as though he didn't want to talk to me either. "I said we were simply caught unaware, and there was nothing wrong in either of our reactions. But, Fawn?" His voice dropped to a whisper. "I lied. I noticed you that day. Even before you bumped into me."

I turned my face away.

"Every time I came over here to work, I noticed you. Every time you brought me an iced coffee. Every time you tied my gloves around your wrists with ponytail holders."

What?

"And I know what you're thinking, because I've heard you say it enough times." He shook his head. "I didn't notice you because you did anything inappropriate. *You didn't.* I noticed you because you're kind and you want to be a good mother. You're helpful and giving." His eyes closed briefly. "Do you remember what you and Ruthie were talking about right before you bumped into me?"

All I could remember from that entire day was the expression on JohnScott's face when I came out of the water, and the expression on his face moments later, when he wouldn't look me in the eye.

"No." My mouth formed the word, but no sound came out. I cleared my throat. "I don't remember what we were talking about."

"You had gone to see your obstetrician. And you were saying the baby had an irregular heartbeat." He rubbed a palm across his face. "And, Fawn, right then, I was so scared for you." He clenched his jaw. "And so darn jealous of Tyler Cruz. I wanted to be the one at the doctor, helping you. You probably didn't even think about it at the time, but I turned around and stared at the cattle like an idiot ..." He shook his head. "I couldn't even look at you."

A tear threatened to slip down my cheek. "And then Grady pulled you in the water."

His eyes held mine. "That day in the holding tank, your physical beauty caught me by surprise. I had forgotten how attractive you are on the outside because I had become so taken with the real you."

His eyebrows sloped down toward his cheekbones, and I wanted to run my hands across his forehead to ease his tension, but I didn't. I wouldn't.

"So when we had that long discussion on my porch about how I slipped and kissed you accidentally? I lied a big fat send-me-straight-to-hell lie, because I had been wanting to kiss you all along." His gaze darted from one of my eyes to the other, and his tone changed, becoming desperate. "Say something."

I flinched.

My life bore scars from vanity and selfishness, scars that might never heal. Yet one by one, tears trickled down my cheeks, and my scarred heart dared to believe him. "I don't deserve those words, JohnScott." His name stuck in my throat with a small sob.

He took two hurried steps toward me, leaned over, and kissed my cheek. The softest, lightest kiss. And when he pulled away, a question lay in his eyes.

His face hovered inches from mine, imploring me to respond. The sincerity in his eyes, the wrinkles on his forehead, the droop of his cheeks all asked the same question, but my insecurity paralyzed me, and when I didn't move, he took a hesitant step away.

Then the inches between us became a chasm as wide as the Caprock itself, and panic snapped my nerve endings like a leather horsewhip. I stepped toward him quickly, wanting to convey the feelings bursting in my heart. Feelings I couldn't voice.

His stiffness melted, and he slowly, gently, cautiously slid one arm around my shoulders and the other around my waist. He bent down, burying his face in my neck, and relief swept over me like a warm summer breeze. The tension in the room, in the town, in the whole world blew away in an insignificant puff of smoke.

I nestled my head against his shoulder and let him hold me—a cold glass of coffee and a big, round baby between us.

CHAPTER
THIRTY-TWO

"Let's get Oreos," Ruthie said.

"Only if JohnScott has milk at his house." I was strolling through the United grocery store with Ruthie later that day, snatching items for a cookout at JohnScott's double-wide, while the coach and the preacher got soft drinks from the next aisle over. Ansel had offered the four of us free steaks if we would drive the four-wheelers to his back pasture to check the pump on the stock tank. But JohnScott could get steaks anytime he wanted, so Ansel didn't fool me with his thinly disguised ploy.

Besides, it didn't take four people to check a water pump.

But we'd had a great time riding around the pasture all afternoon, and I didn't mind sharing an ATV with my arms wrapped around JohnScott's waist. He didn't seem to mind either.

"We could get ice cream, too," Ruthie said. "And crumble Oreos on top. Or make sundaes."

"Velma probably has an ice-cream maker. How about homemade cookies and cream?"

"Do you have a recipe?"

"No, but I can look it up on my phone."

"Not in here, you can't," Ruthie said. "The Wi-Fi in the United is terrible. I think it's the metal roof or something."

The store intercom squeaked, and the manager's voice came through loud and clear. "Ruthie Turner … I hear you."

She tilted her head back and called over the shelf, "You sound like God when you do that, Gene."

Dodd came around the corner carrying a couple of two-liter drinks, which he placed in our shopping cart. "JohnScott went after potatoes." He swept his hand down Ruthie's spine. "Giving your manager a hard time again?"

"He deserves it."

"I'm craving homemade ice cream." I pushed the cart toward the front of the store but jerked to a stop when I almost ran into Sophie Snodgrass.

"Fawn, look at you." She chewed her gum noisily. "Haven't you had that baby yet?"

I slipped my bottom lip between my teeth before answering. "Not for a while now."

"Well, darlin', you still look good. I bet you haven't gained fifteen pounds." She parked her cart and leaned her elbows on the handles as though settling down for an extended conversation. "Land sakes, with my first baby, I gained over sixty." She giggled. "Not sure I ever lost all that fluff, but you sure don't have that problem. If anything, you're underweight." She lifted her chin to Dodd and Ruthie. "Wedding plans coming along all right?"

"Everything's falling into place." Ruthie pulled Dodd down the aisle. "We'll go find the ice-cream ingredients, Fawn. Meet you at the register in a few."

I could have kicked her for leaving me, but just then, JohnScott rounded the corner behind the hairdresser. His steps faltered, but just as she turned, he strode toward me and put a bag of potatoes in the cart.

"Why … *Coach Pickett.*" Her jaw fell open comically, and she looked back and forth between us as though she were seeing an apparition. "You've … got yourself some potatoes, there, don't ya?"

"Yep. Cooking steaks on the grill, so I've got to have baked potatoes."

"Sure enough, you do." Sophie grinned, nodded, then spun her cart around. "Good game last night, Coach. See you later, Fawn."

I wondered if she paid for her groceries or merely abandoned her cart so she could get to her Suburban and start calling her friends.

"I think we just went public," JohnScott said. "In a pretty big way."

Doubt immediately rankled my confidence, but when smile lines spread across JohnScott's cheeks, I couldn't help but smile back. Going public would undoubtedly have negative effects on both our lives. But for the moment, it felt really good.

An hour later, I sat with Ruthie at an umbrella-covered table on the back deck of the double-wide while JohnScott sizzled steaks over charcoal and Dodd tended a screeching ice-cream freezer.

"So, I guess this is a double date?" Ruthie looked at me over the rim of her glass as she sipped her Dr Pepper.

I glanced at JohnScott and shrugged.

Ruthie squinted at him and yelled over the din of the motor. "Is this a double date or what?"

He walked closer to us. "Well, little cousin, I wasn't sure until I saw Sophie, but now I've decided it might as well be."

"True." Ruthie sipped her drink again. "A double date ... Fawn, this is sort of creepy, but Momma once told me she and your mother double-dated back in high school. I don't know who the two guys were, though."

"I can't picture Susan and Aunt Lynda doing anything together," JohnScott said.

"One of the guys was probably my dad, but—" I swallowed my words.

JohnScott whistled, then slowly backed away from us. "I think I'll go back over there where I can't hear you."

Just then, the ice-cream freezer stopped.

"You're stuck now," Ruthie deadpanned.

"Am I missing a juicy conversation?" Dodd stepped across the deck.

"The girls are discussing how Fawn's dad dated both their mothers in high school."

He frowned. "Man, I've heard that one. Anything new?"

"No, but there will be by Monday morning," JohnScott said.

"Sophie?"

"Not to mention Luis Vega bagged our groceries." JohnScott's cell phone chirped in the pocket of his cargo shorts, and he answered it as he forked the steaks onto a platter.

A few minutes later, he pocketed his phone and set the steaks in the middle of the table. "That was Dad. My quarterback's grandfather gave him a call a little while ago."

I frowned. "He called your dad with football business?"

"Uh-oh …" Ruthie crooned the word like a door chime.

"He's worried I'm distracted and won't be able to focus on the remaining games of the season."

"You only went public an hour ago." Ruthie leaned her head back. "The fun begins."

CHAPTER
THIRTY-THREE

Even as thoughts of JohnScott filled me with nervous energy, apprehension about his quarterback's grandfather zapped my strength, leaving me exhausted. Late Monday afternoon, I dropped by the United for groceries and ended up talking to Ruthie for way too long. When I finally trudged home, Rowdy was waiting for me on the front porch.

I scratched behind his ears, leaving comb marks in the black-and-gray fur, and then I lowered myself carefully to sit next to him on the steps. "How did you get out here, old man? You're supposed to be in the house where it's cool."

He rolled to his side.

"I feel the same way." Leaning an elbow on the porch, I arched my back slightly, attempting to ease the achiness. "Another week or so, Rowdy. Then my back won't hurt anymore."

The dog whined softly as though speculating which of us was more pathetic.

Five more minutes. Then I'd lumber into the house, trade my jeans and T-shirt for soft pajamas, and point all the vents of the air conditioner straight at the recliner. Even though temperatures had started falling at night, the afternoons and evenings were still warm as blazes.

Rowdy rested his head on my arm, silently begging to be scratched again.

"You know what?" I put my face close to his and whispered, "I like JohnScott."

The tufts of hair above the dog's eyes lifted, and his silver eyes seemed concerned.

"I know it's not ideal, but it could work."

He whimpered, echoing a doubt in my heart, but I rubbed his neck absentmindedly while I prayed. *God, JohnScott's a good man, and I think I could be happy with him. Just please let him be what the baby and I need.*

The dog's ears twitched, and then he lifted his head and woofed softly.

Three seconds later, the sound of an approaching vehicle invigorated my tired muscles. Hoping JohnScott was dropping by after practice, I pulled myself up and leaned against the porch rail, but when a black F-150 sped around the curve, I sighed. Behind me, it sounded like Rowdy did the same.

Tyler pulled to a stop and climbed out of the truck with his hair falling rakishly over his eyes. That look once would have sent shivers down my spine, but my attraction for him had withered away like a buttercup at the end of the season.

"I thought you'd never get home, babe. Where have you been?" He reached into the bed of the truck and retrieved a large box.

His words jumbled in my head, but the comfort of the recliner still called to me, and I hoped he would leave soon. I motioned to the box he carried. "What's this?"

He spun the box around with a flourish, holding it up for my inspection. "Figured you'd need one."

"An infant car seat." My spirits fell. "Thank you, Tyler."

His eyes flashed for an instant, but then he lowered his chin like a kindergarten teacher softening his discipline. "You sound funny, but that's all right. You're welcome."

Rowdy padded around him, sniffed his leather sandals, then perched on the step between us.

"If I sound funny, it's because I'm wondering if there are strings attached."

Tyler's jaw moved a fraction to the side before he grinned broadly. "No, Fawn. No strings attached. I just wanted to do something for my son, if that's all right with you."

I rubbed a hand across my forehead. "Of course it's all right. I'm just tired and stressed."

He held the box toward me. "I got the most expensive one."

I knew he didn't mean to brag—he always bought the most expensive things—so I softened my tone. "It's the one I wanted. It has a base."

"A base?"

"It stays in the car, but you can also use a seat belt. Like that." I pointed to the picture.

"Seems like an awful lot of trouble."

I sighed. "I've been reading. You can't imagine what it takes to be a good parent."

He rested the box on his hip, and I wondered if he was listening.

"Marry me, Fawn." His body language still said alpha male, but his voice held a desperate quality that seemed out of character.

I pulled the car seat roughly from under his arm. "No strings, remember?"

"Right. No strings."

"I do appreciate the car seat, though."

He laughed, but not his usual chuckle of controlled masculinity. Instead, a high-pitched giggle slipped between his teeth, sending a shiver across my shoulder blades. "You should take a look in your house, babe."

"What do you mean?"

"Come and see. You're going to love it." He leaped up the porch, opened the door, and stood to the side.

Rowdy pushed against my legs, seeming to herd me away from Tyler, but I snapped my fingers to get him to cooperate. Just inside the door, I froze.

Boxes covered the loveseat and stood piled in the corner, their labels revealing a bassinet, a swing, a walker. Shopping bags lay on every horizontal surface, including the floor, and a large see-through bag near the kitchen doorway held a coordinating crib set.

I was speechless.

Tyler nudged me farther into the room, then shut the door. "I probably went a little overboard, but the salesgirl said this stuff will come in handy."

My breathing became shallow. "How did you—"

"I unloaded it all before you got home. You know, you really should get your locks fixed."

"Tyler ..."

"I never knew a kid needed so much junk." He took the car seat from me and set it on the floor near a stroller box. Then he lifted a smaller one. "Look at this thing. He sits in it and plays with all these little toys."

I shook my head. "This is too much. A car seat is one thing."

"Ty needs it."

"Ty?" My feet stumbled toward a huge box leaning against the window. A full-size crib that could convert to a toddler bed, dark-stained wood, beautiful. I'd seen it in a magazine at the United. "I can't accept all this."

He reached for a box, not acknowledging I had spoken. "I know you'll like this white bassinet thing. I can set it up for you real quick."

"No, don't open it."

His actions and speech increased in speed. "You're going to need it as soon as Ty is born. That and the car seat." He quickly slit the tape with what I thought was a pocketknife, but as he shoved it back in his pocket, I recognized it as a loose razor blade.

"Why are you calling him Ty?"

"If the kid's not going to have my last name, he might as well have my first. Check out those bags of tiny, little clothes. And shoes. I've never seen shoes so small."

I stepped back. Tyler's uncontrolled zeal took up too much space in the room, and I felt out of control and sick to my stomach. He pulled parts from the box, still talking, talking, talking, and dread pressed against me with the inescapable force of gravity.

"Tyler, stop." I inhaled to slow the energy in the room. "I can't, *cannot*, take this."

His smile vanished, his chatter stilled, and he cocked his head at what seemed an unnatural angle. "Can't or won't?" He spoke softly, but his words were laced with a threat.

Rowdy barked once and pressed against my legs, and I considered following the dog's advice and running away. But that was absurd. "You said there wouldn't be any strings, but this must have cost you hundreds of dollars. I would feel I owed you."

"More like thousands." He sorted through hardware, comparing bolts and brackets to a diagram on the instruction sheet. "I'm determined to get this thing set up before I leave."

The possibility of him staying long enough to assemble the bassinet made me want to cry. "Don't worry about putting that together. JohnScott can—"

"You shouldn't keep bothering the coach." His words were clipped. "That man's only doing his Christian duty, caring for the widows and orphans—not that you exactly fall into either category—but he's bound to get tired of coming all the way up here every day."

"He doesn't come every day."

"Well, he practically does." He let the hardware fall to the floor, and then he shoved the box with his foot.

Tears seeped to the corners of my eyes but remained safely hidden. "You obviously don't have a very high opinion of JohnScott."

"I'm sure *Coach Pickett* means well, but give me a break. He's out of his league where you're concerned. Look around you." He pointed a stiff finger at a stack of boxes. "This is what Ty needs from you." His eyes held mine for three long seconds, and then he snickered. "Has JohnScott Pickett brought you anything for our son?"

My gaze fell to Rowdy. JohnScott had brought me the dog, but he had brought me so much more than that.

"I didn't think so." Tyler lifted his chin and sauntered to the door. "It's only a matter of time."

"Until what?"

"Until the coach pitches you on your butt." His gaze dropped to my stomach before he crooned, "He's not the type to settle for damaged goods."

CHAPTER THIRTY-FOUR

As Tyler pulled away from the house, I stared at the boxes scattered over my living room. Most expectant mothers would have been anxious to open them, to set up the gear, to play house, but I couldn't bear to look at them. Every box represented Tyler's attempt at control, and I considered piling them on the front porch. Or maybe throwing them over the cliff. But things wouldn't seem so dire once I got some rest.

Drifting into the darkened kitchen, I flipped on the light with trembling fingers and reached for the instant-coffee mix. One more glass of iced decaf might send me to the restroom in the middle of the night, but I didn't care. I turned on the faucet and trudged to the bedroom while I waited for the water to heat.

Tyler's accusations about JohnScott knifed through my heart, but in spite of the hatefulness, his behavior confused me. He had acted strange—manic—with all his spending and excessive energy. He once mentioned he took medication, but I always assumed it was for attention deficit or something like that. Now I wondered.

I slipped off my sandals and tugged my shirt over my head. Probably he was just stressed because of his dad's death, but his prediction about JohnScott sounded all too rational. I braided my hair down one side, then leaned through the doorway to peer toward the kitchen. Steam rose from the sink, so I reached for a cotton nightshirt and hurried into the kitchen in my bra and athletic shorts.

Filling a glass halfway with hot water, I added a spoonful of instant coffee and a spoonful of hot cocoa mix. Probably I was addicted to the stuff, but there were worse things. Plenty of things. When the powders dissolved, I added water and ice, then leaned against the counter and swallowed the pungency sip by sip.

No comfort food could erase the gnawing truth that JohnScott could have his choice of women in Trapp. Even in Garza County. Probably the surrounding counties.

I set my glass on the counter, unhooked my bra, and let it fall to the floor. As I slumped into the living room, I slipped my nightshirt over my head, wondering why I ever thought I could have JohnScott Pickett for myself. I fell into the recliner and pulled at the handle until the footrest lifted beneath my feet, then I turned on my side and buried my nose in the headrest. Even surrounded by boxes, that chair was safe. It smelled of Ansel and Velma's house, but the comfort melted as a memory niggled my brain. Something Tyler had said but I couldn't quite remember.

The wind rattled the beams in the attic, and something shifted on the porch. I ignored it and reached for a textbook, but Rowdy perked his ears.

"It's all right, boy. It's the wind." When I dropped my hand over the armrest and snapped, he obediently came to me. "You'll probably leave me too." I scratched behind his ears, and he laid his head on the armrest. Mentally I shunned the possibility of life without JohnScott, but the thought of losing Rowdy brought tears to my eyes. "You're a good friend, Rowdy."

The dog growled low in his throat.

"What was that for?"

He snorted an apology and nuzzled my hand.

"Don't you get weird too." I took his face between my hands and cuddled him.

He barked then, backing away from me and growling.

I stared at him in surprise. "Rowdy, stop it. Come here."

His jowls were low to the floor, and he continued to growl, edging toward the front door. He sniffed once and then barked.

When I flipped on the porch light, a hollow buzz sounded from the gap beneath the door and echoed off the walls and ceiling as though it came from every corner of the room.

Rowdy inched backward with each deep-throated bark as though the effort released a strong wind that could annihilate the danger. Then he ran forward, growled, and pushed against my legs, trying to herd me deeper into the room.

Chills spiraled down my legs as I peeked out the window, but I couldn't see the snake. I pulled Rowdy by the collar, rubbing his neck. "It's all right, boy. We're safe in here." My words didn't console me, and I searched beneath every piece of furniture and around every box. I considered going out the back door and around the house to my car, but darkness kept me rooted inside.

Fumbling for my cell phone, I dialed JohnScott's number.

"Sorry I haven't called. Practice ran late tonight, and I'm bushed." He sounded as though he was lying in his own recliner, probably watching old football tapes, half asleep.

When I heard his voice, the emotions I had suppressed since Tyler pulled into my yard came seeping over the edge of my heart, and I sobbed once, then stifled the rest of it.

Rowdy barked again, growling at the door, and I pulled him back toward me like a barrier.

"What's wrong?" JohnScott sounded wide awake now, and I imagined him standing up, reaching for his boots, checking his watch. "Are you all right? Is it the baby?" I heard a thump over the phone and wondered if he had knocked something over.

I laughed and cried at the same time. "It's not the baby. It's a snake." My last sentence came out in a desperate whine. "I'm sorry to bother you."

"You're not bothering me." A door slammed, and he panted slightly. "Where is it? By the woodpile again?" A car door slammed, and his truck started.

"It's on the front porch. Rowdy heard it or smelled it or something. I had just thought about going out …" My voice trailed as I considered what might have happened if I had put the boxes on the porch. "He's going nuts."

As if he understood my words, Rowdy set off into a new round of barking, and I could barely hear JohnScott.

"Keep him between you and the snake."

"Believe me, I will." I pulled my feet up and held the dog's collar. "Don't drive too fast."

"Are you all right if I let you go? I'll be safer with two hands."

"Sure, I need to go to the bathroom anyway."

He sighed heavily. "Take the dog with you."

I had to drag Rowdy to the bathroom, because his instincts told him not to turn his back on danger, and when I finally got him in the bathroom, I shut the door—a habit I had gotten out of—in order to keep him with me. He waited, conveying his impatience by whining periodically and giving me the proverbial puppy-dog eyes. I washed my hands and opened the door quickly, releasing him with a frenzy of claws against tile. As he leaped toward the living room, I heard a noise behind me.

A hollow scratching. Only for a brief second, and then it stopped. My heart raced, but I froze like Clyde had told me to do. Through the hallway, I could see Rowdy crouched on his haunches by the door. I snapped my fingers softly, trying to get his attention, trying to get him to come back, but he wouldn't budge.

Slowly I turned, expecting to see a snake in the corner of the room or in the bathtub. Nothing. I heard JohnScott's truck approach with its blessed squeaking, and nothing had ever sounded so good. Rowdy ran into the bathroom, turned around, and barked at me once, wagging his tail. When he rushed in, the piece of plastic I'd pulled off the shaving cream tumbled across the floor, and the hollow sound repeated. I rolled my eyes and let out a deep breath.

Returning to the living room, Rowdy and I looked out the front window as JohnScott lifted a J-hook out of the back of his truck. He raised his hand toward me, then scanned the ground. The porch light didn't reach all the way out there, so he fumbled in his truck for a flashlight, which he swept back and forth as he approached the house. Soon he stood on the steps, studying the boards in front of the door. I couldn't see the snake from the window, but JohnScott held up one finger.

I supposed I should have been glad there was only one, but I worried there were more. And for the first time since I called him, I worried about JohnScott. I didn't even know what would happen if a person got struck by a rattler.

By the time I decided JohnScott could handle things, he had handled them. The diamondback was safely stuffed in a burlap bag, which JohnScott tied and placed in a box in the back of the truck.

When JohnScott opened the front door, I wanted to rush into his arms, but I didn't. "You're all right."

"Me?" He removed his cap and scratched his head. "I was worried about you."

"I had just been thinking about going outside. I would've gotten bit."

"Naw, Rowdy would have." The coach crouched in front of the dog, rubbing his neck and shoulders. "Good boy. You did good."

The possibility of Rowdy getting struck made me shudder. "What would have happened to him?"

JohnScott tilted his head as he rubbed the dog's ears. "Aw, Fawn." He shrugged. "Clyde says the bites cause swelling."

"What else?"

"Well ... a couple of things."

"Like ..."

"Okay." He stood. "The venom circulates through the body and prevents blood from clotting. So any bleeding can't be stopped. Then the venom sort of … digests the body from the inside out." He looked past me to the boxes, and his eyebrows lifted. "What's all this?"

His description of venom poisoning turned my stomach, but his casual question spurred another rush of the same panic I'd felt moments before. What would JohnScott think about Tyler coming by? If I backed away slowly, maybe fate wouldn't strike. Maybe the coach wouldn't get the wrong impression. Maybe he wouldn't scurry away from me.

"Fawn?"

I returned to my perch on the edge of the recliner. "Tyler brought it."

"Oh." He scanned each box. "Looks like you've got everything an eight-pound human could possibly need." He rubbed his chin and frowned.

"I don't know what to think," I said cautiously. "Tyler seemed strange tonight, agitated, and when I mentioned you, he got upset."

"I bet." He bent slightly as though he were going to ask me a question, but instead he turned away again, his head swiveling from one side of the room to the other.

I dropped my head into my hands with my elbows on my knees, and the baby protested at the tight squeeze by kicking against my ribs. I ignored it. I watched JohnScott's boots, the only part of him visible without lifting my head. His feet were planted shoulder width apart, facing toward me, and I imagined his face contorted in disgust. Or anger. When he still didn't move after a few moments, I lifted my gaze.

He looked at least ten years older. His eyes drooped at the edges, weary and overwhelmed. "Do you want to be with him?"

"No, JohnScott, that's not what I want."

"Then tell me."

A tear ran down my cheek. "No good Christian man should want me. Tyler says so. My dad says so. You shouldn't even be here." I sobbed once, feeling small.

Small and insignificant.

But JohnScott knelt in front of me, and one callused hand pushed my hair away from my face. "No, no, no." His soft touch diminished my doubts and kindled my hope, but still I shook my head in protest.

Exhaustion—both physical and mental—drained me of energy, and I wanted to curl up in Ansel's chair until all my problems evaporated.

His fingertips nestled behind my neck, and he wiped my tears with his thumbs. "I want you to be happy, and I'm going to help you get there."

I sniffled. "You ... what?"

"Happy." He pulled a cloth handkerchief out of his jeans pocket and wiped my eyes.

"Tyler said you'll get tired of me."

"When did we start listening to Tyler?"

"He and I are just alike."

"You have a lot in common, I'll give you that much. But you have more things that aren't."

"Like what?"

He pulled me to my feet, wrapped an arm around my shoulders, and led me into the kitchen. "Well, you were both raised by parents who were somewhat controlling, but you're trying to break into independence." He found my half-empty glass of coffee, handed it to me, and watched while I sipped it. "And you're both hung up on material possessions, but you're breaking free from that, too. And you both grew up with strict religion, but you're starting to believe God likes you."

I took a deep breath and set my glass on the counter. "You must think I'm an emotional wreck."

"No, I think you're a hormonal wreck." When I looked at him in surprise, he continued. "I've got older sisters. I've seen the havoc pregnancy can wreak on a woman's mental balance, and it ain't purty."

I popped him on the shoulder and tried to smile.

He took my hand in his then, holding it against his lips for a few seconds. "I'm not going anywhere, Fawn." Leaning his hip against the counter next to mine, he looked down at me. "I'm right where I want to be …" He let his left hand rest lightly on the baby. "And I'm staying."

My heart did a somersault.

He leaned closer, his face inches from mine, then slid his other arm around my shoulders. "I want to kiss you again. Badly. But if you don't want me to, say so."

In response, I reached my hand to his cheek, rubbing the backs of my fingers across the rough stubble on his jawline. I slid his cap off his head, letting it fall to the floor behind his back. "I'm not going to say so."

His eyes shifted, and I recognized determination and confidence before his lips touched mine.

Then every ounce of tension drained from my muscles, and I relaxed against him, running my fingers through his hair. He responded by gripping my shoulders more firmly, supporting my weight, and for the first time in months, I felt carefree, as though JohnScott's arms were strong enough to carry my burdens.

CHAPTER
THIRTY-FIVE

Tyler hadn't been gone from Fawn's house five minutes, and he already missed her. She hadn't reacted to his gifts as he expected, but she could be difficult at times. He cut his headlights half a mile from the scenic overlook so he wouldn't run the risk of Fawn noticing. Lucky for him the full moon illuminated the outline of the white-rock road.

She had turned into some sort of nature girl, fanatical about living in the middle of nowhere, but she didn't even like being outside where she could experience the land. She only wanted to look at it, sitting on the porch, feeling the wind. Whatever. He'd buy her a set of cushioned lawn furniture, or a chaise lounge, or a hammock. Anything she wanted.

He sat on a cement picnic table and rested one foot on the bench, then unbuttoned his shirt and threw it on the table behind him. He stretched his arms over his head and flexed his muscles, remembering how she liked him in jeans and a wife-beater. She always griped about the nickname for his undershirt, though.

He grunted. Tyler slapped her around a bit, but he would never really hit her. He got the impression Fawn's dad might have taken a few punches at her mom—her parents were messed up that way—so no wonder she preferred the term muscle shirt. But that didn't bother him in the slightest because he spent a lot of time and money on his muscles. He rubbed a thumb over his left bicep, gingerly inspecting his healing wounds. One more letter, and he'd have the tattoo finished.

But before that, he'd check on Fawn. She'd been in a tizzy when he left her place, practically pushing him out the door. But if he knew her, she'd be soaking in a bubble bath by now.

He raised the binoculars to his eyes and adjusted the controls. No movement at all in the kitchen. When he scanned the living-room windows, where all the boxes were piled, he cursed. The baby crap partially obstructed his view. He should have thought about that, but at least he could still see the recliner.

Then he saw her, and his hands tightened on the binoculars. She had come into the kitchen to mix herself a glass of coffee. Tyler increased the magnification, inspecting her undergarments and swollen belly. Good Lord, she was beautiful. But she acted like a tramp, undressing in front of the windows, even if the nearest house was miles away. She ought to know better. She ought to save herself for him.

He stroked the binoculars as he watched her drink her coffee, and when she removed her bra, he increased the magnification again. He was addicted to her—physically, emotionally, mentally—but he didn't care. It had gone beyond a claim to his inheritance, and he had to have her.

She curled up on the recliner, and the dog came to her.

Stupid dog. Stupid coach.

He clenched his teeth and lowered the glasses. He should've taken care of JohnScott Pickett at the street dance, and he would have, if the stinking team hadn't interfered. But he'd have another opportunity to set the coach straight. He would see to that.

Pulling the razor blade out of his back pocket, he rubbed his thumb across the smooth surface. He had never worked on the tattoo at night, but he could use the glowing light from his cell phone and finish the job. He'd come to enjoy the release he experienced when he cut himself. As much tension as that woman caused him lately, he might have to carve her last name in his arm too. He'd have half the alphabet running all the way down to his wrist.

He held the phone between his teeth and surveyed his work. No last name needed. FAWN. Carved neatly in block letters across the bulge of his bicep. She had kissed him there once, and she would kiss him there again.

He clenched his teeth as the blade sliced into his skin, then cut twice more, almost dropping the phone. She'd like this. And for once, she would realize how much she meant to him. The blood ran down his arm, dripping from his elbow to the cement table, but he let it flow unhindered. Every drop that trickled out of her name relaxed him that much more.

He needed a beer. A beer and Fawn through his field glasses. He stuffed the blade back in his pocket and stepped to the truck. Taking a can from the cooler, he guzzled the liquid, then resumed his position on the table, lifting the glasses to his eyes. The bathroom light glowed, but he couldn't see in that room much at all.

The woman used the toilet every five minutes. Even back when they used to drink together, she had a small bladder. She'd nurse a wine cooler for fifteen minutes and then have to take a leak.

She had always been a pain in the neck. The wine coolers, for one thing. Who drinks wine coolers? Tyler took a swig of beer, then crushed the empty can before tossing it to the ground. It clanked against a growing pile, and he considered Fawn. She used to toss her empty bottles into a concrete drainage ditch as they drove by, making him slow down so she could hear the glass shatter against the concrete.

In the darkness he turned his head toward the cliff, wondering what shattering glass would sound like as it bounced down the hill. He might have to bring bottles next time.

Headlights approaching Fawn's house caused him to raise the binoculars again. The idiot drove too fast, slamming on the brakes at the curve where the road hugged the cliff, then hurrying to the house to stop outside the swell of Fawn's porch light.

The coach.

Tyler would have to do something about that guy. One way or another, he'd get that message across to the farm boy. Tyler leaned back and rested his elbow on his bent knee, watching the coach get out of his truck. To have been in such a god-awful hurry a second before, he sure moved slowly now. And peered all around the truck like a fool.

JohnScott reached into the back of his beat-up truck for some sort of pole and then crept toward the house. Maybe Fawn didn't know he was out there. Usually when she heard cars approaching, she opened the front door. The coach stepped carefully onto the porch and swept the pole toward the doormat, then jerked it and took a step back.

Holy cow, a snake. On the *front porch*.

Tyler stood and gripped the binoculars with both hands as the coach deposited the snake in a bag. *What a wuss.* If it'd been Tyler, he would have shot a bullet through the blasted demon's eyes. The only good diamondback was a dead one, and he had a collection of rattles to prove it.

But a nerve twitched in his jaw. How did JohnScott Pickett know how to catch rattlesnakes?

Fawn opened the door then, and the dog leaped toward the coach.

Don't go in that house. Tyler gritted his teeth.

But he did. JohnScott went right in as though he owned the place.

Tyler lowered the glasses and rubbed his eyes, still not believing the rattler on Fawn's front porch. He had just been over there and could have stepped on the thing. He hadn't even been thinking about snakes. Hadn't even been looking for them. He opened his second can of beer and downed it quickly, then reached for a third. He'd have to be more careful, that's all.

He bumped the binoculars against his forehead as Fawn and the coach moved into the kitchen. He wished the coach were out of the picture, but he'd take what he could get. Fawn's slender fingers pushed a stray curl toward her braid, and she turned around, leaning against the sink. Even pregnant, she was the most beautiful woman he'd ever been with. He flexed his bicep, thinking of her kisses.

But what he saw next made his back stiffen. The coach was touching her. Not just hugging her this time. He stood close, talking, leaning into her. Tyler rose to his feet and took three steps toward them, then readjusted the glasses. The wuss pulled her toward him, kissed her, devoured her with his mouth. And Fawn—the two-timing slut—kissed him back. She had hold of his neck, and Tyler could see the muscles in her arm flexing as she drew him closer.

He lowered the binoculars as every muscle in his body tightened. A low rumble started in the base of his lungs, then erupted out of his throat in a raspy scream that drifted over the rim of the Caprock. He gripped the binoculars in both hands, wrenching them back and forth, wanting to feel the fiberglass break beneath the grasp of his muscles, but they frustrated him by not budging. He growled and hurled them powerfully over the edge of the rock face, and after a few seconds, he heard the field glasses break into pieces as they hit the rocks below.

CHAPTER THIRTY-SIX

For twenty-one years I had attended Trapp church, but not until I stood on the sidewalk Wednesday night and watched JohnScott walking toward me did the place feel like home.

In the back of my mind, Tyler's accusations about the coach still prickled uncomfortably, but I pushed them away, choosing to remember JohnScott's assurances instead. My face warmed. JohnScott certainly didn't act like he planned to abandon me.

It surprised me to see Clyde following close behind him, and I wondered if JohnScott realized how bringing the ex-convict back to this congregation might ruffle a few feathers. Then again, maybe JohnScott viewed it as a welcome diversion from his own presence.

"I'm impressed," I said. "When you dared me to come to church with you in Slaton, I didn't really think you'd follow through on your end of the bargain."

"I couldn't let you show me up."

"I might be a wild card, though," Clyde said. "If it gets too sticky, I'll wait for you in the car."

"Is it that bad?" I asked.

Clyde shuffled across the tiny foyer. "They weren't any too cordial last year when I dropped in on them."

"But a lot has changed," I said.

"That's a fact," Clyde said, "but I don't want to push." The large man looked down at his feet, suddenly appearing smaller and more timid. "Anyway, I've got my reasons for trying it again."

Three elderly men stood near the coatrack, and when they noticed Clyde and JohnScott, they studied them intently for a few moments before one of them, Lee Roy Goodnight, broke away from the group and approached us.

He leaned heavily on a wooden cane and extended his other hand toward JohnScott. "Coach Pickett, good season so far."

"Thank you, sir."

"Wouldn't hurt to give Quinten Snodgrass a tad more playing time, though. The boys down at the feed store are figuring it could make a difference."

The coach nodded as though considering the suggestion, but I knew what he was thinking. Quinten Snodgrass was second string for a reason.

"I'll keep that in mind, Lee Roy. Thank you for the advice."

The old man ran his tongue over his lips, then worked his mouth as though to recapture the moisture. "I'd heard you were attending over in Slaton, but it's good to see you here. I'm glad to know you've found the Lord."

JohnScott nodded. "It's good to be here, Lee Roy."

"Clyde." Lee Roy extended his hand again, but when Clyde shook it, Lee Roy seemed to hold on to him for longer than necessary. "I'm awful glad you're here, son. Awful glad."

"Thank you, sir."

That seemed to be all the interaction Lee Roy could handle at the moment, because he turned and hobbled down the aisle to his usual position in a front pew.

"So far, so good." I didn't point out that the other two men by the coatrack were frowning at Clyde, clearly befuddled as to how they might welcome their celebrity coach without soiling themselves through interaction with the ex-convict.

As I started toward a pew where Ruthie sat, Clyde cleared his throat. "If it's all the same to you, I'll sit back here."

"Then we'll sit back here too," JohnScott said.

"No, now you two go on down there with Ruthie and them. That's where you need to be. But me? I belong back here." He shrugged. "For now anyways."

JohnScott hesitated, then nodded almost imperceptibly and turned to lead me down the aisle. When we reached the pew, he moved aside so I could sit next to Ruthie. "Hey, little cousin," he said.

"JohnScott?" Ruthie said. "Don't look now, but you're sitting in the middle of the Trapp church." She rested her palm against her cheek in mock alarm. "And you said you'd never come to church with me."

He leaned toward her and whispered. "I didn't come with you. I came with Fawn."

"Actually, you came with Clyde," I corrected.

"Clyde's here too?" Ruthie looked over her shoulder until she caught his attention, then crossed her eyes at him. "What next?"

I asked myself the same question every time JohnScott and I were together. Not because of anything he did or said but because of who he was, what he represented, and the perplexing discovery that I wanted him for my own. Badly.

Right before the devotional started, my mother sat down on the pew in front of us, followed soon after by Milla Cunningham and Pamela Sanders, who sat on either side of her, sandwiching her between their goodness. Mother glanced back at me and smiled faintly, then nodded at JohnScott.

When she turned back around, my lungs seemed to have stopped working, and I had to consciously inhale and exhale. Mother sat *right in front of me*. Not on the far side of the room, not alone on a pew, but right next to Milla Cunningham. And she had greeted me silently.

And … she had acknowledged JohnScott.

Ruthie elbowed me, and JohnScott leaned over and whispered, with his lips so near my ear, his breath tickled, "I take it that's not typical behavior."

I flattened my palms in my lap, patting my thighs nervously. My heart didn't know what to do with the sensations racing through it, but after a few more inhalations, I calmed my pulse and let my hands fall to the wooden pew on either side of me. When I last saw my mother at the feed store, she had openly told me she loved me—not something our family expressed verbally—and now this.

JohnScott's hand rested on the pew next to mine, and as Dodd stepped behind the podium to give his devotional talk, the coach touched the side of my hand with his pinky. Not a caress, but definitely a statement. A silent expression of support. I dropped my gaze to the pew, not touching him back, just looking at our hands side by side against the stained wood. His rough knuckles and my pale fingers, side by side, as though he were waiting for me to be ready to reach out.

Dodd spoke on the Damascus road conversion of Paul, and I couldn't help but wonder if he had been saving the sermon until Clyde Felton showed up. Or JohnScott. But when he said a short prayer at the end, I realized he just as likely could have intended the story for my benefit. Even though I had been raised within the walls of the church building, in the past several months, I had experienced as dramatic a transformation as the coach or the convict, and I certainly was just as sinful.

When Dodd finished his prayer, I kept my head bowed.

Lord, forgive me. Please. You seem to have blessed me with a strong Christian man I don't deserve, yet my prayers have been selfish. That was wrong. Please change me, not him. Make me what JohnScott needs.

After the devotional, Clyde, JohnScott, and I ended up on the small front lawn outside the church, just as we had in Slaton, and I decided I wouldn't mind making it a habit.

Clyde kicked at gravel on the edge of the sidewalk. "I know y'all pondered this a spell, but I want you to know I think the two of you are a good thing."

JohnScott looked at me and gestured to Clyde. "We talk."

"Oh." I nodded, not fully accepting that JohnScott and Clyde were good enough friends to discuss me. The man seemed nice enough, and he certainly knew a lot about snakes, but something about him still seemed … off.

"This town's unmerciful when it comes to gossip." Clyde shook his head. "But maybe they'll go light on the two of you."

"I don't know about that." JohnScott chuckled. "The head coach and a pregnant girl?"

"Stranger things have happened."

"Naw, they'll have a heyday with this one."

My stomach turned. "You guys aren't making me feel any better."

"It'll be all right." Clyde leaned against JohnScott's truck. "I should know."

I lowered my eyes, smoothing my shirt.

"You think it was bad when I came back?" Clyde chuckled. "You should have heard it before I left."

I answered without thinking. "What happened?"

JohnScott coughed, and I immediately felt like an idiot.

Clyde's smile was gentle. "That's all right, Fawn. I was talking in riddles, dodging the truth of it. But so you know the particulars, I stayed in jail in Lubbock before my sentence came down. I had a couple friends who would visit me there. We tried to make sense of things." He shrugged. "But when I transferred to South Texas, we lost touch."

"So they weren't your friends anymore." It angered me to think of those friends turning their backs on him.

"Aw, nothing like that. They got busy with their lives." He squinted toward the street, where Lynda Turner passed by in her hatchback. "Just a big tangle, and it was easier—better—for them to let it go."

JohnScott looked at him quizzically. "Who were those friends? Anybody I know?"

Clyde shifted, putting his weight on his other foot. "Now Coach, don't tempt me to start rumors. You got enough gossip to worry about."

"Thanks for reminding me."

Clyde shrugged. "You about ready to go?"

"Yep, we've had enough excitement for one night." JohnScott's gaze fell to my lips, and he chuckled. "Wouldn't it be something if I kissed you? Here?" He turned away, still laughing.

As I walked to the back of the parking lot, I realized Clyde had become one of the more interesting people in my life, and I wondered if I would ever stop underestimating him. Whatever had happened all those years ago, it surely wasn't enough to send him to prison for twenty years. He just didn't seem the type.

A vehicle pulled up behind me as I unlocked the Mustang, and when I turned, my heart faltered. My father had come to pick up my mother, and she sat in the passenger seat of his truck, looking worried.

He slid out of the cab without killing the engine. He frowned at the Mustang, then made a slow sweep of his eyes toward JohnScott's truck farther down. "What's he doing here?" he demanded. "Tyler's been telling me how the coach follows you all over town. Is he harassing you?"

"I asked him to come." I started to leave it at that but decided I'd better give him some sort of explanation. "A few nights ago, JohnScott took care of a rattlesnake on my front porch. It's the third one we've found out there, and I'm getting a little nervous." I glanced at my mother.

"*We've* found three snakes?" His face screwed into a sneer.

I looked away from him and crossed my arms. People at the side of the building were beginning to notice.

I could see my dad out of the corner of my eye, staring me down, waiting for me to crumble, but when I didn't, an exasperated rush of air pelted from his lips. "You're with the football coach." He shook his head. "You'd think you could set your sights a little higher than that."

A pain shot between my legs and subsided immediately. I recognized it as one of the symptoms Velma had told me to expect—something about my cervix—but the brief intensity caught me off guard, and I inhaled to steady myself. "Coach Pickett's a good friend."

"A good friend?" His voice rose. "If he was a good friend, he wouldn't spend hours and hours at your house. Anybody in the area could see him turn down your drive and let their imaginations fill in the rest."

He was right. That's how things worked in our little town. Two cars in a parking lot or a driveway or behind a store. And gossip would run rampant. "That's not how it is." I hated the whine in my voice, not to mention the lie.

He spit in the gravel between us. "The football coach. Seriously?" His gaze dropped to my waist. "You're just like your mother."

I blinked. I expected him to degrade me and to insult JohnScott, but I didn't expect him to say anything about Mother. *"What?"* I glanced at her sitting on the edge of the passenger seat, and I wondered if she could hear us over the engine. When she shook her head slightly, I realized she had rolled her window down. I turned back to my dad. "What do you mean?"

Clyde's voice called from behind me. "You're right, Neil. She's a lot like her momma." The ex-convict strode toward us. "Only stronger. Harder to push around. I reckon you noticed that, though."

My father spoke through clenched teeth. "Stay away from my family. You have no business with us."

"I got no business with Susan," Clyde corrected. "And I don't bother her."

I stepped between them. "I didn't even know you knew each other."

"Oh sure, Fawn." Clyde spoke smoothly compared to my father. "We graduated high school together, back in the day."

"We don't know each other at all," snapped my father.

Clyde sighed and glanced into my dad's truck.

"Keep your eyes off my wife."

The huge man raised his palms, and I thought of a powerful lion lying next to a herd of deer, not hungry. "Don't make an issue where there ain't one," he said.

"I won't make an issue as long as you stay away from Fawn."

"Not without a court order. And with Susan's daddy dead and gone, you don't have that kind of power."

"You might be surprised what kind of power I have."

"No, I don't think so." The pity in Clyde's voice rang louder than my father's threats, and I realized Clyde had compassion—for whatever reason—for my father.

But that didn't answer my question, and suspicion set off a chain reaction of dread. "Will one of you explain what you're talking about?"

JohnScott walked toward us, but Clyde lifted his hand and waved him away. "It's about time you knew the truth, Fawn, but I'll let your folks explain all that."

"I could have you arrested," my father taunted Clyde, but the ex-convict just walked away.

My father stomped to his truck, leaving a trail of fury like the angry spray of a rabid skunk, but he halted with his hand on the door handle and stared through the window at my mother.

She looked at me, and regret filled her eyes.

I lifted my shoulders questioningly, but she only dropped her gaze to her lap.

Another pain nicked my cervix, this one milder than the last, but my skin jittered from the sensation, a mirror of my heart. I couldn't fathom what happened between my parents and Clyde, but I sensed my life would soon rip from front to back. One more time.

CHAPTER
THIRTY-SEVEN

JohnScott asked me out on an official date the next night, but he didn't pick me up until after dark, and he wouldn't tell me what he had planned. I had never been one for surprises, and I couldn't help but wonder how well JohnScott really knew me. And me him.

We had literally known each other our entire lives, but we had been friends less than a year, and serious friends less than a month. We were moving fast. Maybe I wasn't the person he thought I was.

As we pulled from my drive onto the highway, he turned toward Trapp instead of Lubbock, and my curiosity about the evening increased. "Aren't we getting a late start for a Thursday night? You have the big Slaton game tomorrow. You need to be rested so you can thoroughly stomp our rivals."

"Naw, I'm good."

I cut my eyes toward him. "We both know Trapp shut down two hours ago."

He smiled knowingly but only shrugged.

"Well, everything except the Dairy Queen, and if that's what you have in mind, who am I to criticize? I'm happy to spend time with you in any of our local establishments. I only wish you hadn't told me to wear sneakers, because the DQ definitely calls for heels."

He chuckled. "We're not going to the Dairy Queen."

"Hmm." I rubbed my chin. "The Video Barn? You might want to reconsider that, because they have yet to convert all their movies to DVD."

"We're not going to the Video Barn either."

"The United?"

"Actually, I've already been to the United and got everything we need. And Ruthie, by the way, is sworn to secrecy. Not that anyone in town would believe her even if she told them what I bought."

He eased to a stop at the flashing red light, the town's only traffic signal, then made a left turn and pulled into the car wash.

"Oh, I see." I nodded. "We're going to deep-clean your truck. That's classy."

"Not quite." He drove through the parking lot and into the dark alley between the washing stall and the drugstore.

"We came all the way into town to go parking? Couldn't we have done that at my house?"

"Interesting idea. Maybe next time you can choose what we do." He opened his door, illuminating the inside of the cab. "Here's our loot." On the seat between us rested a United shopping bag filled with no less than ten bottles of blue and white shoe polish and window paint.

I lowered my voice reverently. "Are we going to paint the town?"

"In honor of Trapp's game against the Slaton Tigers, we're going to paint every shop window on Main Street." He pulled a pocket-knife from his jeans and cut the plastic from each bottle.

I giggled as I slid across the seat, getting out on his side of the truck. "This is my best date ever."

"We haven't even done it yet. If we get arrested, it won't rank that high."

"Like either of our cops would arrest a Blaylock or a Pickett, especially for something like this."

"Someone's coming." He pulled me away from the truck and shut the door quickly, leaving us once again disguised in darkness. We snuck around the corner and jogged past the streetlamp to another dark spot, where we went to work on the drugstore windows. In bubble letters, I painted *Trapp the Tigers* while he drew a lopsided football.

We eyed each other's artwork skeptically.

I shrugged. "Not bad. I suppose."

He scoffed. "That's girly cheerleader stuff. I'm representing the men in town."

We quickly filled in the drugstore's front door with dots and stripes, then moved to the gas station across the street, where each window of the garage received a different starter's jersey number. As we went the long way to the bank to avoid the streetlamp, I asked, "How often do you do this?"

"I've never done this in my entire life." He paused to draw a Panther paw print on the back door of the bank. "And the only reason I'm doing it tonight is so I can spend time with a beautiful woman in the dark."

"Well, you're going to have to try harder to impress me, JohnScott, because that Panther paw print looks an awful lot like a Tiger paw print, and we can't leave the citizens of Trapp confused."

"Ha! It's a cat fight." He jogged three steps and called over his shoulder, "Can you draw a cat?"

I giggled as I caught up to him and drew a simple cat figure, to which he added Tiger stripes and what looked like drops of blood.

A pickup stopped at the red light, and we ducked into the alley, then stopped, both of us breathing deeply. "You know what, Fawn? A few weeks ago, I worried about being too old for you. But now I don't feel that way."

"Well, you are older than me, and don't you forget it." I punched him in the chest. "And you draw like a preschooler."

"You run like a duck."

I giggled loudly, and he clapped his palm over my mouth.

An hour later, we had painted every shop window and several of the players' houses.

"I'm glad you asked me out, JohnScott." I smiled at him in the darkness. "I wanted to see you."

He covered the distance between us in two large strides. "What did you say?"

"I wanted to see you."

We were approaching a streetlamp, and he pulled on his earlobe. "I didn't quite hear you. One more time."

"I wanted to see you, but I'm beginning to regret it."

He grinned, his hat perched on the back of his head. "Probably you wanted to kiss me."

"What makes you think I'd want to kiss you?"

"Because I've wanted to kiss you again ever since your kitchen." He laughed out loud as he covered my lips with his, and his humor entered my soul, spreading warmth down to my toes. His arms slid around my waist, and he held me tight while his lips brushed across my cheek. He could switch so quickly from homespun farmer to sultry football coach, and I couldn't figure out which personality I found the most attractive, but I knew I liked all of him.

"Let's go to the top of the elevator," I whispered.

"You're nine months pregnant. You can't climb the grain elevator."

"It's no big deal," I teased. "I hear it's a good place to make out."

A pickup crept by on a side street, and we slipped between two parked cars. "Was that Tyler?" JohnScott's body stiffened.

I gazed after the vehicle as it disappeared behind a house. "It sure looked like his truck, but he wouldn't be in Trapp in the middle of the night. Probably a teenager wishing he had thought of shoe polish first."

JohnScott still peered uneasily at the corner of the house. "Well, whoever he is, the kid should watch out," he declared. "He's likely to get blamed for our mischief."

CHAPTER THIRTY-EIGHT

It took a lot of talking to convince JohnScott I could climb up the grain elevator, but in the end he agreed because I told him I had done it before.

"So, you've been up here lots of times?" he asked as we climbed the curving steps around the tower, barely illuminated in the moonlight.

"Oh sure," I said, gripping the handrails tightly.

JohnScott had insisted I go first so if I happened to stumble, he could break my fall, but I could feel one of his hands on my belt loop nonetheless. "And you mentioned this is a great place to make out."

"I never said I kissed anyone up here."

He paused a few seconds before he blurted his next question. "*Have* you ever kissed anyone up here?"

I ignored him. "You said you've climbed up here plenty of times too."

"I've only ever been up here with one other girl, and I never kissed her."

We were walking up the catwalk now, almost to the lifts, and JohnScott resumed his sarcastic banter. I found myself wondering if it had been the girl he dated in college. "You brought her up here more than once, and you want me to believe you didn't kiss her?"

"I didn't bring her up here, she brought me."

"That's just pitiful, JohnScott." I eased down to sit on the metal platform, swinging my legs a hundred feet above the ground.

JohnScott sat next to me, resting his arms on the railing. "I can't believe I let you climb up here."

"I can't either. Some protector you turned out to be."

He peered at the ground far below. "I'm serious. I shouldn't have let you do this. It's not safe."

"I'm not sure you *let* me." I bumped his shoulder. "But you seemed to lose all train of thought when I used the phrase *make out*."

The worry lines around his eyes lessened, and his smile lines returned, and I found myself very glad the moon had come out so I could appreciate them.

"Tell me who you came up here with," he said again.

"Why do you want to know?"

"I'm not sure." He laughed. "But I … I think I'm jealous."

"You shouldn't be."

"Why do you say that?"

I lifted my chin. "If I tell, will you tell?"

"Sure."

I giggled. "The only person I've ever been here with is Ruthie."

He stared at me in disbelief, and then he chuckled deep in his lungs.

"Now you have to tell me, JohnScott." But I knew before he even said.

"Ruthie," we said in unison.

We laughed softly, enjoying the commonality and looking into each other's eyes. I felt so comfortable with him, so at ease. I wondered if that's what a normal family felt like.

"I really, really like you, Fawn. Especially when your shield is down." With his index finger, he traced a path across one of my eyebrows and around my cheek, ending at my lips.

"Is it down now?"

"Oh yes," he whispered.

"How can you tell?"

"Because when it's down … you're the most beautiful girl I've ever seen in my life."

His words intertwined through my rib cage and wrapped like a cord around my heart, pulling me toward him.

"Fawn—"

I kissed him then. I didn't care what he was going to say next. He liked me. A lot. And he thought I was beautiful. Not only that, but he took me out on a *playdate* and laughed with me and helped me forget my troubles. I wanted to give to him and make him as happy as he made me.

I put my palms on either side of his face, feeling the movement of his jaw, and then I wrapped my arms around his neck, binding him close to me. When I touched the tip of my tongue to his lips, he sighed into my mouth and gently laid me back, flat on the platform, with one of his arms supporting my head.

I didn't let go of his neck. Not when his kisses became frenzied. Not when his free hand began to roam across my body. Not when his thigh found its way across my knees. I had never felt anything so strong in my life, and even while my brain screamed for me to stop, my body wouldn't obey.

But suddenly he moved his arm from under my neck, and my head bumped against the metal. His hands gripped my wrists as he pulled my arms from around his neck, and he stood to pace across the landing, breathing deeply and looking into the distance. Finally he sat five feet away with his back to me, pressing a clenched fist against his forehead.

My feet had been dangling over the side of the platform, but I slowly lifted them, feeling sprawled and exposed, and I rolled onto my side away from him, drawing my knees up to my stomach and curling my arms around my head.

I had done this.

The metal grate of the platform dug into my shoulder and hip, but it seemed like a subtle punishment for my poor behavior. I wondered if JohnScott would ever look at me the same way again. I had no self-control. Or decency or morals or simple common sense. He had already talked to me about it, more or less, on his front porch that night. He didn't want this.

But I had done it anyway.

"Fawn, I'm sorry." He exhaled, long and hard, and I heard him turn toward me.

Maybe he would simply leave me here. I could climb down by myself later so I wouldn't have to look at him, meet his gaze, see his disappointment.

But then he scrambled across the platform. "Fawn? Fawn, no." He cradled my head. "It's not your fault. I didn't mean that at all. It's not you, Fawn. It's me. I shouldn't have brought you up here."

He lifted my arm off my head and nestled it by my chest, then he brushed my hair away from my face. Curls were stuck in moist tears, and he gently fingered them away from my cheeks, wiping my eyes, and kissing my hair.

"You didn't do anything wrong." He lay down behind me and pulled me against his chest, and I thought I felt him sob. "Fawn, please forgive me." His voice broke. "I'm sorry. I'm so sorry."

I closed my eyes and rubbed my cheek against his bicep, which acted as my pillow. I couldn't speak, but I didn't want him to think I was mad. I patted his other arm and kissed his knuckle, and he buried his face in my hair.

We lay like that until our breathing calmed.

He ran his fingers across the back of my hand, and I rubbed my thumb in circles on his elbow, and neither of us spoke. I could think of no words to explain my feelings. Other than *shame*. And *regret*. And *fear*. But I had used those words so much lately that I felt sure he would be sick of hearing them.

But I had to say something. I swallowed and said the first thing that came to mind.

"When I was little, my father never played with me much. I guess he stayed real busy on the ranch, but I always thought he didn't like me for some reason, like I had done something wrong. And my mother always suffocated me, like she was afraid to let me make my own decisions."

His fingers stilled.

"But it's weird," I continued. "Even though I craved a better relationship with my mom, I never, ever wanted to be closer to my dad."

He cleared his throat softly. "Maybe you looked to boyfriends instead?"

I nodded, then chuckled. "You must have taken freshman psychology."

"Okay, smarty-pants." He ran his fingers through my hair. "I don't know about me. I've got lots of older sisters, so I understand women. But some of my sisters are half siblings because my dad was widowed. I spent more time with Ruthie, even though she was younger. I sort of assigned myself as her guardian and protector."

"I'm sure you're suffering from some sort of psychosis like me."

He hummed. "You take any other psych courses?"

I shook my head.

"Yeah, me, neither."

I scooted onto my back, bending my knees. "You're insecure because of the girl in college?"

"I guess so." He intertwined his fingers with mine. "I just know I don't want to do that again. I want to make a relationship the right way."

"God's way."

He nodded.

"Yeah, me, too."

We looked down at our locked fingers, fought the weakest thumb war ever, then rested our hands on my abdomen.

"It's going to be hard for us to wait," he said.

"Clearly."

The baby nudged me, and JohnScott lifted his head. "No way." He raised up on one elbow and spread his palm across my side. Then he smiled as he got kicked two more times.

With the heel of my hand, I pressed against a knee or a foot or an elbow. "I think he could be a kicker for Texas Tech. He'll probably break all your records."

"But first he'll be a kicker for Trapp High School, home of the Fighting Panthers."

"Well, yes. I hear they have a good coach over there."

"I don't know about that. They say he's real distracted now and can't concentrate on his job."

I shook my head, sighing. "Thank you for caring."

"I care an awful lot, Fawn." He leaned over me, and his eyes were sad. "I want to build up that low self-image of yours, but it seems like I'm making it worse."

I frowned. "Low self-image?"

His eyebrows lifted. "I guess so, yes."

I sat up slowly. "I never considered myself to have a low self-image. Everyone's always telling me I'm a vain and arrogant Blaylock."

He eyed me skeptically, as though weighing my good and bad characteristics. "I've always considered low self-esteem and vanity to go hand in hand. One often masquerades as the other."

"How so?"

He squinted. "They both cause people to think of themselves more than they should."

I stared across the rooftops of Trapp. A cat sneaked from bush to bush. The red traffic light flashed endlessly. A pickup turned onto Highway 84, headed out of town. Resting my forehead on the rail, I considered my self-esteem, my self-image, and my self-confidence.

Thinking back over the past few years—my years with Tyler—it suddenly seemed clear. Of course I had low self-esteem, and Tyler had thrived on it. All those years I viewed myself as a snotty rich girl, I was hiding behind the image.

I laughed at the irony of my concerns earlier in the evening. I had worried that JohnScott and I were moving too fast. I thought he might not know me as well as he thought he did. But my doubts had been upside down.

If anyone needed to get to know me better, it wasn't JohnScott. He knew me better than I knew myself.

CHAPTER
THIRTY-NINE

"You look a little bloated." My mother critiqued my appearance as we wandered the aisles of Babies "R" Us in Lubbock, aimlessly picking up items without seeing them. She had called to ask if I'd like to go shopping for nursery items, and I had agreed even though I knew I couldn't possibly need anything.

Judging from the look on her face when she picked me up at my house, I guessed the shopping expedition held a higher purpose than she let on. Maybe the scene my dad made in the yard of the church on Wednesday night had finally compelled her to do something about it.

"Let's get something for the baby to wear home from the hospital." She picked up a white smocked gown gathered at the feet with a ribbon.

"Too girly. How about this?" I held up a blue sleeper, not as fancy as the gown, but high quality, which I knew would please her.

She fingered the fabric. "Maybe if we got a blanket to match."

Tyler had bought at least two blankets on his shopping spree, and I saw no need for another one, but I let her buy what she wanted. Spending money had always been a means of therapy for her.

Freshman psychology. JohnScott would have been proud.

Someone on the other end of the aisle repeatedly squeaked a baby toy, and my head started to throb dully. When the clamor didn't stop, I glared.

"Hey there, Fawn." *Squeak squeak.*

It was Ruthie and her mother.

Lynda's gaze bounced from the squeak toy to the floor to the back wall—anywhere but to Mother and me—but Ruthie strode down the aisle and hugged both of us, somewhat brazenly. "Any day now, right?"

"I guess so." I could feel an electric current traveling between our two mothers that might cause them to spontaneously explode if either of them took a step toward the other. "I'm due in a week."

"I hope that baby comes soon, because you're so skinny, your body can't support much more weight." She chuckled. "When you were walking up the bleachers last night at the game, you looked like you might topple backward any minute."

"Oh, nice, Ruthie. Thanks."

"Great game, don't you think?" She looked directly at my mother, dragging her into the conversation, and Mom's eyes widened.

"I don't know," she said. "I didn't go."

"How could you not go to the Trapp-Slaton game?" Ruthie grinned. "My cousin was amazing. He had those boys so pumped, they could've won the state championship last night." She shrugged her eyebrows. "Too bad they only had the Tigers to contend with."

"JohnScott is doing an excellent job with the team, Ruthie. I'm sure you both must be proud." Mother peered to the other end of the aisle, where Lynda stood with arms crossed, studying the fine print on a pricing sign.

At the lag in conversation, Lynda turned her head hesitantly toward us. "Yes." She swallowed. "Thank you, Susan. I'm extremely proud of that boy."

Ruthie must have decided she had tortured her mother long enough, because she tossed the toy onto the shelf with one last squeak. "Momma, we'd better go find Aunt Velma. She's probably hiding a few aisles over so Fawn won't see what she bought."

The four of us spoke or mumbled our good-byes, and as Ruthie disappeared around the corner, the last thing I saw was her hand. *Who cares?*

My mother became energetic with nervousness. "Do you need anything else? Do you have enough bottles? You'll need to sterilize several at once."

Her chattering seemed like an obvious attempt to prevent me from discussing Lynda Turner, but I figured I shouldn't broach the subject in the middle of Babies "R" Us anyway. My abdomen tightened slightly, and I paused, waiting for the precontraction to ease. "I have three bottles, but I probably won't use them much. I'm planning on nursing for the first year, at least."

Her fluttering ceased. "You're not serious."

"Yes, Mother, I'm breastfeeding. Everyone does it now."

"But you won't have time for that, with your school."

"I'll be taking online classes mostly, so I won't be away from the baby much. And when I have to leave him, I can pump breast milk for the sitter to use."

"Oh, Fawn … darling."

"That's what I need. A breast pump." I walked toward the feeding supplies section.

"You want me to buy you *that*?" She said the words as though the mere mention might cause a naked breast to appear in midair.

"You asked me what I need, and that's it." I squatted to read the packaging on three pumps, located on the bottom shelf.

"Oh, Fawn, get up off the floor." She pulled at the shoulder of my T-shirt and yanked the most expensive pump off the shelf. "Let's go get coffee or something."

Fifteen minutes later, we sat in Starbucks, sipping iced latte and ignoring the proverbial elephant in the room. I wanted to find out what my father had been talking about in the church parking lot, and I knew she wanted to tell me, but after more than twenty years of ineffective communication, it would take us a while to unearth the details.

I decided to sneak up on the conversation from a different direction. "So … Ruthie says you and Lynda went on a double date once."

Puzzlement showed on her face, but then her eyes clouded with memory, and she nodded. "A double date. Yes."

I waited for her to expound, but she only folded the corner of a napkin and lifted one shoulder. "Your father still thinks you should be with Tyler."

Not this again. "Does he not understand I'm old enough to make my own decisions?"

"That's a luxury few women can claim."

"Are you speaking from experience?"

She stared out the window, where car after car eased past the drive-through. "I haven't made a decision for myself since I was sixteen."

I rotated my cup. "When you married Dad."

"Even that decision wasn't entirely mine."

"What do you mean?" I had long since learned that questions regarding my parents' courtship were taboo, but I had always known they married when my mother was sixteen and my father was twenty-one. And that Mother was already pregnant. From recent revelations, I had deduced that my dad had been dating Lynda when he got my mother pregnant. Hence Lynda's attitude.

Mother twirled her straw in her cup until it honked softly, then she dropped her hands in her lap. "Your father means well, but he's not good at communicating."

"That's an understatement."

"He tries."

"Does he really? Because I don't see it."

"He's been trying lately … since things went bad with the church."

I sipped my drink, swallowed, then set my cup on the table. "Will he ever go back?"

"I think so. I don't know. Maybe." She shook her head. "He's always been a leader at that congregation … for generations. Now they look at him differently."

"They ought to."

She frowned. "Yes, Fawn, they ought to, but he *is* trying."

"Like the way he treated Clyde in the parking lot."

"It's different with Clyde."

"How so?"

Her face wrinkled painfully, but she didn't speak.

"I bet they had some kind of disagreement, and Dad can't forgive him. Dad doesn't do that. He holds grudges and remembers things forever and stews on them and gets angrier until he explodes." I smirked. "As Lynda Turner could tell us."

Her head twitched as though she'd been struck, and I regretted my words.

"I'm sorry, Mom. I shouldn't have said that."

"Maybe not, but you're right. He doesn't handle conflict well."

"He doesn't handle people who won't give him what he wants."

She blinked slowly. "No."

Out the window I noticed the sky darkening to a dull red. "Looks like dust is blowing in."

"Fawn, your dad loves me. In his own way."

My emotions clouded like the dusty sky. "Tyler is a lot like him."

"I know," she whispered.

Anger burned behind my eyes as another precontraction hit. "Yet you expect me to be with him."

She clasped her hands together, and her rings clinked. "He would take care of you."

Dirt skidded down the pavement, and I hoped the weather wouldn't turn into an all-out dust storm. We could be stuck at Starbucks for a while. "Tyler represents everything I'm trying to get away from in Dad. I don't want to live my life like you lived yours."

Her lips flattened before she snapped, "JohnScott Pickett has no money."

Heat spread from my sides, around my lower back, and over my shoulders. "What if I don't care? I'd rather have happiness than material possessions. Is that so hard to believe?"

"It's unwise."

The air outside the window began to swirl with dust, and I could feel the temperature dropping. I scoffed. "You've lived so long with a man who pushed you down that you can't imagine anything else. I know back then everybody married if they got pregnant, but adding one mistake on top of another is foolish. I'd be miserable with Tyler. Probably more miserable than you and dad. At least you guys loved each other when you got married. Tyler and I don't even have that going for us."

My mother's lips moved, but I didn't hear what she said.

"What?"

"I didn't love your father," she whispered. "And I didn't want to marry him."

The scent of dust and coffee filled my nostrils. "What do you mean?"

"I hardly knew him when we married."

"But you grew up in the same church. You'd known each other your entire lives."

She twisted her hands, avoiding my gaze. "He was older than me and had been away at college. I had my friends and he had his." Her eyes fogged, and she mumbled, "Though Clyde was older too."

Dust plinked against the windows like sleet, and I shivered, but my mother stared at the table, unblinking.

"Did you know Clyde?" I asked.

"Yes." She peered out the window but didn't seem to notice the accelerating dust storm. "He was your dad's age, but he didn't go away to college."

I searched for a thread of understanding as a thick dust cloud blocked the sun. I could barely make out her Audi in the afternoon's premature darkness.

"Did you ... *date* Clyde? Before you got married?" The idea was absurd.

"He was different back then." She seemed lost in memories. "But the same."

I did the math and frowned. "Did you date him when you were fifteen?"

She blinked once, slowly, seeming to will me to read her mind. "No, I dated him after I turned sixteen."

A cramp, more intense than the last, distracted me, and I couldn't make sense of her words. I waited until the contraction passed. "But if you were sixteen when you dated Clyde ..." I didn't like the image forming in my mind. "What are you saying?"

Her eyes were red, but there were no tears. "Clyde ..." She swallowed, lifted her chin, shook her head.

My jaw dropped, and I slumped against the back of my chair as gears turned in my mind.

Her spinelessness infuriated me, and I gritted my teeth as my life began to make sense. Why my parents had such a stilted relationship. Why my dad treated me as though he didn't love me. Why my mother seemed so distant yet desperate to show love. Always in the wrong ways. Always too weak to stand up to my father. "Say it." My voice rose, mirroring the screeching wind outside the coffee shop.

She took a shallow breath. "I'm too ashamed."

My anger exploded, triggering another contraction, and I began to wonder if the pains were real labor, but I didn't have time to think about them. "What are you ashamed of?" My hands trembled. "Ashamed of getting knocked up by Clyde Felton or marrying Dad or lying to me for twenty-one years?"

"All of it!" She threw up her hands. "I'm ashamed of the way your dad treated you, and I'm ashamed for allowing it. I'm ashamed of staying with him all these years."

"Why did you?"

"What could I do? I have no family left. No money. Your father has control of everything."

I envisioned Ruthie and Lynda working blue-collar jobs. "We could've managed."

She dabbed her eyes with her fingertips. "I can't live like that. I'm not strong. I've never been able to stand on my own."

A tear fell from her cheek onto the table, but I felt no compassion, no connection. I wanted to shake her.

"I'm sorry I didn't tell you about Clyde long ago," she said. "Your dad wouldn't let me."

And of course she wouldn't stand up to him. My posture drooped from weariness. "So why do you keep insisting I marry Tyler? It seems like you would understand if anyone would."

"He's the father of your baby. I assumed you loved him."

A preposterous idea swept through my mind, illuminating the truth like a spotlight. "You love Clyde."

Her head shook back and forth once, almost imperceptibly. "Then. Not now."

I sighed, finally understanding her motivation for the way she had been treating me since I had gotten pregnant. "You didn't marry the man you wanted, so you're trying to figure out the man I want."

"You deserve to be happy."

"JohnScott makes me happy."

She rolled her eyes and glanced out the window, finally seeing the storm. "Oh, good Lord."

As she stared at the thick wall of dust, I stared at her, seeing her for the first time. I wondered who she really was, beneath all the makeup and lies. I might never know.

"So, I'm assuming you married Dad for his money? And turned your back on the love of your life because you were too good for an ex-con—"*But wait.* Twenty-one years ago, Clyde hadn't even been to prison yet. My stomach tightened in disbelief, and nausea swept over me. "You? You were the statutory rape victim."

She picked at something beneath her thumbnail.

"You accused him of rape because you were too embarrassed to be with him?"

"No!" She glared at me then, her timidity shoved aside. "I loved him, and I gladly would have left my family to be with him, but my father wouldn't hear of it. He had Clyde arrested before I had even been to the doctor for a test."

"You could have fought it."

"I was *sixteen*, Fawn, and ashamed and alone and terrified."

Her adjectives knocked the wind out of me, and I nodded in understanding. I knew what that felt like. "You married Dad so he could take care of you."

A bitter puff slipped through her lips, far from a laugh. "Did I marry him for his money? No, Fawn. The Blaylocks didn't have two dimes to rub together. Mr. Blaylock ruled the church, and my father ruled everything else, and when the two of them got together, they worked out a plan that would be … *best for all concerned*."

A constant ache had settled above my thighs. "Explain."

"My daddy gave Neil the ranch." She tapped the table with two fingernails. "He gave him the ranch and married me off to a man so Christian, nobody would doubt us."

I covered my face with my hands, not wanting to believe her crazy tale, even as the jagged pieces of my life finally fell into place. It all made sense now. Almost. "Why did no one ever mention this to me? Half the town must know the truth."

"Nobody knew. Clyde and I kept our relationship a secret because of my parents. Then my father used his political connections to have Clyde jailed away from town, and nobody asked what happened to him." She shrugged.

Injustice flamed through my veins, and I snapped at her. "Surely the news would have gotten around Trapp. There would have been police involved, and judges, and jurors."

"My father bought them all."

"But someone in Trapp must have known. You could have been seen together."

She sighed and nodded. "Before I got pregnant, Clyde and I double-dated with Lynda and Neil. They were practically engaged.

I remember them telling us to wait. Clyde and Neil were good friends." She shook her head. "Even after my father ruined all of us, Lynda promised not to tell. Probably more for Clyde's sake than mine."

My eyes finally filled with tears as I saw myself in my mother. A vain, spoiled rich girl, so insecure she couldn't see the good in herself.

She fumbled with her necklace. "You've changed, Fawn. I don't even know what to think of you, but I know you're going to be all right."

"We're both going to be all right." A strong contraction overtook me without warning, and I gripped the table as the pain radiated around my midsection and settled in my back. Just when I wanted to cry out, a balloon burst inside me, and water ran down my legs, splashing to the tile floor.

CHAPTER FORTY

I settled back into the chair, more out of fear than pain. The novelty of childbirth intimidated me, but starting it in a coffee shop during a dust storm brought me close to terror. After my water broke, the contractions came closer together, and I leaned against the window, where sand scratched as though etching the glass.

Mother sat across the table, wringing her hands. "Are you all right until the storm blows over? Labor usually takes hours."

"I don't know. I'm scared, Mom."

I slid my cell phone out of my purse. JohnScott had made me swear I would call him, so I tapped the screen, chastening myself for not adding him to my Frequently Called list. It hadn't seemed important.

He picked up and started talking without saying hello. "I hope you're indoors somewhere. This is a bad one."

The sound of his voice prompted a juvenile reflex inside me, and I yearned to be coddled—lifted out of this harsh, unpredictable situation and transported to safety and shelter.

Another spasm hit, and I held my breath.

"Fawn? Can you hear me?"

"I'm here." The phone slipped in my sweaty palm, and I gripped it tighter. "We're at Starbucks."

"Oh, that's right, the shopping expedition." He chuckled. "Well, at least you're somewhere with food. Believe it or not, I'm stuck in Cliff Worlow's barn on the far side of Slaton, and we can't even get to our trucks. They're a mile up the road." His voice drawled lazily. "I can't complain, though, I'm lying in a bed of hay."

When I didn't reply, he repeated, "Can you hear me? I don't think we have a good connection."

An agonizing wave cinched the nerves in my lower back, causing me to squirm in the chair, and I whimpered involuntarily. "JohnScott? I'm in labor."

Disbelieving silence filled the phone for three seconds. "Are you sure it's real labor?"

A break in intensity allowed me to take a much-needed breath. "My water broke."

"How far apart are the contractions?"

"A few minutes, I guess."

"Can you get to the hospital?"

"We can't even see the car."

"Tell your mom to call 911."

"Someone already did." The pitch of my voice embarrassed me yet, at the same time, felt like a cleansing release of fear and tension. "JohnScott, I'm scared."

"You got this." He sounded as though he were deliberately calming his voice. "Women have babies all the time."

Fine-grain dust crept through the crack between the doors of the café, blowing across the tile floor to pile against the counter. "Not like this, they don't."

"Aw, you're a West Texas girl. What's a little sand gonna hurt?"

Another contraction began its slow anguish across my body, and my muscles tensed as I anticipated another crush to my spine. My abdomen tightened, and amniotic fluid trickled between my thighs and onto the floor. A man across the room craned his neck, and humiliation suffocated me as the pain intensified.

My mind shut out everything except the contraction and the sound of JohnScott's voice reaching through the phone to comfort and strengthen me. "It's another one, isn't it? Keep breathing, Fawn. You can do this."

Obeying him, I tried to inhale, but a moan hijacked my lungs, and I blurted, "Can you come?" Even in my panicked state, I knew the request sounded absurd, but my fear wouldn't deny my voice the hope of deliverance. I sobbed openly. "JohnScott, I'm so scared."

"You're doing fine."

A siren wailed through the roar of the wind, and soon a male and female paramedic came through the door with a gurney.

"How far apart are the contractions?"

"Hardly any breaks." I spoke through clenched teeth.

"Is that your husband on the phone?" Another pain swelled, and the paramedic laid a palm on my abdomen. "Maybe you should tell him to meet you at the hospital. I think you're going to need both hands for this."

Mother took the phone. "I'll talk to him."

"Alrighty." The man lightly gripped my forearm. "Time to lie down on the stretcher. What's your name?"

"Fawn." I stood, but my legs refused to cooperate, so I leaned against the gurney, letting the paramedics lift me onto it.

"Relax now, Fawn."

The woman motioned to my mother. "You better ride with us. I wouldn't want you driving in this weather. Cover yourself with this sheet."

They worked another sheet over me, tucking it in around my legs. "Fawn, we'll have you loaded in a few seconds."

I held the sheet over my face, but when they pushed me out onto the sidewalk, the wind yanked a loose piece of fabric, exposing my legs to the elements as tiny needles hurled at my skin. The gurney jolted and bumped, and then the tempest whistled past the closed doors of the ambulance.

I straightened my legs, feeling powdery dust matted to my moist skin, and the female technician wiped it away as another cramp inched through my core. The sharpness rose faster this time, and I pushed her hand away, irritation accumulating inside me until I nearly cried out. The tissue around my spine burned and then heightened into blue flame, and I moaned loudly.

"I'm sorry." I sobbed, embarrassed by my outburst, yet terrified of what would soon happen to my body. "Is this normal? Is it supposed to be like this? Mom?"

The paramedic patted my arm. "So far, your labor has all the signs of being perfectly normal. We'll know more when we get to the hospital. Fawn, I'm going to start an IV so you'll be all set when we get there. All right?"

I nodded, relaxing as the pain ebbed.

She wiped my arm with a sanitary cloth and then opened another. "Got to find a clean spot first. Too much dirt."

The needle pricked as the ambulance shifted, turning a corner. It felt like we were crawling down the street. "Can't he drive faster?"

"Not in this storm, he can't. But we'll be there in plenty of time, don't you worry."

Of course she was right. Besides, getting to the hospital sooner wouldn't necessarily ease my pain. "Can I get an epidural?"

"Depends on how quickly your labor is progressing." The ambulance came to a stop. "Fasten your seat belt, Fawn. We've got to get out in the dust again, but only for a second." She tucked the fabric far under my legs and torso. "We're not losing this sheet again, though."

By the time the door opened, I felt like a caterpillar in a cocoon, and dust only smattered my hand, which held the sheet over my face. But then I didn't notice the dust anymore. I didn't notice anything. Pain took over my thoughts, my vision, my awareness of everything around me. I arched my back and groaned as we bumped over the threshold into the emergency room. I had the overwhelming urge to bear down, and I held my breath and tensed.

"Not yet, Fawn." The man yanked the sheet off me. "Keep breathing and don't push. Give us a chance to get you into a delivery room, maybe even cleaned up a little."

"No," I wailed, struggling to breathe as he had said, but the need to bear down challenged the limits of my control. They lifted me onto a bed, and nurses scurried around me, pulling my clothes off, washing my skin, rolling me to my side, slipping my arms into a gown. "I need to push."

"Not yet, you don't." An older nurse lowered the end of the bed, propped my legs in stirrups, and covered my knees with a sheet. "You wait five more minutes. Now breathe." Her commanding voice compelled me to comply. I focused on the black dots of the ceiling's acoustic tile, trying to find a picture among them, but all I could envision were tiny grains of sand. Then misery wracked through me again, and I breathed fast and deep and clenched my fists.

The drill-sergeant nurse laid a strong hand on my shoulder. "Breathe slower, or you'll hyperventilate." When I obeyed, she patted my thigh. "Here comes the doctor. You made it."

"Well, hello, Miss Blaylock." Dr. Tubbs strolled in as though he had all the time in the world. "You're right on time."

My mother materialized from the corner of the room. "Is everything all right?"

"Sure, it is. This little guy wants to meet all of us." He studied a computer screen, then moved to the foot of the bed. "Okay, Fawn. You're clear to push now."

The relief of those words took control of my body, and I pushed with every bit of my strength.

"Well, he's practically here already," the doctor said. "One more push should do it."

My face burned from the exertion, as though I struggled against a brick wall, and I almost cried out in frustration, but the nurse abruptly moved away from my side to stand at the foot of the bed.

For a long second, I didn't realize the baby had whooshed out, because the agonizing pain in my abdomen continued. The doctor was busy, but I couldn't see what he was doing. Lifting my head, I strained to see my baby as another contraction, lighter this time, fell over me. My breathing came easier, and I sucked in air as though I had sprinted a hundred-yard dash, wiping sweat out of my eyes. I collapsed against the pillow.

"There we go," the doctor said. "Healthy boy. Looking around like he's in charge."

I heard a tiny cry, and the nurse laid my son across my stomach, right back where he started from, only now I could hold him in my arms. Curls matted against his head with whiteness that covered his scalp and trembling limbs, and his wail melted my heart.

Flat on my back, I shifted him closer to my chin. "Don't cry, baby." At the sound of my voice, he fell quiet and squinted as though startled to discover the face that went with my voice. "So you're the one who's been kicking me."

The drill sergeant bustled around the end of my bed, doing Lord knows what, and I realized Dr. Tubbs had gone. She barked at my mother. "Granny, can you raise her bed for her?"

My mother jerked to attention, following orders, and soon I found myself sitting up and peering into the most beautiful face I had ever seen. The baby blinked at me, and for a moment we did nothing but worship each other.

"He's precious, Fawn." My mother laughed and cried at the same time, and I reached for her hand for the first time in years.

"He's perfect."

The nurse clanked the stirrups back under the bed. "If you're breastfeeding, go ahead and do it. This is your bonding time. After that, he'll go for a bath."

The woman lacked a decent bedside manner, but at least she let me know what I should do. I pulled his teeny body to my chest, feeling his skin against mine. Velma had said sometimes babies know what to do, and sometimes they don't have any idea. It looked as though my son had things figured out, and relief trickled across my worries like healing ointment. *Thank You, God.*

"Five minutes each side," the nurse said.

I nodded and inspected the baby's toes and fingers, his ears, his eyelashes, his hair. My mother straightened from where she had been leaning over the two of us. "I need to make a few calls."

"Thanks for everything, Mom." With those four words, I tried to convey the feelings I held for her. Compassion at the discovery of her past. Understanding for the decisions she had made. Gratitude for raising me as best she could. In the past hour, she had become a different mother than I'd had that morning. Or maybe I had become a different daughter.

Her lips curved into a sad smile before she slipped from the room.

I turned the baby to the other breast and pulled the sheet over him, afraid he would get cold in the air-conditioning, then hugged him closer to my warmth and thought I would never let him go. He was beautiful. I fingered a wisp of thick, black hair near his forehead and let tears fall down my cheeks as I watched him nurse. His dark eyes, alert and attentive, studied me, and we spent the next five minutes memorizing each other's faces.

My heart had never loved, never dreamed of loving, so thoroughly as this. I'd only been a mother fifteen minutes, but already I knew I would do anything—anything at all—for this child.

His mouth formed a tiny *O* as I pulled him away, laying him across my lap while I tied my gown back in place. And then he filled my arms again, and I kissed his forehead and rubbed his small fist against my cheek.

"He about ready for his bath?" the nurse asked.

Before I could answer, the door flew open with a loud metallic clunk, and we both startled.

A man panted in the doorway with hazy, red powder crusting his hair, and his skin and clothing were reddish brown from grit. He stared at me, holding my gaze with a fierce intensity that exposed savage fears and raw tenderness. Affection pulled a fresh sob from my throat, and my heart fluttered higher in my chest until I thought I might float off the hospital bed.

JohnScott.

CHAPTER
FORTY-ONE

"Touch nothing." The nurse demanded, "Are you the father?"

JohnScott didn't answer. Didn't even seem to hear. He stood three feet inside the door, out of breath and staring into my eyes. "You're all right." When he stumbled forward, tears left clean trails down each of his cheeks, revealing a spot where the storm had worn his skin away like sandpaper.

A year ago—less, even—I would have been offended by his bedraggled appearance, but now joy bubbled in my chest, and I giggled and cried, holding the baby slightly higher to draw JohnScott's attention.

His gaze fell away from my face, landing on the bundle in my arms, and laughter escaped his lips along with a sigh. "Look at that."

I couldn't speak for the emotions pummeling my heart. Too much blessing. Too much happiness. Too much love.

He bent his knees, bringing himself down to our level but careful not to lean over lest he get us dirty. He and the little guy looked at each other. The baby made sucking motions with his lips, and

JohnScott grinned with his mouth slightly open, his eyebrows lifted in amazement. "Look at that," he repeated.

Pride swirled around me like a soft summer whirlwind. Pride at what I had done and for the perfect human I held in my arms. I had never felt such deep elation, and the fact I wanted to share it with the likes of JohnScott Pickett left me feeling uncertain and fragile and fresh. As if I were the newborn.

I shook my head as tears stifled my vocal cords. "You're here."

He removed his hat, causing a waterfall of dust to glide to the floor.

"Enough," the nurse said as she swept the baby from my arms. "Too much dirt."

My heart wrenched as though a lifeline had been severed, and I watched longingly as she swaddled the baby tightly, placed him in a rolling, plastic cubby, and pulled him toward the door.

"I'll bring him back after his bath."

We watched mutely until the door clicked behind her and the room filled with his absence. Then JohnScott laid his palm hesitantly on the side rail of my bed.

"He's all right?"

"Yes." I grinned, aware of the cheesy pitch of my laughter but not caring enough to stifle it. "I can't believe you came. You could've waited for the storm to blow over."

"Probably should have."

"I thought the truck was a mile from the barn."

He ducked his head. "I ran."

An image of JohnScott battling the dust storm quickened my pulse, and I wanted to jump out of the bed and dance around the room. But physical exhaustion and the lingering pain of childbirth rooted me firmly between the sheets. "I'm so glad you're here."

He shrugged, nodded, looked away. "What are you naming him?"

"I guess I'll call him Nathan. It means *gift from God*."

"I like that."

His lips parted as though to say something, but then he turned and pulled a chair toward the bed. When he sat, his head slanted in an uncomfortable position. I considered lowering the head of the bed, but before I could, he stood again, clearing his throat.

"Fawn? When I couldn't get out of that barn, I did a lot of thinking." He fingered the brim of his cap. "Or really, I did a little thinking very quickly."

My chest warmed from the energy he radiated. Energy that covered me with a gentle glow of security, but not the kind of security that comes from money. A different kind. And I enjoyed the foreign feeling.

He exhaled sharply. "I know this isn't the place for it, but I need to run some ideas past you."

He sounded as though he had developed a new strategy to add to his playbook, and I smiled at his uneasiness. But just as quickly, my smile slipped, and a wave of guilt pulsed through my veins. The tone of JohnScott's voice left me hoping for something I never thought I could have. But I had just given birth to another man's child, and I quivered in shame.

"When do you suppose they'll bring the baby back?" I asked.

His shoulders fell, but he grinned. "You're already a mommy." When he leaned over and brushed my lips with his, I smelled the dusty scent of the storm as tiny grains fell from his hair onto my cheeks and pillow. He pulled away, leaving his mouth hovering a centimeter from mine. "I'll go check on the little guy."

When he left the room, I turned on my side, watching the door he had gone through, wanting him to come back. But then Nathan filled my thoughts, and the sweet miracle of his birth floated around the room like a gentle promise. I yearned to have him back in my arms, feeding him, caressing him, counting his fingers and toes, but I gradually realized I wanted JohnScott to be the one bringing him to me.

Maybe fatigue dulled my shame, maybe euphoria blurred my vision, but at that moment, I couldn't imagine life with anyone other than Nathan and JohnScott. I didn't care if I would live in a mobile home instead of a ranch house. I didn't care if I would sit at football games instead of cattlemen's corporate dinners. And most surprisingly, I didn't care what my parents thought, or even the church.

I lay on the bed, alone in the room. No nurse. No mother. No baby. Now, no JohnScott. Looking around me, I pulled the sheet up to my chin, and my laughter bounced off the sterilized walls, filling me with warmth and goodness and something that felt an awful lot like love.

For the first time in as long as I could remember, I didn't feel alone.

CHAPTER
FORTY-TWO

Even though exhaustion smothered me, I no sooner could have taken a nap than done a set of jumping jacks. Adrenaline laced my veins, and every swoosh and thud coming through the walls jerked my attention. So when the nurse propped the door open and laid Nathan in my arms, my muscles jittered as though I won first place in a long-distance race.

His face had pinkened as though she had scrubbed him until his circulation increased, and I felt the urge to unwrap the blanket and inspect him all over again. Instead, I pulled at the tiny pink-and-blue knit cap until his curls—now downy clean—were exposed and beckoning to be touched.

Like JohnScott's.

A twinge of guilt brushed across my neck, and I forced my thoughts in a different direction. Nathan had my curls, not his.

I lifted my gaze to the nurse, standing silently at the foot of my bed, her head bowed over a clipboard.

"That husband of yours is a mess," she said, "but to tell the truth, he's not the only man who showed up looking like that today. Worst storm I've seen in years."

"Oh …" My face warmed. "He's not my husband."

Her pencil momentarily stopped scurrying across the page, and then she shrugged. "That's the way of it nowadays. Young people do things out of order, but it all comes out in the end."

Shame compelled me to be honest even though I wanted to crawl under the bed and hide from the truth. "Actually, he's not the father."

Her eyes briefly cast judgment before she veiled them with indifference. "Well, he's a keeper. Came down there asking questions. Was the baby healthy? How bad was the labor? Did you seem afraid? Yes, that one's a keeper." She jotted something on the clipboard and then hung it at the foot of the bed. "I gave him a set of scrubs and showed him where to find a shower. My name's Georgia. Push the call button if you need anything."

Her description nudged my heart as I imagined JohnScott's slow drawl, and I whispered to Nathan who slept soundly. "I bet he drove her crazy."

I swept Nathan's soft hair to one side in a swirl, then fluffed it into a mini-Mohawk. I pulled him close to my face and rubbed my nose on his head, smelling his heavenly baby scent as though it were my new life's breath.

Excited voices in the hallway signaled guests, and Velma, Ruthie, and Lynda breezed through the doorway, descending on our quiet intimacy.

"We've been stuck at Raising Cane's Chicken," Velma said. "Went there for lunch and thought we'd never get to leave."

"Let me hold him," Ruthie said, wiggling her fingers.

"Oh … of course."

Velma snickered. "You don't want to give him up yet, do ya? Can't say as I blame you." She peered at the baby through her bifocals. "He's a pretty little fella. But how could he not be, considering his momma and daddy." Her gaze swept from the baby to me. "How're you doing?"

"No worries."

"And how about the feeding? Is he taking to it all right?"

"I think so, but I've only fed him once."

Ruthie reluctantly passed the baby to Velma. "Was delivery as bad as they say?"

Already it seemed months ago, but the echo of fear still pressed sharply against my memories. "Absolutely."

Lynda peered over Ruthie's shoulder, inspecting Nathan. "At least you had a short go of it. Ruthie took twelve hours to get here."

Ruthie picked up Nathan's cap, stretching it between her fingers. "That might have been a blessing in this case, considering the dust. They're calling it a *haboob* because it's the worst storm Lubbock's had in years." She inspected the few items in Nathan's crib—a pacifier, a suction bulb, a package of alcohol swabs. "And I can't believe JohnScott. He looks like he's been sprinkled with cocoa powder."

"Doesn't smell like it, though," Lynda said.

Velma shook her head and returned Nathan to my arms. "That boy."

I heard boots scuffing the tile hallway, and I looked up, anticipating a clean and scrubbed JohnScott. Instead, it was Tyler, leaning against the doorframe, holding a bouquet of flowers upside down at his side. Disappointment shadowed my happy glow but immediately changed to embarrassment when I realized I hadn't even thought to call him.

"Hey there, babe. I hear we've got us a little boy." He sauntered to the side of the bed.

"He's healthy," I said quickly, "and I'm calling him Nathan."

"No ..." Tyler said under his breath, "you're not."

Velma waved Ruthie toward the door. "We've got a few errands to run, but we'll drop back by before we leave town."

"Don't go yet." I sat up so quickly, my stomach muscles protested, but Ruthie gave me a meaningful frown behind Tyler's back.

"We'll be back later," she said.

"Thirty minutes at the most," called Velma.

Then we were alone. The three of us.

I hadn't told them about Tyler's visit to the house, and they didn't know the uneasy feeling gnawing in the depth of my stomach. I told myself not to worry, because the concerns weighing me down were probably only my imagination.

The baby stirred, and I focused my attention on him, wondering if I should nurse him again and wishing Velma was there to tell me. I patted his bottom like she had done, and he settled back into deeper sleep.

Tyler's gaze traveled around the room, inspecting the television bolted to the wall, the plastic pitcher of water next to the bed, the window overlooking an adjacent roof.

"You can hold him," I said.

His gaze returned to the bundle in my arms, but his eyes seemed empty, detached. "Of course."

After I fumbled the baby from my arms to his, he held our son awkwardly against his chest with his elbows pointed out.

"Try it like this." I pressed my hand against his arm, but when he shifted, the tight sleeve of his T-shirt rolled, exposing a cut. I gasped. "Tyler, what have you done?"

Pulling at the sleeve, I suddenly felt as though I were falling from the rim of the Caprock with nothing beneath me to cushion my fall. My name was carved in his skin. The *F* and *A* had healed into transparent scars, but blackened scabs formed the *W*, and the *N* appeared to be a fairly fresh wound.

A corner of his mouth pulled away from his teeth. "It's my way of showing how much I care."

"But—" My breathing became shallow, and I couldn't fill my lungs with enough air to satisfy. It would be odd enough for him to get a regular tattoo, considering we weren't really together, but for him to carve my name in blood? I snapped my mouth shut and swallowed. "Those scars will be on your arm forever."

"That's the idea." He rested one hip on the edge of the bed and smiled down at the baby, who had opened his eyes. "Ty Cruz? Everyone in Trapp's going to know I'm obsessed with your mommy."

I gently drew the baby from his grip, and my gaze shifted to the nurse's call button on the side of the bed. "You needn't have done that."

"Oh, I think I did." His faced turned to stone. "I couldn't seem to get your attention."

"But, Tyler—"

"This is *my son*, Fawn, and I'm going to have him. Just like I have you."

His words, his mannerisms, his instability suffocated me, and I fought the urge to shove him away and call for the nurse—or to scream for JohnScott.

"Tyler, I told you I can't marry you."

He laid his fist on the top of the bed so his mutilated arm rested directly in my line of sight. Slowly he leaned toward me, squeezing the baby between us. He ran the backs of his fingers along my cheek, then pressed his mouth forcefully against mine. When I tried to turn my head, he gripped my chin tightly, keeping my lips shoved against his teeth until I thought I would smother.

The baby squirmed in discomfort, and Tyler pulled away, but his face hovered inches from mine. "Yes, Fawn, you can marry me." A muscle bulged in his temple as he clenched his teeth. "You can and you will."

CHAPTER
FORTY-THREE

"Is JohnScott with you?" My voice quavered when Ruthie answered her cell phone, but she didn't seem to notice.

"No ... he said he was showering, and we left him to it."

I shouldn't have called her. Tyler was gone now, and I would be fine. I sat in a rocking chair in the corner of the room, my arm cramping from holding the baby one-handed. JohnScott had been gone longer than expected, but he would be back any minute, and he'd know what to do about Tyler. "So are you guys coming back soon?"

"Actually, Velma's Chevy broke down." Ruthie groaned. "Ansel's on his way, but we probably won't make it back to the hospital till tomorrow. Aunt Velma's about to have a conniption fit to see the baby again. Here, she wants to talk to you."

The phone twanged. "Fawn, darlin', I can't believe this blasted old tank called it quits today of all days. I'm itching to get back out there. How's our sweet fella?"

"Sleeping like a baby." I smiled at my own joke, feebly trying to calm my nerves.

"Well, you watch him, make sure he wakes up often enough to eat a good meal. When JohnScott was a wee one, he nearly slept himself to death. Ansel finally took a wet washcloth to the bottom of his feet."

I frowned at Nathan and jostled him slightly.

"No need to worry about that, though. I'm just rattling because I'm flustered. Oh, there's Ansel. Here, talk to Ruthie."

The phone boinged again, and Ruthie said, "I better go, Fawn. Sorry, but I need to help Ansel."

"Okay." I steadied my voice. "Good luck with the car."

Ansel's voice hummed in the background, and it sounded as though Ruthie were getting out of the car. "Kiss the baby for me."

I did just that. Dropping my cell phone to the floor, I held Nathan close, trying not to think about Tyler's arm or his threats. The man was used to getting his way, and I knew from experience what that could do to a person's behavior.

Nathan gave a bleating cry, then opened his eyes and looked at me. Tears pooled on my lashes, and I gushed like a sappy Hallmark movie, saying a prayer of thanksgiving as we rocked together, the baby comforting me as much as I comforted him.

A tap at the door prompted me to lift the blanket to cover myself. I wiped beneath my eyes and smiled, but when the door opened, disappointment pulled a sigh from my throat.

My mother stepped into the room with my father right behind. "I brought your dad to see the baby." She spoke gently as though to soften the tension snapping between the three of us.

My mind went numb. This hospital room acted as a revolving door, spinning people in and out of my presence, allowing them to jerk my feelings up and down, back and forth, but my post-delivery hormones weren't keeping up. My heart had gone from joy to love to peace to fear, and anything my parents heaped on me would necessarily be kept at arm's length as a precautionary measure.

My father leaned against the wall, hands in his pockets.

"Oh, heavens." Mother pulled back abruptly. "If you're feeding the baby, we can come back later. I wanted to get flowers from the gift shop anyway."

"No, it's fine." The baby relaxed into slumber, and I lifted him slowly to my shoulder, dreading the inevitable. "Mom told me about Clyde Felton."

For the first time in my life, my father looked away from me uncomfortably. I had never approached him so boldly, never stood up to him. Sure, I had rebelled against his strict ways, but always in a passive-aggressive manner he could choose to ignore.

He inspected a fire-escape diagram posted on the wall by the door, and silence filled the room, broken only by a soft burp. I curled my arms around Nathan as though to shield him.

"We should have told you before." My father's shoulders dropped a centimeter. "When Clyde came back to town last year, I knew it was only a matter of time."

"You should've told me a long time before that."

"Maybe."

Scores of angry accusations perched on the edge of my tongue, but every ounce of energy had been squeezed from me. I didn't even have the stamina to explain Tyler's alarming behavior for fear I'd have to debate them, backing up each accusation with a convincing rebuttal.

My father slowly touched the corner of the fire-escape notice, his shoulders hunched forward around his heart.

I had never seen him like this. Even when things went bad with him and the church, it only increased his false confidence. Now he had no more secrets to hide behind, and I hardly recognized him.

"Dad, I'm sorry."

At my apology, my father's feet grounded shoulder width apart in his usual pose of power, and I wondered if he was bolstering himself, climbing back up the crystal tower he had fallen from. But his eyes told a different story. They were sad and tired, and surprisingly affirming. He said no words to convey his regrets, but he held my gaze for a split second before he nodded. Then his eyes hardened to their usual coldness. "Susan, we should leave."

He opened the door and stepped one fancy leather boot into the hall, and my mother scurried after him, but she turned back and said quietly, "Fawn, you're a stronger person than either of us ever were."

The door closed softly behind them, echoing in my thoughts, and I leaned my head against the back of the rocking chair, exhausted, and stared at the ceiling. My soul needed a good cry, but my body didn't have the strength. Every tear had been milked by the emotions of the day, and my eyes and my heart had dried out in the process.

Another knock at my revolving door barely caused me to lift my head. Only the nurse, Georgia.

"One more check before I leave for the day, but I'll be back tomorrow. I'll see my reality-TV star again before you're discharged."

Her comment cut, but it didn't make a dent in my rusty armor of detachment. "So I'll be able to go home tomorrow?"

"Probably in the afternoon." She took the baby's temperature, checked his umbilical cord, and changed his diaper—something I hadn't remembered to do—then swaddled him tightly again.

When she handed him back, I drew him close. Already he was my strength, my reality, my motivation.

The nurse's lips clamped into a frown, and I wondered what I had done. My life was so repulsive, even strangers were offended. "Thank you for changing him, Georgia. I had so much fun holding him, I didn't think to do it."

"You'll be a good mother if you like rocking your baby." Her eyes softened, and she sighed.

"What is it?" I asked quietly, not sure I wanted to know. Not sure I cared what this strange nurse thought of me anyway. And not sure I could bear it.

Her nose wrinkled on each side as if she smelled something foul. "I met the baby's daddy."

"Oh." I had no response, no rebuttal, but I wondered what Tyler had done to make such a vivid impression on her.

"He kissed you," she snapped.

My cheeks warmed until I felt sure they were scarlet, the color of the letter branded to my chest. "His doing, not mine."

She watched me for several seconds, then seemed to reach a verdict. "I suppose your life is different, so the rules are different." She stepped to the door, unable to hide her scorn. "You've had a busy day, and you need rest."

The door closed behind her, and I wished for the old recliner and Rowdy. I wanted to lie back and sleep for a week, or forever. I wanted to talk to JohnScott. Where was he? He hadn't wanted to leave. Not even long enough to shower. He had wanted to come back.

The door opened again, and Georgia thrust her head into the room. She remained partially covered by the door as though she preferred not to get mixed up in my business. "Your filthy man?" She shook her head. "He also saw you kissing the other one." She planted her hand on her hip as though I had thrown away a winning lottery ticket. "I liked the dirty one. I liked him a lot."

The door closed behind her, and my heart burst open, releasing all the tears my exhaustion had been holding at bay. No wonder JohnScott hadn't come back. No wonder he had abandoned me and left me to fend for myself against my family and his, against Tyler and his threats.

I could only imagine what JohnScott thought.

CHAPTER
FORTY-FOUR

JohnScott pulled out of the hospital parking lot, steered the pickup toward Trapp, and tried to lose himself in the hypnotic drive across flat terrain. He didn't want to think. Or feel. Or hurt. He wished he could drive indefinitely, far away from Fawn Blaylock. So fragile, so easily influenced, and when she held the baby in her arms, she only became more beautiful.

He prayed. Right there in the truck, driving down the highway. He wanted the best for Fawn, but apparently her self-esteem had sent her running back to Tyler and his blasted security. He gripped the steering wheel, thinking the kid seemed more consumed with himself than with the good of the baby or Fawn. But JohnScott knew from experience that God could make something out of a mess of flesh.

He stopped the truck in front of his double-wide. As the engine died down, so did his hope. He peered thoughtfully at his home, then around the cab of his truck, and finally up the road to his parents' small house. No, he had nothing to offer Fawn, and he had been a fool to ever consider she might want him.

He fingered his key chain, hanging from the ignition. The idea of going inside his house depressed him. A three-bedroom setup he undoubtedly would never share with anyone. He would stay close to his parents and look after them as long as they lived, and then he'd be older, set in his ways, even more settled into his bachelor lifestyle. Get up in the morning. Work all day. Head home to a book or a show. Go to bed and start over the next day.

He stared at his front door, but he couldn't go inside. Couldn't take on that life just yet.

He started the truck and backed away, avoiding his folks' place, too. He wouldn't check the cattle or rework the back gate or set out a new salt lick. He could do all that later. It would still be there. Even as he headed back up the Caprock, he knew it was irrational, but one more visit to her place wouldn't hurt. After that, he'd embrace his destiny. Then he'd be good for it.

When he pulled into the front yard, he felt the stillness. The house lay deserted, of course, because Fawn was at the hospital. With Tyler. She had Neil and Susan, for what they were worth. And Ruthie. Even his own mother was there. To be so alone, Fawn had quite a matrix of people taking care of her. She didn't need him.

He slammed the truck door, startling himself with its hollow echo. The wind breezed lightly in contrast to the blustery sand fiasco of earlier in the afternoon. The temperature was cooler than average, and he knew it had gotten close to freezing in the night. Summer had come to an end, autumn had set in, and winter would blast by soon enough. Nothing stayed the same for long.

He slumped against the truck and looked around the yard, now standing empty except for the old woodpile in the side yard, not twenty yards from her back porch. He really ought to move it farther from the house because the stack would undoubtedly attract reptiles. He spit in the sand. She would need a fresh woodpile come winter. He could keep a handful of logs in the house when winter set in and leave the bulk out in the pasture. Away from Fawn and the baby.

He caught himself. He wouldn't be doing that.

Most likely Tyler wouldn't leave her here a week, much less till winter. In fact, she might not return to this house at all after she left the hospital.

He plucked his cap from his head, and dust sprinkled his cheeks. He'd showered, but after he saw Fawn with Tyler, he had changed out of the clean scrubs and back into his work clothes, and his cap was still caked from the storm. He slammed it against his thigh three times and then dusted the resulting red powder from his jeans. He imagined Fawn's giggle, and he ran a hand through his unruly curls and shoved the cap back down to his ears.

He might as well check on Rowdy.

The doorknob turned easily in his hand, and he shook his head at Fawn's irresponsibility. But then he realized the lock was broken. He made a mental note to repair it as soon as possible, but when he turned around, the boxes of baby goods assaulted him. He had forgotten about that. The stuff turned his stomach, and he gritted his teeth as the dog nuzzled his palm.

At least Rowdy wanted to see him. In his slow-moving canine way, the dog bestowed all kinds of affection on JohnScott. Sniffing his boots, sitting at his feet, looking up at him expectantly. "I know, boy. It's just me this time." He patted the dog's head and went to the kitchen to fumble around until he found a bag of dog food. "This'll make you feel better, though." JohnScott wished he had a good plate of chicken-fried steak to make himself feel better.

After spending thirty minutes getting things ready for Fawn's return, he patted Rowdy. "Sorry, buddy. You're staying." Walking to the truck, he opened the door quickly, planning to drive away and never come back. Instead, he stood with one hand on the door handle, staring into space. He reached behind the seat and retrieved his work gloves, then marched to the rotted woodpile and started moving it to the side pasture.

The physical labor felt therapeutic in a way, and he lost himself in the work, his thoughts temporarily suspended as his brain mapped out the details of the move. The logs that were still usable could be shifted against the fence, close enough to the gate so as to be easily accessible. But some of the smaller logs were so deteriorated, they fell apart in his hands. He would need to shovel the rot into a pile and burn it later or spread it over the pasture for mulch. But he didn't mind the work. He wanted to labor away every memory of Fawn. Every image of her hesitant smile, every kick he had felt from the baby.

He fell into a mindless routine of loading the wheelbarrow, trekking across the bumpy pasture to unload it, and then trekking back. He'd made about fifteen trips when he stopped for a rest. He removed his cap and let the breeze cool his scalp. In another thirty minutes or so, he'd go in the house for a drink and let Rowdy out. He replaced his cap and reached for another log.

Past his gloved hand, gray bark slithered near the base of the woodpile, and even without a telltale rattle, he knew what he'd seen.

He backed up and surveyed the pile. Apparently he had been right to want to move the wood farther from the house.

He retrieved his J-hook out of the truck, and after gently moving a few more logs, he captured the elusive reptile. Part of him wanted to kill the beast. He wanted to hurt something because of the pain he felt and to purge himself of his bitterness toward Tyler. Instead, he trapped it in a five-gallon bucket he had in the back of his truck. The lid no longer snapped on tightly, so he rested a large rock on top.

He would have a hard time getting the thing off the property. The lid wouldn't stay on past the front yard, and he could hardly leave it at the house for someone to stumble upon. No matter. He'd figure that out after he got the woodpile relocated. He busied himself with logs again but heard a faint buzzing before he even got the wheelbarrow full.

Not his day.

When he stepped away from the pile and surveyed the wood, his stomach tightened. Bark appeared to be in motion in two different places, but the skin of the snakes blended so well with the wood, he could barely make them out. One of them slithered beneath a rocky ledge that had been partially covered with wood for decades. In the past hour, JohnScott had exposed it.

From a safe distance, he squatted and peered into the musty-smelling crevice, but he was too far away and couldn't make anything out. The woodpile now lay motionless. If Clyde were right, then the snakes wanted away from him as much as he wanted away from the snakes.

He walked back to his truck, scanning the terrain as he went, laughing at himself for being so antsy. He leaned the seat of his truck forward, digging through farm supplies until he found his old six-volt flashlight. He flicked the switch but had to hit the flashlight against his palm a few times before it shone brightly.

He returned to the woodpile, eased a tiny bit closer than last time, and shined the light into the crevice. He sensed movement, but the flashlight went off again. He popped it against his thigh until it came on, and then he leaned closer to the crevice, his head almost against the ground.

What he saw sent shivers up his spine, and he fell backward and away from the woodpile, scurrying on all fours before he leaped to his feet and ran another ten yards. He breathed deeply and jerked around to check the ground around him. The flashlight lay near the wheelbarrow, still shining brightly, mocking him as he pulled out his cell phone.

He slowly walked to his truck, stunned from the fear of what might have happened to Fawn. He pushed a few buttons on his phone.

"Clyde, it's me." He pulled his shirt away from his chest. "I'm out at Fawn's place. Pretty sure I stumbled on the diamondback den."

"Thank the Lord," Clyde said. "Where is it?"

"Under the wood—" A much-too-close angry rattle shook JohnScott's nerves, and he spun around. The lid of the five-gallon bucket lay toppled on the ground, but before he could locate the snake, a violent pain shot through his calf with the burning pressure of a red-hot coal.

JohnScott dropped the phone.

CHAPTER FORTY-FIVE

"You mean JohnScott was at the hospital—the hospital we just left—and you didn't tell me?"

"Fawn ... darlin' ... you need to get on home." Velma rotated the steering wheel on her Chevy, and Ruthie turned around to peer in the backseat.

She sifted her fingers through Nathan's hair. "JohnScott said the hospital's no place for a baby. All those germs."

"But he's okay?"

"He'll be fine." Velma's statement drifted as though it needed an anchor to weigh it down. To make it believable.

"They say the critter didn't get a good hold on him," Ruthie said. "Only one fang made it through his boot. And the ambulance got there fast with a shot of antivenin."

I shuddered. "Why was he even at my house yesterday?"

Velma and Ruthie looked at each other.

"What are you not telling me?"

Ruthie fiddled with her ponytail. "When we asked him why he disappeared after he showered, he wouldn't answer. He only said things weren't going to work out for the two of you."

Velma gripped the steering wheel with one fist at twelve o'clock. "Makes me want to knock a harelip on that boy. Snake or no snake."

I took a deep breath as we turned onto the gravel road leading to my house. "When you hear what I have to say, you may want to knock me instead."

"Aw, girlie, don't go talking that way."

I couldn't bear her kind words, and I blurted my confession quickly. "Tyler kissed me."

They were paralyzed in the front seat, and I wondered if they were holding their breath.

"At the hospital. After the baby came." I rushed the last of it.

Ruthie let her hand fall to her lap, but Velma reached back blindly and patted my knee. "I bet you have a good explanation." She peered at me in the rearview mirror. "Don't you?"

I shrugged and looked away. "I didn't kiss him back." It seemed like a bad idea to tell them about Tyler's strange behavior. It felt like an excuse. "He didn't ask. He just did it."

"Sounds like Tyler," Ruthie mumbled.

Velma scowled. "Did you set him straight?"

"I tried, but he wouldn't listen."

Ruthie looked over her shoulder, and her lips quivered as she suppressed a smile. "And JohnScott saw him kiss you."

"He'll probably never speak to me again. I know your cousin seems confident, but he actually has an insecure streak."

Velma popped her hand against the steering wheel. "Girl, you're right when you say that boy is insecure, but he also has a logical mind. I suggest you grab him by the collar and lay it out for him. As long as it's the truth, he'll come around."

We eased past the cliff and pulled into the yard, where Clyde's sedan was parked haphazardly next to Dodd's El Camino and, farther past them, two pickups I didn't recognize. I leaned forward. "What's all this?"

Silence filled the car. "Well, it sure ain't a welcoming committee," Velma said. "Come on. Let's get inside out of the wind."

"But what's going on?"

Ruthie squinted. "Clyde said it had something to do with the snake that bit JohnScott yesterday."

I laid a hand across the baby's car seat. "Didn't they catch it?"

"Um … I'm not sure."

I peered at the vehicles, and a cool sensation washed over me as I realized Clyde—*my biological father*—was here at my house.

And he didn't know I knew.

I laughed nervously, and Ruthie raised an eyebrow. "What's funny?"

"It's too much, you know? What next?"

I followed them to the steps, looking on and under the porch, wondering where JohnScott had found the snake.

"Oh, Fawn. You got a bassinet." Ruthie squealed as she entered the house, but then she hesitated, surveying the living room with a confused frown. "And a *lot* of other stuff."

"Tyler's doing. Oh—" I stood in the doorway and looked across the room at the bassinet, fully assembled. "Who finished putting it together?"

Velma grunted. "That would be the insecure, logical one."

"But …" I stared at the baby bed, perplexed.

His mother patted my shoulder and reached for the car seat. "When JohnScott's upset, he works."

"He works?"

"Yes." Ruthie nodded.

Velma talked baby talk as she unbuckled Nathan. "And when he's frustrated, he works. And when he's irritated, he works. And when he's sad, he works hardest of all."

I settled into the recliner. "That can't be right. He works every time he comes over here. Has ever since I moved in."

Each of them looked at me with an eyebrow raised.

"He works?" I asked feebly.

"He works when he's trying to solve a problem, and you've been his biggest problem so far." Ruthie looked at the bassinet. "But I think he's getting things figured out."

"That boy of mine hit a little snag, what with that kiss—and the snakebite—but he'll get back on track." Velma laid the baby in my arms. "Time for a feeding. I'm heading out back to see what's going on."

I shivered as I pulled Nathan close. They could be wrong about JohnScott. He might not work things out logically.

Ruthie brought me a glass of ice water from the kitchen. "Georgia said drink."

"And what Georgia says do, I must do." I didn't miss the straight-talking nurse, and thinking of her reaction to Tyler's kiss reminded me of the fragility of my relationship. "She called me a reality-TV star."

"Did she?" Ruthie snickered, but when she looked at me, her smile faded. "JohnScott'll come around, Fawn."

"You think?"

"Momma says she's never seen him like this. Not that he's dated much, but he's never treated another girl like he treats you."

My bottom lip pulled between my teeth. "How is your mom? You don't talk about her much."

Ruthie frowned. "Are you changing the subject?"

"Maybe." The recliner creaked beneath me as I rocked. "People are saying she's with Clyde."

"Not a chance." She dug through a shopping bag, perusing the baby items. "She's still waiting for Daddy to come back."

"After twenty years?"

"Fourteen."

Emptiness swept through me as I considered Lynda Turner. Neil had dumped her, and then later, her husband abandoned her.

"So how does he treat me?"

"Who … JohnScott?" Ruthie held up a footed sleeper. "Like he would do anything to make you happy. Anything in the world."

Anything except talk to me.

"Why did they hold him overnight if the snakebite wasn't bad?"

She sighed. "They wanted to give him more antivenin injections."

I leaned back, visualizing JohnScott sitting next to me sipping coffee.

The back door opened behind me, and Ruthie smiled. "Hey, Clyde. Come on in."

I shifted the baby to my lap as my pulse pounded. In the past Clyde had made me uncomfortable, but now that I knew the truth about him, I felt nothing but anticipation. Like Christmas morning and the first day of school and homecoming all rolled into one.

He ducked his head in greeting, and his eyes bounced from Ruthie to me and then to the baby, where they stayed. "Heard everything went dandy for you and the little one."

I tilted him toward Clyde. "Other than coming in the middle of a dust storm."

"In less than two hours." Ruthie squatted to pet Rowdy.

"Two hours." Clyde hummed. "Well, I guess that's to be expected."

"Yeah, my mother delivered me real quick."

"I never knew that," Ruthie said.

I wiped a drop of milk from Nathan's mouth. "Yep." I looked at Clyde, wondering how many details he knew about my mother's pregnancy and delivery. A chill crept down my arms. It all seemed so absurd. Humiliating. Unforgivable. "Clyde, have a seat."

"Oh no, ma'am." He hadn't taken his eyes off the baby. "I couldn't do that. You must be tuckered out."

"I'm tired, but I can't settle down." And I had too many questions. About the snakes, about JohnScott, about the trucks in my yard. About my mother. "You can hold him."

His eyebrows lifted with the hungry anticipation of a child in a toy store, but he shook his head. "Naw, I'd probably get him dirty." He leaned closer, and his blond hair fell to either side of his face. "Look at his little fists. He's all pink and everything. What's his name?"

"Nathan."

"That's good. Does he have a middle name?"

Ruthie huffed. "She won't tell any of us."

"His name is Clyde," I blurted before my courage waned. "Nathan Clyde Blaylock."

Ruthie stared between the two of us, but Clyde's gaze never wavered from the baby. His eyes filled with tears, and he stood motionless as though the slightest movement might shatter his strength. Then he looked at me hesitantly, fearfully, a blend of doubt and hope falling across his eyes.

"Mom told me," I said softly.

His face turned dark and his cheeks trembled and he nodded firmly. "He's a fine boy, Fawn."

Ruthie slipped from the room, the back door opening and closing quietly, and she left me alone with him. Alone with my father. My dad. I couldn't imagine ever calling him either.

The purr of the air conditioner shifted to a low hum as the compressor cycled, its predictable regularity quieting my blaring thoughts. Thoughts of the two men who called me their daughter. They couldn't have been more different.

Nathan squirmed in his sleep, gave a disgusted half sigh, then settled back into his dream.

The corner of Clyde's mouth lifted as he ran a callused finger across the swaddled blanket, but then he straightened suddenly. "I'm so sorry. About everything."

The pain chiseled on his face made me want to hug him, but I didn't. He may have been my father, but I still barely knew him. "It's all right."

"I want to make it up to you. Or if you don't want the truth out, I'll take it to my grave." He waved toward the back door. "Ruthie and them won't talk."

After the emotional tornado I had endured the past two days, Clyde's simple compassion soothed my frayed emotions like a warm bath. "I don't want any more secrets."

"All right, then, but if there's anything I can do, just let me know." His eyes searched the room. "Do you need another air conditioner? Or maybe a space heater now that the nights are cool? This place could use a lot more work."

I stared at him as one more piece of my life fell into place. "You own this house."

I wouldn't have thought a man that large could shrink so dramatically, as though humiliated by his own good deeds. "It belonged to my grandpappy. Guess that would make him your great-grand." He scratched the side of his neck. "Wish I had something nicer for you."

"You've seen the view. It doesn't get much better than that."

He gazed out the window. "No, I don't suppose it does."

"There is one thing you can do for me."

"Anything."

I smiled. "I just want to know what's going on in my yard."

"Nobody told you?"

"They act like it's the apocalypse."

"Don't want to scare you, I reckon." He took three steps across the room and then paced back. "JohnScott came across the rattlesnake den out near your woodpile."

If he had said those words to me a month ago, I would've reacted in horror, but now the news only perturbed me. My emotional energy level couldn't take another hit. "The den you searched for years ago?"

"That's the one. Been there thirty years or more."

My scalp tingled as I recalled what he had told me about snakes returning to their den every year. "Were there very many?"

Clyde blew air through his teeth. "I called a couple hunter friends to come out and help. Between the three of us, I think we've done all we can. Dodd and Grady are out there taking pictures with their cell phones."

"But you got all the snakes?"

"Probably not. The gas we use drove most of 'em out, and we snared 'em. Others will fall asleep and come out later. But don't worry, when those wake up, they'll leave and stay far away till the den airs out. That could take a year or more."

I nibbled a fingernail, trying to get my mind around all he said. "So what did you do with the snakes?"

"Loaded them in the vehicles. We'll take 'em out when we go."

Other than Velma's Chevy and my Mustang, four cars were parked in my yard. My voice broke. "*Four* vehicles?"

"Aw, Fawn." Clyde ran a hand over his whiskers. "We've corralled about sixty so far."

"*Sixty?*" My skin jittered as though spiders crawled all over me.

He lowered himself to one knee so he would be on my level. "You could stay with Ansel and Velma for a few days."

I glanced out the window. "But this is my home."

"JohnScott said you would say that."

My heart tugged. "Is he really all right? Velma and Ruthie act like he got a bee sting."

Clyde chuckled. "Probably it's worse than they let on ... but not as bad as you imagine. He ought to be home in a few days."

"Do you think I could call him? Get his advice?"

"JohnScott?" He shoved his hands in his pockets. "Better not just yet. His head's in a bit of a scramble still."

I nodded but didn't say anything. If I spoke, I might cry, and if I cried, I might never stop. And if I never stopped, I might die.

Clyde sighed long and full, but his sigh didn't echo the despair I felt. Instead he sounded content. And maybe slightly humored. "Wait and call in a few days."

I fussed with Nathan, trying to stifle my tears so Clyde wouldn't see.

"Velma said she'd stay with you, but I'd feel a lot better if you went on home with her. This place will be safer in a week."

Ansel and Velma's house, right across the pasture from JohnScott's double-wide, suddenly sounded like the best place in the world. "Okay, Clyde. I'll stay with Ansel and Velma."

CHAPTER
FORTY-SIX

JohnScott stayed in the hospital three days, but he wouldn't answer his phone. Ruthie said he was in *a mood* and not to worry, but worry had become my second skin. She and Velma seemed to have divided their caregiving responsibilities. Velma stayed home with Nathan and me, and Ruthie checked on her cousin before and after her classes. When she and Dodd finally drove JohnScott home, I was watching from Velma's living-room window.

Standing on tiptoe, I could see the El Camino stop at the side yard of the double-wide, and JohnScott's silhouette limped across the front deck. Dragonflies swarmed through my lungs as I watched him, but not once did he pause with his hand on the doorknob. Not once did he turn and peer longingly across the pasture to his parents' house, where I waited. Not once.

Ansel said the snakebite was nothing short of a miracle, because only one fang pierced JohnScott's skin. The other one had been found later, stuck in the top edge of his boot. Even though the venom swelled his leg to twice its normal size, there hadn't been enough to do permanent tissue damage. Clyde was given most of the credit because he got there so quick and knew what to do. They were both written up in the *Trapp Times*, and I studied the grainy picture of the coach's leg at least ten times a day.

Beginning on Wednesday, I watched JohnScott's truck as he left for school every morning, and again in the evening as he bumped back home after practice. But he never stopped. Nathan settled into a routine of eating every four hours, round the clock, and Velma deemed him an easy baby. I spent two hours a day online, catching up on my classes as my body transformed from its soft, liquid-feeling state into a form that promised to be firm again at some point in the future.

On Friday morning, Ruthie shoved my feet off the couch and sat down next to me. "It's time you got out of the house. Come with me to the game tonight. It'll do you good."

"I can stay with Nathan," Velma said. "If you feed him right before you leave, you'll have three and a half hours to yourself, if not more."

"I couldn't leave him. Not yet."

"Why?" Ruthie's determined expression told me she had come prepared for battle, and I got the impression she and Velma had planned their attack ahead of time.

"He's not even a week old. He needs his mother."

Velma shuffled around the room, halfheartedly dusting end tables with a crumpled paper towel. "I know you've read those books telling what a momma needs to do for her baby, but sometimes, taking care of yourself helps the little tyke more than anything else."

"I am taking care of myself," I argued. "I eat good food and get plenty of rest. I walk with Rowdy outside in the sunshine, and I'm going a little farther every day."

Ruthie rolled her eyes. "Yeah, you've made it all the way to JohnScott's house and back. But sitting in a rocking chair on his front porch when he's at work is not the healthiest thing emotionally."

My face warmed, and I looked away.

"Forget my moronic cousin, Fawn, and think about something else for a while."

Velma settled in a chair and lifted her slippered feet onto an ottoman. "If you get out, your problems won't seem near so big."

I smiled, not feeling it. "But he won't talk to me. I've left messages."

"He's just stressed from work," Ruthie said. "Put him out of your mind for four hours and give yourself a break."

Work was Ruthie and Velma's number-one excuse for JohnScott's behavior, and when I shoved my self-pity under the rug, I had to admit they were probably right. Even though the Panthers remained undefeated, the anticipation of a winning season left our small community expecting more and more from the coaching staff. The parents demanded more playing time, the boosters demanded more practices, and the other teachers demanded equal time for their own extracurricular events. And no one seemed to care that JohnScott was still recovering from the bite of a western diamondback rattlesnake.

I picked at a hangnail, remembering my prayer that I might become what JohnScott needed. Maybe if I went to the game, if he saw me there, it would somehow be an encouragement to him.

"Okay, I'll do it."

"Excellent," declared Ruthie. "Sophie Snodgrass will never believe you already fit in those fancy jeans of yours."

At Ruthie's insistence, I wore my favorite shirt, a crepe peasant top, which fit differently now that I was nursing, but Velma said it was fine. And I wadded my hair in a messy bun on top of my head, leaving a few stray curls hanging around my neck. I felt like a fake—a liar—dressing up like a college girl when I was really a mom.

Velma pushed us out the door early so we would have time to take a plate of home-cooked chicken strips by the field house. I knew her actions were motivated by something other than JohnScott's hunger, and I only hoped she and Ruthie weren't pushing him too far.

"What if he's not in there?" I quizzed Ruthie as we walked across the parking lot.

"He is. I texted him, and I'll text him again when we get to the door."

"He might send one of the other coaches. Or a player."

"He wouldn't risk his chicken. Velma's cooking is too well known."

My skin jittered. Ruthie wanted to surprise him by bringing me, but now that it came down to it, I wondered if I should go along with it. I might be invading his territory, but the hope of seeing him drew me toward the field house like a colt on a lead rope.

We stood outside the cinder-block building as players in full pads bumped through the metal door, heading toward the field for pregame warm-ups, and my pulse felt like the booming of a bass drum during a halftime show. "Text him again."

"I did."

"He's coming to the door?"

"Relax, Fawn."

And then he was there. Three feet away from me. So close I could have reached out and touched him, hugged him, pressed my nose into that soft spot at the side of his neck that always, *always* sent his arms circling around me. My chest ached when I noticed dark shadows beneath his eyes, but he smiled.

"Thanks, little cous—"

But then the smile lines disappeared. He never took his eyes off Ruthie, but I could clearly see he knew I stood beside her.

"Aunt Velma sends her best," Ruthie said hesitantly. "She said there ought to be enough chicken to share with the ag teacher, should he show up."

"Sounds good." His gaze still hadn't left her face, and he stared blankly, void of emotion. "I'll see you later, Ruthie."

"Is there anything else you need? From the concession stand? Or ... anything?" Her voice trailed, but he had already answered her with a shake of his head.

The door closed behind him, then immediately opened as two linemen stepped past us, but JohnScott had disappeared.

I spun on my heel, then froze. My lungs sucked in oxygen in a deep, uncontrolled spasm, as though someone had forcibly covered my mouth and nose, and I was only just able to escape. A moaning sob floated out with the exhale, and Ruthie grabbed me by the elbow and steered me to the restroom.

By the time we entered the small, stuffy building, tears wouldn't stop spilling down my cheeks no matter how many times I wiped them with the back of my hand.

I dampened my fingertips with water from the faucet and dabbed at mascara even as I kept crying. A few women and girls looked on with interest, and I wanted to end this pitiful performance before anyone else witnessed it.

"I'm so stupid," I whispered. "Stupid."

"Oh no you're not." Ruthie thrust a brown paper towel at me and slammed the handle for another one. "I have never in my life been so angry with that cousin of mine."

"It's not his fault. I shouldn't have come here, not now. He needs to focus on the game." I dropped my voice. "He looked exhausted."

"I don't care if he's tired. I don't care if he was bit by a snake. I don't care if he has half the town breathing down his throat. He has no right to treat you like that." She wiped my cheek with the paper towel, then leaned closer, inspecting my jawline. "Are those bruises?"

"Oh, it's nothing." I ran my palms across my face in an attempt to redistribute my tear-streaked makeup.

"Those are Tyler's fingerprints." She held her own fingers up to my cheek, checking her supposition.

"They're almost gone," I said lightly. "Don't worry about it."

"Fawn ..." She lowered her voice as she glanced toward the toilet stalls. "You said he kissed you, not mauled you."

"He didn't maul me, but when I tried to turn away, he got mad."

"Stop defending him."

I slumped against the sink, peering at myself in the mirror, scrutinizing the yellowish blotches on my chin.

She let out an exasperated sigh. "My idiot cousin better get his act together, or I'm going after him with an electric cattle prod." Shaking her head, she looked at me as though I were hopeless. "Come on, let's go."

We drifted out the door and through the growing crowd, then found an empty spot where we could lean against the chain-link fence adjacent to the concession stand.

In the time we had been in the restroom, the team had huddled around the gate, preparing for their grand entrance. Apparently JohnScott reigned somewhere in their midst, because the mob was growling sporadic responses to his prompts.

I hooked my fingers through the wires of the fence. "It's no wonder he hasn't called me this week."

"No, he should have called you." She stretched her neck, looking into the stands. "Dodd's up there somewhere, saving us seats with Milla and Grady."

"Do you care if we stay down here for a while? I might call Ansel to come pick me up."

She bumped me with her hip. "If you want to go home, I'll take you. Ansel's probably in the recliner holding Nathan, and he won't want to leave."

My eyes watered, but I blinked the sensation away. "Now … don't be talking about my baby, or I'll really want to go home." Suddenly I longed to hold him, rock him, kiss his fluffy hair. Hide away with him.

The team thundered past us, and I watched numbly as JohnScott followed behind the team, limping slightly. He had never even held Nathan.

An accusing snarl right behind me grated my nerves like gravel on asphalt. "Where's my boy, Fawn?"

It was Tyler, and he was drunk again.

His sweaty body pressed me into the fence, and I clung to the wire to keep from veering sideways as his solid arm circled my waist. "Where is he?"

I breathed in his odor, tasting alcohol on my tongue. "Velma's babysitting."

"You shouldn't have left him there, babe."

Ruthie snapped, "The baby's fine."

He wore a muscle shirt in the cool fall air, and as he fisted the top rail of the fence, his bicep, with my named carved on it, lay exposed for everyone to see. The tattoo looked worse than before. He had reopened the wounds, and the letters were blackened with ink and scabs, the skin between them flaring scarlet with infection.

I shifted, trying to pull away from him discreetly, knowing if I made him angry, he would accelerate. "I'm about to go home anyway."

"Home?" His lips pressed into a hard line. "You may be staying at Ansel Pickett's place, but it's sure as heck not your home."

"That's not what I meant."

His fingers slipped beneath my shirt and gripped my belt, yanking me back to his side. "Next time, call me."

As the band began playing the national anthem, I looked past him to the hundreds of people who had turned toward the flag. I trembled, wondering how many of them noticed the tension passing between the three of us standing not thirty feet from the flagpole.

"If you're going to go sleazing around town," Tyler said, "the least you can do is bring the baby to me. I would never leave him alone."

"She didn't leave him alone," Ruthie insisted. "Nathan's perfectly safe with my aunt and uncle."

His eyes hardened into slits, and he leaned across me in slow motion. "Shut up." His gaze traveled down the front of her body before returning to her face. "And stop filling my wife's ears with your trashy lies."

"What are you talking about?" she demanded as the band finished playing. "I don't lie to her. And Nathan isn't alone." She took a step forward and lifted her chin. "And Fawn's not your wife."

With his free hand, Tyler shoved her hard, and she sprawled into a huddle of people behind us. Then he jerked me toward the entrance gate, oblivious to the crowd watching us. "We're leaving, Fawn. We'll get Ty first and then go on home. I've been more than patient."

With both hands I pushed at his arm, but my muscles felt lax and soft, and he only tightened his grip around my waist.

Ruthie struggled to her feet. Several bystanders stepped toward us. And humiliation rippled over me like the soft fluttering of the flag above our heads. Tyler wouldn't get away with this, but I would never live it down either.

"Mr. Cruz, is there a problem?" Eldon Simpson, one of Trapp's two police officers stood in front of us with arms crossed.

I wanted to run, or disappear, or turn into a scissortail and fly away. I could go somewhere nobody knew me, where Nathan and I could live in peace, without anyone watching, judging, talking. Then I would be free.

"Took you long enough to get here, Eldon," Tyler slurred. "But you have other big business to tend to." He guffawed. "Like shoe polish on shop windows."

Eldon nodded. "You all right, Fawn?"

"Ruthie and I were just leaving."

"You hear that?" Eldon's gaze dropped to Tyler's fists, still locked around my waist. "She's leaving with Ruthie."

"No, she's not."

Eldon laid his palm on Tyler's arm. "Go ahead and let go, and we won't have any trouble."

"Get your hands off me, Eldon. I could sue you."

The cop tightened his grip around Tyler's wrist, but the drunk's body convulsed in anger. He lunged at Eldon, pinning me momentarily between the two men before I was shoved toward Ruthie.

CHAPTER
FORTY-SEVEN

When we got back to the Picketts' house, Velma and Ruthie tried to encourage me, saying things weren't as bad as they seemed, but before I went to bed that night, the news reached the house. Tyler had been arrested. And if that weren't enough, the Panthers had barely won the game. With a score of 3–0, Trapp's state ranking fell into question thirty minutes after the final whistle blew.

Velma wrung her hands and fluttered around the kitchen, grumbling to herself and working off her frustrations exactly like her son would have done. Ansel lifted the remote control like a saber, silencing the evening news with a punch of his thumb, but he continued to sit in his new recliner, staring at the blank screen.

I cried myself to sleep.

The town would blame JohnScott. Not only for the scandalously low score but also for the scandal in front of the concession stand. And by association, I would be blamed too. And really ... honestly ... we were both at fault. But I was tired of being put down by people who expected something of me without ever giving in return. And I was finally realizing I didn't have to believe them.

So the next morning, I showered, ran a comb through my hair, and put on jeans and a T-shirt. The baby whimpered in the living room, but he couldn't be hungry, because I'd fed him right before I got in the shower. From the sound of it, Velma rocked him back to sleep.

I flicked off the bathroom light, then stepped down the hallway, expecting to see Velma.

Instead, I saw JohnScott.

My heart quivered, and I put my fingers over my mouth. He had his back to me, and he leaned over Velma's old cradle, rocking it gently.

"He asleep again?" My words came out wobbly.

JohnScott didn't turn around, didn't even flinch. "Yep."

"I was surprised to hear him cry. He ought to sleep for a while. He's got a full tummy."

"He needed to burp. It woke him up."

"Did your mom burp him?"

"Naw, I did it." He looked away from the baby, out the sliding-glass door.

"I'm surprised you knew that's what he needed." I laughed lightly.

"Twelve nieces and nephews." His easy answers couldn't hide the pain in his voice.

I stepped to his side, entering an invisible cloud of tension. He smelled of soap and cologne, which blended with Nathan's baby lotion until I couldn't separate the two and didn't want to.

The baby blanket had come unswaddled, but JohnScott tucked it around the edges. Nathan's lips moved in and out in a blissful nursing dream, and JohnScott moved the pacifier to the corner of the crib.

"He's been like this since birth," I said. "Eats and sleeps."

"Let's hope it lasts."

He still hadn't looked at me, and his disinterest pulled a string of frantic blubberings from my mouth. "You're probably thirsty. I could get you a Dr Pepper. Or some iced coffee. Did your mother already offer you something?"

"She's not here."

"Sure she is."

He ran a hand over his chin. "She left."

I glanced toward the kitchen. It seemed odd Velma would leave without telling me. "She'll be back soon?"

"Not for a while." He stepped to the bookshelf in the corner of the room, favoring his bad leg, then stared blindly at the titles. "I didn't want to bother you, but she told me if I didn't come over here, she'd strip the starter out of my truck." He crossed his arms. "She's done it before."

My fingers tightened around the wooden trim of the cradle. "Very resourceful."

He turned suddenly. "Fawn, everyone and their dog has been telling me you're finished with Tyler, but I don't know what to think. You tell me one thing, and then I see the two of you making out—"

"We were not making out." I deliberately glared at him, partly to convey my disgust and partly to encourage myself I wasn't as tainted as I felt.

He leaned against the wall and peered at me silently. Blankly.

"Come sit down." I motioned to the couch, but when he didn't budge, I sat next to the crib and looked at the baby, gathering strength from his innocence. "When you showed up at the hospital, it felt right and made me happy."

"I was out of line."

"You were the only person I wanted to see," I added hurriedly. "Of course, I needed your mother there. She's a tremendous help with the baby, but you're the only one I wanted, just because."

He sighed, and his muscles thawed with the release of air. "I don't blame you if you want to be with him. He's the father of your baby."

"Please stop calling him that. It makes me sound like I should be on a talk show where families yell at each other on national television." Driven by nervous energy, I stood up abruptly, but then found I had no where to go. And I had no way to escape the tension that hung in the room like a cloud of smoke. "I know you saw him kissing me, but it's not what it looked like."

"How so?" He monotoned the two words, bored, indifferent.

"It's not like I wanted him to kiss me." My words tumbled. "He still insists he's going to take care of me, but I told him again that it isn't going to happen. I don't want to be with him."

JohnScott's shoulders withered.

I walked around the couch and stood on tiptoe, forcing him to look at me. "I don't want to be taken care of the way Tyler would take care of me."

"He's the father of your baby." He winced at his use of the phrase. "That sort of gives him a natural right to a relationship."

"With the baby. Not with me."

He blew air through his teeth. "Tyler Cruz has it all, Fawn. Looks, money, confidence. Girls want guys like him."

"He doesn't have integrity or compassion. And he doesn't love me. Not really."

"But he's the father."

A jab pierced my temple. "Every time you say that, it reminds me I had sex out of wedlock, and I feel like a harlot."

He stepped away from the bookshelf. "You're not … that."

"I feel like it though, so what's the difference?"

He ran a hand through his curls, then sighed, and his next words sounded like a begrudged confession. "The difference is your heart."

"Not everyone sees it that way."

"Of course not." He shrugged. "There's always somebody who will tear you down, but you're a good person. You'll land on your feet."

"Well, I'm not going to land on my feet next to Tyler Cruz." A tear of frustration welled in the corner of my eye. "And if I have to shake you by the shoulders to get you to listen, I'll do it."

The corners of his mouth pulled down, and his eyes locked with mine. He frowned, but in the shadow of his gaze, I saw a dilemma, a debate, as if I were an opposing team that had to be analyzed.

My body felt crippled. I had just threatened to shake him by the shoulders, but his scowl withered my confidence, and I realized there was nothing I could do. I couldn't make him hear me, believe me, love me. He either did or he didn't, and I would have to pick up the pieces and get on with my life either way. The wetness in the corner of my eye grew into a puddle and slid down my cheek.

JohnScott took a step toward me and touched the tear with his fingertip, as though checking to see if it was real. His brows eased.

"You don't have to shake me." His finger trailed across my lips. "I hear you."

I melted into him, slipped my arms around his waist, and nestled beneath his chin. We hadn't hugged since the baby's birth, and without Nathan between us, I felt incredibly close, almost as though I stood inside him. "I've missed you."

He ran a hand through my wet hair and pressed his lips against my forehead.

"JohnScott, I've had so much on my mind. Motherhood isn't what I expected. It's so much different and so much better. And your mom and Ruthie have been great, but I wanted to share it with you." I kissed his chest, then rested my ear against the spot, listening to the steady rhythm of his heart. "Ruthie said you were sad."

His hand trailed up and down my back. "I have a confession to make."

I lifted my head to meet his gaze.

"I'm a pouter."

"I'll say you are."

"I like to work through my problems, but I'm not sure that's what I've been doing the past week."

I fingered his sleeve. "I won't complain about your juvenile behavior if you won't complain about mine."

"Deal." He pulled me against his chest and rested his chin on the top of my head, and we swayed in the corner of the living room. My mind emptied and my heart settled, and I clung to him, feeling like a rescued child.

"Ruthie said you have bruises."

"It's nothing."

He bent over me, running his fingertips across my jaw with feather-soft tenderness. Then he kissed each yellow spot. "He's not going to get close enough to hurt you again."

As I stood in the shelter of his arms, my paranoia about Tyler seemed trivial. "I'm worried about you."

"Me?" He laid his palms firmly on my shoulders. "Oh, you mean my leg? It's okay now." He chuckled. "But when it happened, it felt like a branding iron."

"Not your leg. Football. It's eating you alive."

"Yep." He brushed a strand of hair away from my face, and his bewildered gaze traveled to my ear as he gently nudged the wayward curl behind it. "The school board, more or less, told me to get my act together or else."

"Or else what?"

"I didn't ask." A corner of his mouth wrinkled. "I think I'd better take these boys to the play-offs or look for another job."

"If that's all they want, you have nothing to worry about. I thought you were going to say they told you to break it off with me."

"At this point"—he chuckled—"I think they've decided I'd be more productive if I kept you."

"You'd be more productive if you would talk to me."

He rested his forehead gently against mine. "I didn't want to look weak."

I shook my head, rubbing my nose against his. "Not weak, just real."

"Real." His mouth grazed my temple, then circled my cheekbone before settling familiarly against my lips. His kiss felt soft and warm and cautious, but as seven days' worth of fear and doubt fell from my shoulders, my response gradually escalated, and I silently conveyed the desperation of all the words we had left unsaid.

Settling back against the bookshelf, he drew me closer, answering my unspoken plea as his lips begged for confirmation. And I wordlessly answered him, willing him to believe my regrets, my intentions, my love.

When the baby cried, we pulled away from each other and looked toward the crib. We couldn't see Nathan, but the cradle shook slightly from his kicking, and we both smiled.

CHAPTER
FORTY-EIGHT

Tyler reached for the binoculars on his dashboard, then slammed the door of his truck. He hadn't counted on being jailed for the night, but it didn't matter. He'd still had plenty of time to set things up over at Fawn's house before she returned from the Picketts'.

Earlier that day, he had spread a new tablecloth on her kitchen table, and right in the center, he positioned a pot of flowers, a live plant so it wouldn't wilt. Beneath the salt-and-pepper shakers, he placed a greeting card and a new Bible. Then he filled her small freezer with dinners and her refrigerator with milk and fruit.

Before he let himself out, he set up the baby monitor, taking one of the receivers to keep for himself. And so it wouldn't be obvious what he had done, he took time to unpack a few other baby items, making it appear he had thoughtfully prepared for his son's arrival. He considered leaving the diamond ring on the table next to the flowers but thought better of it. He wanted to see the expression on her face when she saw the size of the rock.

She had come home this afternoon. He knew she'd come back to him eventually. She spent the first thirty minutes walking around the front yard, carrying his son in one arm and pointing at the horizon with the other. Tyler watched her through his new field glasses, itching to give her the ring and get his life moving forward, but he bided his time. He had things to take care of before that.

She went inside the house, and since the sun hadn't set, she was out of his line of sight. But no matter, he could listen on the monitor. A cloud of dust appeared to his left, and he gritted his teeth as the coach's truck approached the house. Tyler needed that jerk out of the picture, so he had a plan for JohnScott Pickett. Or rather for the brakes of his truck.

His plan seemed simple. When Fawn and JohnScott were busy in the house, he would slip over there and tamper with JohnScott's truck. Tyler had parked closer to her house this time, only a half mile away in a mesquite thicket. Neither of them would know he had been there, and the coach's brakes would fail a few minutes after he left the house. He'd probably make it to the highway, accelerate to fifty-five, and lose control.

If his father were still alive, Byron Cruz would have slapped Tyler on the back and said, *Well done, Son.*

Tyler snickered when he realized the new binoculars were stronger than the last pair. He opened the door of his truck, flipped on the monitor, and reached for a beer.

"Fawn, I'll change Nathan's diaper." JohnScott's voice sounded muffled and distant over the intercom, and Tyler figured the idiot was in the bedroom.

He clenched the beer can and cursed. This would be the last day JohnScott Pickett would find himself anywhere near his wife's bed.

She answered him, and her voice sounded nearer, louder. "You change diapers?"

"Well … only wet ones."

"Impressive." She moved farther away, probably nearer to the coach, and when the baby fussed, both of them made whiny baby-talk sounds.

"He's probably hungry," crooned Fawn. "Then he'll be sleepy."

"I'll stay in here." JohnScott's voice got loud, and Tyler turned down the volume on the receiver.

Silence for a few seconds, and then Fawn followed him. "Would it bother you if I … just covered with a blanket?" The baby's cries almost drowned out her words. "I hate for you to sit in here all by yourself."

"Whatever you want to do is fine with me."

Tyler squirmed in the seat of the pickup. Of course the coach didn't mind ogling a half-dressed woman. Fawn may not have had the body she had a year ago, but she was still gorgeous, and the pervert had no business being in the room when she fed her baby. *Their baby.* His and Fawn's.

She laughed nervously. "This is all so new to me."

"Not to worry." Tyler heard a thump, and then JohnScott said, "I'll put this swing together and pretend you're not here."

The baby finally stopped crying, and Tyler turned the monitor back up a notch, guzzling the rest of his drink.

"Who put these other things together?"

Fawn hesitated so long, Tyler figured she hadn't heard him. "I guess Tyler. He must have stopped by sometime before I came home from your folks' place."

Tyler heard two clanking sounds and then a click as though two parts of the swing had been snapped together.

"I don't like it," JohnScott said.

Fawn answered quickly. "He got these things ready for Nathan and left some groceries and flowers. It's probably his way of apologizing for making a scene at the game."

"Fact is, we don't know what he meant. Baby toys and groceries tell me one thing. Flowers say something different."

Tyler tested the binoculars, but the sun hadn't set enough for him to see in the house. Another few minutes, and he should be golden.

A stretch of silence followed, broken only by the squeaking recliner, and Tyler pictured the coach reading instructions. "If I start putting all these gadgets together now, I should have them finished by Nathan's first birthday."

Fawn laughed, and Tyler gripped the monitor tightly. *She shouldn't laugh at something so stupid.*

When she stopped, she said, "I really ought to take some of it back to the store. Do you think I could, even without the receipts?"

"Will he mind?"

Finally Tyler could see them through the living-room window. Fawn rocked the baby in the recliner, and the coach stood with his back to her. The flake must have come straight from football practice, because he wore coaching shorts and a Trapp High School polo shirt.

"I don't know." Fawn's shoulders slumped.

JohnScott turned and watched her for a few seconds. "Hey."

She looked up at him with a slight smile, and the fool went to her.

"Everything's going to be fine, you know." He kissed her on the lips.

Tyler had the urge to pull JohnScott out of the house and beat him to death. The coach had nerve to kiss Fawn while Tyler's baby sucked on her.

Sickening.

When the baby made a smacking sound, JohnScott cleared his throat and turned away.

"About time you got embarrassed," Tyler yelled. "Get *away* from her."

Tyler clenched the steering wheel with one hand, calming his anger while he watched what happened behind the coach's back. Fawn laid the baby across her lap and adjusted her shirt and underthings. He only saw skin for a second, but he could see that Fawn wasn't flat-chested like she used to be.

"Here, let me burp the little guy."

When Fawn smiled at JohnScott again, Tyler spit in the sand.

The coach reached for the baby and walked to the window, holding him like a receiver cradling a ball. "You're a good boy, Nathan. You're going to grow up and be a strong Christian man, but before that, you need to burp so your momma won't worry about your tummy." He lifted the baby to his shoulder. "That's better. Now you can take a little nap in your bassinet. Notice how nicely it's put together. So sturdy."

Fawn stood behind him, and the coach kept talking. "You're going to need a tough cradle, because you're going to grow, and then you'll be a big, strong baby. And when you're in high school, you can play football for Uncle JohnScott. You'll probably be a lineman."

Tyler gritted his teeth. Not only would his son never play ball for Trapp High School, but he would never call JohnScott Pickett *uncle*.

Fawn picked up a blanket. "How could he be a lineman? Tyler and I aren't that big."

"You've got a point." JohnScott held the baby out from his chest, looking into his face. "You might not be a lineman, but what about a running back? Or a receiver? Or the quarterback?" He pulled the baby close to his face. "Or if you're really lucky, we might let you be the *kicker*."

Tyler came out of the truck, breathing deeply. The coach wasn't merely trying to take Fawn. He had set his sights on the baby, too, but Tyler would never let another man lay claim to his son. A new idea formed in his mind. An idea so obvious he didn't know why it hadn't occurred to him before—much better than the brakes on the coach's truck.

He lifted the binoculars and stared.

JohnScott swayed with the baby in his arms while Fawn hovered near his elbow. The three of them were wrapped in a nauseous, sappy glow that made Tyler spew curse words like a Fourth of July fireworks show. He stepped back to the truck so he could hear what they were saying.

"He's about asleep again," Fawn murmured.

"I have that effect on children."

"It's true." She took the baby from him and laid him in the bassinet. "I slept through most of your history classes."

JohnScott laughed but caught himself and quieted, and then the two of them stood over the bassinet, gazing down at the baby. Then the coach slipped his arm around Fawn's shoulders and hunched over her like a vampire attacking his prey.

Tyler leaned against the hood of the truck, intrigued. Then he pressed the binoculars against the bridge of his nose and watched closely as Coach Pickett ravaged Fawn for what would probably be the last time.

When the animal finally released her, JohnScott asked, "You holding up all right?"

Tyler turned up the volume on the monitor when the wind whirred through the cab of his truck.

"Besides being exhausted all the time?" Fawn said. "Yes, but I feel a little stir-crazy."

JohnScott rubbed the back of her head, and Tyler imagined her hair getting tangled. Fawn would hate that.

"Let's go for a walk."

Tyler cackled. "Excellent idea, Coach."

Fawn stared at the baby. "I couldn't leave Nathan."

"Five minutes. And we'll stay in sight of the house." JohnScott reached toward the end table by the window and unhooked the second monitor from the charger. "You'll be able to hear him the entire time."

Fawn peered hesitantly into the bassinet, and Tyler cursed. "Go on the stupid walk, Fawn. Go with the stupid, stupid coach."

"It's getting cool outside."

"You can wear my hoodie."

"I guess five minutes wouldn't hurt." She spread a blanket over the baby, and a few seconds later, she and JohnScott went out the back door.

Tyler counted to twenty-five before starting his truck and speeding toward the house. He only had a few seconds, and he didn't dare pass up the opportunity. He would rescue his son, and then Fawn would see how things ought to be. He would use the car seat, and then she would see what a good father he was. He might even buckle up himself. Tyler laughed, feeling an instant high.

Fawn and Ty would be his at last.

He slid to a stop in front of the house, and the light from JohnScott's flashlight swung lazily, reassuring Tyler that they were still walking away from the house. Thank God for the wind whooshing through the cedars, blowing dust past the house and giving Tyler more time under the cover of its sound.

He pulled the screen door open, gripping it firmly so the wind couldn't wrestle it out of his hand. Then he stepped into the dark room and closed it softly behind him. His hands shook uncontrollably, and he studied them for a brief second, feeling another charge of adrenalin. The porch light cast shadows across the living room, and Tyler could just make out the bassinet.

He stepped toward his son.

CHAPTER
FORTY-NINE

"Stop worrying, Fawn." JohnScott tapped the screen on his cell phone as he opened the back gate. "Only five minutes."

"Five minutes there and five minutes back, or five total?" The wind swept a curl across my eyes, and I turned into the onslaught, letting the air hit me full in the face. Stress seeped from my pores, spiraled down my hair, and snapped from the end of each wind-tossed curl.

"How about four each way?"

"Good deal."

JohnScott led me in a wide berth around the pile of bark that had once been my woodpile.

"Is it safe to walk at this time of day?" I asked.

"Not the best idea we've had, but at least there's a full moon."

"We need Rowdy."

"I'll bring him back from Mom's house tomorrow. Should've already." JohnScott activated the flashlight on his cell phone and slipped his hand into mine.

My body had almost gotten back to normal, and I had pent-up energy longing for release. The four-minute time limit created a mental safety net around my maternal instincts, and I picked up my pace.

"Slow down," JohnScott said. "I can't keep up."

"You too old?"

"Now ... don't go there."

"You listening for the monitor?"

He held the receiver to his ear. "Not sure I'll be able to hear much in this wind." He adjusted the volume control, and we both heard the baby cry slightly.

My heart lurched, and I spun around and began walking back to the house.

JohnScott laughed. "So much for our four-minute sprint."

I reached for his wrist and turned his phone to see the screen. "Three and a half. That's not bad."

The baby cried louder, and my milk let down, instantly moistening the pads I had placed inside my bra. *Thank goodness I had done that.* The personal problems associated with breastfeeding were not something I wanted to share with JohnScott.

I pressed my forearms against my chest, pretending to straighten my necklace, but when I heard a man's voice over the intercom, all thoughts of leaking milk were lost.

"Hush up, boy."

Gravel ground beneath my feet as I jerked to a stop, gripping the intercom between sweaty palms. "What's Tyler doing here?"

JohnScott kept walking, faster now. "Probably just came to see Nathan."

We were halfway back to the house. *No need to worry.*

But when Tyler spoke again, his stilted voice made my skin go cold. "Daddy's here, Ty, and you're never going to be a kicker."

In the moonlight, JohnScott looked like a mountain lion, ready to pounce, and when the screen door slammed, he took off at a sprint, his flashlight swinging crazily as he hurdled cactus.

I ran after him, stumbling across the moonlit pasture with my soft insides jiggling in protest. But even as I considered the possibility of crossing the path of a rattlesnake, anxiety propelled me faster and faster. Branches lashed my shoulders, and tall grass slapped against my jeans.

The glow of Tyler's headlights shone around the side of the house, and guttural sobs choked from my throat. My legs felt weighted as I clunked past the new woodpile, feeling clumsy and inadequate and slow.

JohnScott charged around the corner just as Tyler's truck spun, sending a shadow of dust into the wind.

He wouldn't take the baby, would he? My chest heaved as I ran across the front yard. "Where's Nathan?" I screamed the words and lunged toward the porch. My baby would be safely in his crib, right where I left him. But JohnScott grabbed my arm, wrenching me toward his truck, and as my skin burned from his grip, I remembered Ruthie giving me a two-handed sunburn in first grade.

"Get in!" He lunged for the driver's door, but time moved in slow motion, and a mired-in-quicksand frustration pressed against me as though I were in a nightmare. My fingers clawed at the handle, but I couldn't take my eyes off the road.

Tyler's brake lights fishtailed lazily, illuminating the jagged drop-off each time the truck swung to the left. A low grinding filled my ears as the tires locked and slid across gravel, but the sound gave way abruptly, unbelievingly when the truck sailed over the edge and into a free fall. For a long moment, I heard nothing but the soft purr of the engine echoing against the caliche walls.

My feet were cemented to the ground, but I took one faltering step before the oxygen around me thickened with the paralyzing racket of metal on rock. The vehicle carrying my baby—my world— had just dropped fifteen feet and slammed to the uneven ground below. I could no longer see the truck, but I stared into the blackness as the Ford rolled end over end down the Caprock's steep decline, its taillights casting a beam into the night sky like a grand-opening celebration.

Suddenly the wind slacked, and sounds became amplified in my ears. The horrifying crunch of the truck's frame. The shatter of breaking glass. The thick snap of a cedar. The rumble of a small avalanche of rocks and pebbles.

Then horrific, mind-numbing, tangible silence pressed against me, holding me captive and suffocating me with the odor of gasoline.

I screamed.

And I screamed.

And I screamed.

CHAPTER FIFTY

Freezing water coursed through my veins, and I ran blindly, not heeding my body's angry protests at being pushed, not feeling the ice that silently froze my heart as I pictured Nathan dead at the base of the Caprock.

When I got to the curve in the road, I saw the truck halfway down, its chrome trim reflecting the moon. It lay on its side, and I registered absentmindedly that a squatty cedar had stopped it from falling the remaining distance. My heart raced as I jogged farther, but when I heard the baby crying, I fell to my hands and knees, scurrying along the brink of the cliff. Thorns cut through my jeans at the knee, and rocks pressed into the soft skin of my palms, but I hardly noticed. Nathan's wails swelled on the wind and then faded each time the breeze shushed past.

The sound of his crying was like nothing I had ever heard. Not the day he was born. Not when he had nightmares. Not even when he got shots. His screams mimicked the cries of a trapped animal, and the sound drove me into a frenzy of desperation. I lowered a foot down the side of the ridge, unable to get to him fast enough.

But then JohnScott's thick arms clamped around my waist, and he picked me up, lifting my feet off the ground. I kicked him. I jerked from side to side. I knocked my head against his chin in a frantic effort to get away. To get to Nathan.

"Fawn, stop!"

I tried to yell. To tell him to get his hands off, but all that came out of my mouth was a strangled shriek.

"Let me find a way down." He held me firmly, coaxing me to comply. "You can't go jumping off the Caprock."

He was shaking too. His arms, his voice, his confidence, all wavered uncharacteristically, and I stopped thrashing. "Hurry, JohnScott."

He ran along the lip, hunched over, peering at rocks and bushes and crags. "Call 911. Tell them to hurry."

I stumbled behind him, trying to still my trembling hands enough to work my cell phone. The screen prompts I manipulated every day now made no sense, and I stared at the keypad, urging my brain to process what the numbers meant. It took me hours to dial. Days to connect to an operator. Years to explain the situation.

And when JohnScott motioned that he had found a way down, I punched the phone off and shoved it back in my pocket, not heeding the questions I was being asked. They weren't important. Nothing was important except getting to Nathan, and I shoved past JohnScott.

"No." His hand gripped my wrist and pulled me back. "Slow down. Let me go first so I can help you."

I screamed at him to hurry, but he was already scaling the short drop. He balanced on a small overhang six feet below, catching me when I slid haphazardly over the edge. We repeated the move again, but I pelted into JohnScott's arms, and we rolled several yards before coming to a painful stop amid rocks and broken glass.

Nathan's cries floated upward, taunting me.

"Get up!" I crawled on hands and knees before stumbling to my feet, but then I fell again, not yet balanced on the hill.

JohnScott pulled me to my feet, but just then, Nathan's cries stopped.

I stood motionless, staring down at the truck, straining to hear a sound, desperate to know he was all right.

JohnScott and I jerked into movement at the same time, half running, half sliding, sometimes rolling down the hill. We pulled each other. We pushed each other. We scrambled over rocks and around cactus, and at some point, Nathan started crying again.

When I heard his cries—proof he was still alive—a mewling whine erupted from my throat, and sobs flowed one after the other. My cries mingled with Nathan's, and I imagined a cord of communication bonding us together. A cottony, soft moan of compassion and comfort.

The roof was smashed halfway down to the dashboard, and a shiver traveled up my spine when I saw the car seat hanging from the seat belt.

JohnScott beat me to the truck, reached through the broken-out windshield, and rested his palm on Nathan's head. "It's all right, little fella."

The baby's cries eased slightly, then increased with renewed vigor.

"Hurry, JohnScott. Get him out." I fumbled for my cell phone, trying to shine the flashlight on the car seat. The light trailed across the seat of the truck, now vertical, and I gasped. Tyler had been thrown across the seat and now looked as though he were sitting up. Blood covered his face, and his left arm was bent at an unnatural angle. He seemed to be compressed between the seat, the door, and the roof. I shuddered. "Is Tyler alive?"

JohnScott sliced the car seat harness with his pocketknife. "I don't know." Holding one hand against Nathan's chest, he carefully lifted the baby out of the seat, beneath the damaged roof, and through the broken windshield.

Nathan frantically kicked and waved his arms.

"He looks all right." A lone sob shuddered through JohnScott as he turned and handed me the baby.

Never in my life would I have dreamed my maternal instincts could be so powerful, so urgent, so driven. When I saw Nathan's chin and lips quivering in terror, and his tiny baby fingers jerking rigidly, I dropped my cell phone and grabbed for him, holding him close to my heart and pressing my lips against his sweaty forehead.

In the moonlight, I could see drops of blood on his sleeper, and I felt him frantically, looking for a source, but found nothing. The pitch of his cries lowered in intensity, and I crooned to him as JohnScott picked up my phone, then returned to the cab.

I lifted my shirt, and the baby nestled into me, sobbed twice more, then finally relaxed. I stood on a flattened rock and swayed from side to side, shushing him. He shuddered, seeming to remember what he had been through, but then settled into a calm rhythm and only whimpered occasionally.

Tyler moaned from the driver's seat. "I'm sorry, babe."

His voice, raspy and desperate, nearly pulled a snarl from my throat, and I stumbled away from the truck—instinctively putting distance between him and Nathan. When I lost my footing, I almost fell, and I ended up standing on a crag with chill bumps creeping down my quivering arms. I tightened them around Nathan.

"Don't talk, Tyler." JohnScott knelt in front of the truck and reached into the cab to hold his hand.

"Fawn? I'm sorry, okay?"

His voice sent shivers up my spine. "I know, Tyler. It's all right." It felt strange to comfort him. Right and wrong at the same time.

Without warning, the muscles in my legs gave way, and I crumpled to a sitting position. I slowly rocked back and forth, back and forth—aware of Tyler's moans, aware of pain all over my body, aware of sirens and flashing lights and people approaching from above and below.

But I was unable to do anything except pray.

CHAPTER
FIFTY-ONE

The doctor said Tyler was a miracle. His left arm was broken in two places and had to be set with plates and screws, and he underwent surgery to repair bleeding on the brain. Other than that, he had bruises on almost every surface of his body, and his left kidney was so damaged, he might lose it.

But he would survive. He would eventually return home and carry on a healthy life.

But he would do it alone.

I had never considered Tyler's loneliness until I sat in his lawyer's office a week later. His family had always been surrounded by a whirl of people—ranch hands, businessmen, moochers—but when it came down to it, he only had Nathan. No wonder his father had been adamant he marry me. The lawyer said Byron Cruz had done everything within the limits of the law to force Tyler to marry me, even going so far as to withhold his inheritance until we married.

"So, will Tyler inherit anything?" I felt detached as I stared at the corner of his mahogany desk.

"Actually, yes." The man leaned on his elbows. "Even unmarried, Mr. Cruz stands to inherit almost everything, but not until he's forty years old. Until then, the estate will fall under the management of an executor, and Tyler will receive a substantial monthly income." He interlocked his fingers. "But … concerning the wreck … I'm assuming you pressed charges?"

"No, but he'll be arrested anyway, as soon as he's released from the hospital, because of the DUI and endangering a child. How will that affect the legalities?"

"He'll inherit either way, but there are concerned parties with the power to see he's treated for alcoholism before he gets a dime. Not to mention the psychotic behavior." He ran his palm quickly across his mouth, and I wondered if he was supposed to be telling me all that. He shook his head slightly. "But nothing Mr. Cruz does will affect Nathan's college fund. It will be put in place now that I have your signature."

My head hurt. From the discussion, from all that had happened, from the stress of it all.

As JohnScott and I walked to his truck, I couldn't meet his eyes. Neither of us spoke. We slid into the dingy cab, buckled the car seat, and gazed at the baby.

"Where to?" JohnScott laid his arm across the back of the seat and fingered one of my curls.

"Somewhere there are no people."

He stared out the windshield as his wrist lolled over the steering wheel, and only after he contemplated his options did he start the truck. The engine coughed a few times before sputtering to life, and then he revved it to keep it alive.

I sat in silence as he drove from Lubbock to Trapp, and my mind filled with thoughts of Tyler's obsessive love for me. So painful and dangerous. Yet so passionate.

The truck pulled to a stop on the edge of town, and JohnScott slowly turned left.

My house.

I didn't want to go back up there, but I didn't have the strength to argue with him. Instead, I stared at the mesquites streaming past the side window, and my mind drifted to hollow emptiness.

JohnScott crept down the road, slowing to a crawl at the curve near the cliff. A fresh mar in the sand reminded me of the sound of Nathan's cries far below, and I clenched my eyes shut.

We pulled into the yard, but instead of parking, JohnScott shifted into reverse and did a three-point turn so the truck faced the cliff. Then he killed the ignition. My eyes focused on a random point miles across the mesa, giving my soul a blessed sense of uncluttered simplicity. My nerves relaxed as though all my stress had been poured out onto the rolling plains.

"How did you know?"

"I've seen the way you look at this view."

"It's beautiful."

He kept his gaze on me. "Yep."

I smiled at his intended meaning but didn't look at him. Not yet. "It's not the beauty of this country that strikes me. It's the openness. I used to sit out here, looking into the distance, and it made me feel small. It made my problems feel small." I grasped the hem of my skirt, wadding the fabric until it wrinkled. Just like my wrinkled, imperfect life.

I jerked the truck door open and slid out, but I caught myself before slamming it. It would never do to waken Nathan. Instead, I left it open and leaned against the warm hood with my back to JohnScott.

He left me there for a good five minutes before he joined me. "What are you thinking about?"

"Tyler," I whispered. "I'm thinking about sitting in that waiting room, not knowing what would happen to him."

JohnScott's dress boots kicked at a beetle.

"But then my brain began working through the options. What might happen, and how it would affect Nathan and me."

I stared to the farthest point I could see. It would be so nice to go that far away and never come back, to escape from my wrinkled life, my upside-down world. But I would never be able to look JohnScott in the face if I didn't confess the truth.

I steeled my heart. "I thought it might be easier if he didn't recover."

A cool breeze swept past, lifting one curl and blowing it across my face.

JohnScott tucked it behind my shoulder. "The same thing crossed my mind. I'm not proud of it, but it's natural for our brains to go down that road. That doesn't mean we wanted it to happen."

"It feels like I wanted it."

He pushed away from the truck and faced me. "You acknowledged that Tyler makes your life complicated, but that's different than wanting him dead. It's very different." He squinted into the sun. "Half the town's thinking the same thing."

"That doesn't make it right."

"I didn't say it did."

"But how can God forgive me for thinking something like that? It's repulsive."

"Are you talking about God forgiving you or you forgiving yourself?"

I turned away, exposed, but JohnScott didn't offer comfort. He didn't even move. The sun tingled the skin on my arms as I pondered his question. "Both, I guess."

He left the silence alone for a while and then said, "The two aren't interchangeable. God wants our best, and He's patient while we work on it, but we're never going to be perfect Christians. He doesn't want or expect that. If we were perfect, we would have no need for Him."

My eyes wandered from the top button of JohnScott's shirt to the bend in the road near the cliff. "Why do I do that? I've finally gotten to know God on my own, but I still have trouble believing His promises. He forgave me for my sins with Tyler. He forgave me for rebelling against my parents. He forgave me for turning away from Him."

"He'll forgive you for whatever you've done. He's cool that way."

"I know He will, but sometimes it's so hard to feel Him, and to know for sure He's there, and that He'll keep forgiving me."

JohnScott grinned.

"What?" I asked.

Without answering, he turned toward the expanse beyond the edge of the Caprock as his smile created happy lines across his cheeks.

I followed his gaze, perplexed. But then I heard the whisper of wind purring through the cedars, I saw the reflection of the sun bouncing off sandstone, and I smelled the earthy compost of nature itself. And I knew.

I had been feeling God's love all along.

"He's pretty big, isn't He?" asked JohnScott.

"Yes," I agreed. "He's incredibly, amazingly, perfectly big."

CHAPTER
FIFTY-TWO

Four weeks later, Ruthie and I sat on the Picketts' couch as the ending credits of *Runaway Bride* rolled across the television screen. In the morning, she would marry Dodd, so we were enjoying a mini-bachelorette party. It was only the two of us, but we had watched a string of romantic DVDs and eaten loads of sugar-filled treats.

"I wonder what Dodd and the guys did tonight," Ruthie said.

I rotated my plastic cup, swirling the ice left in the bottom. "If I know JohnScott, football happened at some point."

She tilted her head to the side. "And just how well do you know my cousin?"

I set my cup on a coaster and hugged a throw pillow. "Pretty well."

"He's happier than I've ever seen him." Ruthie's approval showed in her eyes, but then she faltered. "But what will that be like for you … if the two of you get together?"

"What do you mean?"

She sat on the couch cross-legged, her bare toes wiggling nervously. "I can't picture you in a double-wide. Sorry."

"I know. I've been thinking about that for months—"

"For *months*?" The corners of her mouth teased.

"At first I couldn't imagine living like that. Not that there's anything wrong with a mobile home. It's just different—less—than what I'm used to." I chuckled. "And that's only the beginning of the differences. But now that I know JohnScott better, and now that I know *myself* better … I don't care anymore. I want to be with him, and if he's in a mobile home, or a mansion, or a shack on the Caprock, that's where I want to be."

She slurped her straw. "Well, it's not likely to be a mansion."

I twisted the fringe on Velma's crocheted afghan and then smoothed it out neatly. "I don't need a mansion." It had been a wild few months, and I had only recently begun to settle into a routine of school and work and baby love. The shattered pieces of my world had fallen into place, creating a patched and mended, uniquely beautiful work of art. I was learning to accept myself for me—who God wanted me to be—not what others thought I should be. And certainly not something as unattainable as what I had imagined I ought to be.

But still, a piece was missing.

Ruthie lowered her voice even though Ansel and Velma had gone to bed hours ago. "Has JohnScott asked you?"

"No." I looked away.

"I bet he will soon." She leaned over and hugged me. "And then you'll have everything. Just like me."

I rolled my eyes, remembering my tantrum at the Laundromat. "I already have everything."

"You always did."

I chuckled again as the baby started to cry in the back bedroom. "I knew he would wake up soon."

"Will he go back to sleep?"

"As soon as his tummy's full." I set my cup in the sink and stepped toward the hallway. "Ruthie?"

"Hmm?" She leaned back on the couch, staring at the ceiling.

"Have fun tomorrow."

"Thanks. See you in the morning."

Ruthie was so different from me, yet so much the same. If we weren't careful, we might end up being best friends after all.

Slipping into the back bedroom, I fed Nathan in the cricket rocker Velma had dragged in. My thoughts wandered in the same direction they always took lately. *JohnScott.* Even though we had grown so close we could talk about almost anything—how Nathan should be raised, the messiness Tyler would smear on our lives in the years to come, even our own unconditional love for each other—we never discussed marriage. And I wasn't sure why we didn't.

I got the feeling he was old-fashioned. After all, he was Ansel Pickett's son. I wouldn't have put it past him to wait until football season was over. The Panthers were headed to the state play-offs, and JohnScott had enough to think about without planning a wedding, too.

Nathan's head lolled back in sound sleep, and I lifted him to my shoulder, rousing him to burp before he finished his midnight snack. I heard Ruthie straightening the living room, carrying dishes to the kitchen, flipping off the lights.

The curtains swayed from the gentle breeze coming through the open window, and I rested my head on the cushion of the rocker and rubbed Nathan's back. Life frightened and exhilarated me, but when I looked down at my son, I knew we would be all right. God wasn't angry with me, wasn't holding a grudge, wasn't waiting for me to prove myself. God was God. So I didn't have to be.

I laid Nathan down, giving the cradle a gentle nudge before I put on my nightgown. But when I crawled into bed, I heard a muffled commotion through the window. Stepping to the curtain, I peered through the screen. The holding tank lay fifty yards away, beyond Velma's garden. I could see JohnScott and Dodd, along with a few other men, standing on the side of the cement cylinder with the moonlight gleaming against their bare chests and legs.

They all wore underwear, mostly boxers, but a few sported white briefs that glowed in the brightness of the autumn moon. Even though they weren't close enough for me to see anything revealing, I felt like a Peeping Tom. I started to turn away when I heard a heckle.

Grady held his hand in the air as though signaling the start of a race, and two stragglers ran from JohnScott's double-wide, stumbling as they kicked off clothes. "A one!" called Grady, and then he said something I couldn't understand. "And a two!" He said something else, and several men made catcalls to Dodd. "And a three!" In unison, they cannonballed into the water, splashing a wave over the cement sides.

For a few minutes, I watched them banter and listened to their squealing protests about the freezing water. Then I crawled into bed, remembering the day I swam in the holding tank and bumped into JohnScott. So much had happened since then. So much had changed.

Something scratched against the window screen, and my heart fluttered when I heard JohnScott whisper loudly, "Fawn? You awake?"

I scrambled out of bed and pulled back the curtain. "What are you doing here?"

"I had to see you." His breaths came in short bursts, and he looked over his shoulder to the holding tank, still swarming with bodies. He popped the screen off the window and leaned it against the side of the house.

"Should you be taking that off?"

"Done it a million times." Water dripped from his hair and ran down his chest, and his teeth chattered slightly. He wore jeans, which were still unbuttoned.

"You shouldn't be here." I said the words, but I smiled, not wanting him to leave. His presence tugged at a tender spot in my chest, and when he leaned through the window, sliding his hands around my waist and pulling me into a wet kiss, I leaned toward his shivering body willingly.

The pitch of his voice dropped. "I love you, Fawn."

"I love you, too."

"Marry me, then."

I pulled back and giggled. "All right."

"Thursday."

"Thursday?"

"That's the first available date."

His words whirled through my brain. "What?"

"Tomorrow is Dodd and Ruthie's day. Sunday the justice of the peace is closed. Monday is the first day we can file for a license, and it takes seventy-two hours. So we can go to the J.P. on Thursday." He placed his palms next to mine on the sill and leaned with his face inches from mine. "I don't want to wait,

Fawn. I want you sitting on my couch Thursday night and sipping coffee on my back porch Friday morning. And next week I want to look up in the stands at the state championship and see my wife."

His gaze dropped to my gown, now wet, and then he glanced away, running his hands through his wet curls. "And if we work it right, I can get you on my insurance next month, and then Nathan's doctor visits will be covered." He peered past me into the bedroom and lowered his voice. "Where is he? Is he asleep?"

I chuckled. "That's the most I've ever heard you say at one time. Except maybe that day you were harping on me for being a cheerleader."

"Yeah, I remember that."

The moon filled the sky behind him, casting his face into shadow, but I could make out his eyes. "Yes. Thursday," I whispered. "But not at the courthouse."

"Then where?" His hands slipped over mine, and he drew them toward his lips and kissed my palms. "The Caprock, right?"

"Yep." I ran my index finger through the curls above his ear, intoxicated by the knowledge that I would soon be able to fluff his hair whenever I wanted.

"Perfect." He cupped my chin, and his thumbs caressed my cheeks, but just as he leaned toward me, a muffled whoop echoed behind him, and he was tackled by three wild animals, none of whom had taken the time to put on jeans.

I pulled the curtains shut and sat on the edge of the bed, listening to them wrestle. JohnScott's laughter sent joy ricocheting through my chest, and I laughed. Even though I knew I wouldn't sleep a wink, I peeled off my wet nightgown, settled down on the mattress, and pulled the blanket up to my chin.

And I sighed. Deeply. Thoroughly. Cleansingly.

My life remained upside down from what it had been last year, but I realized it would probably always be that way. One way or another. But God could work with it. He could take my mistakes and my messes and turn them into something good. Something worthy. Something beautiful.

He already had.

after words

... a little more ...

When a delightful concert comes to an end,

the orchestra might offer an encore.

When a fine meal comes to an end,

it's always nice to savor a bit of dessert.

When a great story comes to an end,

we think you may want to linger.

And so, we offer ...

AfterWords—just a little something more after you

have finished a David C Cook novel.

We invite you to stay awhile in the story.

Thanks for reading!

Turn the page for ...

NOTE TO THE READER

When I started writing, I never dreamed how much fun it would be to interact with readers. You guys are by far the best part of publishing, and I'm having a blast writing for you and interacting online and elsewhere.

This second story has been a challenge for me, probably because I'm like Fawn. I give myself a tough time and end up trying too hard. If you have the same tendency, I hope her story has helped you knock away some of those annoying, little expectations we place on ourselves. And I pray we can all accept the fact that *God is big enough*.

I wish I could have included a photograph of the Caprock Escarpment, because I know my feeble words don't do it justice. But really, pictures don't either. You've just gotta go there. So if you're ever in West Texas, drive north on Highway 84 and gaze over the rim. Then email me at varina@varinadenman.com and tell me if you see God. I bet you do.

If you read both *Jaded* and *Justified*, you may have realized that Fawn was pregnant for slightly longer than a normal human. I regret that she had to go through that, but otherwise we wouldn't have gotten to enjoy her story during football season, and those chapters are fun reading. Thank you for your tolerance.

The next book in the Mended Hearts series continues the story through the eyes of Lynda Turner and Clyde Felton. My goodness, those two have been through a lot. So in a few months, meet me in Trapp, Texas (yes, it's a fictitious town), and we can read *Jilted* together.

In the meantime, find me online at varinadenman.com or one of the social-media hangouts. I'd love to meet you!

Thank you for reading,

Varina

ACKNOWLEDGMENTS

What a crazy journey this second book has been. And just like the first, I had loads of help along the path. There's no way to sufficiently thank each of you, but I'd like to at least take this speck of ink and try.

To Don, for your constant encouragement and for propping me up while I learned to navigate publishing deadlines. Thank you most of all for loving me and liking me … even when I'm an unlovable, frazzled wreck.

To my kids: Jessica, Drew, Dene, Jillian, and Janae. And my kids-in-law: Colton and Kelsea. Thank you for your support during all the craziness. I apologize for the times I was a writer first and a mother second.

To Marci for taking on the role of *first reader*. What would this book have become without your eyes on the manuscript? Eww, I can't even imagine.

To Mom and Dad for sharing your expertise on all things Caprock and verbally traveling across Texas with me the past year. Let's do it again soon.

To Ron McWhorter for details regarding diamondback rattlesnakes and the Sweetwater Round-up. If not for you, I would have made many, many embarrassing mistakes. I probably still did, but if so, they are my mistakes and not yours.

To my Facebook friends who serve as a wealth of knowledge for random research questions. Thank you for assuring me Tyler's wreck could happen in the real world. And for helping me dress Fawn in designer brands I've never heard of. And for putting Susan behind the wheel of an Audi, which suits her so much better than an SUV. You guys are way more fun than an encyclopedia, and you know *everything*.

To my agent, Jessica Kirkland, for gently pointing out the lameness of my first draft. You literally made this story what it is, and I love seeing your fingerprints throughout its pages. I can't imagine ever writing a book without you.

To my developmental editor, Jamie Chavez, for convincing me *Justified* was not dreadful, and for doing everything in your power to make it better. If we ever meet in the real world, I'm going to give you a bear hug. Then a fist bump. Then a high five. Maybe even an air kiss.

To my copyeditor, Jennifer Lonas, for cleaning up the loose ends. If not for you, Rowdy's eyes would have changed color midstory and Labor Day would have been late in September. I'm amazed at the way you keep track of details across all three books. I can't even do that, and I wrote them.

And, of course, to all the folks at David C Cook who brought Fawn Blaylock to life. Ingrid Beck, for helping me through the flurry of publishing stages. Amy Konyndyk, for creating another beautiful cover. Helen Macdonald, for making sure the manuscript was spotless. Darren Terpstra, Karla Colonnieves, Lisa Beech, and Jeane Wynn, for getting it out there. And to Karen Athen, Nick Lee, and all the other marketing, editing, and production people whom I've never met and therefore never had the chance to annoy. You guys are the ones who actually make the magic.

BOOK CLUB
DISCUSSION GUIDE

1. In the opening scene, Fawn Blaylock feels as though she's not good enough. For her parents, for the town, for herself. Not even for God. Why do you think she feels like that? Can you relate? If so, what do you think prompted those feelings?

2. Throughout the book, Fawn's personal beliefs are mirrored through the actions of townsfolk like Sophie Snodgrass. How might Sophie's actions help or hinder Fawn's view of herself? Do you ever allow the opinions of others to influence your self-esteem? How?

3. Ruthie Turner is Fawn's "unlikely" friend. How do the two of them draw closer to each other? What do they have in common at the beginning of the book? At the end? What faults must they overlook in each other?

4. Ruthie teases Fawn with her made-up *Who cares?* hand sign. How does this gentle reminder help Fawn chill out? When might this attitude cause more harm than good? Explain.

5. Early in the story, Tyler Cruz decides to woo Fawn back. What prompts this change of heart? Do you think any part of Tyler's decision is sincere?

6. During the scenes when Fawn is at church, some of the members (even her own mother, at first) treat her coldly because of her unplanned pregnancy. Why do you think those women behaved that way? How might their actions have made Fawn feel? Would such a judgmental attitude ever be acceptable? Explain.

7. Fawn can't seem to let go of Tyler even though he is emotionally and physically abusive. How do you explain her actions? Consider Fawn and her mother and their approach to handling abusive partners. In what ways do the two women differ? How does each of them grow and overcome?

8. In the first chapters, JohnScott Pickett views Fawn as spoiled, insecure, and self-protective. Do you think he is justified in his opinion? What has Fawn done to deserve those labels? How does she finally earn his respect?

9. Snakes are a recurring theme in *Justified*. Why do you think the author chose such a repulsive creature? What parallels can you see between the snakes and the story line and/or characters? Are there biblical parallels?

10. Fawn compares herself to Velma Pickett and feels that she falls short, even though Velma is a nonbeliever. Explain why Fawn might feel this way. In the beginning of the story, what positive traits does Velma possess that Fawn doesn't? How might Velma have attained these characteristics without the influence of the church and the Scriptures?

11. JohnScott spends many hours "cleaning up" Fawn's house in an effort to repel the snakes. How do his actions mimic Fawn's previous and current lifestyle? How does Fawn attempt to clean her upside-down life? What things does she do that help? Hurt?

12. Fawn and her mother, Susan, both got pregnant before they married. How might that similarity have drawn them closer together? Did it? What else had to happen before they could heal their relationship? What do you think will become of Fawn and Susan now?

13. Fawn and JohnScott struggle to maintain purity in their relationship. What factors make it more difficult for them? How is their struggle true to real life? What is different? How did their emotional baggage factor in?

14. Clyde Felton educates Fawn about the dangers of diamondback rattlesnakes. In what other ways does Clyde teach Fawn valuable lessons, either directly or indirectly? What other characters are affected by Clyde? Do you think the ex-convict even realizes the influence he has on those people? Why or why not?

15. Neil Blaylock never really apologizes to Fawn. Why might he refuse to admit his faults? Do you think he is sorry for his actions over the past years? Do you think he'll ever be able to verbalize his regrets? Explain.

16. When Fawn's baby is born, Fawn is bewildered by the maternal bond she feels. Why do you think that catches her by surprise? In

what ways does she nurture that bond? What do you think Fawn and Nathan's relationship will look like in the years to come? What kind of issues might they struggle with? Why?

17. Toward the end of the book, JohnScott admits he's a pouter. Why might he behave in such an uncharacteristic and immature fashion? Why does he wait so long to apologize? What finally prompts him to come to Fawn? When have you ever acted in an uncharacteristic way? What helped you deal with it?

18. When Tyler steals the baby, his mental imbalance causes him to become dangerously overwhelmed and desperate. To a much lesser degree, we all have these feelings at times. What causes feelings of desperation? How can you combat them?

19. Just after the wreck, Fawn is frantic to get to her baby but feels helpless. In what times of life have you felt the same way? What have you learned from those experiences?

20. Tyler gradually becomes irrational. What do you think caused that? How long has this character flaw been growing? Will he ever be able to heal? What do you think will be his role in Fawn's life now?

21. At the end of Fawn's story, she finally "sees" God on the Caprock. What do you think she actually saw? Why couldn't she see or feel Him before that? When have you had trouble finding God? What helped Him come into focus?

22. In the last chapter, Fawn states that she doesn't care if she has less than she grew up with. What had to happen for her to finally realize this? What difficulties lie ahead of her? Do you think it's realistic for her to make such a drastic turnaround? Explain.

A Sneak Peek at Book Three:
JILTED

Varina Denman

CHAPTER ONE

My daughter always called me a glass-half-empty kind of person, but she was wrong. Not only was my glass half empty, but a tiny crack shot diagonally from a chip on the rim, and something bread-like hovered in the murky liquid.

But I was planning to toss that glass and get a brand-new one.

Today I sat in my hatchback on the side of Highway 84, smoldering in the afternoon sunshine. When I had left town, I had been driving like a mountain boomer scurrying across hot sand, but I soon settled into a reasonable speed, and now, twenty minutes later, I eased to a stop and shoved the car in park.

I did this a lot.

Sometimes I drove all the way to the lake and stared at the rippling water, but most times, like today, I stopped here. Now I reached across the seat and cranked down the window on the passenger side, allowing a breeze in. Ninety-four degrees in September, but it could have been worse. Last week, we were still in triple digits.

As a truck sped past, my car rocked gently, and I almost ducked. It was only Old Man Guthrie. His index finger made a slow salute in greeting, and I did nothing in response. My typical hello. Clyde Felton called me distant, but really I was just tired. Tired of waving. Tired of pretending. Tired of trying.

I focused my gaze on the cotton fields and hoped no other people would drive by. If they did, one of them might eventually pull over to check on me, and I would have to explain why I was sitting in my car on the side of the highway, staring at the wind turbines. I smiled. Old Man Guthrie never stopped, so maybe he understood.

Those wind turbines, marching across the Caprock like evenly spaced tin soldiers, stretched for miles and miles into the distance. And they settled my nerves like a dose of Valium. Not that I'd had any Valium in the last ten years, but one doesn't quickly forget.

Depression almost killed me.

Twice.

But I got over it. I beat the demon both times and lived to tell the tale, but even after that, it threatened to rear its ugly head. *The nerve.* I had beaten it, trampled it, killed it dead, but depression still haunted me like a villain hiding just beyond the glow of streetlights. Waiting.

So I took to fighting it with a spotlight. They say an ounce of prevention is worth more, so whenever I felt the beast slithering through my heart, I would do a mental escape to protect my happy thoughts. And believe me, I wasn't the type of person to have any extra happy thoughts to lose.

This was one of those days.

I inhaled ninety-four-degree oxygen until my chest couldn't expand any more, then I released it back into the hatchback as the muscles in my neck relaxed. Sure, I was a weirdo, but at least I got out of my house now. I bought my own groceries, smiled at people, and went to Panther football games. I even ate dinner with my daughter and her preacher husband once a week. I was beating the demon. I was.

I squinted at the nearest windmill, watching its slow-motion arms slice the sun as it cast moving shadows over the hood of the car.

The cool grayness slipped along my skin, then sailed to the far side of the highway where it slid across the pavement before looping back to slap me again.

Round and round and round. This was my temporary escape from life. From the beast. From people. From my hometown. I snickered. I never got very far from Trapp. As much as I hated the place, I didn't want to leave it behind.

Flashing lights caught my eye from way down the road, and I leaned forward, resting my arms against the steering wheel and my chin on my wrists. The West Texas landscape lay so flat that I could watch the police car approach from miles away. It seemed to crawl along at a snail's pace before finally coming close enough I could hear the squealing siren. A highway patrolman. He barely slowed before turning on the lake road.

I rested my head on the back of the seat and smiled at the predictability. This happened every so often. A group of fishermen would hole up in a cabin, get drunk, then turn stupid. Last year a couple of them actually started firing shots into the water, thinking they would shoot the fish since they weren't biting.

Yes, Trapp was predictable. Quaint. Simple.

Narrow-minded.

Clearly my daughter was right. I was—and always would be—a glass-half-empty kind of girl, but plenty of other residents viewed the place as heaven on earth. They seemed energized by the same gossip that kept me shut inside myself, locked away along with my heart. But at times, when I stared at the windmills, I wondered if I could be happy again—truly happy, not just faking it—and deep inside, I felt a teensy glimmer of hope.

The moan of another siren swelled on the breeze, and I located a police car in my rearview mirror. No, it was two. And through the front windshield, I saw what looked like a fire truck approaching from Snyder, silently making its way closer. This was *not* predictable.

A lone highway patrolman was to be expected, along with the game warden, but not four emergency vehicles. And now it looked as though an ambulance was following the fire truck. I turned in the seat as the police cars sped past, and I covered my ears to block the screeching wails.

As I started the ignition, curiosity niggled my brain, but I didn't follow the emergency vehicles. Instead, I did a U-turn and headed back to town. I was scheduled to work at the diner, and it wouldn't do for me to be late. I needed the income. Besides, the news of whatever was happening at the lake would probably beat me back to town.

CHAPTER TWO

Clyde Felton peered up and down Main Street, then settled his gaze on Dixie's Diner. He could see Lynda in there behind the counter, frowning at an order slip. Maybe he wouldn't go in after all. He leaned against his old sedan and stared down at his work boots. Why did he even wear boots? His job certainly didn't call for them, but somehow he felt better in them. More confident.

A hot gust of wind brought sand to his eyes and the familiar stench of the feedlot to his nose. More than once, he'd heard strangers gripe about the odor when they'd stop on their way through town, but it didn't bother Clyde. He'd smelled worse. But the stench of human waste in the stifling air of a cell block hardly compared to the outdoorsy scent of too many cows in too small a space.

Trapp, Texas, with its foul smells, run-down buildings, and unsurprising people ... was home. And that's where his good memories lay. Memories before prison. Memories of freedom and happiness and friends.

Lynda in particular.

In a strange way, she formed the missing link connecting his past to the future, and he was drawn to her. Had been since he got back to town. Drawn to her in a way he hadn't been drawn to a woman in a long, long time—even though she never looked at him as anything more than a friend. Or worse, a brother.

He shoved away from the car, took two long strides, and pushed open the door of the diner, ducking slightly as he entered.

She had moved into the kitchen now, and when she looked at him through the pass-through window, he thought she might have rolled her eyes slightly. But that was just Lynda.

"Hey, Lyn." He sat on a stool at the counter and reached over to get a menu. Instead of opening it, he tapped it against the Formica. "I'll take pork chops, I guess."

"With carrots and corn bread. I know." Then she really did roll her eyes, but she also smiled.

Every time he came in, he ordered the same thing, and every time, she razzed him about it. He cut his gaze toward her before dropping his eyes to the menu now open on the bar in front of him. Her hair was pulled back, same as always, and some of it was falling down, same as always. She had sweat on her forehead and circles under her eyes, but in spite of it, she looked just fine.

Undoubtedly she looked fine to a lot of men in town. Sometimes Clyde noticed them watching. They would talk to her, try to get her attention, but she wouldn't have it. She hardly seemed to notice and certainly didn't care.

The left side of her mouth curled when she came around the corner. "Dixie gave you an extra chop. I think she has a crush."

Clyde grunted. "Sure she does." The owner of the diner was at least twenty-five years older than Clyde and happily married with a passel of grandchildren.

Lynda leaned her elbows on the counter opposite him. "How are things at the Dairy Queen?"

"Same."

"Burned anything lately?"

"No."

"Me neither."

It was his turn to speak. Taking turns was the way it was done, but he scooped a forkful of carrots into his mouth to avoid it.

Why did she make him so nervous? He knew her better than he knew anyone else in town—anyone left, at least—yet she made him tongue-tied, and today was even worse because he had something to say.

He chuckled to himself. The nightmare of prison life didn't compare to the terror he felt about asking Lynda Turner to go out with him. Or maybe not *go out*. That sounded all formal and stuffy. Official. And Clyde didn't really do formal and stuffy.

He blurted her name before he could change his mind. "Lynda?"

"Clyde?" Her voice overlapped his. "You hear anything about an arrest out at the lake this afternoon? Or maybe an accident?"

Clyde's insides collapsed into a wad of tin foil, but the sparkle in her eyes made him curious. "No ..." He sliced his corn bread with his fork. "What does the rumor mill say?"

"Nothing yet, but I saw a cop headed out that way."

Clyde watched her carefully as she wiped the counter with a dish towel. Then she rubbed the same spot again. "You've been to the windmills," he said.

She folded the towel and shrugged. "It helps."

Right then, Clyde thanked God for the chunk of pork chop he was able to shove in his mouth, masking his smile. If Lynda had noticed, she would have thought he was making fun of her, and he never would have been able to explain that he simply found her very, very ... cute.

Nobody thought of Lynda as *cute*.

Beautiful? Yes.

Sexy? Probably.

Nice or sweet or thoughtful or kind? Not hardly.

The woman rarely smiled. She couldn't keep a friend. Even her family got impatient with her mood swings. But beneath those sharpened porcupine quills was hidden the soft fur of a bunny. A cottontail, not a jackrabbit.

A teenaged waitress slapped a paper on the counter next to Clyde's elbow, and Lynda picked it up and glanced at the order. "Be right back."

For ten minutes, he watched her cook while he finished his lunch. In another ten minutes, he would be back at the Dairy Queen, cooking for someone else. It was funny all they had in common.

He sucked on a piece of crushed ice, then chomped it between his teeth. Ten minutes. He had sworn to himself he would ask her. *Today.* And now he only had ten minutes left. Five, really, because he had to allow time to get in his car, coax it into starting, drive eight blocks to the DQ, get his apron on and hands washed. Now he wished he had walked. It might have been faster.

Lynda stood just on the other side of the pass-through window, side by side with Dixie.

Clyde took one last swig of his iced tea before lifting himself off the stool. "Hey, Lyn." He tried for an offhanded tone of voice. "You need a ride to the game tomorrow night? I can pick you up."

"Naw, that's all right." Lynda waved her hand. "I'll be with Velma."

She kept her gaze focused on the grill in front of her as she flipped steaks, but Dixie looked at him and winked.

What had he been thinking? Of course she would go to the game with her sister. Hadn't she done that every Friday night for the past two seasons?

The cowbell over the door clanked near his ear as he ducked his way out to the street. The breeze still blew from the direction of the feedlot, but he wasn't one to complain. After more than twenty years of waiting, his life had finally become peaceful, and he knew he should leave well enough alone. He had everything he needed.

Everything he deserved.

Clyde started his car, telling himself to forget about Lynda, but he glanced once more in the diner window, hoping she would look at him after all.

CHAPTER THREE

"Lynda, that man wants you."

I pressed my lips together, scowling at Dixie. "No, he doesn't." Clyde had fancied me when we were teenagers, but that was a long time ago. Nothing could come of it now. Not after everything in our past. Not after prison.

But Dixie needn't know all that.

I watched through the window as Clyde ambled to his worn-out sedan, folded his large frame behind the wheel, and started the ignition. His gaze flitted to mine briefly before he backed out.

I set two plates on the ledge above the grill and slammed my palm against the bell. Clyde Felton didn't have the gumption to get a decent job, much less find an available woman to care for.

"Here comes Ruthie." Dixie paused as she sliced tomatoes, motioning to the dining room with a paring knife. "Why don't you take a break?"

I glanced at the clock on the back wall. "Fifteen?"

"Maybe just ten. It's starting to get busy."

Dixie followed me into the dining room where I slid into a booth across from my daughter.

"I was just telling your mother she should date more." Dixie crossed her arms and ignored my short sigh.

"I've been telling her that for years," said Ruthie. "You see how she listens."

My daughter thought she knew everything. She had found the man of her dreams, fallen for him like a bag of cement, and was now living her happily-ever-after. It was nauseating. I glanced around the diner and wished both of them would leave me be. "I've got no need for it."

"I think you should date." Lonnie Lombard sat on a stool at the counter, chewing with his mouth open and giving me a suggestive smile.

I smirked.

"You're all wrong for her," Ruthie said.

Lonnie straightened on the stool. "I'm a fine specimen of masculinity."

"It's true you are, but Momma likes men with hair."

His jaw fell open, and he ran a palm over his slick head. "Bald is beautiful. Or hadn't you heard?"

"Yes, I got that memo, but Momma never did."

Dixie crooned softly, "I was thinking of someone with much more hair. Long and curly."

She looked knowingly at Ruthie, and my daughter's eyes widened just before her gaze locked with mine.

A slow breath labored through my lungs as it made its way from my pride to my lips, and I cocked my head toward Dixie. "Could you give it a rest?"

"I will, but you know I'm right."

A family of five bustled through the door, and I attempted to take the focus off myself. "Here comes a big order." I made to stand, but Dixie's plump palm on my shoulder stopped me.

"You've got nine minutes left, and I'll dock your pay if you don't use it." She spun on her heel and made her way back to the kitchen.

Ruthie opened her menu. She didn't say anything, but her eyebrows shot up, annoying me more than anything Dixie had said all day.

That was Ruthie—*Ruth Ann*, as I called her. Hoby and I named her after our mothers, but she was *Ruthie* to everyone else in town—spunky, straightforward, invasive. It was enough to drive a well-balanced, emotionally healthy person over the edge, and I had never been described in such positive terms. But she meant well. I know she did. She wanted me to be as happy as she was, and she hadn't yet realized happiness could evaporate like mist in a single afternoon.

I pulled the band from my hair, fingered the loose strands back in place, then secured my hair again in a bun on the back of my head.

Ruthie used her menu as a fan while she sipped iced tea and merrily chattered to Lonnie and anyone else in the restaurant who looked our way. She talked like those people hadn't hurt her over the years. Like they were her friends. Like she cared what they had to say. It was strange.

The door opened again, and a strong, hot wind blustered through while Fawn Blaylock backed into the dining room, pulling a stroller. She smiled when she saw us, then bumped past every table as she made her way across the room to sit next to Ruthie. "My one o'clock class got canceled."

"Stop bragging." Ruthie scrunched her nose.

"I'm not. I'm rejoicing."

"Same thing, and it's ugly."

I toyed with the idea of escaping back to the kitchen. "Girl, you want a sandwich?"

Fawn's eyes smiled. "Thanks, Lynda."

I may have been lousy at conversation, but at least I could remember my customers' favorite orders. Fawn was easy. Chicken sandwich and salad. And I knew to add a side of well-cooked green beans for her baby, Nathan. The kid was asleep in the stroller, but any other time, Fawn would have him in her arms, talking to him, tickling his neck, laughing.

Happy, happy, happy.

Ruthie leaned toward Fawn. "Don't you think Momma should start dating?"

Fawn froze in her seat, and only her eyes bounced back and forth between the two of us. "I think so?"

Lonnie called over his shoulder as he slipped from his stool and headed to the cash register. "She won't have a bald man."

My irritating daughter smiled knowingly, then whispered to Fawn, "We're not the only ones who think she'd be good with Clyde. Dixie noticed it too."

My palm slapped against the tabletop. "Stop it, Ruth Ann."

I feared she might fall into one of her uncontrolled giggling spells, but she sobered when she heard a light clearing of a throat one table over. Her eyes grew to the size of prickly pear, and she mouthed silently, "*Blue* and *Gray*."

Fawn snickered at Ruthie's nicknames for the two elderly ladies, but I couldn't find anything funny about the situation.

Ruthie spoke under her breath. "I'm sure they would disapprove of you dating a convict."

"*Ex*-convict," mumbled Fawn. "And he didn't deserve it in the first place."

Ruthie stretched to look down at the baby, and then she settled back into her seat. "You know that and I know that, but Blue and Gray don't care either way. Once a jailbird, always a jailbird."

Their comments rubbed a soft spot behind my lungs. "Clyde may not have deserved twenty years, but what he did was definitely against the law."

Fawn bit her bottom lip.

"But he loved Susan," Ruthie said simply.

I jerked my head from left to right, disgusted with both of them, disgusted with Dixie for mentioning Clyde, and disgusted with Clyde all over again. "If he cared enough about Fawn's momma to have sex with her, he should have cared enough not to."

Ruthie's face pinched into a frown.

I dropped my head into my hands and tilted it from side to side a few times. These two didn't mind pushing an ex-convict into my love life—one who had been convicted of statutory rape, no less—but they strongly disapproved of me pointing out his faults. "Fawn, I'm sorry to talk about your daddy that way, but you might as well look at the big picture. Clyde and I have a lot of baggage in our past, and you girls fancying the two of us could ever have a thing for each other is absurd."

Fawn dug through Nathan's diaper bag.

"Momma," Ruthie moaned, "Fawn doesn't call Clyde *Daddy*."

I could never say things without making a mess of them.

"You're right, though," Fawn said. "He's not without fault. It's just that I get tired of people acting like he's a bad person. He made one unwise decision that affected him the rest of his life."

"There were five of us whose lives went into a tailspin," I corrected her. "Not that I put the responsibility entirely on him. Clyde and your momma just set it all in motion."

We had been talking in low whispers, and I noticed the blue- and gray-haired sisters eying us curiously. They were picking at their peach cobblers and leaning toward our table.

Gray cleared her throat again. "Have you all heard what happened out at the lake? We stopped by the post office before lunch and got it all straight from the chief's wife. Biggest thing that happened here since—" Her face wadded as though she had just remembered a distasteful joke.

"Since a long time ago, Sister." Blue wagged her finger.

"Yes." Gray renewed her speech with fervor. "Biggest thing that happened here since a long time ago." Her lips puckered slightly. "Any who, the chief's still out there trying to make sense of it, but he called Clara Belle on his cellular telephone so she wouldn't be too worried if she heard something about it on the radio or television."

"Radio or television?" Ruthie turned in her seat.

"You'll never believe what they found out there." Blue removed the plastic wrapper from a toothpick. "Over on the south side of the lake. Not a quarter mile from a marina. A couple of hikers were skipping stones on the water—"

"I think folks ought not to skip rocks like that," said Gray slowly. "Could fill up the lake eventually, don't you think?"

"Or at least make it too shallow for boats. I've never been out to Lake Alan Henry. Is it a shallow lake?"

"Well, don't leave us hanging," blurted Ruthie. "What did they find?"

"Oh, land sakes." Gray waved her palm. "They found a bone! A *human* bone!"

The three of us stared at her.

Blue and Gray were the town's most thorough gossipers, but there was no way a human bone could have been found. Not near Trapp. That was something that happened in movies.

Ruthie asked the question I was thinking. "How do they know it's human?"

"It was a *femur*," Blue bragged. "That's a leg bone, and they called a specialist from Lubbock to come right away." She added the last sentence with a sharp nod, as though that tidbit of information verified the entire story. "Not to mention the police are trained in this sort of thing."

A cold chill crept up my back, sending shivers down my arms and legs. But that was silly. I got the same chill when I watched *CSI*.

I stood, knowing I was running away from the conversation, but not caring. "I'll go make your sandwich, Fawn. Ruth Ann, you want a burger?"

Ruthie turned away from Blue and Gray and wiggled her fingers at the baby who was just waking. "That'd be great, Momma. Thanks."

As I made my way to the kitchen, the two sisters puttered to the register at the end of the counter. Gray tucked her chin as though it would prevent me from hearing her say, "Sister? You think our convict had anything to do with that femur?"

"Might at that," Blue said.

I plunged a basket of frozen fries into hot oil, and the sizzle drowned out their last mutterings, but I could imagine what they were saying. For as long as he lived, Clyde would be accused of any crime that happened in our little town, whether it be a bone found at the lake or a candy bar stolen from the United grocery store. *Guilty until proven innocent.* Yet nobody ever took the time to prove anything.

Dixie caught my eye for only a split second before returning to her bread dough, but I knew she was still thinking about Clyde too. I glanced toward the front windows where his sedan had been, and I remembered the way he had looked at me as he backed out of the parking space. His eyes had only met mine for a split second, but in them, I had seen anticipation. And hope. And something else.

Another chill skittered down my thighs. Good Lord, Dixie was right.

Clyde Felton wanted me.

Even now.

ABOUT THE AUTHOR

Varina Denman is a native Texan who spent her high school years in a small Texas town. Now she and her husband live near Fort Worth, where they enjoy spending time with their five mostly grown children. *Justified* is her second novel. Look for other books in the Mended Hearts series online and in bookstores.

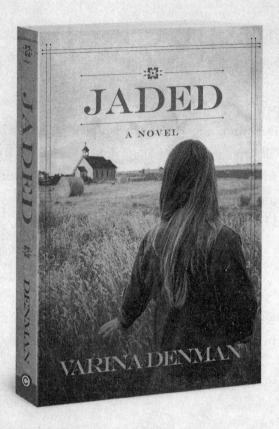

Their small-town church wants them apart.
God has other plans.

As a child, Ruthie was shunned by the local congregation.
Thirteen years later, her heart begins to stir when Dodd Cunningham,
an attractive single minister, moves to town. But their relationship
unearths a string of secrets that threaten to turn the small church,
the town, and her world upside down.

David C Cook
transforming lives together